Susan S. Senstad

Milk and Venom

Austin Macauley Publishers™
London • Cambridge • New York • Sharjah

All characters in this publication are fictitious and any resemblance to real persons, living or dead, is purely coincidental.

A CIP catalogue record for this title is available from the British Library.

ISBN 9781787107830 (Paperback)
ISBN 9781788230087 (Hardback)
ISBN 9781787107847 (E-Book)

www.austinmacauley.com

First Published (2018)
Austin Macauley Publishers Ltd.
25 Canada Square
Canary Wharf
London
E14 5LQ

Dedication

For

Roberta Jessica Tom
Heidi Rolf Damian
Britt Simon
Synnøve

Iole
Julia Ada Sarah
Anne Bente Kirsten Anna Luise Thea Ane

Ed una lupa, che di tutte brame
sembiava carca ne la sua magrezza,
e molte genti fé già viver grame,
questa mi porse tanto di gravezza
con la paura ch'uscia di sua vista,
ch'io perdei la speranza de l'altezza.
E qual è quei che volontieri acquista,
e giugne 'l tempo che perder lo face,
che 'n tutt'i suoi pensier piange e s'attrista;
tal mi fece la bestia sanza pace,
che, venendomi 'ncontro, a poco a poco
mi ripigneva là dove 'l sol tace.

Dante's Inferno. Canto I, 49-60

And a she-wolf came, her scrawny body
filled with craven lust, who had made
so many others wretched
and the sight of her weighed me down
with such heavy terror
that I lost all hope of rising up again,
like a miser, happy while winning,
then when his luck turns and he must count his losses
his every weeping thought fills with misery,
so did I become when facing that frantic beast
who stalked me, closer and closer, step by step,
then thrust me down to where the sun kept silent.

Translation: M. Lombardi,
The Winged Scorpion's Daughters

Prologue

Before she quit her job, Millicent applied for an American Express credit card. She bought one-way tickets for her and Alice, and stuffed their future into two suitcases and a tattered, army-green duffel bag.

With Beary-Bear's head and a Barbie doll's legs sticking out of Alice's carry-on, they flew from Chicago to New York where they would pick up their midnight connection to Rome.

When their flight was finally called, she woke her daughter. As they hurried off toward the gate, an elderly man grabbed Millicent. For a split second, she imagined the assailant to be her mother and so, on automatic, wrenched herself free.

"Isn't this yours?" he asked her holding out the travel wallet she'd left on the bench. Everything she needed was inside: their passports, her international driver's license, her birth control pills, the precious credit card – and all the money she had in the world in the form of the only traveler's checks she'd ever bought.

"Oh, I'm so sorry. Yes. Yes it is. Thank you. Thank you so much!"

The wallet was a going-away present from her sister, Geena. On the gift card, still inside, she had calligraphed, in Gothic script: "Virgil tells Dante: 'Go onward, and in going, listen.' Your big sister adds: 'Start listening to Life when it whispers, Millicent, or it's going to have to scream.'"

I.

1

Millicent waited a few weeks before phoning her sister in California. "So, how's the Roman Conquest?" Geena asked.

"We're winning, I think. You should have seen us at the airport, Geena. Unbelievable. Enrico came to pick us up. In a teeny Fiat *Cinquecento*!"

"With all that luggage?"

"The trunk wouldn't latch – Alice and I had to wait an hour in the parking lot while he drove around hunting for rope. Roman shops close between one and four."

She didn't mention the spring rain, or that the airport swarmed with soldiers carrying machine guns because, as Enrico explained later, left-wing terrorists had assassinated some judge in Palermo the day before. She did not tell Geena how much she'd enjoyed those uniformed hunks winking at her, calling out sexy-sounding words that she couldn't understand.

"Is the apartment some sort of ancient monument?"

"Not a bit. It's in the middle of miles of six story buildings with teeny balconies full of geraniums and clotheslines. It's Bruno's apartment."

When Enrico had formalized his invitation for Millicent to come and teach at his language school in Rome, he'd offered her and Alice a room to stay in at his fifty-year-old partner Bruno's Roman apartment. Enrico camped out there when he wasn't off working in Bologna or Milan. Bruno had set up housekeeping with Silvana, his *amante*, his "hell cat lover from the Roman slums"; his 'real' home was in another part of Rome, where the rest of the anti-Communist Leftist Intelligentsia elite resided. His fancy furniture, his library, his clothes – everything – was still in that other apartment, where he ate lunch almost every day, where, for thirty years, the same maid had ironed his shirts and slacks, even his underwear. "Why get mixed up with these new divorce laws?" Bruno had said to Millicent. "It would only hurt everyone: Silvana's husband, their children, my wife. The mistress is the mistress but the wife will always be the wife."

"Some culture," Geena mumbled. "Didn't you explain to him that the point of running away from home is to get to someplace better? Wait a minute. What am I saying? You tried to run away from our dysfunctional family by marrying Neal!"

"Our family wasn't dysfunctional."

"Right. We got this fucked up all by ourselves."

"Speak for yourself."

"I love you, Mill, but you are a jerk. What about Alice?"

"I've switched her to the British elementary school. It's terribly expensive, but the Italian public school day ends at noon, long before I'll finish work. The Italian mothers all dress up in high heels to bring their kids and pick them up – they never heard of car-pooling and I guess they don't have jobs. Luckily the Brits bus Alice back and forth."

Millicent also withheld from Geena that there was no bedroom for Alice, only a cot set up behind a curtain in a windowless alcove in the living room where the TV kept the kid awake at night. She didn't mention the battered double bed and walnut-veneer wardrobe that crowded the bedroom she used, or the sounds of arguing that seeped through the wall at night. She didn't share her worries about what she and Alice would do if Bruno and Silvana split up. She had no contingency plans and she'd never asked Enrico a single question about how much money he expected her to contribute to the rent and food let alone what child care would cost when she worked late or taught in other cities as he had promised, enticingly, that she would.

"And the Prince? How's it going with dashing Enrico? Are you still crazy about each other?"

"The Prince is just fine," Millicent proclaimed. She didn't admit that Enrico spent less time with her and more time in Bologna than she'd anticipated. Her expectations of their Roman love nest had not quite materialized.

Switching topics, Millicent confined herself to the entertaining details, such as the stiff, waxy, non-absorbent toilet paper, and how she'd learned, the hard way, to avoid peeing on her panty hose when the public toilet was just a gaping hole in the floor with man-sized ceramic foot prints on either side.

"And the shopping. The general store is like a closed-stack library. I have to wait for somebody to ask me what I want – *if* I can remember what it's called, and *if* the woman behind the counter deigns to acknowledge my existence. I asked her for matches yesterday, perfectly, *'Fiammiferi, per favore.'* She climbed a ladder to search for them and looked right through me and carried on talking to the *signora* standing behind me."

"Like a pack-rat with dementia."

"There's anarchy everywhere. They drive the wrong way down one-way streets, park on the sidewalks and then mobilize the guys standing around outside coffee bars to pick up and move double-parked cars that are blocking them. But their salvation is *pasta – maccheroni, penne, tagliatelle, fettuccine,* or *spaghetti* – comforting *pasta* every day. That's within their control."

****

Carefully following Silvana's instructions, Millicent took the bus for twenty minutes then changed to another which ran from the seedy central train station, past St. Peter's Basilica, to the language school's neighborhood near the Vatican.

The receptionist/secretary handed her a sign-up sheet indicating the few remaining hours when the two classrooms and the three meeting rooms weren't already booked, and a list of potential private students for her to contact. Enrico had impressed on Millicent that his bulging customer portfolios were the fruits of years of labor. She would have to earn her own following.

Although Enrico was out of town on Millicent's first day at *Lingua Nuova,* he had instructed Charlotte Caciolo, a big-boned peasant from Marseilles who taught French, to settle her in. She looked shocked when she saw Millicent. "He told us an important colleague was arriving from America," she said in heavily accented English. "But why did he not warn us that you are beautiful?" She let out a throaty, sexy cackle before grabbing Millicent's arm to give her the tour.

Millicent took to Charlotte straight away. She liked her energy and her no bullshit style and was happy, after a frustrating and unproductive morning, to go out to lunch with her. Taking long strides, Charlotte maneuvered her through the midday rush-hour crowds to the *centro storico*. Above the traffic din, she pointed out Gucci, Valentino, the windows of the room above the Spanish steps where John Keats had died, the Bernini fountain marking how high the Tiber flooded in 1598. "The guide books say it's a sinking boat," Charlotte laughed, "but we know it as Rome's largest *vulva e clitoride*."

During lunch, she provided Millicent with information she considered vital for a newcomer – where to buy pirated designer shoes, Rome's best pizza, the world's best ice cream and how to protect her purse from the motorcyclists who raced past and sliced through the strap with a razor. And how to hide income from Bruno and Enrico so they couldn't take their full cut.

As Charlotte accompanied her back to the office, she pointed out a discreet little hotel and shared a secret, which Millicent suspected might be public knowledge: married Charlotte held Wednesday afternoon trysts with a virile university student fourteen years her junior, in the French *cinq-à-sept* tradition. "Maybe someday I will let you see him!" Charlotte said and then kissed Millicent on both cheeks. "*Bella,*" she exclaimed, "my new *Lingua Nuova* friend!"

****

Jocasta de Koning was the name at the top of Millicent's list of potential clients. She wanted her eight-year-old son to receive English lessons at their home. Bruno delighted in leaking *Lingua Nuova* gossip to his beloved Silvana, who relished spreading it. In quirky English and with a grin, Silvana told Millicent that Jocasta, a Greek Cypriot, had secured a male heir for her Dutch Canadian husband and his de Koning dynasty, whom she had insisted they name 'Atlas'. Jocasta had always presumed her husband had divorced his thirty-year-old first wife because she was barren, but when Jocasta turned thirty, four years ago, he had dumped her, too. His lawyers forced her to relinquish claim to all de Koning assets except the sprawling penthouse in the center of Rome. She received no alimony, only access, at a specified monthly rate, to the interest earned by the de Koning Trust Fund established for their son. Once Atlas came into his money at eighteen, Jocasta would revert to being her own family's burden.

Now the mistress of an aristocratic politician, she was living in Roman luxury, but was cash poor. This was presumably why she'd chosen a mid-level status school like *Lingua Nuova* to improve her son's mastery of his absent father's language. "That's me: the bargain basement teacher," Millicent thought but checked herself from saying it aloud to anyone.

Jocasta's rickety elevator left Millicent unprepared for the elegance she encountered on the sixth floor. When the oversized brass knob on the glossy red door turned, a gray-haired maid escorted her along a corridor lined with pedestals, each bearing an ancient sculpture. Wide marble steps led up to an airy expanse of living room, where the maid left her. The view through the glass doors, which covered one entire wall and opened onto a roof terrace, stretched across the *Tevere* and up the *Gianicolo*. In spite of the panorama, Millicent's irritation about being kept waiting increased, until she recalled that she was being paid by the hour.

At last, Jocasta made an entrance. Her eyes and wavy hair were black; even her aura, despite a patina of gracious formality, seemed dark. During the short interview, as Jocasta probed for details, Millicent imagined herself as the obsequious governess in some Victorian novel granted an audience with the haughty lady of the manor.

Atlas, frail and no taller than Alice, though six months older, reminded Millicent of a miniature, middle-aged man. Silvana had said he still wet his bed.

He remained mute during their work session at the kitchen table, until Millicent asked to see his school notebooks in an attempt to find a way through to him. He knelt on his chair and, in a mixture of broken English and Italian, began an animated narration of his drawings of axes, knives, shields, chains, cannons, tanks and exploding bombs. No people. His assignment for their next lesson, she concluded, was to draw pictures of knights.

2

True to his word, Enrico arranged for Millicent to teach one Saturday at *Lingua Nuova*'s Bologna branch. Silvana agreed, though with an unexpected reluctance, to take care of Alice from Friday afternoon until Saturday night.

Millicent worked her way through the crowded train corridor to her Second Class compartment. There, she and seven Italians were crammed onto two worn leather benches, facing each other. Once installed, she melted into the background so she could eavesdrop. What were they talking about? *Melanzane,* eggplant; *pomodori,* tomatoes. *Piselli,* green peas…or might they be discussing someone's penis? It was one of those quirks of the Italian language.

Her Bologna hostess, the teacher whose English class she'd be teaching, met her at the station and spent that evening talking her through the lesson plan, which Millicent followed scrupulously the next day.

On the train back to Rome that evening, she had a whole compartment to herself. During the next three hours, for the first time since her Roman adventure began, she had time to take stock. She watched her reflection in the train window as the Italian landscape swept by, then closed her eyes and let her mind drift. Her daughter, Alice, was almost eight; her confidence in her teaching performance was growing, it seemed she was more than adequate, maybe even good; she'd have a *career* soon, not just a job, one she might even have a talent for. How elegantly cosmopolitan she was starting a New Life in the Old World, and she was no longer alone with Alice now that she was here with Enrico, The Prince. Look how far she'd come!

Geena was right – she'd been an idiot to imagine that marrying Neal would fix anything. She'd gone through a wild phase. Working as a temp after college, her new friends had introduced her to drugs they promised would make sex even better. She wasn't good at taking drugs but she had always been told she was very sexy. Even her own mother used to say it for god's sake, to her and to everybody. Sexy was what she was.

She managed to preserve her virginity, technically, until she left for college at seventeen, then immediately started on the pill and a course of study her sister called 'Intercourse 101.' "Your university transcript will say: 'Major in English, Minor in *Shtup.*'" She tried to be a responsible person. Phoning her father's lawyer's med-student son a few days after their one-night-stand, she warned him that he might have caught a yeast infection from her. He called her a slut, a dope-moocher, a selfish fuck and hung up.

The day she renewed her driver's license, she met Neal Kadison. A skinny, lower-middleclass, low-level Department of Motor Vehicles bureaucrat, he seemed a godsend that would get her life on a safe track: he was funny, had almost no libido, and, best of all, he wasn't mean. Her mother dripped with disdain for him, but she knew her parents wouldn't protest: he was Jewish.

Geena begged her not to, but in June Millicent married him, a year after graduation and four months after they'd met. On their wedding night, in the bridal suite of San Ensayo, California's best hotel, after the extravaganza wedding her mother had insisted on and stage-managed, Millicent stepped out of the ivory shantung gown and, for one fleeting moment, allowed herself to think, *Shit. What have I done*?

To her mother's undisguised relief, the newlyweds moved to Chicago, two thousand miles away. Three months later, to Millicent's genuine joy, she realized she was pregnant. She loved Alice so much she forgot to be afraid of motherhood.

But, marriage. They bickered constantly, ostensibly over housework and money, but really because she yearned for contact while he wanted to be left alone. When seducing him failed, she'd begged, then nagged, then bitched. When she started shrieking insults intended to wound, she knew she'd crossed a line: she'd have to give up or else become this terrible person she didn't want to be. His silences grew warmer then, as he mistook her resigned distance for permission to withdraw in peace. Divorce was unthinkable – an upheaval, especially for Alice. Millicent stayed for three more years, until she feared she might die of loneliness. She took their daughter and left.

Neal could have had Alice with him Wednesday afternoons and every second weekend, but seldom did. Though Alice could be great company, after two years alone with her, Millicent felt entitled to self-pity. Stuck at Northern Chicago Community College in a secretarial job she hated, and with hardly ever anyone to fuck her, she took periodic vacations into depression.

One day, she heard the buzz around NCCC about some visiting, thirtyish, *homme de femme*. She'd caught sight of him, Enrico Benassai. He held court in the English Department lounge, semi-reclining with one leg draped over the arm of his chair, and with a coterie of young, female students gathered around him. He smiled indulgently at them as if each were his little girl, delightful, enchanting, perhaps, a bit silly. Millicent saw the sex. She knew before he did where this would go.

"Oh, the fucking is fabulous, Geena. Day and night!" Millicent effused. "He's Italian. From Italy. Elegant. More handsome than Mastroianni – he has acne scars, so his face is rugged instead of pretty. With blond curls, like a Renaissance Prince."

"What's he doing there?"

"He married (and divorced) an American, so he has to spend a month in the US every year to keep his Green Card."

"What is he doing at Northern Chicago Community College? Is he a student?"

"No way! He's a man. A grown-up."

Millicent explained that Enrico and his business partner, Bruno, co-owned a language school with branches in Rome, Milan and Bologna. Enrico also taught Italian to middle-aged businessmen, diplomats, their wives, and, even better, he'd said, to their daughters. He hoped to convince Millicent's boss, an old friend of his, to grant college credits to NCCC students if they'd use their year abroad to study Italian at one of *Lingua Nuova*'s schools.

"He walked into the English Department and there I was, sitting on the floor with all the folders spread out around me, re-organizing the filing cabinet. You know what he said? 'We trEEt our bEEautiful women much better in *Italia*. We let you sEEt on chairs.'!"

They'd recognized each other as kindred. She invited Enrico home after telling Neal he'd have to take Alice a lot over the next few weeks. Millicent told Enrico that she'd married to escape from sex and then divorced to reclaim it. Free now to unleash her unabashed sexual enthusiasm, she couldn't keep her hands off him, alone or in public. His muscular forearms, the nape of his neck. Whenever she sat next to him, she removed one of her shoes to rest the sole of her foot against his thigh. She soon had him exulting over her hair-trigger orgasms saying he felt more desired by her than anyone ever before. Millicent began to moan "*Sì!*" whenever she came.

Gradually, a plan emerged: Millicent would use the eleven months until he returned for his next Green Card renewal to learn how to TESL, "Teach English as a Second Language." By then, he'd know if he could offer her freelance work as the Roman branch's only American teacher of English. Her B.A. would enhance *Lingua Nuova*'s professional status.

With new determination, she pulled her daily life together: she washed their clothes more often, kept her apartment cleaner, almost neat, and seldom ran out of food or toilet paper. In the car, Alice whined that she wanted to listen to "*Sesame Street*"; instead, Millicent played the tapes she'd bought to teach herself Italian.

As the months passed, the double entendres in her letters to Enrico were replaced by business ideas. She devised advertising proposals to entice corporate types to study American rather than British English. Some of her executive father's savvy might have seeped into her after all.

She couldn't help noticing that she signed all her missives, "Love," while, Enrico's short notes, scribbled on paper torn from a spiral notebook, offered only "*Un abbraccio,*" a mere hug. But, she understood, he had a whole school to run while she was just a student/secretary/mother.

When Enrico returned, Alice was there too. He called them "Mill-ee-CHEN-ta" and "Ah-LEE-tchei" and Alice called him "REE-coh." He'd bought Alice her very first Barbie doll, which Millicent, at her feminist sister's urging, had long refused to do. Alice spent hours in Barbie-talk and dunking her doll's hair into cups of water. Sometimes he held Alice on his lap and read to her, letting her twirl a piece of his long, blond hair around her finger while Millicent watched from the corner of her eye. Other times, all three of them talked together and laughed and cuddled. Once, Millicent even baked cookies. When Enrico spent days and nights elsewhere during that visit, Alice cried.

So did Millicent. But Enrico declared with pride that he wasn't the stereotypical, *macho* Italian man with a double standard. Yes, he required liberty, but he granted Millicent her freedom as well.

"*Millicenta*, I want to be perfectly honest with you right from the start," he said. "I will never marry you."

"That's fine. No problem," she'd responded, thinking that lots of couples lived together without getting married. She knew better than anyone that marriage didn't solve anything.

And now, here she and Alice were – in Italy. With The Prince!

As the train pulled into Rome's *Stazione Termini*, her trusty internal radio switched itself on playing Johnny Nash, '*I Can See Clearly Now'*, the perfect refrain for the moment, reminding her that the outlook was bright and the pain of her life wasn't there anymore at all.

****

Alice was asleep when she arrived from the train station.

An ashtray on Millicent's nightstand overflowed with lipstick-stained cigarette butts that weren't hers. Neither was the gold bracelet next to it.

"Who was here last night, Silvana?"

"Enrico," Silvana answered, her back to Millicent, then added, softly, "and Mariangela."

"Who?"

"Hasn't he told you?" Silvana looked away from Millicent as she revealed that Enrico had been bringing nineteen year old Mariangela from Bologna to this apartment for almost a year.

"Alice? Did Alice see them together?" She felt faint.

Silvana nodded, slowly.

When Silvana left the kitchen, Millicent crammed the ashtray and the bracelet into an empty milk carton which she shoved deep into the trash. She ripped the sheets off the bed she could no longer think of as 'ours', hurled herself down and cried deep sobs.

She'd been aware of his distance. She'd known but refused to admit that his passion for her derived primarily from luxuriating in her passion for him. He'd found her body too womanly, not girlish enough, he felt daunted. Almost unmanned.

"I was honest," he declared the next night, with a belligerence that seemed forced. "I said I'd never marry you."

"You didn't say you'd be with someone else. With my daughter next door!" Millicent hissed. "We came over from Chicago, Enrico."

"Mariangela is devastated. Her father gave her that bracelet."

"I should give a fuck?'

Millicent watched herself play the "wronged woman" to Enrico's "honorable but insistently 'free' man." She wept, he expostulated, they both talked at once, until, all of a sudden, they stopped. They looked at each other, with matching, sober smiles.

Look at us playing out this silly scene, she seemed to say during that silence.

Addio, amore, he seemed to respond.

Goodbye, my dearest, Millicent's sad smile said.

Whereupon, they resumed the process of ending their relationship.

Maybe she should have taken a lesson from Bruno's wife and Silvana's husband: laughed, tweaked his cheek and said, "Grow up, jerk. Fuck her until you're done – in her bed, please, not ours. Then, let's get on with it." He might have answered, "Give me some time. You and Alice moving here scares me shitless," which probably was true. What if they had married? Had built up *Lingua Nuova*, raised Alice plus children of their own, grown old together, accepting each other's foibles with indulgent humor since they knew all too well how imperfect they both were.

"It was weird, Geena. Like a whole alternative life trajectory was playing itself out in front of us. One I hadn't expected. We came all the way over here, you know? This morning, I looked in the mirror and asked myself, 'Do you want to go home? You have an American Express Card. You could leave today.'"

"And you answered?"

"We're in Italy. Geena, we're in *Roma*."

3

Geena mocked Millicent's penchant for drama until, a week later, the stakes shot up. A weeping Silvana informed Millicent that she and Bruno were splitting up and moving home to their respective spouses. As an act of mercy toward Millicent, Silvana's husband would wait until the last minute to remove the furniture. She had until the end of the following month to find a place to live.

In a foreign city, a foreign language? Could she afford to take over Bruno's lease and buy the furnishings? Or rent a smaller place in that same complex? She approached the *portiere*, a man in his fifties with a five o'clock shadow and a sweat-drenched shirt stretched tight across his belly. He was in the courtyard sweeping up the previous day's bougainvillea blossoms and he knew who she was. She'd locked herself out of the apartment a few weeks ago and he'd used his master key while grumbling something snide in broken English about the comings and goings in *"l'apartamento del professore comunisto."*

Millicent asked him about a rental in her best Italian. He looked her straight in the eye. With raised shoulders and upturned palms he shook his head. "*Signora.* A woman, alone? With a child? A…divorced woman? *Ma signora*. *Non è possibile*." The sexual revolution may have been in full swing in America, but it hadn't reached Italy.

Charlotte already knew by the following day. Millicent guessed that Charlotte was no stranger to break-ups and she felt sure she'd detected something sardonic mixed with a bit of sympathy. What had Enrico said, and to whom?

By Wednesday, when she met with Atlas, Jocasta knew too – the Silvana rumor mill seemed to work in both directions. Her diatribe focused on retaliation. She considered vengeance a moral imperative, a matter of self-respect.

"Invite a mother and child across the ocean and put them out onto the street. *Che stronzo*!" Millicent flinched. *Uno stronzo*? A piece of shit, a fucker, an asshole, a cocksucker?

"Leave it to me," Jocasta continued, seething. "I am not without resources and connections. I will throw you a dinner party."

****

Eight Men of Power and their assorted wives and paramours gathered around the elegantly set, roof-terrace table. (Jocasta had let it be known that this very garden was soon to be photographed and featured as the centerfold in the glossy magazine, *Ville Vive*, showplace of the homes of the *ricchi e famosi*.) Millicent struggled to interpret the group's absence of merriment. Were the silent signals they emanated conspiratorial? Were they all pissed off? Paranoid? Or maybe they just didn't like her.

"Is something going on?" Millicent asked Sergio Lo Chiano. Jocasta had seated the journalist with nicotine-stained fingers beside her since his wife had recently left him.

"This morning, there was another assassination attempt. This one in *Bologna*," Sergio explained in sophisticated English. "No wonder we call the times we're in now, *gli anni di piombo,* 'the Years of Lead.'"

Despite the somber mood, the gathering fulfilled Jocasta's intention to rescue Millicent: one of the women knew a diplomat named Colin Sanford. He'd been subletting the rooms in the *Via Scarlata* apartment in Rome's *centro storico* that he rented to a twenty-year-old Algerian demi-monde named Enchantée, and her German Shepherd, Désirée. She had kept a queue of paunchy, balding Arab "friends" on the stairwell and consistently "forgot" both to pay the rent and to clean up after her pet. Everyone laughed. Perhaps Colin Sanford could help with some accommodations?

Colin phoned Millicent the next day. He had two furnished bedrooms and a bath to rent out at a price she could afford, in a 3-bedroom apartment spread over the three top floors of a 16th century *palazzo* in Rome's historic center.

"We're across the bridge from *Castel Sant'Angelo*," he explained, "immortalized by Dante in his Eighth Circle of Hell, the one reserved for Panderers, Seducers and False Flatterers. It's where the Popes' escape tunnel from the Vatican led and the setting for Puccini's *Tosca* – the gullible *fanciulla* jumps to her death from those very ramparts when she realizes the bullets they'd shot at her lover hadn't been blanks after all. Remember: the etymological heart of the word 'romance' is *Roma*. Can you come this afternoon?"

The elevator was stuck so Millicent and Alice walked up the three narrow flights of stairs.

"Ah, *madre e figlia*," Colin greeted them at the door. "How lovely, I thought to myself when my colleague suggested you as a replacement for disreputable Enchantée *e il suo cane*: wholesome domesticity to brighten my hearth." While Alice was off inspecting what might become her room, he whispered, "I am also pleased how luscious you are. You will take it won't you?" Millicent appreciated this urbane banter and his reputation as a rake, particularly since their co-habitation would be simplified by her not finding him, with his forty-ish balding pate and flushed, plump cheeks, at all attractive. She wondered, too, whether the thrust of his sexual inclinations pointed elsewhere.

"You'll be living here on borrowed time," he warned. "Property managers adore embassy and consulate tenants: no Roman would move in without a rental contract and none of us from the peripatetic diplomatic corps dares to be bound by one."

He explained how the neighborhood, like much of Rome, was vertically stratified: a coffee bar and stores on the ground floor, poor folks and petty law-breakers one flight up on what they call the first floor, *il primo piano*, shopkeepers on *il secondo piano*.

"Up here where the sun shines, on our third, fourth and fifth floors, there's the likes of us – and the Neumanns, a retired American couple who live across the landing. They've been away because he was sick, but I think they may be back now."

"We'll take it," Millicent said, greatly relieved.

They moved in the following weekend.

4

While Millicent was drilling Atlas on the past perfect continuous tense, or, as she called it, the "happened-and-kept-on-happening time," a crew carrying photographic equipment filed past Jocasta's kitchen door. Atlas had finally managed to say, "The soldier has been shooting," instead of his usual, "the soldier shoot and shoot." Millicent cried out, "Hurray!" and a man walked in asking for a drink of water. Around her own age, soft-spoken, taller and more broad-shouldered than most Italian men, his short, black beard, loose pants and smock-like shirt reminded her of Caravaggio. His left hand ring finger was bare.

He seemed not to notice her. Having been so recently usurped by Mariangela, she had collapsed into the certainty that no one ever would. She was wearing a paisley tunic made from a faded Indian bedspread over her old Levis with the eagle rump-patch. Both had been scrounged from a Point Acuerdo, California, Free Box half a decade ago. With her long, straight, black hair parted in the middle, she could hardly have looked more American.

As she was leaving the apartment an hour later, he spoke to her. He introduced himself as Fabrizio Donizetti, the photographer on this *Ville Vive* assignment, and switched to English: "Maybe you wish to ate a dinner with me late tonight?" he said with a thick accent. He said that he lived in Milan and would enjoy some company while in Rome.

Her frantic search for a babysitter yielded a cash-poor opera student, the sister of Charlotte's *cinq-à-sept* "Wednesday Boy." Unsure how the evening might pan out and wanting to be certain that Alice would be looked after, Millicent arranged for the sitter to sleep over.

At the restaurant, she learned that Fabrizio, like many Europeans, wore his wedding ring on his right hand. Nonetheless, she accompanied him to his hotel when he invited her, partly in the spirit of 'if you can't beat them, join them', and partly because she was lonely and in need of sexual solace. After the second of the evening's four fucks, she asked him if he minded her being easy-to-get. On the contrary, he said, he preferred her *"onestà americana"* (her "American honesty") to the hypocritical games Italian women played. Clearly this wasn't his first extramarital foray. He asked if he could call her again after the summer.

At 5 a.m., she took a taxi home to be there before Alice woke up, and as she slipped into her own bed, an unexpected wave of grief over the loss of Enrico flooded her. How pathetic that she was still in love with the *stronzo*.

****

Everyone who could escaped to the seaside in August, leaving hot, sunny Rome to Millicent, Alice, the tourists and a skeleton crew of shopkeepers. There would be no Enrico and Mariangela to rip open her wounds, no Jocasta to toady to, no Fabrizio to remind her that every attractive Italian man had a wife somewhere. But somehow she needed to figure out how she and Alice would make it through August without any income. She hated the idea of making Alice change schools again, but she couldn't afford to keep her in the British school in the fall, and paying less for an Italian private school meant she could just about eke out her earnings so that they'd survive.

Alone together, she and Alice played house. While Alice decorated a Barbie world high up in her bedroom's built-in *armadio*, Millicent scrubbed and organized her own closet, and the kitchen cupboards. She bought an Italian cookbook, in English, and experimented with unfamiliar cuts of meat. She learned that if she acted slightly irritated, the grocery store lady here would give her precisely what she wanted and sometimes even smile. Inspired by the begonias covering one entire wall of the butcher shop, Millicent went straight to the florist. She lugged home a philodendron giganteum, with huge leaves. It had air roots so it could nourish itself.

"It's a St. Bernard plant," Alice said.

"Only we don't have to walk it," Millicent added.

Colin came and went – Millicent never knew whether for work or pleasure – and sometimes he invited them to dine at one of his avant-garde haunts. She loved how the staff indulged his every whim. He had initiated Alice into the delights of *Monte Bianco*, a chestnut extravaganza with liqueur, chocolate and whipped cream and winked to the waiter to make sure her serving was huge.

And he took it upon himself to spare Millicent from future disgrace by whispering discreet correctives: *Pasta* wasn't undercooked when it was *al dente,* firm between the teeth. If she wanted more than a lonely slab of meat on a plate, she'd have to order *un contorno,* some vegetables or potatoes. And, oh horror of horrors, Millicent! Only boors and Americans drink *cappuccino* after breakfast time.

For much of that month, Millicent and Alice were tourists. At *Piazza Navona,* they ate ice cream from tall fluted glasses with long handled spoons. They tossed coins in the *Fontana di Trevi* and made wishes. They imagined wearing colorful togas and shopping two thousand years ago at the *Mercati di Traiano*. They stalked tasty Christians at the Coliseum, while roaring and laughing. After *la catacomba sulla via Nomentana*, however, they both had bad dreams. Those weren't Disney skeletons. Real bone dust had gone up their noses, from real dead people.

Inside a series of Roman churches, Millicent dropped 100 *lire* coins into the metal boxes and lit "holy" candles, reveling in the echoing silence and all that art while Alice mouthed conversations for her dolls. The only doors barred to them were to Rome's lone Synagogue which was closed that August due to a bomb threat.

They had tried to find summer companions for Alice, but it had been a struggle. Millicent sent her down to the small piazza at the end of their street to play with the neighborhood kids, but whenever she looked out, Alice was sitting alone on the curb, hugging her knees. A bucked-toothed girl around Alice's age lived only one floor below them, but her shopkeeper father forbade her to enter any foreigner's home. Alice visited her once, and came back in tears clutching a Barbie torso. The girl's big brother had torn blonde-haired Barbie limb-from-limb and kept the head. On Alice's behalf, Millicent looked forward to summer's end and the beginning of school.

5

Some of Alice's former classmates from the British school finally returned to Rome toward the latter part of August. One of the longed-for play dates Millicent organized for Alice freed her to visit a local clothing boutique in an attempt to make herself feel more like the elegantly groomed Italian women she encountered every day.

"*È americana, Lei? Ma è piccola, come se fosse una di noi!*" ("You're American? But you're as petite as if you were one of us!") the bored owner gushed before embarking on educating Millicent, the day's only client, in how to put outfits together, "*come un'italiana.*" She showed her a gray silk dress in a subtle rose print, with dozens of tiny, fabric-covered buttons running up the back, up the high collar, up the long, narrow cuffs. Millicent shook her head, no – she hadn't yet learned the Italian words for "prim" or "nun-like."

The storeowner knew her craft and insisted she try it on. The minute she looked in the full-length mirror, Millicent saw the piquant, almost perverse, contrast between the dress's buttoned-up modesty and the tantalizing way the silk slid over her hips with every movement and then continued swaying long after she stood still. *Any man,* Millicent thought, *who had ever touched a woman, would long to caress the soft, firm hips hidden, yet revealed, beneath that silk.* With less tuition to pay, she worked out she still had enough to buy herself the dress and the accessories the boutique owner recommended: a soft suede blazer, high-heeled boots, purse and earrings. Donning her purchases in front of her bedroom mirror that night, she fantasized about Fabrizio's admiring photographer's glance.

****

When had she last had a makeover? Five years ago, her "Free Box" transformation before Geena's first sculpture exhibition. Geena had urged her to fly from Chicago with two-and-a-half-year-old Alice to attend the opening of her show at Beau Jangles, the Point Acuerdo café that transformed into a discotheque on weekends. She had also, eventually, convinced Millicent not to tell their parents – neither about the exhibit nor that Millicent and Alice would be in California without visiting them.

"I'm showing three pieces," Geena had said. "They're made of wood. Like your husband's head."

"We'll only be gone a week," Millicent had reassured Neal who stood, in an icy rage at Chicago's O'Hare airport, his crossed arms clutched so tight against his skinny chest he barely breathed, his thin lips pursed so hard they turned white. She'd performed as elaborate a display of sorrow-at-leaving as she could mock up while hating him for his constant, punitive, silent displays of resentment.

Geena greeted Millicent at the San Francisco Airport with a hug, nibbled Alice's neck and stood back to have a look. "What a pair of 1958, Leave-it-to-Beaver throwbacks," she exclaimed. "But we'll fix that."

"I don't have money. And Neal…"

"Not to worry," Geena laughed as they climbed into the cab of her flatbed truck. She rammed the stick-shift pole into gear and roared off, her muffler a rattling misnomer. She drove them across the Golden Gate Bridge, westward as far as the continent stretched, and up the coast to what was left of downtown Point Acuerdo now that back-to-landers, dope-growers and arty types had driven the fishermen, loggers and sheep farmers out.

She parked in front of the health food store. "Our village *couturier*," she said pointing to the "Free Box" with a handwritten sign over it, "Put in whatever you're done with. Take out whatever you like." Geena pulled out a tie-dyed t-shirt for Millicent and a pair of bell-bottomed Levis with an embroidered eagle patch on the rump. For Alice, she unearthed toddler-sized overalls just like her own, and little hiking boots.

Geena turned onto an unmarked dirt road leading to the combination cabin and studio she was buying cheap since the dope-dealer selling it was in jail. Once inside, Alice climbed happily into the plastic laundry basket that Geena had filled for her with a rainbow of fabric remnants. While Alice conversed with a long purple frill, Geena showed Millicent her sculptures.

Two of the three oversized, carved wooden heads hanging on the white wall appeared to balance on the five-foot long pikes she had rammed up into their necks. Their tongues lolled in silent screams while their lifeless eyes blared in horror. "I've called it 'The Insane Despot and Her Thieving Mate'," Geena grinned. No mistaking it: here were Phyllis and Herb Milner. Geena and Millicent's parents.

"You can't do this to them," Millicent whispered, her face pale. "It's like you've assassinated them." She stared down at the floor, then over at Alice who was falling asleep with her thumb in her mouth, her fingers stroking a swatch of blue flannel.

"Amazing, huh? Made them from an old telephone pole. That's why it stinks of creosote in here. Carved them, blow-torched them, plunged them into a tub of water. When they were dry, I brushed, them, hard. With this." She smiled again, displaying a stiff, steel wire brush. "The burnt summer growth is softer. Brush it away and you're left with just the winter grain." Geena looked across at Millicent's downturned face. "Great texture. Go ahead, stroke it."

Millicent refused, feeling faintly sick.

"Creating destruction isn't the same as destroying, you know Mill."

The third carved head was completely different: Millicent and Geena's faces, cheek-to-cheek, shared one pair of ears and were framed by the same mane of curly hair. "Siamese twins, joined at the temple," Geena said. "No pikes for us, honey. Looks like we're hovering in mid-air, doesn't it?" Geena had sanded the sisters' faces silky smooth then painted them pantomime-white. Their eyes were closed, their smiles vapid. "Frozen, hostess smiles," Geena crowed like a roost-ruling cock from her bar stool perch.

"You can't exhibit these, Geena. They'd never speak to you again."

"I should be so lucky."

"You don't really mean that. He does love us, you know, and she can sometimes be nice, too."

Geena looked at her, hard. "Oh, absolutely *charming*. What's with you, refusing to get it? Amnesia? Or Stockholm syndrome?"

"What's that?"

"Kiss up to your torturer, maybe she won't kill you." Geena squinted at her sister. She flung open a cupboard drawer, selected a tube, squeezed a worm of paint onto a fresh sheet of palette paper, rummaged through a ceramic crock filled with brushes until she found the one she wanted.

"Don't!" Millicent cried as Geena approached their mask.

"I'd never harm you," Geena said, softly. "I just realized I've left part of the story out."

With great care, Geena painted Millicent's carved lips vermilion.

Lying on the folding cot at Geena's that night, Millicent thought how her sister always exaggerated. Really. She made their mother out to be some cruel madwoman who had constantly beaten them. Sure, there had been spankings, like when they'd broken her red glass lamp. And, oh…that time…when they'd forgotten to rinse out their day-camp thermos and she had grabbed Geena and slammed her against the wall and – yes – *beaten* her with the padded lunch bag, raising red welts. "You! Disgusting! Pig!" she'd yelled. Millicent had only cried. She didn't try to stop her. How could she? Nobody could.

But, Geena always left the good stuff out. Their mother would sometimes want a cuddle, or would perform songs for them. She loved to tell everybody how beautiful Millicent was; she paraded her almost. But now, as she lay in the still night, she remembered the time her mother held her when she was crying and stroked her hair. Then, without warning, shoved her away like she was an ugly freak, stood up and started hollering, "Look what your snot has done to my good silk blouse!" Her eyes were slits. "What do you have to snivel about, you selfish brat? If anybody should be crying here, it's me!" Her mother had looked so desperate that of course Millicent had felt sorry for ruining her blouse. But surely, their mother didn't mean to hurt them. She wasn't perfect, but surely, she only wanted the best for them. And didn't Daddy, too?

It was too confusing. Millicent fell asleep.

The next day, while several of Geena's friends helped swaddle the heads in blankets and load them onto her truck, Millicent sat on a stool holding one pike in each hand, straight up.

"Some weapons you got there, Mama," L.D. said, the bearded Mountain Man who was Geena's boyfriend, sort of. Millicent tried, in vain, to ignore his sheepskin vest turned pelt-side-out, his horn belt buckle, the solidity of his thighs, the fading of his jeans where that bulge had abraded the dye. *Mama*? He'd called her? Because of Alice? Because her bureaucrat-wifeness shone through despite the denim Geena had encased her in?

At last, Geena shouted for him and the disturbing block of maleness left, with the inevitable quip, "Your big sister sure gives good heads."

After the exhibit, Millicent and Alice flew back to Chicago, to Neal, dressed in Free Box garb, her first overt act of marital rebellion.

Now, here she was in Italy, in her thirties and alone again. She examined her face in the mirror and decided she'd better start wearing make-up. She had learned it was the obligation of any self-respecting Italian woman to take care of her looks. "*Laciarsi andare,*" to let oneself go, was the cardinal sin. When Enrico and the staff of *Lingua Nuova* re-convened after the summer and Fabrizio called, Millicent would be ready.

6

Though scheduled for ten o'clock, the first *Lingua Nuova* staff meeting of the new semester began, *alla romana*, at around eleven. Over the summer break, Enrico and Bruno had signed a corporate contract for Millicent to teach a full semester of day-long classes in Milan, every second Saturday, well paid. Millicent smiled: Fabrizio lived in Milan. She'd have to pay her travel costs but *Lingua Nuova* offered her the use, free of charge, of the one-room apartment they maintained there. She was pleased that Enrico had come through for her in this, at least.

She started planning: the day train up on Friday – eight hours from Rome to Milan, as far as the distance between L.A. and San Francisco – spend as much of that night with Fabrizio as he could finagle, teach on Saturday and, after class, be with him again until the night train left for Rome.

The problem would be finding sitters. Daniela, the dour, young maid she'd hired to pick Alice up from school, clean the apartment, do the laundry, shop for and cook their weekday dinners, had been forbidden by her bus driving fiancé to work evenings or weekends.

The *coloratura* student, her very first sitter, agreed to cover Friday and Saturday night of Millicent's first trip north. All went well that first time, but when Fabrizio and Millicent arrived at *Lingua Nuova*'s apartment for Millicent's second *Milano* trip, the phone was already ringing. A frantic Daniela was on the other end of the line; the Singing Sitter had not shown up – something about "*una grande occasione*," a chance to be a stand-in in the chorus at the opera.

"Daniela? Could you take Alice home with you?" Millicent had to work not to panic. Daniela had agreed, it being the only solution they could come up with. Then, when Millicent returned home Sunday and was tucking Alice into bed, Alice told her, "They sleep three in a skinny bed at Daniela's and with me that made four!" Millicent stroked Alice's head, whispering, "sweetheart," until

Alice let out the sob she'd been stifling. "Mom, I didn't know people could be so poor." Millicent promised that Alice could come with her on her next trip to Milan (so, no Fabrizio). The following day, she raised Daniela's salary.

****

"You need a wife," Geena said, laughing, when they talked at the weekend. "How do you like the teaching, by the way?"

"You may not believe this. I think I'm actually good at it."

"That wouldn't surprise me at all."

Millicent had wholeheartedly embraced the use of games and role play and literary texts and had plunged right in with her students.

"Bet they love that," Geena said.

"We're on verbs of existence, verbs of sensation, linking verbs, helping verbs."

"Such as?"

"*'Be am are is, was were been being, may can, must might, shall will, could would should, have has had, do did does*.'"

"How could I have forgotten?"

How grateful she was to have Geena to phone. "Turns out my eighth grade English teacher didn't tell us the official grammar-book category these all belong to. Know what that is?"

"I'm waiting."

"…'*Copulative verbs*'."

"Ha! You're kidding!"

"You know, like 'bound together'. I *be-am-are-is* at my best when I come to class straight from underneath Fabrizio, having had his Italian injected into me, up and down."

"Smiling at both ends!" Geena said. "Don't forget to shower before class, babe. The scent of fuck-dust lingers."

7

A taxi driver lugged Hermina Neumann's baggage up the flights of *Via Scarlata* stairs to her apartment, across the landing from Millicent and Alice. She opened the shutters, removed the sheets from the tables and sofas, and saw everything in the late summer light, unaltered: her Etruscan figurines, their books and papers, Sam's *libretti*, recordings, tapes, everything. She phoned *la donna* who cleaned and cooked for them. She rang their few friends in Rome, those of a certain age who had known that Sam was sick. Then she left to buy food.

The shopkeeper gathered a bouquet of oregano, rosemary and sage for her after learning of her husband's death. The butcher, a kind man whose wife tended the shop's wall of begonias, held onto her hand when giving her the half kilo of *petto di pollo* she'd asked for – too many chicken breasts for one person and they both knew it. He looked into her eyes with solemn tenderness and refused her money.

She trudged up the stairs. When she entered the apartment, Sam's absence exploded out at her. The shock wave hurled her down onto the entry hall sofa. Her grocery bags hit the floor. Why in hell was she still alive?

Now, Hermina, you'll feel much better if you get up, she heard Sam say each day. *And dressed. You'll feel better if you make the bed. Now, get on with it.* The weeks passed and she knew she ought to deal with his clothes. She came as far as opening his side of the *armadio* and forcing her fingers into contact with the frayed cuffs of his tweed jacket, the one she'd been threatening to throw out for years. "You'll have to bury me in it," he'd joked, but they'd left it behind in Rome. If one piece of clothing might still retain the scent of Sam, this would be it. She inhaled. No. Only musty wool.

She emptied the pockets onto the bedspread and found a 100 *lire* coin, a balled up handkerchief and two slips of paper. One was the receipt for the shaving cream he'd bought when they realized they needed to see what was beneath his beard.

A beard had once represented poverty and Jewish orthodoxy, both of which he'd escaped. After he sold the business and retired, freedom from shaving seemed luxurious. But last January, they'd needed to see his face.

She had known something was wrong: he'd lost his appetite and too much weight; his nails were yellow; he was complaining of a metallic taste; he seemed panicky when the elevator didn't work or when he grasped how far a museum was from the bus stop. She was sure he knew, too. But it took her accusatory look, as if he'd been cheating on her, to make him shave.

She'd placed that day's *La Repubblica* across the bathroom sink and handed him her sewing scissors. Sam said the clumps of beard falling onto the papers reminded him how the fake snow had hit the stage during a performance of *La Bohème*; the snow machine lost its grip and chunks of white plastic thudded down while the undaunted chorus belted out their cheerful song.

When he'd cut all he could with the scissors, Hermina had folded the newspaper the way she'd folded tablecloths around crumbs after the dinner parties they hosted for eccentric, successful musicians during those years when Sam had found his way onto the Philharmonic's Board. Their American home had had all the glimmering elegance of late 19th century European aristocrats, yet all the camaraderie and warmth of early 20th century European immigrants. He'd made his *stetl*-born mother proud. Hermina would have preferred smaller, less formal affairs but she did those gatherings dutifully and well. She liked hearing fresh concert-circuit gossip and then, in her participant-observer fashion, running the analytical, cultural play-by-play for Sam once the guests had left.

Now, ten years later, he'd dug into the archeology of the closet to unearth his old shaving brush, the heavy razor and a little paper-wrapped packet containing one, last, double-edged blade. Hermina had protested at the *La Traviata* song Sam was humming as he shaved – Giorgio's aria to convince Violetta that leaving his son Alfredo would be a supreme gesture of love.

When they were young, Hermina had stood behind Sam, her body pressed against his naked back, and watched him shave. He'd used a straight razor then and she'd exclaimed how brave he was holding a murder weapon to his own throat every day; she'd kissed the back of his neck challenging him to keep a steady hand. But not now. She stood behind him without touching him, her arms crossed, her fingers clutching at her sleeves, her eyes wild.

After Hermina had stuffed the newspaper containing what was most likely Sam's final beard into the kitchen trash, they looked at his face in the mirror. They could see clearly that he was not a well man. They'd both known: fate might be a shock, she'd said, but it is rarely a complete surprise.

The Italian specialist declared the three-quarter inch, asymmetrical, scallop-edged, reddish black patch of skin just above his jawbone to be the harbinger of a Stage IV, aggressive, metastasizing, malignant melanoma. They'd left immediately for the States.

8

When Hermina returned from her walk, a little girl raced past her shouting something down the echoing stairwell to her young mother. She soon flew past as well, laughing and flinging a breathless, "*Mi scusi signora*!" at Hermina, who held onto the stair rail and watched them as they bounded up.

"I won! Again! *Come sempre!*" came the child's voice from the top floor. The two had already closed their door by the time Hermina arrived at hers. It seemed that the other tenant, the sad girl and her scruffy German shepherd, had been replaced.

Hermina saw the mother and child a second time on the street one afternoon and nodded. The mother nodded back politely with no sign of recognition. Over her morning *cornetto* and *Caffè Hag* at the local bar, she noticed them seated at a table in the corner. From professional habit and sheer human curiosity, she observed the intensity of their exchanges, the young mother's tender patience, the way their language swung between an educated east or west coast American and an acceptable Italian, with, at least on the part of the little girl, a bit of a Roman accent. To Hermina's trained eye, they looked more like Ashkenazi Jews than Italians.

"You can stop *working* as an anthropologist, but apparently you can't quit *being* one," Sam had said; he enjoyed teasing her about her analytical approach to life. Since her retirement, her curiosity and her reading had focused less on cultures and more on individuals. Often, she and Sam played the game of creating lives for strangers; actually, she made up the tales and Sam embellished them. She still talked to him, sometimes even out loud on the street. As she sipped her coffee, she observed them discreetly and from the minute details she registered about her neighbors she wove a story from the threads.

The mother and daughter, she noted, breakfasted weekdays at the coffee bar. Whenever a man came into the bar, the mother seemed uncomfortable, self-conscious, which suggested to Hermina that she was unattached. Since it was statistically unlikely for someone that young to be a widow, she might be divorced, Hermina concluded, although, these days it was no longer improbable for someone even of her apparent social class to have borne a child out of wedlock. Perhaps she was a lover of the diplomat who rented the apartment and sublet the extra bedrooms, but Hermina doubted that; he seemed too eccentric for her and, at the same time, too dull. Besides, he was hardly ever home.

The child was, perhaps, seven or eight. She watched her climb onto a stool to initiate a loud conversation with the bar owner above the roar of the milk steamer as her mother continued to read the *International Herald Tribune* at their usual table. The child seemed well-socialized, indicating some discipline at home, yet, Hermina noticed a tinge of chaos about her, both in the urgency with which she spoke and in how oblivious she seemed as to whether or not someone listened to her. She was not a neglected child. Absolutely not – the affectionate tenderness between the mother and daughter moved Hermina. But she was not completely secure. Though, what child ever is? Not even David had been, her own son.

Perhaps the woman's ex-husband was Roman, Hermina hypothesized, on her way to buy a ticket to the Picasso retrospective, which Sam would have wanted her to attend despite his death. No. had she been here that long, her Italian would have been better. If the father had moved back here on his own, perhaps, she'd followed to ensure their daughter's contact with him. Italian men may cling to their progeny as property but often drop them like stones – especially their daughters – once they become inconvenient responsibilities. Had the young woman forged a bond with her parents-in-law and wanted her daughter to grow up near them? Hermina stopped on the street and laughed at herself. Sam would have teased her, as a mother-in-law herself, for coming up with such a transparently self-aggrandizing scenario. Perhaps she'd been alienated from her own family. Such a history might account for her edge of desperation.

Entering her building, Hermina noticed an article of doll clothing lying on the lower stairs, a tiny, iridescent purple peignoir with matching fake-fur trim, probably for the doll called a 'Barbie'. Would she have permitted a daughter or granddaughter of hers to possess such a toy? A plastic woman with disproportionately long legs and large breasts? Now Sam chided her for being doctrinaire.

This train of thought brought her back, again, to what their lives would have been, hers in particular, if she had not delivered a stillborn daughter in her fifth month of pregnancy, two years before David was born. Although sons are valued above daughters in most cultures, Hermina suspected that her own maternal nature might have grown more ardent and her career ambitions proportionally less so, had that girl-child, Inanna, lived. Would David's politics have turned to the Ruthless Reagan Right if she had been softer? If they'd had a daughter (and/or a granddaughter?), would Hermina still be in Rome now that she was – and she could barely think the word, much less apply it to herself – a widow?

She and Sam had rarely had the opportunity to check out how well their invented life histories jibed with reality. She decided to use the doll's nightgown as an excuse to knock on the neighbors' door. No one answered. She'd try again some other day.

9

Millicent had never thought about the elderly woman in their building and failed to recognize her when she came knocking on the door. She had found what Alice called "a doll 'clo'" – a perfect example of internalized grammar since if "dolls" is a plural with the singular being "doll" then "clothes" must be plural and the singular must be "clo'."

The interruption came immediately after Millicent had heard from Fabrizio that he couldn't meet her on her next work trip to *Milano* because "they," that awful word, were having company. If she bumped into him at the train station, he warned, she must not greet him, like that Dylan song, she thought but didn't say, '*She Acts Like We Never Have Met*'. Rather than stay alone all evening at the Milan apartment, she'd take the Friday night train, which she hated. She couldn't afford a private sleeping compartment and would have to share one with five weird hags. She'd teach badly the next day, deprived of both sleep and sex.

Millicent thought the soft knocking she heard was Alice tacking up another princess drawing on the hall corkboard. The name of the American old lady standing there on the landing was something like *hermana*, Spanish for 'sister,' a word she had learned while helping Geena study for high school quizzes. Longing only to shut herself in her room with her Fabrizio misery, Millicent would have refused the invitation for coffee and cake, but Alice wanted to go. She pulled on her mother's arm, hung on it and mobilized all her facial features into the high-eyebrowed, stretched-smile pleading she reserved for things she knew were possible. Irresistibly cute, sweet Alice. (She used a different approach when begging for impossibilities – a twelve-inch lollipop or a six-foot teddy bear – involving histrionic sighs and the tilting of her head while her eyebrows pulled together into a deep furrow.)

Millicent found their shoes, locked their door, pivoted on the landing, and entered through the open door facing them. The lady hadn't just moved in. This was an established American-European home, where even the entry hall was furnished; a table with a stack of magazines and a lamp on it stood beside the door, next to a faded, burgundy velour sofa. Family photos covered the walls. As if all that weren't bad enough, Millicent noticed a menorah standing on a bookshelf. This was a Jewish home.

She didn't want to be involved in any of this and fought the instinct to flee in panic. Instead, she followed the old lady up a few steps into the bright living room; the apartment seemed to be a mirror image of the one they shared with Colin, only smaller, well-furnished and without a loft. Somehow, a piano had been maneuvered up the building's narrow stairs to occupy a corner of the room. Next to it were rows of phonograph records. Leather bound books shared another wall of shelves with yellowing paperbacks, along with dog-eared papers and magazines. Small clay figurines appeared to live there, like tiny inhabitants of an ancient village.

The coffee table was set with porcelain plates and lacy paper napkins. The silver forks, Millicent noticed to her relief, didn't match. The woman produced a pot of *espresso* for Millicent, almond-flavored milk for Alice and a brass tray full of pastries – cream-filled, chocolate dripped, whipped cream topped, even one containing *zabaglione*, which happened to be Millicent's favorite. The whole scene upset Millicent terribly for some reason. She stiffened, turned *polite*, revealing, in a dependent clause, only that she was here teaching English. She asked *polite* questions and carefully avoided filing the answers.

Alice, on the other hand, loved the almond milk and ate two pastries, using better table manners than Millicent remembered teaching her. And she talked. The woman listened, asked questions and commented on Alice's answers. So Alice talked some more. When the woman expressed curiosity about Barbie dolls, Alice cried out, "Wait! Mommy, can I go to our house and get them? Please? Pretty please?"

"We don't have time for that," Millicent said, wanting just to leave. She stood and snatched up her purse but Alice persisted. Millicent yielded – on the condition that she remember to turn the key three times when locking up – and Alice soon returned with her favorite dolls and a shoe box.

"Look at this 'clo'." Alice launched into a discourse, expounding the coherent trains of thought she invested in her toys in even greater detail than usual.

While the woman focused on Alice, smiling and encouraging, Millicent sneaked a look at her. Not much taller than Millicent's five-foot-three, she wore a basic old-lady dress and matching bolero. Her tight hairstyle was probably called a 'bob' in the old days. She'd done nothing about how her gray hair had yellowed and her eyebrows were an unplucked nature preserve. She had appeared twisted when she'd walked across the room, with one of her hips held higher and farther forward, but not crippled. She didn't look sick. She looked like an old lady with old skin, although with very few wrinkles.

Millicent had once heard an actor comment that, while people presume it's the nose that makes someone look Jewish, it's actually the lips. This woman had Jewish lips: fleshy, indomitable, Tevye-lips. And her eyes…even from the side, Millicent could see that her eyes were sad. That's right. She had referred to herself as "recently widowed."

Unaccountably, an image arose of this stranger holding Millicent's face between her hands, looking at her, into her, with those sad, kind eyes, and Millicent felt terrified. Then angry. She stood up abruptly. "Say thank you to Mrs…Mrs…?"

"Neumann. Hermina Neumann."

"We ought to be leaving now. We both have work to do."

And Millicent got them the hell out of there.

****

Hermina had planned to elaborate on the meeting for Sam the moment her neighbors left. Except, she had felt uncomfortable about Alice's parting hug and was ashamed to admit that to him. Why in the world should a child's hug upset her, he would chide.

During the months in California as Sam was dying, she had grown accustomed to the cautious, obligatory embraces of twelve-year old Ethan. She understood that he'd undoubtedly been frightened off by the sights and smells of sickness which his grandparents had brought into his home but not much warmth had been forthcoming from David, either. He was losing his father; as his mother, it was her job to comfort him and not the reverse. She knew David's Protestant wife, Jill, loved her and Sam, but in that chilled *goyishe* style, from across a cultural chasm reinforced by the lack of proximity.

Now, without warning, Alice – a little girl unknown to her until now, had hugged her, intensely. That intensity probably wasn't personal; perhaps, it belonged elsewhere. To a grandmother far away? She replayed the scene in her mind. In her left hand, Millicent held the shoe box into which she'd gathered all the dolls and their clothes, except the red-headed Barbie which Alice carried. Millicent extended her right hand to Hermina with a brusque formality; mother and daughter then turned on the landing to face their own apartment door. While Millicent fumbled with the lock, the child turned again to face Hermina. Resolutely, and, it seemed, with urgency, Alice wrapped her arms around her, pressing her cheek against Hermina's breast as Barbie's stiff legs jabbed into her hip.

At first, Hermina's arms hung at her sides. She hadn't expected this. She'd intended the visit only as a neighborly gesture and (if she was honest) as something she could talk to Sam about. Slowly, her arms rose to wrap themselves around the girl's slender body. She realized now the source of that discomfort. The embrace was the natural consummation of a genuine encounter between two – here it was, the telling word – an encounter between two *lonely* individuals. Alice's body had pressed against Hermina's and Sam's body never would again. After being held in Alice's embrace, Hermina could not deny that Sam was gone. That was her own reaction, but what of Millicent's? As Hermina had rested her cheek on the top of the girl's head, she'd looked up to see Millicent staring at them with an expression resembling absolute horror.

10

The second slip of paper that Hermina had found in Sam's jacket pocket was a note dated January 12th informing him that a record he'd ordered at his favorite music store had arrived. That was how abruptly they'd left to seek medical treatment for him in the States; the last thing Sam would neglect was a new recording.

"Damn it!" Hermina said when she heard the knocking on her door. *Now, Hermina,* Sam's voice suggested, *won't you feel better if you answer that?* She stuffed the note into her pocket.

Alice stood on the landing, her arms out straight, displaying a blonde Barbie. "Look," she said. "I just made her a poncho!"

"Let me see," Hermina said, squelching a curt dismissal under pressure from Sam. She reached for the doll but Alice held onto it, detailing how she'd cut a circle, a small head-hole, in the poncho, but Barbie couldn't get it on and off without taking her head off first.

"That would be funny, huh?" Alice laughed, "If we had to take off our head, every time we got undressed! I have something to show you." As Alice tugged at her sleeve, Hermina relented, crossed the landing and entered her neighbor's apartment for the first time. Alice's bedroom lay just off the entrance hall the way Sam's music room did.

Alice pointed out the rope ladder her mother had asked Colin to hang from the ceiling; she used it to climb into the playhouse she'd made on the top bunk of her wrought iron bed. It also helped her monkey her way up into the Barbie World she'd created in an upper cupboard of the built-in *armadio*. The Barbies had a plastic swimming pool complete with its own tiny ladder, and also a lipstick-red car, an apparently hand-carved wooden convertible. "My aunt Geena made that. She's a sculpture."

"A sculptor? She makes sculptures?"

"Uh-huh."

"Is Geena your mother's sister or your father's?"

"Mommy's. And here's Ken, and here's G.I. Joe. They're the boyfriends and the Barbies always fight. POW! 'Go away!' 'No! You go away.' Hit. Hit. 'I'm the girlfriend, not you.'" The red-haired doll seemed to win on many accounts, including the privilege of wearing the fur coat made, Alice explained, a little sadly, from a real rabbit. She lamented that her dolls lacked the big Barbie house, which her mother said cost too much. She'd made rooms herself out of shoe boxes. "Here's their school, in this box my boots came in. They hate school."

"Are you alone here?"

"Daniela's upstairs. She babysits me."

"Do you think she or your mother would mind if you came on an errand with me to a record shop?"

With the excuse of finding Daniela, Hermina looked around. Millicent's entry hall was empty except for a telephone with a long cord and a bulletin-board covered in princess drawings. Millicent's bed, a mattress and box springs placed directly on the chipped, hand-painted floor tiles, was neatly made, but the crocheted bedspread had holes in it and a water-stain along the hem. Her bathroom had a uselessly big tub given the tiny electric water heater hanging over it. (Sam had installed a gas burner providing them with unlimited hot water.) Hermina climbed the stairs from the hall up to the kitchen; the door to a third bedroom, which she presumed was Colin's, was open. Clothes and books lay scattered around an unmade single bed; an uncurtained window faced an opening hardly bigger than an air shaft. Hermina realized that Alice's room on the floor below shared that same dark view.

More books lined the living room where blocks of foam rubber covered in orange and blue synthetic silk served as sofas. Milk crates served as end tables to hold a few bulbous lamps.

Hermina considered it an appalling act of architectural vandalism that someone had cut through half the living room ceiling, exposing the 16th century *palazzo*'s massive wooden beams and peaked roof, to create a third-floor loft area. At the top of the stairs, two sling-backed chairs stood on a shaggy orange rug in front of a fireplace. A sliding door and metal grate opened onto a roof terrace where Hermina found Daniela smoking a cigarette. Dried dirt and cigarette butts filled the six cement planters. The terrace overlooked a wilderness of TV antennas, chimneys and tiled roofs slanting in all directions. Hermina explained to a skeptical Daniela who she was and where she intended to go with Alice.

The gesture of taking Alice's hand to cross *Corso Vittorio Emanuele II* came automatically; neither let go once they'd reached the other side.

The woman at the record shop said she usually did not keep unclaimed orders for so many months, but this one was special. "I searched hard to find this exact recording which *il signore* Neumann said was an early birthday gift for his wife. That is you, *signora*? Are you sure he wants you to ruin the surprise?"

Once again, Hermina ran the widow's gauntlet of public grieving. This clerk, too, had cared about Sam; he'd given her buying tips, she said, had stood listening with her to new releases, evaluating with her the qualities of six different recordings of Mahler's 8th Symphony.

"*Per favore signora*, wait one moment." She disappeared into the back room.

When she presented Hermina with the record she'd just gift-wrapped, she said, formally, "Happy Birthday from your husband." The clerk looked shaken and Hermina squeezed her hand.

"It's your birthday?" Alice exclaimed. "I didn't know."

"Actually," Hermina said, "my birthday was in July."

"Mine was in June."

Hermina heard Sam make a suggestion to which she yielded. "Then you, too, should have a belated present in September. And perhaps, a pastry, too? But first we'll tell Daniela, so no one worries."

In the crammed toy store located between the flower shop and the butcher, Hermina saw the Barbie house Alice wished for, but she and Sam agreed it would be too lavish a gift. Alice, who seemed to grasp it would be wrong to take advantage of Hermina's generosity, walked past the luxurious Barbie gowns to select a tennis outfit, complete with racket and miniature ball. Hermina insisted Alice turn away while the clerk gift-wrapped it which made Alice laugh.

At the coffee bar, after they sang "Happy Birthday, Alice and Hermina," Alice opened her present. "Just what I wanted!" she cried in hammy astonishment then bounced the tiny tennis ball off their table and chased it across the room.

Once they'd eaten their *profiterole*, it was Hermina's turn. No amount of *Now, Hermina*'s could prevent two tears from sliding down her cheeks. "This is hard for me to open," she explained, so the child wouldn't be frightened by seeing her cry. "My husband, Sam – you two would have liked each other – died only ten weeks ago. This is the last birthday present I'll ever have from him. I'm sure you understand that it makes me both happy and sad."

Alice grew solemn. "Maybe I should open it for you."

"No, thank you." *Hermina!* "Why, yes. That may be just the thing."

This classic early 1950s recording of Prokofiev's *Peter and the Wolf*, narrated by Eleanor Roosevelt in her crackly falsetto, had been David's first version. He'd taken their copy with him when he left for college. Just recently, when she and Sam had referred to Mrs. Roosevelt's courage facing her husband's illness, the war and his love affair with her private secretary, he had said Hermina reminded him of Eleanor. Both women had forged places for themselves in a man's world and maintained their self-respect and their kindness, even under fire. And Hermina's voice, Sam said, also turned screechy whenever she was angry.

"Alice. May I tell you something?"

"What?"

"I'm grateful you knocked on my door today. Thank you."

Alice smiled. The two walked back to Hermina's apartment and Alice listened to *Peter and the Wolf* for the first time. They sat side by side on Sam's favorite listening sofa, with Hermina's arm around Alice's shoulder.

11

When Daniela met Millicent at the door and confessed that Alice had gone off with the *signora,* Millicent fumed, as if Hermina were an interfering old woman out to co-opt her daughter while she was away working her ass off.

She knocked hard on Hermina's door. When it opened, Alice threw her arms around her mother. Millicent stemmed the torrent of tales of birthday cakes, Barbie 'clos', grandfathers and wolves.

"Thank you for your generosity to my daughter, Mrs. Neumann," she said through tight lips while attempting to shove Alice into their apartment. But Alice had suddenly remembered that she'd left behind the gift Hermina had bought her. "Well, go get it, then," Millicent snapped. She had no idea why, but she wanted everything of theirs extricated from that woman's clutches. "Come on," she called out to Alice while looking Hermina in the eye. "Move it!"

"Thank you again for today," Hermina leaned down to tell Alice. Millicent noticed this wasn't the fake, primary colored voice people usually laid on thick when talking to children. Also absent was any trace of an apology for the abduction. Hermina took Alice's face between her hands and, in an apparently heartfelt rendition of the standard Italian salutation, placed actual kisses, first on one of Alice's cheeks and then on the other. From her vantage point behind her daughter, Millicent had a view of the Eastern European, Jewish eyes into which Alice had gazed before wrapping her arms around Hermina's neck. Millicent watched Hermina's eyes close and felt the urge to slap her. Why this vicious anger? It didn't make sense. It was like an allergy, or something.

Although Millicent mentioned the annoying old lady across the hall to Geena, she didn't say anything about her confusion – nor did she forbid Alice to go back there, or tell Daniela to keep her at home. Because Hermina was inviting Alice over often, Daniela was providing less and less childcare over the week and an idea began to take shape in Millicent's mind. She paid through the nose for sitters to cover her weekend work trips to Milan, and she'd already called the three sitters on her list and none was available for her next trip. If Fabrizio ever invited her to escape with him mid-week, as he'd mentioned he might, finding a sitter would be even harder.

"I just came up with a brilliant solution," Millicent told Geena. "Maybe I can get that irritating Hermina across the landing to babysit."

"Now you're cooking," Geena said. "What you can't escape, you might as well exploit!"

Millicent donned her most business-like blazer and smeared a smile over the emotional maelstrom the old lady inexplicably provoked within her. When Hermina opened her door, Millicent offered her the pleasure of Alice's company, the opportunity to babysit for Alice during the next weekend trip, from Friday afternoon until she returned on the night train from Milan, early Sunday morning.

Hermina accepted.

****

Sam had always stacked the scores, *libretti*, program notes and boxed reel-to-reel tapes that he'd been using onto the guest bed in his music room until he was ready to replace them in his archives. He had followed a color-coded filing system Hermina had never dreamed of invading and thus did not understand. Whenever she cleared the bed for guests, she transferred all the piles to Sam's desk, turning each one ninety degrees to maintain his categories. She left the records standing on the floor next to the desk lest they warp.

Since Alice would be sleeping over, what should she do? Heave it all from the bed straight into a garbage bag? That image brought a wave of nausea. Given Sam's arcane tastes, it seemed unlikely that any school or collector would want his archives, though, someone would want Sam's VPI turntable vacuum for cleaning LP's. She'd have to make some calls. Soon. Before she died, she'd promised David.

I'll have to deal with it all when I move home, Hermina heard herself say as she stabilized the tower of riches against the wall at the back of Sam's desk. She froze and looked about her with hare-in-the-headlights eyes. She hadn't been aware that such a decision was taking shape.

"Not yet, Sam!" she said out loud. The grief and effort of stripping this place, exposing the dirty rectangles on the cream colored walls where framed posters and autographed photos now hung, would have to wait. She would do it slowly over the next six months or a year. Maybe longer. She showed, unfortunately, no signs of dying.

In the meantime, she had bright, generous Alice who, over the course of the weekend, revealed a stubborn streak that rivaled her own. If Alice preferred to lounge the sunny afternoons away reading *Topolino*, or Italian translations of *Asterix,* why try to force her into any outings? There seemed to have been more than enough chaos in the child's life; let her control what she could. It pleased Hermina, a woman who had re-shaped a corner of the American field of anthropology by dint of will, to lose battles to a bulldozing eight-year-old. *Get strong, little girl. Life does not favor meek females.*

****

Over the next weeks, Millicent didn't ask Daniela about what Hermina-jaunts had taken place in her absence, nor did she encourage Alice to further embellish her reports on the increasingly frequent visits back and forth: outings, lunches, tea parties, Barbie talks, record concerts, encyclopedia explorations, hair brushings. But, *bubble baths*?

"You take *bubble baths* with Hermina?" Millicent exclaimed. "Together? With her in the tub?"

"No, Mom! Hermina, without her clothes on?" Alice snickered and shook her head.

"Hermina!" Alice called from the tub.

"Ready to get out?" Hermina asked through the closed door. Since Alice had assured her she could swim, she allowed the child privacy.

"Come! Look what I can do!" Hermina entered and seated herself on the toilet seat lid with a large bath towel held in readiness, an appreciative audience for Alice's feats of breath-holding, feet-kicking, belly-sliding, and the splashing of water all over the floor. Admonitions of bathtub hazards gave way to cries of, "My, oh my!" and "Now, will you look at that!"

"My mom always washes my hair for me." Alice sat in the tub as Hermina sudsed her scalp. The room was full of phantoms. The shade of Hermina as an eight-year-old kneeling on a chair in front of the kitchen sink holding a washcloth over her eyes (the way Alice did now) while her mother rinsed her hair with pitchers of water at just the right temperature. Her mother, Hannah, would die before Hermina reached sixteen.

Hermina had named their stillborn daughter Inanna, posthumously, in Hannah's honor, after the Sumerian goddess who reaches the Underworld and manages to return. She would have been a decade older than Millicent now. "I couldn't save our girl," Hermina had wept to Sam, though, he tried to convince her that sometimes babies die *in utero* without it being anyone's fault.

Hermina had never ceased imagining lives for Inanna, following a myriad of potential trajectories. She pictured Inanna at eight years old, here, now, her black hair like Alice's, hanging mid-back when wet but curling to shoulder-length once dry. Inanna could have wrapped herself in a bath towel toga and a hand towel turban as Alice did now. Hermina might have bundled that eel-slim, slippery little body, too, in a towel and watched her girl pretend to suck her thumb like a baby for one delighted moment and then laugh, like Alice, at her own silliness. Sam was here, too, *kvelling* as tenderly over a daughter as he had over his son.

In the midst of this ectoplasmic horde, stood Alice-of-this-moment, singular, alive and smiling.

"Shall I brush your hair for you?" Hermina smiled back.

'*O glaube, mein Herz, o glaube: Es geht dir nichts verloren!*' 'Believe, my heart, oh believe. Nothing is lost to you!' Gustav Mahler and Sam Neumann reassured Hermina. Again.

****

Since the first overnight visit had gone well, when Millicent asked Hermina to repeat the favor for the next trip, and the one two weeks after that, Hermina answered that Alice was no trouble. On the contrary, she had enjoyed having her. But when Millicent snarled sweetly that she could only pay her what she gave the other sitters, Hermina had nearly thrown her right out of the apartment. Claiming she had something boiling in the kitchen, she stormed off. The insolent ass! *Now, Hermina!* Sam admonished, sternly.

She stood beside the stove, cross-armed, taking deep breaths until her fury abated and she could hear Sam's moderating explanation: *Empathy, Hermina.* Millicent is in pain for some reason. She might hate to need anything, to be beholden to anyone. Maybe she even felt a little ashamed. Hermina could grant her this.

An apparently serene Hermina returned to Millicent in the front hall to clarify that she was functioning as a friend, not as a paid sitter. And, as such, she invited Millicent to lunch with her and Alice upon Millicent's return from Milan next Sunday. Millicent's tight acceptance left Hermina with a "gotcha" grin that illumined the remainder of her afternoon.

12

Before each encounter with Fabrizio, Millicent booked herself in for a manicure, a facial and an eyebrow wax. He was a photographer. He saw. She liked the way he'd said his fashion models were "steel dusted in gold," while she was, "an ingot, solid gold through and through." She'd scanned for sarcasm, but found none. He'd organized a hotel room for them this time, around the corner from the shoot. As usual, she'd packed candles and matches plus a scarf to drape over the lamp to soften the lighting. She packed massage oil and a vibrator, her pills, a cassette player and music tapes ranging from fuckable rock to romantic classics. She knew how to do this. It was the one thing she had always been good at.

As she packed only her newest clothes, she thought of those back-to-school wardrobe shows for Daddy that her mother had stage-managed each of her pre-teen and teenage years. As directed, Millicent had swept in through the kitchen door, flounced over to the sofa and then pivoted, slowly, while the emcee – her mother – exhorted the proud, though, embarrassed audience – Daddy – to applaud for "the glamorous allure of the *hot* little model" – Millicent.

She didn't want to know how Fabrizio explained these nights away, nor did she choose to interpret the smile on his lips when once he let slip that his wife's name was Teresa. She refused to look at photos of his kids. He had explained that as his photography studio was in their home, Millicent could never phone him. So every phone call and every encounter required Fabrizio's initiative, which Millicent took as proof that he wanted to be with her.

He'd given her the number of a friend of his in Rome whom she could call in case of emergency, a man named Massimo, but he discouraged her from using it. Fabrizio had narrated adventures he'd had while crewing with Massimo on a cruise ship years ago – joking about how they'd once bet on which of them could seduce a honeymooning bride. Fabrizio claimed to have won.

She hated it when he said things like, "Don't think about me too much," reminding her that he had a life elsewhere. She would have to make damned sure that Fabrizio would find it hard to stop thinking about her: what she lacked in brains, she thought, she made up for in body. She had learned already by puberty's start where the essence of her existence lay, her currency, her stock in trade. Her mother rhapsodized – to everyone, all the time – how graceful and petite their *younger* daughter's body was. How *sexy*. Early on, she'd invented a secret rotation against the seam of her pants, the arm of the sofa, her beloved bicycle seat, to bring on 'the delight'. Later, she pulled off the same trick while straddling a boy's thigh. Her impact on his physiology intensified her joy – insignificant, little Millicent Milner had power!

Her eyes would search out males, of any age, and if they didn't notice she was sexy, she tried harder. At fourteen, she'd whispered to their family doctor that she was afraid she was a nymphomaniac, and then was mortified that he asked if she was a virgin, which of course she was.

****

Her train arrived before his photo shoot finished and she took a taxi to the hotel room the client included in his fee. She asked for the room key in her irritable, entitled, grocery store voice, as if she had as much right as any other grown-up to check into a charming, old hotel in sophisticated *Milano* near the famous Gothic Duomo Cathedral. In the movies, people tipped bellboys, but she had no idea how much. She carried her own suitcase.

Once inside, she locked the room's door. The fading wallpaper, polished dressers, and landscape paintings in gold curlicue frames reminded Millicent of someone's grandmother. She perched on a needlepointed chair to wait, not daring to disturb the floral print comforter on the narrow double bed. Would he show up? A strip of paper like a Miss America sash had been placed around the toilet seat, probably to reassure guests of its virgin purity. Millicent slid it off, peed and carefully replaced it. She couldn't afford to pay for the room if Fabrizio stood her up; maybe, if she hadn't despoiled the bed or bath, the hotel management would just let her leave.

She heard a knock. "Who is it?" Millicent asked in a high peep without opening the door.

"Who do you think?" Fabrizio said.

She wondered later if, when she'd opened the door, his photographer's eye had registered her fear.

****

Hermina carried in a brass tray filled with *antipasti*. "To Americans," she said, "Jewish cooking means the cuisine that Ashkenazis – Poles, Russians, Hungarians, Romanians – brought to the New World around the turn of the century."

"Like my grandparents," Millicent divulged. She caught herself; she owed this woman nothing more than good manners.

"Roman Jews comprise one of the oldest Jewish Communities left on earth. They are neither Ashkenazi nor Sephardic, but purely Roman," Hermina continued. "Will you have water with bubbles or without, Millicent?"

"*Gassata*," she answered, putting the lecturing pedant in her place.

Alice filled her plate with the cheesy eggplant she'd refused to try earlier, until Hermina had hypothesized, theoretically, that it might appeal particularly to younger palates.

"These are all dishes that my husband…loved. I flinch each time I combine his name and a past tense verb. As a language teacher, you must have a refined sense for such grammatical subtleties."

Wanting the dead not to be dead, subtle? Try predictable or banal, Millicent thought as she dipped the tip of her fork into one of the *antipasti* she'd spooned in tiny portions onto her plate. She'd stopped buying ready-made foods when Colin informed her that what she'd brought home was fried squid not onion rings.

Alice stood up apparently used to clearing the table here. Hermina invited her to stay seated between courses.

"Told you she's nice," Alice said the minute Hermina left for the kitchen.

She returned with *il primo*. *Tortellini*. Low labor intensity, Millicent thought – *just boil water*. They were Alice's favorite, prepared her favorite way, with butter and parmesan and a sprinkle of sage. "My mom makes me these too, anytime I want, almost," Alice said, unaware of having quelled a wave of maternal guilt; this pasta was fresh rather than the packaged brand Millicent bought.

"I've specialized in easy meals," Hermina said when she brought out *il secondo*. "The only thing complicated about this, also

Sam's favorite, is to remember to spike the beef with garlic the night before. The rest, the slow oven cooking – with celery, onions, rosemary, nutmeg and a little water – takes care of itself."

She picked up her napkin to dab at some tears. "Alice, I hope, is accustomed to my crying a little now and then. See? Passed already. More wine, Millicent?"

By *il dolce*, some laughter had found its way to that table, mostly in response to things Alice had said. After lunch, Hermina invited them to leave the table for the sofa, though, Alice said she'd prefer to read her *Topolino* in Sam's music room, which Millicent noted she called "my room."

Sitting awkwardly on the front edge of the sofa cushion, Millicent searched for an exit line: Fabrizio might phone. But before she had a chance to strike, Hermina deftly stepped in to ask her about her teaching approach. Perhaps it was the *way* she asked her – not just a cursory interest but a genuine enquiry – that caused Millicent to reveal more of herself than she meant to, about Alice's dad and how they came to be in Rome.

"An intelligent young woman with such a fine daughter and yet you're alone?" Hermina said, with genuine surprise.

"I have a married lover in Milan," the truth slipped out.

Millicent noticed Hermina stiffen. There it was: the inevitable attack, the slap after the cuddle, the knife in her gut the moment she relaxed her guard. Millicent stood up. "You can wipe that look off your face right now! Thank you for your hospitality, but we're going."

"I beg your pardon?"

"You damned well should! I make my own choices. I don't need your approval and certainly not your disapproval." Millicent picked up her purse. "In future, Mrs. Neumann, limit your involvement to Alice and leave me out!"

"I spent decades curing arrogant students of projecting their concepts of their own culture onto that of others," Hermina's voice had dropped an octave. "I am a foreign entity to you. You know almost nothing about me. I know little if anything about you."

"I'm not interested in your opinions."

"Nonsense! Or you wouldn't have reacted like that. You share a confidence with me, concoct your own story about my response to it, then have the gall to reproach me when you don't like your own fiction!"

"I saw your face!"

"Yes," Hermina's voice softened. "My face. Sam says…said…I wear my heart on my eyebrows. You registered a look, something intense. In that, you were right. But you'll have no idea of the content of that intense thought unless you ask."

"All right. I'm asking."

"Then, please sit down."

Millicent sat, stiffly upright. "Yes?"

Hermina looked down at the backs of her hands, turned them over and looked at her palms. Cupped them. Millicent saw tears well up then watched one fall into Hermina's open right hand. "I thought of my empty hands. When you mentioned a married lover, I pictured what it must be like to love someone and have him leave you, again and again. That's what I was thinking, what my face expressed. How empty your hands must be."

Millicent sank back into the sofa.

****

Man plans, God laughs, Hermina recited to herself sitting in a café the following morning as people in their prime raced past her in a blur. She had planned to die before Sam, but seventy-three proved not to be an advanced age for a woman in their culture. Nor had she lived in such a way as to ensure an early demise: she didn't smoke, drank only moderately, took an hour-long walk nearly every day, fed herself and her husband well. Was it her own fault she was still alive? Was it Sam's that he was dead? She couldn't blame Sam for having abandoned her. He was three years older than she and, as it turned out, only human, *ergo*, mortal.

She looked down at her clasped hands as one thumb and then the other stroked the life line of the opposite hand's palm. She recalled her awe as a child when she'd examined her hands in the moonlight and had whispered, *One day, these hands will be old and wrinkled and then dead and buried, everything gone except my bones.* They were old and wrinkled now. And empty.

Her skin had begun to hang in matching accordion pleats from her biceps and inner thighs; it draped in more delicate folds across her kneecaps. Loss of visual acuity supported the illusion of taut facial skin but the magnifying mirror she reserved for plucking chin hairs revealed, once she'd re-located her reading glasses, a rubbled landscape reminiscent of Pompeii after the lava flows cooled. Loss of head, eyebrow and pubic hair pigment reminded her of the riddle: Why does the hair on our head turn white before the hair between our legs? The answer isn't that the bush below is fifteen years younger. It's that the head has only worries. Down there, there's only joy.

Joy. Even close to the end, to their mutual, grateful surprise, Sam could enter her and she would cup his buttocks to feel the goose bumps that always accompanied his orgasms. Her hands throbbed now with the memory of his flesh. Then ached.

Since she was likely to go on living, she'd bloody well better find something for her old, empty hands. She'd tried working with clay in the past, enough to get the luscious feel of it but not enough to create anything – how she wished she could replicate those Etruscan figurines inhabiting the bookshelves in the apartment. But she'd never been able to make the clay obey her will. She promised herself she'd fill her hands now that Sam was gone. Create something.

Hadn't the Creation followed *Yahweh*'s loss of His *Shekinah*, His Sabbath Bride? Hadn't He picked up a lump of clay to fill His aching, empty hands? Were they old and wrinkled?

****

"Empty hands?" Geena exclaimed. "What did you say to her?"

"Not to pity me. That I'd never been so well loved in all my life. I didn't say it, but she's the one who is lonely, not me."

"Mother would dance a jig if Daddy died – all that insurance."

"Geena, you're awful!"

"So what are you going to do about the witch widow across the hall?"

"I don't know. As little as possible?"

13

A huge bouquet of red roses, white baby's breath and green fern fronds stood in a cut glass vase on the receptionist's counter when Millicent arrived at *Lingua Nuova*.

"A birthday?" Millicent asked.

"No," the receptionist answered without looking up. "We took up a collection on Friday for Enrico and Mariangela."

"What's the occasion?"

"You don't know?" She glanced up on the alert for some telltale expression. "They're getting married next month. Do you want to sign the card?"

Millicent exercised strict control over her face until she was behind the locked bathroom door. She'd worked hard during the half-year since she and Enrico broke up to hide her humiliating grief and cool her burning rage. She'd 'black-holed' Mariangela, treating her as non-existent, a torment the girl would be powerless to prove. She'd savored how sweet Enrico continued to be to her while she was cold to him. As if she'd never loved him. As if she didn't love him.

And now he was marrying the brat? Mariangela was nineteen, for chrissake; she couldn't be his partner, his friend, certainly not his wife. Millicent had wanted to punish him and make him suffer, but she didn't want him to ruin his whole life.

She splashed cold water on her face, flushed the toilet and, with a determined stride, approached his office.

"*Sì?*"

She entered, closed the door and leaned against it. "Don't do it," she said softly. Enrico's forehead furrowed. "You don't have to marry her to get rid of me. No need to: I hereby set you free."

His face went slack then his shoulders and finally his chest; he reminded her of a demolition film she'd seen of a dynamited high-rise pancaking down onto itself. As the dust settled, Millicent thought she saw tears in his eyes.

"I told you. Even *before* I married Neal I knew that it was a mistake," Millicent pushed on. "I thought I had to go through with it because the invitations were already mailed. It's not too late to call it off, Enrico." Despite the shame of her unremitting unrequited love, she had to admit, "I love you too much to watch you screw up your life like this."

He shrugged. Then as Millicent turned to leave he whispered, "*Grazie, Millicenta.*" He hadn't called her that since she'd arrived in Italy.

Striving to impersonate a competent career woman, Millicent made it back to the receptionist's counter without screaming without hurling pastries or flowers or furniture or ripping her clothes from her body or the flesh from her bones. She made a generous contribution and signed the card. During the staff meeting, she conducted herself for all to witness, particularly Charlotte the cuckold-expert, who checked her out from across the meeting room, as if she were simply fine. She joined the applause accompanying the presentation of the bouquet "*Da tutti noi*," then forced her hands into her lap so no one would see them tremble.

When she reached the limit of what she could bear, she cut short the lesson she had before the lunch break and fled home. He'd said nothing, no explanations, no excuses much less any apologies. Not one single word of comfort. Might he actually love the girl? That concept cramped in her guts.

Millicent unlocked her door. Daniela was picking Alice up at school and the frozen emptiness of the deserted apartment echoed. Suddenly, she remembered that Alice had told her she'd left doll "clos'" at Hermina's. Reclaiming them that moment seemed imperative.

She stepped across the landing and rapped on the door. For a long moment, it seemed as if that home, too, was empty. The door swung open and Millicent without warning burst into tears before Hermina. After a moment's hesitation, Hermina wrapped her arms tightly around Millicent and stroked her hair.

Through wave upon wave of crying, Hermina held her. The first upsurge filled Millicent's mind with, *Why not* me*? What's wrong with* me*?* Although, only sobs came out of her mouth. After that wave broke, Millicent registered, fleetingly, that she was huddled in a cold hallway, in the arms of an alien woman, at risk of letting comfort in. Then an undertow of images dragged her back out: Enrico slumped behind his desk today, Enrico in bed with her, his head on her breast, Enrico's head resting, now, on Mariangela's breast, and those images roiled up more sobs and unspoken words, *Fucking bitch! Son-of-a-bitch!*

The next ebb left Millicent beached on the landing as the full force of Hermina's kindness permeated her. But far from soothing her, that feeling rubbed salt into some festering wound. She wrenched herself loose and pulled herself upright. Just in time! *Before* the knife, before the cruelty that always follows a caress. She backed off, dried her face with her sleeve and performed the internal maneuver at which she'd become an expert: she slammed herself shut and shoved spikes out through all her pores. *Don't take what just happened personally!* she thought but only said, "Pardon me." She raised her eyebrows and pulled both sides of her mouth down, as if accusing Hermina of having invaded her.

Hermina's now empty arms dropped to her side and she said, softly, "Someone must have hurt you terribly."

"Just the usual soppy love story."

"No. Something more than that. Do you want to come in?"

"I'm better off alone."

"It doesn't seem that way."

The sound of the street door opening reached them. Daniela and Alice. "Wait here one moment," Hermina said. She returned quickly with a wad of tissues so Millicent could blow her nose. "Feel free to come back. Anytime."

Alice, running, reached the landing before Daniela. Her mother and Hermina turned to greet her, but she raced on by them and in through her own door. *"Mi scappa la pipì!"* she shouted. She had to pee.

****

Millicent couldn't swallow any of the lunch Daniela had prepared. She watched as Alice ate and chattered on relentlessly. Alice was never intentionally mean, but Millicent, it was dawning on her, had been treating her neighbor awfully. Alice could keep visiting Hermina if she wanted to, but maybe Millicent shouldn't. Maybe she should protect Hermina from her own nastiness by withdrawing from all contact. Or she could just apologize? Maybe even tonight?

When she came home in the evening, Alice was doing her homework at the dining room table. Beside her stood an arrangement of sunflowers in a red glass vase.

"Did you buy these, Daniela?"

"*No signora*."

Then Millicent noticed a heavy, white card propped against the vase, with 'Dr. Hermina Neumann' embossed across the top. A message written in cobalt blue fountain pen ink, in a slanting handwriting Millicent recognized as the Palmer Method, the style her mother learned during the 1920s, read:

> *Dear Millicent,*
>
> *Though clouds obscure the light within you, still you shine. Nothing essential can be lost.*
>
> *Sincerely, Hermina.*

After Millicent was certain Alice had fallen asleep, she knocked on Hermina's door. They sat on the entry hall sofa in order to stay close to both front doors, open in case Alice woke up. The extension cord on Millicent's phone reached into Hermina's hallway.

"Well," Hermina began, "please tell me as much or as little about yourself as you would like to share."

****

Retirement had released Hermina from her strict anthropologist interviewing discipline, like taking off a tight girdle. "You're free now to be just as opinionated and judgmental as you really are," Sam had teased. She felt guilty, but suspected that most of her colleagues harbored this same yearning to indulge a hidden – or not so hidden – conviction that their way was the right way.

Though she was out of practice, Hermina was able to engage what she termed her "split-screen mind" – immersing herself emotionally in Millicent's tale while simultaneously stepping back to parse it. What secrets might Millicent be protecting without even being aware of it? Sam referred to such ignorance as people's 'life lies', the Henrik Ibsen expression that Sam enjoyed. To which she'd respond, gloating, "Now which of us is the judgmental person?"

Hermina let Millicent empty her bucket of *Rotten-Enrico* rants. When her tears and protests seemed, for the time being, to have taken the edge off her desperation, Hermina asked, "What about your family? Your parents? Are they alive?"

Yes. Herb Milner, her tall, balding father, was a successful businessman and a fine person. "Really, it was 'Melnikov', but my grandfather thought that sounded too Jewish."

“My immigrant father changed our name, too, when he arrived in New York,” Hermina said, “but for a tricky reason. My maiden name, ‘Szivesen’, isn’t a name at all; it’s Hungarian for, ‘You are welcome!’ He loved forcing Americans to say that to him every time they called his name.”

Millicent described her father as reminding her of the biblical Patriarchs, or, with his hard, round, ‘executive belly’, of the cigar-smoking, Captain-of-Industry fathers in early Katherine Hepburn films. Her bosomy mother, Phyllis, was his helpmeet. And, Geena, Millicent’s Bohemian big sister, was her best friend and champion. They all were looked after by their loyal, live-in cook and maid, Deniza Vukovic, who’d been with them since Millicent was ten. Few, if any, had lucked out as she had in the family department.

“A mite too good to be true?” Hermina blurted out and saw Millicent freeze. She heard Sam gasp, *Judgment!* Millicent’s jaw was clenched, her lips pursed, she narrowed her eyes and crossed her arms, short-circuiting their emerging rapport, and Hermina winced. She had violated a core tenet. The aims of an investigation should be communicated as clearly as possible to the informant *in advance*. Millicent might well feel lured into an enquiry designed primarily to satisfy Hermina’s curiosity.

What now? Should Hermina continue to be in harness, or attempt to “stop working and simply care,” as Sam had often chided her for not doing? Would Millicent give her another chance?

“I must apologize,” Hermina began. “It may seem as if I’ve tricked you.”

“Tricked me? What are you talking about?”

“You were telling me about Enrico and I changed the subject, pursuing my own agenda as usual. I’m an incorrigible anthropologist, you must remember.”

Millicent seemed confused for a moment, but then her expression transformed from a smile to a grin. Finally, she laughed. “Now you’re the one doing it!”

“What?”

“Making up a story about what I’m thinking instead of asking me what’s actually going on! That’s what you said I did with that ‘empty hands’ thing. And you were right. I should have asked you. Now you should ask me.”

Though it took her a moment, Hermina realized that the joke was on her. This tickled her. Few people besides Sam ever caught her at her own game. “So: Why did you seem to freeze up?” she politely enquired, smiling.

"'Too good to be true,' you said. That hit a nerve. I can't tell if it's really like that or if I just want to paint it like that. And then I was thinking of the flowers you gave me," Millicent said. "That red vase," she went on, softly. "And it reminded me. I was six, so Geena would have been nine when it happened."

"When what happened?"

The Milners had moved from the city to a suburban bungalow so small that she and Geena could play "furniture tag," making a complete circuit of the living room. From one big easy chair they'd hop onto the end table with a red glass lamp on it, to the sofa, the other end table with its matching red lamp, the second easy chair, the coffee table and back to the first chair, without their feet ever touching the floor.

On the day Millicent now recounted, Geena had knocked one of those lamps off the end table. Its red glass vase-shaped body shattered, sending shards all over the rug. "It crashed! Mother ran in. She looked like she hated us and she grabbed hold of the skin on Geena's upper arm, dragged her into our bedroom and slammed the door." Millicent heard the spanks on Geena's bare skin and the rhythmic screeching, "You. Fat. Clumsy. Brat!"

She was ashamed now that she hadn't begged their mother to stop, and also that she still wished she'd punched her in the stomach with all her might. Hurt her. "I knew I should have told Mother it was my fault, too," Millicent said, "but I just ran out and grabbed my bike and pedaled away faster than the pedals could go."

Soon, though, Millicent had become hungry and wanted to go home, as if a string was attached to her that only stretched so far and only for so long, something about how the living room felt when the curtains were closed, how they hung in neat folds and how the light spread out from the red glass lamps (now there was only one of them), with Daddy in an easy chair reading the paper.

Millicent had wrestled her bike down the bulkhead cellar stairs at the back of the house and managed to close the slanting cellar doors, like the ones that locked Dorothy out in the tornado in *The Wizard of Oz*. She'd passed her mother at the kitchen stove then went in and flopped onto her carefully made bed. She knew she was a traitor and hated her stupid self for that.

"Close the door, jerk," Geena had growled from the other bed, without looking up from her book. Millicent had stood up and closed the door.

14

A long pause followed. Hermina went to the kitchen and returned with two glasses of water. "What you describe, Millicent," she shook her head, slowly, "is not a safe home."

"But it was our fault. We were racing around Mother's living room breaking her stuff."

"You don't beat Alice though, do you?"

"Of course not!"

"She doesn't doubt whether she's entitled to exist or that she is loved. You never look at her with hatred. You may get annoyed at her nonsense sometimes, but not at her very being. I never feel the need to protect her from you." Hermina chose not to mention her desire to protect Alice from some of Millicent's *decisions*. How proud Sam would be to see her tread so cautiously. "What you've described is not how love should be."

Millicent looked bewildered. "That's just how it was."

"But your mother's behavior was not acceptable. Can you not see that? Oh, I'm trying to remember…What was that girl's name? We were eleven…Betty Krasner!" Hermina laughed. "Imagine retrieving that from sixty-two years ago. Betty Krasner used to tease me at school, calling me 'Quasimodo' because of this bent spine of mine."

"What's wrong with your spine?"

"A mild scoliosis, rarely painful. Anyway, when I cried and told my parents what she'd said, you know what they did? They marched me immediately to Betty's house. In front of her parents, my mother and father told her that they were sure she didn't mean to be unkind deep down, but her name-calling had been hurtful. Cruel. They said they'd like it to stop and that they'd be watching."

Hermina's mind switched back into its split-screen mode. Now that she had laid the groundwork, the opportunity arose for her to make her point: "Do you see the difference, Millicent, between being well treated and being badly treated?" Whereupon Millicent's phone rang, and the reverberating pause Hermina had built up to so that this message might sink in, was ruined.

"*Pronto*?" Millicent seized the receiver before the first ring had stopped. "It's him!" she mouthed to Hermina with a huge smile. Clutching her phone, she ran across the landing and locked her door.

****

Fabrizio had called to invite Millicent to stay with him an extra night after her next Milan class. She swallowed hard when she asked Hermina if she would keep Alice longer, apologizing that it would also involve a bus trip early Monday morning to take Alice to school. Millicent noticed no hesitation or any sign that Hermina condemned her for leaving Alice to go away and play, and with a married man – or maybe that was coming.

Exhilarated in anticipation of the night with Fabrizio, she devised a lesson plan for Milan that was particularly upbeat. She divided her students into four groups to perform the excerpts from James Thurber, P.G. Wodehouse, Joseph Heller and Oscar Wilde that she'd culled from Colin's library. She countered a barrage of protests by declaring that this was a non-negotiable certification requirement. Humor, she explained, is the shortest path to the soul of a language, and it would be fun.

The lighthearted atmosphere continued after class and the students decided to head out to a restaurant together, pressuring "*la dottoressa*" to join them. She would have gone if she'd been on her own or if Fabrizio weren't married to somebody else.

He was waiting for her in his car just outside the building. She climbed in and initiated an intense bout of deep kissing, which was interrupted by a grinning male student who knocked on the fogged-up car window and winked.

"I was afraid you wouldn't wait," she admitted to Fabrizio.

"Are you crazy?" he said, using one of his heavily accented English phrases. He had planned this trip with care. His excuse for the clandestine get-away involved dealings with his cousin early the following morning in La Spezia where Fabrizio had grown up. Millicent didn't want to know the details.

They'd driven three hours south to *Porto Venere* ('Venereal Harbor', as Geena called it later). Famed for being so beautiful that Minerva forgot all about Athens, it seemed to Millicent now, in an autumn thunderstorm, more like a perfect setting for the opening of

Macbeth. Fabrizio parked beside a hotel built into a parapet overlooking the site of an ancient temple to Venus Erycina, "Goddess of Love, Beauty and Prostitutes," he explained with a leer. When Millicent got out of the car, she caught him shoving one of his wife's red high-heeled shoes surreptitiously under the seat.

Once inside their top floor room, he opened the balcony doors wide. "To let in the sea and the wind," he said. He removed Millicent's coat, her dress, her underwear, "*Sono l'unico dei tuoi studenti a vedere la maestra nuda.*" ("I'm the only one of your students to see the teacher naked.") They made love. Again and again and again.

In the morning, she sprawled smiling across the bed, still naked, as he dressed to leave. He'd order *un cappuccino* and *due cornetti* sent up for her and promised to be back in a few hours.

"What if you aren't?"

"Are you crazy?" he said again, lifting her chin. He laughed, kissed her and left.

Millicent closed the balcony door against the morning chill. She pulled the blanket up over her shoulders and called out, "*Puo aprire*," when a knock came announcing the arrival of breakfast. An embarrassed teenage boy placed her tray on a small table and hurried out. Fabrizio would have to tip him later.

Carrying the tray to the bed, she luxuriated in the soreness of her well-used parts and in the thudding of the waves which even a closed door could not shut out. Again, she thought about how things were beginning to turn around for her: she reflected on her students' performance the day before and savored her pride in their accomplishments. What a success she was making of her life.

But as she dipped *un cornetto* into the foamy *cappuccino,* the old, familiar Devil made his entrance.

Her image of herself as a career-woman began to burn and blister like a frame of film stuck in a movie projector: Was she successful? She didn't really know what she was doing; she'd taken one dumb TESL course back home and that only half-assed. In Truth – a self-evident *ah-ha* now trumpeted forth posing as a major revelation – she was a fraud. A Charlatan. Her students would realize soon that she couldn't teach – only entertain. They'd turn on her, complain to *Lingua Nuova*, to Enrico, who was marrying Mariangela and not her. All that "*Dottoressa*" bullshit. Why had she let them inflate her status on the brochures? She was still the whore she'd been when she'd fucked the sons of all her parents' friends.

And now, she was a harlot-home-wrecker. Alice was cursed to have her for a mother.

It would serve her right if Fabrizio dumped her here. Should she dress and pack in case she had to leave in a hurry? Or stay naked and try to win him back if he did show up? Why the hell was she even alive? She curled up in a ball and cried herself back to sleep.

She was awakened by the sound of the key in the door. Fabrizio was stripped naked and inside her, entering her from behind, before she was fully awake. With the covers pulled down her breasts were cold but she didn't dare tell him.

Shivering, she turned toward him afterwards. As they lay together, he twirled a strand of her hair in his fingers and laughed about how he'd just met a guy he'd gone to high school with who worked now as a car mechanic. Fabrizio had imagined bragging to him: *A naked woman is waiting for me in a castle by the sea. While you're lying under your car fixing your muffler I'll be between her wide open legs. While you breathe stinking exhaust, I inhale the wind from Arabia, and the salty smell of strong women.* "No wonder I had a hard-on the whole way back here."

15

Hermina showed up for their evening out wearing an elegant, pale blue, raw silk suit.

"Beautiful!" Alice cried.

"This is the first time I've dressed up since we discovered Sam was sick."

Alice had on her purple castle dress. Barbie wore her spangled gown and real fur stole, Millicent her silky gray.

Colin had introduced Millicent to *L'Acqua Vitale*, a restaurant frequented by the Vatican elite, or as he called them "the Ordained Eunuchs." Millicent warned Hermina that at a certain moment during the meal, *L'Acqua Vitale*'s slim, sari and dashiki-clad nun/waitresses would silence the guests in order sing a hymn. Millicent reconstructed Colin's explanation of the place, mimicking his droll tones: "These women serve those of God's servants not inclined to serve each other, men whose patina of chastity hides a tumult of desire and an aggressive lusting after power. . . ." Hermina laughed. Sam, she knew, would not even have smiled; he was allergic to hypocrisy, no matter how lovely the hymn.

When they returned home, sated, Hermina sat on the edge of Alice's bed and sang a Yiddish lullaby. Millicent recognized *schlofn*, "sleep," and *kleyne meydel*, "little girl," and resisted the urge to snuggle into bed beside Alice and be sung to.

In the loft, Millicent lit the compressed sawdust fake-log fire and offered Hermina one of the sling chairs, hoping she wouldn't find it too uncomfortable. She sat on the rug by the hearth in the warm glow and asked, "How did you and Sam meet?"

"At a concert in New York. Mahler's 2nd Symphony."

"How old were you?"

"I was 28. Sam was 31. Mahler was important in our household while I was growing up. My parents made sure to take me to hear his music performed whenever they could. Do you know Mahler?"

"No." Millicent had no recollection at all of music being played at the Milner home.

"We have a recording I'd love for you to hear."

"But how did you find each other? Did someone introduce you?"

"I was alone, several rows in front of Sam at the concert. When the last notes faded, a stunned silence fell over the audience. Unbridled applause followed and I remained in my seat for a long time. He noticed me. As we jostled through the crowd queuing to descend from the balconies, I noticed him. 'Beautiful!' he mumbled, looking at me. He seemed full of emotion. I was grateful to have someone to speak to about what we'd all just experienced."

She'd proclaimed to Sam that Mahler's 2nd was a confirmation of Life having meaning, with no need for religion to redeem mankind. She paraphrased for Millicent what she could remember having read to Sam from the program notes as they descended the staircase to the lobby. "The notes, in Mahler's own words, spoke of there being no such thing as eternal judgment, thus no sinners, no punishment or reward. There was only an overwhelming love that lightens our Being. We just know. We simply are." She continued to marvel at having blurted out all of this to someone she didn't know, someone, she'd slowly discover, who knew everything she did about music and much, much more.

"He didn't dismiss me as a pedant, as many have done. Later he told me that I had reminded him of a complex fugue, one whose score he longed to study." She'd never forgotten that, or his admission that he had declared within himself, there and then, that he would marry this girl, if she would have him.

"Sex? Sex had nothing to do with it?"

"My dear. If sex is the main attraction, it won't stand up over time," Hermina said, and loosed a bawdy laugh. Millicent looked at her in shock but said nothing.

They watched the fire.

"Millicent. Thank you for asking about Sam. I'm sorry the two of you will never meet. It's a relief for me to talk about him." While Millicent stood up, poked the fire and slid open the terrace door to let the smoke out, Hermina kept right on talking. "He couldn't see anything from the back of the top balcony, but his ears were what conveyed to him the meaning of the world. He valued words most when they were sung."

She fell silent and after a long pause, added, softly, "'*Sterben werd' ich, um zu leben*!' 'I will die, that I might live!' That's from the 2nd Symphony, the fifth movement choral poem. It sustained us as Sam lay dying."

Another pause, and then, "'*O glaube, mein Herz, o glaube: Es geht dir nichts verloren!*' 'Believe, my heart, oh believe. Nothing is lost to you!' Mahler brought us solace. Also when Inanna died."

"Inanna?"

"I lost a baby." Hermina spoke softly. "Inanna. She was stillborn."

"Oh, Hermina." The sympathy in Millicent's voice was real and deep.

Then, they were quiet, together.

Once in bed, Millicent kept thinking of Hermina's quip: "It won't stand up over time." Talk about a long double-take! Only now did she register what Fabrizio had said at *Porto Venere*: he had bragged to his friend about inhaling the salty scent of "*donne forti.*" Strong *women*. Plural. Were there others? Besides her and his wife? What did that make her? A whore in a harem? What would happen when great sex wasn't enough to hold him, when he moved on to someone new – a younger model – like Enrico had? Where did love come into this, she wondered and then fell asleep.

"I think Millicent was a little shocked at my double entendre," Hermina exclaimed to Sam that night. "The arrogance of the young to think they invented lovemaking. They take it as a given that we in our seventies are left with only a distant memory of some boring bits from our missionary-position past."

Hermina had apologized to Sam when her circulation slowed and flannel pajamas such as the ones she put on now replaced her silk nightgowns. He'd kept his promise that no elastic waistband would ever defeat him.

"Imagine Millicent thinking sex may not have played a part in our falling in love." She rubbed one cream onto her face and a second around her eyes.

She approached the bed.

Occasionally during the forty-four years of their marriage one of them had slept in the guest room because of the flu or more rarely an argument. Sam had taken the odd business trip, she'd traveled to conferences, been hospitalized for one stillbirth, one birth and two D and C's when her periods wouldn't stop. The other sixteen thousand plus nights of their marriage, Hermina and Sam had slept together.

Whenever she came to bed, Sam would turn onto his side and extend his arm; even in his sleep he somehow registered her arrival. She'd place a kiss and then a pillow on his outstretched arm. He'd burrow his free hand up under her nightgown, later her pajama top, to cup one of her breasts. Sometimes when she slid her rump toward him she encountered hardness, gradually less enduring but almost always welcome. Other times she reached behind her to invite it.

Then Sam died.

At first, dreading their bed, Hermina had tried sleeping on the couch but lay awake until exhaustion, mercifully, knocked her out. Her attempts to fill Sam's side of the bed by sleeping on it caused vertigo, as if she'd been thrown off a cliff. Sprawling across the bed and occupying the entire mattress might have felt luxurious during Sam's business trips, but terrified her now, lying there, ungirded, exposed. She had piled his side of the bed with her books and papers and assumed her customary sleep curl on her own side of it, with her arms wrapped around Sam's pillow. Her spine had felt chilled in that position until it occurred to her to place the guest room pillow behind her. Barricaded: that's how to sleep like a widow.

16

Natale con i tuoi, Pasqua con chi vuoi. "Christmas with your family, Easter with whomever you wish." Fabrizio would be spending Christmas with his wife and kids, Enrico would be off flapping Mariangela's wings, *Lingua Nuova* would be closed, Millicent's classes over for the year, her students all *con i suoi*. Jocasta would be traveling with Atlas to her family in Cyprus – no great loss since Jocasta treated her more like a servant than a friend – or a court jester, expecting Millicent to stay on after her lessons with Atlas and entertain her with anecdotes and adventures from her life. Colin would probably be off on some unsavory tryst with a French Intellectual's embodiment of Skinny-Woman-as-Phallic-Symbol. So, Millicent imagined, she would be left to wallow alone in the shame she deserved, like the hussy home wrecker mistress she remembered from some black-and-white 50's movie. At least, she'd have Hermina for company.

Alice had always spent Christmas with Neal, who, though Jewish, did the whole Bing Crosby routine, complete with purple, flocked tree and rotating angels, leaving Millicent in peace to do nothing. This year, for the first time, Alice would be with her. She pictured them here, in their half-furnished draughty apartment lighting ersatz Chanukah candles and arguing over endless games of Clue and Monopoly. Meanwhile, Millicent imagined, dynasties of Romans would be devouring turkey-free feasts, drinking, belching and all talking at once. She assuaged her internal "you're a rotten mother" tirade that the approaching holiday provoked by buying Alice gifts she knew would bring a smile. At least, as long as it took Alice to notice that getting things she wanted didn't make her nearly as happy as she'd expected.

Cold comfort though it was, Charlotte had invited Millicent to a pre-Christmas party before Rome closed for the holidays. Charlotte's sister-in-law lived at EUR, *Esposizione Universale Romana*, the 'Great Fascist Ideal' suburb Mussolini had built. At least, it would add some gravitas to Millicent's Rome experience so far – or provide some stories to gossip about with Geena.

She hung her cloth coat among the furs in the entry hall, to the accompaniment of her standard refrain: *Will any Man ever want me for a Wife?* When she entered the L-shaped living room/dining room and surveyed the balding, paunchy, bureaucrat males, the lyrics changed to, *Will I ever find a Man I want for a Husband?*

If any of the female guests (besides Charlotte), in their A-line skirts and color-coordinated, brand-name silk foulards, had lovers on the side, there was no way to know. Their role as Mothers of their Husbands' Children, Colin had explained to her, obliged women of the bourgeoisie to eschew any trace of libido. *La donna borghese* was Wife the way Elizabeth II was Queen: her function took precedence over her person. As Millicent had trouble decoding what she termed the 'cultural bee-dance,' she directed a warm smile at each unwelcoming woman. Surely beaming the message, 'I'm a nice person,' at every clenched face would work. Right?

She approached a small group of women and did her best to imitate the jocular manner of Italian matrons. No matter what topic she broached, however – the disciplining of children, the necessity of salting eggplants – her words were followed by a beat of silence; the group's conversation then went on as if she hadn't spoken. If her utterance clearly demanded a response from these scrupulously polite women, one of them would begrudgingly start to answer her and then stop mid-sentence, to call out to some other woman on the other side of the room.

Millicent gave up on the women and gravitated toward the men whose on-going conversation focused on the latest political scandals. She read the papers, was familiar with all the stories and had even formulated opinions. But citing columnists from the leftish *La Repubblica* which she bought primarily for the movie reviews, simply resulted in the men changing the subject. They based their opinions on the conservative *Corriere della Sera*, which they bought mostly for the stock analyses. The clash of cultures between them and Millicent was not just because she was foreign.

The boldest man among them, the one with the fewest flaccid chins, asked Millicent about herself, perhaps hoping to flatter her with his interest. How could he have foreseen that his probing would send her off across the room on the excuse that she wanted a toast and eggplant canapé. How could she describe her life and situation? A woman alone with a child? In a Roman Catholic country, that had finally legalized divorce but would never consider it respectable? A divorcée sharing a huge apartment in the historic center of Rome with a man everyone would presume was screwing her? A woman claiming to offer "private" English lessons? Had there ever been a husband? She certainly couldn't answer, "What brought you to Italy?" with the truth: "I came for a man I was having an affair with, but he had another girlfriend so I left him." Had this gathering taken place in Chicago or California – Point Acuerdo or even San Ensayo – Millicent's Roman life would have seemed enviable. As one friend back home had gushed, "You're living out every girl's favorite chapter." But in Italy it didn't feel like that. The rules were different here. Turns out it would make a better story than it did a life.

Since all alcohol made Millicent feel lousy, she kept adding water to the same glass of white wine rather than make a fuss and ask for a glass of something soft. The other guests had no such problem and once their blood-alcohol levels had risen sufficiently their hostess proposed playing party games.

Her Italian wasn't good enough for charades, so Millicent sat quietly on a sofa beside the host as one contestant after another acted out who-knew-what and she laughed and hooted when everybody else did, pretending to get all the jokes. During a lull at the end of one round, raucous laughter erupted from three women.

"*Bilanciarsi sulla bottiglia!*" the shortest woman in the group called out. Her heavily sprayed hair sat rigid on her head like a helmet. "Charlotte! What's your girlfriend's name? She can play first!" All the women, except for Charlotte, gathered around Millicent, all talking at once and she started to have a sinking feeling. She laughed with them tentatively, although she couldn't grasp what was expected of her. Where was Charlotte when she needed her? Finally, the "helmet-woman" held an empty wine bottle high above her head and demanded silence. "What you have to do, Millicent," she declared to all assembled, "is to *Sit* on this bottle. Put it down on its side on the floor and *Balance* on this bottle, with your legs off the floor, and without using your arms either, until we all count, *One. Two. Three!*"

Instead of refusing to play and attracting yet more scorn, Millicent carefully placed the bottle on the carpet and proceeded to make a number of attempts to sit on it, much to the hilarity of the surrounding guests. Momentarily finding some equilibrium, she crossed her ankles and made a show of lifting her legs from the floor and waving her arms about to distract the tipsy crowd from her surreptitious use of the edge of her left high-heel to maintain balance. The faces of the women encircling her made Millicent think of a WWII photo her high school history teacher had used to illustrate the meaning of *schadenfreude*. In it, a joyful, smiling pack of French women taunted a terrified girl whose shaved head marked her as a "fraternizer," the lover of a German soldier.

Uno! Due! Tre! They now called out, men and women together.

Millicent struggled to her feet and took a bow, to a chorus of male voices shouting, *Brava! Ha vinto lei!* She had won.

She dramatized her mortification the next day while Hermina made coffee. She played it for laughs but evoked none. Hermina only shook her head as she reached for the sugar bowl from the cupboard.

"Okay then, why were those women so mean to me? I wasn't chasing any of their awful men."

"You have that backwards," Hermina said pulling out the drawer and searching for the coffee spoons. "Your sin was not that you were out after their husbands, but that their husbands were out after you. Of that, you are guilty as charged."

"Men's fantasies are *my* fault?" Millicent asked. "Am I supposed to be neutered or something?"

Hermina, still holding the drawer handle and with her back to Millicent, failed to choose her words carefully. "You're so worried you won't be noticed that I suspect you raise the volume a bit high." When she turned, she saw the look of wounded shock on Millicent's reddening face. She smiled and took Millicent's face between her hands.

Millicent flinched. "Look at you!" Hermina said. "You're a dear, good person, an exciting, exotic woman. If you don't acknowledge and accept all that, you won't be able to show mercy toward women who feel fear and self-contempt in your presence, who worry – perhaps, rightly so – that they pale in comparison to you. You can afford to be generous." Her hands still on Millicent's cheeks, Hermina placed a kiss on her forehead.

Millicent disengaged herself slowly and with a fragile reserve exited Hermina's front door and went back to her own apartment.
Later on that afternoon, Millicent heard a soft tap at the door. Hermina stood on the landing. "Millicent, my dear. I have something to tell you," she said and handed Millicent two small giftwrapped packages. "Little Chanukah gifts for you and Alice. I'll be leaving the day after tomorrow to spend the holidays with my son. With Sam gone, David thinks I should be with them. It seems

the right thing to do. It'll only be for a few weeks. Here's his number just in case."

Millicent's solar plexus cramped sharply. Why should that matter? But it did.

****

A week after Hermina left, and just before the end of the semester, Geena called.

"Mother wants us home, Mill."

"Why, what's happened? Is everything OK?"

"Yes and no."

"What, Geena. Tell me what's up?"

"It's Daddy's business, Mill. It's in trouble. He wants his daughters home with him for Chanukah. Can you believe…?"

"Oh, Geena! Is he OK?"

"Well, it's not as if we haven't been here before, is it?"

"Oh, come on, Geena. That's unfair. Will you go?"

"Wouldn't miss it for the world! What about you?"

"Of course we'll come." It was only when she put the phone down that she wondered how, after paying the airfare, she could cover her next month's rent.

When her students asked her during their final class what she'd be doing for the holidays, she put on the forbearing smile of a dutiful daughter, the newly fledged, international career-woman quietly making a sacrifice to provide succor to her father in his time of need. She gave her shoulders a proper Italian shrug and answered, "*Natale con i tuoi, Pasqua con chi vuoi.*"

17

Alice discovered that if she clutched her own elbows hard while hugging Raffaella's hamster she could vent her love full force, the way she could with Beary-Bear, and not kill it. Alice really wanted a hamster too but Millicent said no. The one living creature she happily took care of – Alice – was plenty. Alice said she'd do everything for the animal herself, but Millicent said such arrangements rarely worked as planned.

A *Cicciobello* doll, then? A baby doll like Raffaella's who looked alive; she could hug him with all her might without even holding her elbows. She lingered a long time in front of the Christmas crèche window display where *Cicciobello* as Baby Jesus was surrounded by ornaments made of chocolate. "We can't afford it, sweetie," Millicent said.

Alice wrote to *Babbo Natale*, though she pretty much knew he didn't exist. It wasn't Santa Claus who gave bad kids lumps of coal for Christmas; she knew that because she and her mother had bought the black coal candy themselves, at *Piazza Navona*. "You could feed real twins for a month on what *Cicciobello* costs," Millicent had explained to Alice. But, since Phyllis had ordered them home without offering to contribute to their airfare, she'd have to charge the trip to her credit card; might as well add the price of that doll to her debt.

There were cheap *Ciccio* imitations available, but Millicent had hated it when her parents substituted made-in-Korea knock-offs of a toy she'd said she wanted. They'd never paid much attention to what the girls asked for, although, they'd bestowed lavish presents on each other – like the muskrat coat for Phyllis and brand new Oldsmobile for Herb which they'd upgraded a few years later to a mink and a Lincoln Continental.

Millicent acknowledged that Alice hadn't had the piano lessons, ballet classes, religious education, horseback riding that she had been given. She didn't have two parents who stayed together. Poor

Alice. *Schlepped* across the globe and parked with a stranger. Hermina was a sweet stranger, but still. Millicent hadn't ever hit Alice or humiliated her; she had rescued her from Neal – neglectful, stingy-hearted Neal. He loved Alice. But, badly.

She'd been thinking lately that her own father could have, maybe *should* have, rescued her and Geena. Instead, the few occasions he'd come into their room at bedtime had been after they had, as their father put it, "driven" their mother to violence. "See my fingers?" he used to say, holding up his hand. "If one of my fingers is injured, my whole hand hurts. A family is like that. When you hurt your mother, you hurt our whole family." The sisters felt sorry then for causing their father pain by making their mother miserable. Millicent had begun to wonder, though, *why the pain their mother inflicted on them never hurt their father's fingers?* Where were she and Geena on that hand of his?

Yet, she was homesick. She longed for the luxury awaiting her there: percale sheets, deep carpets, the gleaming china and crystal, Deniza's elegantly served meals, the building's heated indoor pool. Why, she wondered, had Hermina greeted this description with a look of consternation? She'd looked Millicent straight in the eye and said, "Remember: Life is real. *You* are real."

Millicent phoned Hermina at her son's to inform her that she'd been commanded to spend Chanukah in California. The thought of the dear girl returning there filled Hermina with concern. Millicent's description of the uptown luxury apartment that Phyllis and Herb had bought once both the girls had left for college had sounded to Hermina like a *concept* of home rather than the real thing. Yet the girl clung tenaciously to her rosy, fictional version of the Milner family. Like the photo she'd shown Hermina that their father had taken of Phyllis and Geena. Looking seductively into the camera, Phyllis straightened a wisp of her own hair with one hand and held a cigarette to her lips with the other. Meanwhile, one-year-old Geena, looking terrified, seemed to struggle to stand up, not to fall off her mother's lap. Phyllis wasn't holding her. Not even touching her. Millicent had shown off that picture *fondly.*

For now, Hermina didn't feel she should name it. Nor had Millicent given any indication that she'd welcome Hermina contacting her at the Milner's home.

18

Millicent placed the gift-wrapped *Cicciobello* in the overhead compartment explaining that it was a present for Geena. The moment the fasten-your-seatbelt light turned off, she took the package down.

"You'll be at your dad's such a long time, I can't wait. So, here!" Millicent glowed. Alice ripped open the box and clutched the new baby to her heart. Embracing the two of them, Millicent tried hard to picture herself back home, and soon Alice, too, with *Cicciobello* and with Phyllis holding all three of them.

After delivering Alice to Neal in Chicago, Millicent stood before the mirror on her flight to California and applied cover-up to mask a huge zit. Stupid skin – erupting now. She wanted her mother to admire how she looked, to appreciate that leaving for Italy had not just been an impulsive, immature decision.

When Millicent came out of the gate, Geena ran to her. "It's *you* at last, Geena," Millicent cried, "not just your disembodied voice!" They held each other, pulled back a moment to smile and wipe away each other's tears and then continued hugging.

"Check out my brand new very old truck," Geena said as she rammed her stick-shift into gear and sped onto the highway

"*Flash Bulletin*!" Millicent yelled into a make-believe microphone. "*Modern invention – a muffler – now available at your local automotive store!*"

"I've missed you, Mill." They laughed together. "But I hate having to deliver you to those shits."

"What do you mean?"

"Our parents, jerk."

"Geena! Daddy's in trouble. They need us. Maybe we can help them."

"Yup. You bet."

"You're just dropping me off. Not staying?"

"I'll drive down again in few days. I promise."

Deniza opened the apartment door with a broad smile and went to get Mrs. Milner. While Millicent was in the entry hall hanging up her coat, her father caught sight of her through the library's wide doorway, put his magazine down and shifted his bulk up from his leather chair. He offered his usual hit-and-run hug, but he seemed to smile only with his mouth, without the joy that usually lit up his eyes at the sight of her. Something was, indeed, wrong.

Phyllis, however, came into the hall and enfolded Millicent with precisely the perfumed softness she had been waiting for. Her arms still encircling her daughter's slim body, Phyllis pulled back. The way she knitted her eyebrows in a look that was surely maternal concern awakened an awareness in Millicent of how frightened she'd been during her ten months in Italy. But just as she was preparing to pour out her story, her mother exclaimed, "Millicent! Is that a cyst on your forehead? Or a pimple? If your period is coming, Deniza has to remake your bed with old sheets." As usual, her mother was right – she was premenstrual.

When Deniza lifted Millicent's suitcase, Phyllis ordered her to spread a sheet over the carpet in the bedroom to protect it from the dirty luggage. "Once she's unpacked it, store it in your room, Deniza."

****

Geena came for the first night of Chanukah. Everything was in place – the silver, the crystal, the brass menorah, the embroidered tablecloth. Phyllis kept a watchful eye on Herb's plate. The moment he needed more steak she summoned Deniza by stepping on the buzzer which they'd installed beneath the rug to replace a small brass bell shaped like a woman in a long gown with the clapper where her legs should have been. As usual, Phyllis's complaint that Millicent didn't eat enough while Geena ate too much was met with sardonic asides from Geena which went unacknowledged.

Millicent noticed the way her father's hooded glance directed everybody else's focus during dinner. Was this new? Or had Millicent simply not noticed before how he managed to remain in charge without permitting attention to fall on him? His scrutiny burned. He bestowed approval or levied criticism from a great distance, with an unchanging smile, as if the judgments he passed emanated from his chest. Was she being mean and making all this up? Had her mother always hijacked the conversation whenever Millicent launched into a story, turning the subject toward herself instead? Had Geena always inhaled demonstratively at each interruption or was that Millicent's warped imagination, too? She was still jet lagging, after all.

She'd added to her American Express card debt in order to buy her father a far too costly, butter-soft leather *portafoglio* at a shop in Florence on the famous covered bridge across the *Arno*. His response seemed uncharacteristically subdued.

Her mother's, "Oooh!" when Millicent handed her a gift-wrapped package was followed by a curt, "Mmm, lovely." As soon as she saw the six, antique (well, old) silver coffee spoons, each engraved with a 'P', she searched in vain for a hallmark. "Not much brass showing through the plating," she said, her voice flat, as she heaped the spoons back into the box.

Millicent gave Geena a flapper-era scarf made of black chiffon with heavy, blood-red beading. "This begs for an ivory cigarette holder to go with it," Geena declared flinging it around her neck, "even if I don't smoke. Not tobacco, anyway."

For Millicent, Geena had carved a small, balsa wood relief: one head with two faces recognizable as Geena's and Millicent's, cheek-to-cheek sharing a single pair of ears and encircled by the same head of hair. It was an update of the mask from Geena's exhibit. On that one, the sisters' eyes had been closed and their smiles phony; now, their eyes were open and their lips were parted as if about to speak. Geena had wrapped the relief along with a cardboard-covered empty notebook. "I purposely picked a cheap journal," Geena said. "Good paper can be intimidating but these pages will eat whatever crap you feed them without even a belch."

"Watch your language," Phyllis bristled while her daughters hugged each other.

"Now, it's time for your *big* gift, Millicent!" Phyllis went on, her voice sounding pink.

She dragged a beat-up, three-foot square, cardboard packing carton tied with a twine bow from the hall closet. On a torn piece of paper, she'd written, "Mommy keeps her little girl warm!"

"For me?" Millicent said. All eyes focused on her as she lifted from inside the carton the now-faded, gray-beige muskrat coat her mother had stopped wearing once she got her full-length mink.

"It may be a little big on you," Phyllis said, helping Millicent into it, "but it wouldn't cost you much to have a furrier alter it." She led Millicent to the entry hall mirror. "Well? What do you think?" Phyllis stroked the full collar affectionately. "This was an expensive coat. Think of me as always having my arms around you." Geena snorted.

In the mirror, Millicent saw a young woman lost in the distressed pelt of her mother's ankle-length coat, her head drowned by the immensity of its collar. It was too hot for Rome. And too heavy – they'd already used up their baggage allowance. But her mother wanted her to be warm. Her mother loved her. Was she an ungrateful, selfish brat?

"It's wonderful, Mother." Millicent hugged Phyllis. "Wonderful!"

"Too stingy to buy the kid something of her own?" Geena called out.

"You always put everything in the worst possible light," Phyllis shouted back. "She likes it. You like it, Millicent. Right?"

"Yes, Mother. I love it."

"You seem to forget, Geena, why your father and I wanted all of us together this Chanukah." Phyllis stood in the doorway to the dining room with her hands on her hips. "I told you both that Daddy's business is in trouble."

"That's enough, Phyllis," Herb said softly out of the corner of his mouth and then returned to his hot apple pie, complimenting Deniza on the lightness of the crust. Phyllis stormed around the table gathering up the used wrapping paper. She crushed it into a hard ball which she slammed onto the silver tray Deniza carried, nearly upsetting the carafe.

Geena and her parents exchanged no gifts.

"I'm tired," Millicent yawned. "I think I'll lie down." She took the heavily perfumed coat and retreated to the same room where she'd dressed for her wedding nearly a decade ago.

Later that night, she was awakened by the sound of her parents' raised voices. She couldn't make out the words, but her mother's voice seemed caustic, accusatory. Worse: demeaning. Had they always fought? She opened her door a crack. "I get no support," she heard her father say. Were there tears in his subdued voice?

"You? I'm the one who keeps this extravaganza running. If I wasn't racing around like a circus plate-spinner, trying to keep up appearances, everything would crash down around us."

"Close the door, Phyllis. This is nobody else's business."

"It's your business, and you've mismanaged it."

"*Our* business, and you've been in on every deal, contract, loan, every…" The door slammed.

Millicent was about to close her door when Geena arrived on tip-toe. "Did you hear what he just said?" she whispered. "That she's been in on every '*bribe'?*"

"He didn't say that."

"Oh, yes he did. But what a bitch she is."

"They are having money troubles."

"Yeah. Right. We're poor, our maid is poor, our chauffeur's poor, our gardener's poor. And that fur coat smells so bad it even stinks up my room. Go hang it in the hall closet."

"Oh, Geena, I've missed you."

"It's weird, all four of us being together again here," Geena said. "Makes me homesick for my chainsaw."

When Millicent lay down for a rest the following afternoon, her mind flooded with images from her childhood. Things she hadn't thought about for years – like the scary scene from a movie from long ago. She'd been four and Geena seven when their parents had dropped them off at what they said was a children's film but it wasn't. In it, somebody cut the air hose of a man in a bubble-headed spacesuit and left him floating outside the ship, drifting farther and farther away. Nobody tried to help him. They left him to float off into dark, icy emptiness. Totally alone. Forever. Millicent had known exactly how he felt.

She remembered the game she'd started playing when she was around eleven. She'd lie in her bed and try to think of the exact word that matched the feelings churning inside her. Wrong words went 'thud,' like the comedian Ernie Kovacs in a gorilla suit on TV when he'd raised his drumsticks over a kettle drum; everybody expected a thundering thump, only the drum turned out to be full of pudding. Right words triggered something physical in her body. *Afraid* flushed through her so her forehead sweated and her guts cramped like diarrhea. *Angry* forced her eyes to squint, her teeth to clench, and made her dizzy, as if her head was a giant balloon full of poison gas. At the word *ashamed*, she shrank into a ball so tight and tiny that not even a sound could slip out, like when kids made fun of her or when her mother taunted her – "*Ha. Ha. Ha.* Get used to ridicule. Life is hard!" *Sad* made tears gush from all her pores. Not even good feelings were easy. *Happy* hurt – she was small and it was gigantic and threatened to burst her apart, like Niagara through a garden hose.

She wondered now what the word might be for whatever was behind the new deadness in her father's eyes. Logic told her it would be *sad* given that his business was failing. But that went 'thud.' Working her way through alternatives *depressed* did it. He was *depressed*.

It was just how he'd been when he lost his other businesses to bankruptcies. Or to that fire just after her wedding. She and her father had held each other among the fire trucks while the buildings burned, and ashy water streamed down the front of his beloved stores. Phyllis had raged at him later as if the fire were his fault, another betrayal, another example of his incompetence putting her future at risk. Millicent was the one attuned to him, to his loss, his pain.

What if he were to become ill? Everybody knew it was common for illness to follow loss. Was she too late? Was he already sick?

He was in the master bedroom with the door closed.

"Come in," he said, softly. Through the gloom, she saw he had his eyes shut. She thought she saw him smile. "I'll get up soon. I just have a headache." That's right, he often had headaches.

"You don't have to answer me," she said, "but I want you to think about something." The authority in her voice startled her, its depth, how it resonated in her chest and belly instead of just in her throat.

"Daddy," she felt the pitch of her voice rise. "You need to look after yourself. You will get through it. Just, don't let this kill you…" it rose higher. "Without you," and higher, "I'd…I'd…*die*!"

19

Phyllis insisted on throwing a dinner party two days after Christmas even though Herb protested that this was no time for "putting on the Ritz."

"Maintaining the appearance of abundance matters most during hard times," she'd countered.

Phyllis had invited the Rademachers, wealthy retired neighbors from two stories up. She'd been meaning to entertain them for a long while and if ever they needed to cultivate potential backers, the time was now. A party of eight was no extravagant shindig. Besides, she proclaimed, she didn't have many opportunities to show off her happy family. She went to the safe for her matching ruby necklace, earrings and armband along with the custom-made, mother-of-pearl "poison" ring Herb had given her. The other guests were Sydney Baines, the Milner's lawyer (who knew everything anyway) and, unavoidably, Rosalyn his "nasty lush of a wife" as Phyllis liked to describe her. Her menu centered around filet mignon served on the gold-rimmed Minton china, accompanied by an apparently unlimited supply of the right wines, decanted, and poured into the appropriate Waterford crystal.

The place to Herb's right at the table was reserved for Mrs. Rademacher whose husband had the place of honor at Phyllis's right. Millicent sat beside him and, since he was practically deaf, spoke only to Sidney's wife. Rosalyn had Herb to her right, but she said nothing to him. Phyllis had wanted Geena to sit next to Rosalyn since she owned a prestigious art gallery, but Geena had refused. "You're the ass-kisser," she'd said, "not me."

Millicent would have preferred the seat Geena ended in, next to flamboyant, flirtatious Sydney who trimmed and waxed his mustache and eyebrows so he looked like a comic opera devil. She'd had a one-night-stand with his medical school student son – the yeast infection incident during what Geena referred to as her "Willy-Wild Years" before Neal. She feared Rosalyn might still hold it against her but Rosalyn either didn't know or didn't care. She'd studied art in Italy and her interest in Millicent's life there seemed genuine. Her knowledge of Roman art and history exposed Millicent's ignorance, but their conversation made Millicent homesick in the opposite direction.

Rosalyn apparently had a well-established arrangement with Deniza to keep her wine glass filled. By the time the banana-cream pie was served, Rosalyn was far gone. Waving her dessert fork in the air with one hand, she tried in vain with the other hand to force a strand of expensively dyed chestnut hair back into its *chignon*. In a loud, conspiratorial stage whisper she said to Millicent, "It's easy to get rich when you know how. Screw your business partners, milk the assets, slurp the cream and when you're bankrupt, Ahoy! Call for help…"

"Shut up, Rosalyn," Sydney grumbled, though Millicent heard resignation in his voice.

"Sorry to upset you, dear," Rosalyn said to Millicent, at full volume, "You're a very nice girl, but you've got s.o.b. parents. How can my husband look in the mirror with such *ganiffs* for clients?"

Phyllis shoved back her chair as if preparing a physical assault but, interrupted by Herb's stern, "Phyllis!" she sat down.

A long silence ensued which Phyllis broke with a compliment on the gold necklace worn by her neighbor's wife, a filigreed, hinged box hanging from a chain. She described her own collection of rings that also opened, one of which she was wearing now. "Instead of poison," she said, glaring at Rosalyn, "I fill them with saccharine for my coffee."

Millicent soon excused herself, politely, and Geena followed.

"Told you Daddy's a crook," Geena whispered to her sister. "Did you see the look on his face?"

"You're totally wrong," Millicent protested. "He's not a cheat or a liar. He's a very moral man. You don't know him the way I do. Remember when they took us to see *Seven Brides for Seven Brothers*?"

"Yup. What about it?"

"We stood in line for tickets and Daddy told us he'd seen the play on Broadway? Well, he hadn't and he came and told me later that he felt awful about lying about it and would I forgive him. He'd just wanted to impress us."

"What did I tell you? He lies!"

"He came at night and confessed – to *me*. I was just a little girl! Our father is a good and moral man," Millicent declared.

"Shit, Millicent." Geena almost walked away but stopped. "Memories? I was 10 and woke up to pee. Their bedroom door was ajar and they were raucous. She was in her underwear wearing practically her entire collection of costume jewelry. He had a fat roll of cash and was stuffing wads of it into her brassiere."

Millicent looked bewildered.

"Kickbacks, Millicent. Bribes. Oh, grow up."

20

Although Neal was really good at choosing birthday and Christmas gifts for Alice, he did nothing else. He paid almost no child support, never phoned, sent a letter or even a card. Even though she'd moved them far away, Millicent wanted Alice to have some sort of on-going relationship with him. She paid Alice's entire airfare from Rome to Chicago and would rather have bitten her tongue off than make any nasty comments to her daughter about his neglect.

Now and then, of course, a vacation from being Alice's only operational parent was lovely. There would be no loquacious kid getting hungry several times every single day, filling her purse with Barbie "clos" and half-eaten apples, requiring her constantly to scope out the public johns in case one was needed at short notice. But when Alice was gone, Millicent had to beat back the urge to phone her at Neal's all the time and often found herself panicking, *Where's Alice?* As if she were a toddler who'd been stolen from the playground.

The hours after Neal delivered Alice to a stewardess in Chicago for her non-stop flight to join her mother in San Ensayo were awful for Millicent – her child hurtling alone across the heavens in a thin-skinned metal cylinder at the mercy of strangers. What if the pilot had had a drunken row with his nagging wife the night before or if she and Geena had crashed on the way to the airport and Alice deplaned only to find no one waiting, no one in the world?

There she was, running from the gate shouting, "Mommy! Geena!" making whooping noises, holding *Cicciobello* and wearing a new, pink, Barbie Doll backpack. As they walked holding hands three-abreast toward the baggage claim, Millicent wanted to shout so Neal could hear it, *she's mine, all mine!* and do a Rumpelstiltskin victory dance.

Alice spilled out tales from the flight – a stewardess had dropped lunch on some guy; the kid in the row in front of her had thrown up in a bag – but Millicent also glimpsed what she read as sadness. *Don't miss your father!* She wanted to beg.

****

When they arrived, Bompa opened his arms wide and lifted Alice up. Dropping *Cicciobello*, she fastened her arms around his neck and twined her legs around his big belly. Millicent watched her father close his eyes and smile fully just like his old self. MiMi (or as Geena would have it, "*Me!Me!*") shoved herself in, spitting on her fingers and plastering her granddaughter's bangs off her forehead. "Let's show off your pretty face," she said, stiffly. The moment Alice was free, Deniza embraced her, saying something tender in Serbo-Croatian.

When Alice was little, Bompa had bought a four-foot long Steiff lion he'd found reclining in the display window of a toy store going out of business. He pulled it from the hall closet and into the library whenever she came and had taken photos of her asleep on his back or trying to wrap her small arms around his mane.

"*Aspetta un attimo*!" Alice cried out, releasing herself from Deniza's hug, her reversion to Italian delighting her grandfather. To MiMi's horror, she threw open her overstuffed suitcase right there in the front hall. "I packed all by myself," she said and dug down to unearth a scruffy replica one fifth the size of the big lion. "I found him at the flea market with my dad! Now the lion will have company even when I'm gone." She ran to the library where sure enough the beast awaited her.

Phyllis raised one eyebrow at Millicent, and with an ostensibly indulgent stage smile, she whispered, "Deniza, get that filthy stuff out of here."

Throughout the meal Geena tickled Alice who ambushed her right back the moment her attention went elsewhere.

"Stop that, children!" Phyllis said.

Millicent and Alice regaled them with funny Rome stories, Alice mimicking the sausage-shaped lady in the dirty housedress who sat all day on a wooden chair on the narrow strip of cobblestones near their apartment. She'd got the woman's vulgar *romanaccio* dialect to a tee. Millicent translated. "You deficient-in-the-brain! You cursed piece of poo-poo!"

Herb beamed. Phyllis laughed. Millicent saw that, despite the weight she'd gained, her sixty year old mother was still beautiful, with high cheekbones, a smooth forehead, symmetrical features.

And when she smiled, as she did now, she seemed radiant. *Charming* was the perfect word.

Dessert finally arrived – Deniza had made the chocolate-pudding walnut pie Alice loved – and that heralded presents! Millicent gave *Cicciobello* a bottle that looked full of milk when standing upright and appeared to empty when tilted. She'd also bought him a newborn-sized sweater. Alice helped him sit on the table to model it for them.

Geena handed Alice a Big Bird pillowcase loaded with gift-wrapped packages. Unwrapped, the dozen irregularly shaped pieces of colored wood made no sense to Alice. Feigning innocence, Geena looked up at the ceiling. Then Alice got it: a puzzle! The handmade jig sawed pieces came together into a portrait Geena had painted of Millicent, Alice and herself smiling the biggest possible smiles.

"You can put us together when we're far apart," Geena said.

To her grandmother's growing annoyance, Alice mixed up the pieces and put them together over and over. "Look, Geena!" Alice picked up one piece. "I'm holding your nose. Now you're supposed to say, 'Well, then, how do I smell?' Go ahead. Say it."

"Well, then," Geena said, obediently, "how do I smell?"

"P.U. Awful!" Alice laughed and grabbed Geena's real nose and the two of them wrestled until Phyllis, not laughing, barked, "Enough of that," and removed *Cicciobello* from her table.

Proudly grinning, Phyllis placed two packages in front of Alice. "I have something for you too, you know. Are you ready for your *big* gifts?" Alice opened the larger one first, a fancy sweater with a lace collar. "It's for New Year's Eve," Phyllis said. "Put it on. I want to see it on you."

"Bit big?" Geena sneered.

"She can push up the sleeves until she grows into it," Phyllis protested. "That's very expensive, hand-crocheted Irish lace. Not much gratitude around this table."

"It's lovely, Mother," Millicent said. "Isn't it lovely, Alice?"

"Pretty lace," Alice said, examining the sweater as if figuring out how to cut the lace off and what to use it for instead. "Thank you, MiMi," she said as she stood, walked around the table and kissed her grandmother.

"See, Geena? She likes it," Phyllis said.

Next, Alice unwrapped an ornate silver-plated picture frame containing a photo of Phyllis and Herb wearing swimsuits, tanned, happy and waving, taken during their latest Caribbean cruise.

"We're saying hello to you all the time." Phyllis smiled as if they were still on that sailboat.

"Egotistical clod," Geena said.

"What's wrong with it?" her mother snapped, her face tightening.

"What every eight-year-old longs for is a picture of her grandparents."

"The frame is high quality plate. When she grows up, she'll appreciate it. Maybe she misses us? Ever think of that? And who are you to talk? You gave her a picture of yourself."

"You don't get it, Mother," Geena said.

"She's only kidding, aren't you, Geena?" Millicent said. "It's lovely, isn't it, Alice? We'll be glad to have it when we're far away in Rome, right, Alice?" Alice nodded.

"And you've *never* gotten it, Millicent," Geena said.

Herb appeared to sink back down into himself, and the sadness Millicent had glimpsed in Alice at the airport seemed to return. She sat with her elbow on the table and her chin propped in her hand, taking apart and putting together the jigsaw puzzle faces.

In the privacy of the bedroom, Millicent brought out Hermina's gift for her. Alice opened the distinctively embossed white envelope and Millicent helped her decipher the cursive writing.

"For you and the ones you love.
With great fondness from, Hermina."

A gold locket in the shape of a book and engraved with Alice's initials hung from a thin gold chain. She opened it. It was empty with space for two pictures.

"See the difference, Millicent?" Geena asked without receiving an answer as she helped Alice fasten the chain. "Don't let MiMi see that, though," Geena said.

"Why not?"

"When she's jealous she turns mean. Or, even meaner."

"Can't I say my dad gave it to me? Please?"

"Great idea!" Geena said.

Millicent shook her head. "That would be lying, Alice."

"White lies were invented for moments like this," Geena countered. Millicent knew that it wasn't the lie that bothered her but the thought of Neal getting the credit for such a nice present.

Alice decided to hide the locket in the pocket of her Barbie backpack.

The three of them filled the remaining days before New Year's with excursions: boarding a cramped, Japanese submarine captured during World War II, and riding a shaky, Science Museum elevator down into a fake coal mine where gas exploded and a stuffed canary keeled over and died. Millicent checked for that little shadow of sadness she'd noticed before, but it wasn't there as they watched the latest Disney movie and Geena tried to teach Alice to throw popcorn up and catch it in her mouth, or when they shopped for shoes to wear with the satiny dress with a swirly skirt and puffy sleeves her dad had let her buy. Millicent said it would be perfect for the New Year's party.

When they got home, Millicent saw through Phyllis and Herb's open bedroom door piles of papers everywhere. Though their actual words were muffled, tones of dispute leached out into the atmosphere. Alice stood up suddenly, complained that her stomach ached and went to her bed to curl up in a ball. Millicent and Geena squabbled over shelf space in the bathroom as though hurled back into their own childhoods, and quickly agreed that this stay with Mother and Daddy was way too long.

21

Herb had been given complimentary tickets to a glamorous New Year's Eve gala, complete with fireworks – the final family event before escaping what Geena called their "Hereditary Hot House." Millicent had insisted Alice nap that afternoon or at least play quietly on her bed. Then the fun of dressing up began, a rumpus of zipping, giggling, spraying of perfume, elbowing for a good place in front of the mirror, all followed by lipstick kisses to color Alice's mouth.

Millicent wore her trusty gray and pink silk number. "Look!" Alice pirouetted before her aunt and mother in iridescent lilac. She played at flinging the dress's matching stole over her shoulder, imitating what Geena did with the beaded scarf Millicent had given her which worked perfectly with the raw-silk, black sheath Geena had decided to wear. Geena would, of course, have enjoyed disgracing her mother in front of "Valuable People" by showing up, yet again, attired in unwashed overalls.

"Mother's going to freak-the-hell-out if Alice isn't wearing that sweater," she said *sotto voce* to Millicent.

"She won't, Geena. Not when she sees how sweet Alice looks." Millicent said.

"Believe whatever you want, my dear. Let's go paint the town vermilion!" Geena announced.

Phyllis stood in the front hall removing her mink from its protective zipper bag. "Where is her sweater?"

Geena hurled a look at Millicent. Unconcerned, Millicent said, "She could bring it with her."

"I didn't say *bring*. I said *wear*." Alice turned to Millicent for help.

"She'll be warm enough without it," Millicent explained as she reached into the closet for their coats. "Her dress has its own stole. She looks lovely, doesn't she?" She leaned down and kissed Alice.

"I told you I bought that sweater for New Year's Eve. People will be there who know us and who can tell the difference between cheap crap and real Irish lace. You never think of what is important to me."

Millicent noticed the look of pleading in Alice's eyes and said, "Let her bring it, Mother, in case she gets cold. Please? Alice is happy in what she has on. Besides, that sweater doesn't go with the dress."

"Change the dress. Make *me* happy. "

"My dad gave me this dress," Alice said.

"And I gave you the sweater. You're in my home. Do what I tell you." Alice stood, arms rigid at her sides, tears pooling in her eyes. "Get that sweater and put it on." Alice didn't move. "I said, *go*! You selfish brat."

"I *won't*! And you can't make me."

Phyllis backhanded Alice, hard, across the face.

"No!" Millicent gasped as Herb cried, "Phyllis!" and Geena, "You fucking bitch!"

Alice ran away, down the hall. Millicent stood in front of her mother and said through clenched teeth, "Don't you *ever* hit my child again!"

Her body trembling with confused fury, Millicent rushed off to comfort Alice.

"See?" Geena called out to her. And, "Happy New Year!"

Herb and Phyllis left for the party alone.

****

Memories assaulted Millicent that night. Raina, the Rabbi's wife, taught the Synagogue's Saturday kindergarten and was very pregnant. Millicent had made a construction paper whale for her and when she and her mother had gone to the Rabbi's house one afternoon, there it stood on the bookshelf.

"I made that, Mommy," Millicent had pulled at her mother's arm but she went on talking. Millicent repeated "Look! Look!" until, without warning, her mother had hissed, "Shh!" yanked her arm away and backhanded Millicent with her knuckles, smashing Millicent's lips against her teeth. She'd tasted the blood. *She didn't mean to*, Millicent remembered telling herself while Raina daubed at her mouth gently with moist paper. Frantic at seeing the blood on the carpet, Phyllis had run for wet toilet paper. She'd rubbed at the spots, breathing hard. "God, Raina, I hope it doesn't stain!"

For some reason, Millicent had stayed there until late. When it was time for them to take her home Raina scooped her up and she'd pretended to be asleep, letting her legs dangle next to that big belly. "You think we have a sweet Millicent growing inside me, Jacob?" she heard her whisper.

"Let me take her for you," he said softly and Millicent had let herself flop into his arms covered with those nice, coarse, Daddy-hairs.

The teenager teaching the class the following Saturday told them that Raina was at the hospital having her baby. "Raina's named her baby *Millicent*, like me," Millicent had said to herself, but out loud. Without checking, the teacher smiled and said they'd all make congratulations cards. She wrote *Millicent* on the board, large, so they could copy down all those straight lines and dots.

Later, in her bedroom, she was playing with her ballerina doll when her mother raced in and grabbed her. She pulled her underpants down with pinchy fingers, flung her across her knees and spanked her, one hard slap for each word, "You! Little! Liar! You! Little! Liar!" Then she shoved her giant face, stinky from cigarettes, close up to hers. "Raina hasn't had a baby named *Millicent*," she'd shouted. "Everybody's calling to say my daughter lied. They're calling *me*!" Millicent exploded on the inside and wasn't there anymore.

****

At Alice's bedtime the next night, Millicent kissed her cheek and forehead and, as was their custom, placed soft kisses on her closed eyelids. She repeated her promise to Alice that she would never, ever let MiMi hit her again.

"Cuddle?" she asked. Millicent slid in behind her and they lay like spoons.

"I missed you while you were at your dad's," Millicent said into the pale light of the waning moon.

"I missed you, too."

"It's weird to be here, isn't it? Especially with Bompa and MiMi fighting all the time."

"Why are they mad?"

"Something about Bompa's business." They were quiet. Millicent stroked Alice's hair.

"Deniza's making me rice pudding tomorrow," Alice said, her voice groggy.

"Mmm. That'll be good." The cuddle continued. "Before you fall asleep, may I ask you something, Alice?"

"Yeah. What?"

"What was it like at your dad's?"

"Fun. He took me to the movies a bunch of times and shopping and we ate Chinese a lot and he made tacos."

"I mean, how were *you* there? What was it like for *you*?"

"Huh?"

"I was trying to find the word that matches how you look sometimes when you're being quiet. Even before that awful mess with MiMi last night, I thought that you looked 'sad'."

Alice was silent. Millicent was about to check to see if she'd fallen asleep but as she touched Alice's face, she felt tears. She let her hand rest on Alice's cheek, kissed her curly hair and waited. Soon, Alice let out a small sob.

"What is it, sweetie?"

"I don't know," Alice said, crying.

"Can I make guesses and you tell me if any fit?"

"Okay."

"Is it some sort of missing? We'll be going all the way to Rome again. Do you wish we were staying here?"

"No. I like it there. I like Hermina."

"Is that why you're sad? You miss her?"

"No. Something else."

Millicent suspected she knew what that might be, but hated the thought. "Is it your dad? Do you miss him?"

Alice cried hard now and Millicent held on tight. She restrained the impulse to rail against Neal who gave so little yet took up so much space.

"Mom?" Alice said as her crying eased. "If I tell you a secret, will you promise not to tell?"

"Absolutely."

"I miss my dad even when I'm with him. All he does is make jokes, all the time. Like it doesn't even matter if I'm there or not."

That shut-down bastard. Loneliness is why I left him. Should I inflict him on her time and again? Millicent managed to snuggle in and only say, "I know your dad loves you, very much, even if he's not always good at letting you know."

But was that true? Was there some universal principle causing all parents to love their offspring? What about Phyllis? Millicent knew it was often her fault when Phyllis was mean. But her mother's words from years ago filled her mind and she winced. "I'm not like everybody else," Millicent remembered her mother telling her one horrible afternoon when she was a teenager. "I don't love anybody. Nobody,"

"Are you sleeping?"

"Yes," Alice answered.

"You know your dad loves you, a lot?"

"Yes."

"That may have to be enough, sweetheart. And, Alice?"

"What?"

"I love you. I may not always do it well, but I love you. You know that. Right?"

"Yeah."

"And your dad and I – we both know that you love us. Both of us."

Alice turned over and they held each other. After a while, Alice fell asleep and Millicent lay thinking about who could love and who couldn't. She loved Alice, ferociously. And Geena. And, of course – Daddy…But had she ever loved Neal? Maybe she'd only loved the fact that she didn't have to be afraid of him. What about Enrico? Or Fabrizio? They were too far away for her to think about right now. And Hermina?

Could it be that Millicent only pretended that she loved her mother? She pitied her, possibly even ached for her. *But did she love her?* If not, what would that say about Millicent? What kind of a monster doesn't love her own mother?

II.

1

Lucky me, I'm leaving, Millicent hummed to herself while waiting for their flight to Rome, then reproached herself for filial *perfidia*. Excited, she and Alice made up stories in Italian about passers-by, imagining it to be their secret language until a businessman near them chuckled too appropriately.

"What will you be glad to come back to?" Millicent asked, and then regrouping, amended her question with unexpected vehemence: "…to come *home* to."

"*Tortellini con burro*," Alice answered without hesitation, "and my Barbie cupboard. I'm going to make a hammock for *Cicciobello*." She grew quiet, then added, "I miss Hermina, too. A lot. What did you miss?"

Millicent quashed a reflexive, *Fabrizio*, especially since Alice made fart noises with her tongue and lips whenever she heard her mother answer the phone and it was him. "Hermina. And *spaghetti aglio e olio* at *da Luigi*'s. Riding the bus with everybody shoving and pushing. Lighting candles in the churches. Hearing Italian instead of English. I missed the Italians."

But really, what did she know about them? Every *napolitano* was presumed by people from everywhere else to be a thief just as all *siciliani* were *mafiosi,* all *piedmontesi* were *tedeschi* ("Germans") and all *calabresi* were *cretini* ("idiots"). Among the indomitable *romani*, those who spoke *romanaccio* were reviled as vulgar while the *Dolce Vita* types were satirized as snobs. Rising above them all were the Tuscan *fiorentini*, the fair-haired Florentine descendants of Dante Alighieri, who considered themselves to be the Only True Italians and looked down upon everyone else in the world.

Millicent used to laugh indulgently at the Italians' antipathies but here she was, ranking the Americans at the boarding gate. Well-attired businessmen and women: thumbs up. Beer-bellied men, teased haired women: down. Anybody with a nasal, New York accent: down. Prim, dishwater-blonde, American Gothic Protestant housewives without style or lipstick: down. Warm, noisy, working-class extended Italo-American families: up. Over-entitled Orthodox Jewish men with small bowler hats and big egos who lorded it over harried-looking wives with flocks of children; strutting sons who aped their fathers in imposing patriarchal authority over their sisters: very, very down. And why were there no black people?

Her ignorance of how to sort Italians into groups had obliged her to evaluate them as individuals. This, she now admitted, meant she was a nicer person when she was abroad. She was better altogether when she spoke Italian. To find the right words and plan her sentences, she first had to find out what she really wanted to say. She had to think. So even when the Italian was wrong, what she finally said came out sounding more real. Much of what she'd become aware of these last weeks had been staring her in the face – Fabrizio kept leaving her, her mother was mean – what else had she been blind to? Alice never mentioned school. She'd noticed her daughter's lack of friends but failed to acknowledge the obvious: Alice was lonely. Their life in Rome might not be good for her. Maybe Millicent wasn't just a consummate shit-eater, but a shit-server as well.

Idiota! She growled at herself as their flight was called, remembering now that loaded into the belly of their plane was a tattered duffel bag bulging with a ratty, smelly muskrat coat.

****

"You're *romana*," the cabbie said to Alice, leaning on his car horn in the busy lunchtime traffic, "but where does *la bella mamma* come from?"

"What a kid!" Millicent said mussing Alice's hair. "You speak like a native, already!"

The taxi driver made a show of how easily he could hoist the heavy suitcases into the elevator. He winked at her and left the fur-filled duffel for Millicent to carry.

Dragging the bags onto their landing, Millicent smiled. Sighing deeply, she turned her unmistakably non-American door bolt through its three reassuring clicks. Once inside, she flung her bedroom shutters open in a joyous gesture reminiscent of Scrooge welcoming in the blazing morning light before bidding an errand boy to buy that Cratchit family a Christmas goose. "Hello, dear

House!" she sang as she sprawled out on her sun-warmed bed. The elephant ear philodendron had a huge new sprout.

"Let's go buy some *tramezzini,*" Millicent called out – she'd missed those moist, triangular tuna sandwiches on soft white bread with the crusts cut off – but Alice had already crossed the landing to knock on Hermina's door.

"Hermina's not home," Alice said. "Shouldn't she be back by now?' A flash of anxiety shot through Millicent until she remembered Hermina having grudgingly agreed to stay on in California for a party her son wanted to throw in her honor. "Don't worry, sweetie. She'll be back in a couple of days. I'm hungry. Aren't you?"

The woman at their corner bar clapped her hands when she saw Alice. "*Pensa! Tornate da California!*" Alice began to thrill her with details of what a taco is and how she'd been down in a mine where canaries die when gas explodes, boom! She couldn't dredge up the Italian for 'coal' but remembered that *Babbo Natale* brought it to bad kids at Christmas.

"*Carbone, cara*! You were so naughty last year *Babbo Natale* brought you the whole *carbone* mine!" the bar lady shouted over the hiss of the *espresso* machine and Alice laughed.

They bought *petti di pollo* from the nice butcher, and then went on to the grocery store. They bought *tortellini* and *burro*. And milk *a lungo conservazione*, irradiated and with an unrefrigerated shelf life of three months. That seemed scary but Hermina used it so it had to be okay. The rectangular carton needed to be cut open with scissors, a feat which not even Hermina managed without milk spurting out.

Millicent carried her groceries up the stairs to the kitchen. When she set the bags on the counter, she saw the mail which Colin had stacked in a neat pile. She shuffled quickly through it, ignoring her American Express bill – she'd confront that shock later – and spotted an anonymous looking, hand-addressed envelope bearing Italian stamps and no return address and her heart rate jacked up. Had he missed her?

She ripped it open, "*…sìa sù che giù, dentro che intorno, tu, e loro, e 'lei.'*" Yes, he'd missed her: "both up and down, inside and around, you, and them, and 'her.'" Such intimacies ought to have aroused her but instead she felt sort of dirty. Cheap. The instant she read that he could be with her in Milan during her new semester's very first work trip, in only ten days, all that was forgotten.

When she called the office to confirm her schedule, the good news was that there were waiting lists for her courses in Milan and for her private lessons in Rome. Ends would meet and American Express would be paid. The maid, Daniela, would come on Monday and Sweet Daily Life begin again. Imagine. She might be building something of a good reputation for herself at *Lingua Nuova* – perhaps, she and her teaching style weren't off the wall.

While Alice disappeared into her Barbie-world cupboard, Millicent dug out her lesson plans and got to work.

As she worked, the sight of the coat-filled bag behind her bedroom chair disturbed her. She shoved the giant, green turd into the back of her clothes closet, although, it occupied far too much of that precious real estate.

When she finally opened the bag a few days later, the scent of *L'Air du Temps* invaded the room. "Mom!" she crooned, reflexively, but she couldn't help hearing how phony she sounded.

Initially, she wrapped the coat around one of the sofa pillows in the airy living room. Every time she passed through on her way to the loft, she suffered a hallucination that her mother was sitting on the couch. Regardless of where she was in the apartment, a sudden draft would transport a few molecules of her mother's perfume up her nose and her guts would clench.

The coat had to go.

She lugged it onto the bus and to the office hoping tall, blonde Charlotte would want it. "*Elegante*! *Raffinata*!" Charlotte oozed, holding some of her fingers back from touching the thing as women do when they utterly detest something.

Home again, Millicent tried it on once more and thought of a movie where a recluse, an aging silent screen diva, commits a murder. The cops come for her and convinced she's still the camera's darling, she sashays down her front steps – wearing something quite like Mother's muskrat coat.

When she asked Alice if she wanted to cut it into pieces to make furry Barbie clothes or blankets for *Cicciobello*, Alice admonished her that there were freezing cold poor people who would love a warm coat. Millicent hadn't seen a Salvation Army in Rome, nothing so Protestant in Popesville.

She rejected the idea of presenting the coat to the fat lady who sat on the cobblestone sidewalk shouting obscenities at her sons.

Finally, she made up her mind: she would air out the coat and then use it to pad the window seat in her bedroom where she liked to sit looking at the sky. And, sometimes, at her handsome neighbor across the street, who seemed to enjoy watching her when she put on her make-up in front of the window. She carried it upstairs to hang it on the clothesline. It stretched outside the kitchen window, across the airshaft between the buildings, looped on a pulley. The worn-out rope snapped under its weight and sent the coat sliding away. Air filled the satin lining as the puffed-up coat wafted down, arms out, like a huge, blond bat. Leaning out the window she saw it land and raise a cloud in the dust of centuries, five stories below.

She thought she might cry. Or did she only feel *obligated* to cry? Colin would help her rescue it. She sort of hoped it wouldn't rain before he came back.

****

She managed to forget all about the fur at the bottom of the shaft. Hermina was still gone and she had less than a week to find a sitter for her next trip to Milan.

During dinner, Alice sat with her head propped up with one hand while she opened and closed the gold book locket with the other. She wore it all the time now, except when she took a bath. She'd found a tiny picture of her mom that fit perfectly on one side. Until she got a small enough picture of her dad or of Aunt Geena, she put the stuffed lion on the other side. She'd scissored right through MiMi's head and body to free him. Then she found a picture of Hermina standing, with a real wide smile, inside the gaping mouth of a stone monster at the Bomarzo Gardens. She put Hermina in the locket, in front of the lion, facing her mom. Hermina should have been back by now.

"Could we call her," Alice said, "and make sure she didn't get sick or die or something?"

Millicent checked her coat pocket for David's number, but it was gone. Then she remembered: in a fit of housekeeping, she'd emptied her purse onto her nightstand – the phone number, a broken Bic, some breath mints, a half-unwrapped tampon fuzzy with purse lint – which somehow reminded her of the fallen fur. As she looked out the window for signs of rain, she heard Alice shout, "I hear her! I hear her!"

Alice flung open their door. Hermina stood on the landing, breathless, fumbling to tip the cab driver who'd had to haul her suitcase up all those stairs since the elevator was broken again.

“You’re back! You’re back, you’re back, you’re back!” Alice sang out, throwing her arms around Hermina’s waist.

“Hello, sweet child,” Hermina said tilting Alice’s face in her cupped hands so she could look into her eyes. “Look at you, my treasure!”

Millicent felt the stab of pain that always came when she saw Alice and Hermina hug, but that reaction now struck her as wrong. She lifted Hermina’s suitcase and waited for them to finish. Hermina reached out to pull her in close too. “Ahh,” Hermina sighed, pressing her cheek against Millicent’s. Millicent stiffened at first then yielded.

With a shy pride, she noticed as she welcomed Hermina home and asked about her journey that a request for Hermina to babysit the coming weekend had not been her first thought.

2

The 'My Christmas Vacation' essays she'd assigned her class proved to be a successful exercise; a number of students transcended what was expected of them to reach something approaching eloquence. Now Millicent was rehearsing her own version, which she planned on telling Fabrizio in her best Italian – about the fur coat, the sweater, and the slap that had finally knocked the blinders from her eyes. First, however, she welcomed him back – stroking him with her long, heavy hair and reacquainting him with all those intimate parts of her that he'd claimed to have missed so much.

In order for Fabrizio to understand the epiphany she'd had, she would have to go back to that time when she was nine. She had come home from school on a winter day and unzipped her jacket as she waited for her mother to answer the door. Her mother on seeing her had slapped Millicent's face, hard. She'd brought her hands up to shield herself but her mother lifted Millicent's skirt and pulled down her tights and panties, there in the doorway, and using her open palm she'd walloped Millicent's bottom and thighs.

"What did I do?" Millicent had cried out.

"Are you trying to get sick? It's snowing, and you leave your jacket open?" her mother had yelled. *She's only worried because she loves me,* Millicent had told herself then and continued telling herself all these years.

Until her mother hit Alice. Then, she described for Fabrizio, something had finally risen up inside her. "'No!' I shouted, 'Don't you hurt my child!'" In the sex-scented darkness, she paused to await the outrage she presumed Fabrizio would express on her behalf. He was asleep.

When had she lost him? She was dense, "thick as a toe," as Geena called her – first she wears the guy out and then, self-involved bitch, expects him to listen to her whine.

****

While Alice was downstairs reading in Sam's room, Millicent confided to Hermina how stupid she'd been, sharing something important with Fabrizio as he was falling asleep.

"Did it upset you?"

"I'm used to people not listening to me."

"Some people simply aren't good listeners. In that way, I may be more like your Fabrizio than I'd wish to be."

"No, you're not. Besides, I don't have to put on a performance for you," Millicent blurted out and then realized what she'd said.

"He does seem to have it all his own way," Hermina responded, before Millicent could formulate a retraction.

"What would you do if Alice as an adult chose not only to endure such exploitation as you accept from Fabrizio but also called it 'love'?" Though Hermina realized she had already gone too far, she couldn't seem to stop herself from adding, "You will undoubtedly make some man a kind and loving wife when, at the smorgasbord of life, you stop selecting the leftovers."

Sure enough, Millicent stood right up. "Don't you dare talk about Fabrizio like that! For your information, I have never been so well loved in all my life. It's time Alice was home in her own bed." Ignoring Alice's objections, she retrieved her daughter. Without looking back, she slammed both their apartment doors behind her.

The pressure wave following Millicent's sudden exit slammed into Hermina's chest; for a moment she felt she might be having a heart attack. Might she be dying? She'd never pictured *her* funeral. *Her* flowers, *her* grave opened next to Sam's. If Sam could die, anyone could. It was all that softness she didn't want to master – it destroyed her precious illusions of invulnerability.

Hermina fumed long after Millicent and Alice had gone. At Fabrizio. At Millicent's defense of that man, who gave her nothing more than crumbs. As if Sam were hard of hearing, she roared to him about men in general. "I hope you feel appropriately ashamed of *your* half of the species. Deficient in conscience, betraying their wives and using their mistresses in whatever way may suit their porcine selves!"

And the pretty little piggies of your half of the species, she could hear Sam tease, *willingly recline on platters with apples stuffed into their smiling mouths.*

After such an exchange, Hermina would have turned her back on him that night. He, in response, would have cuddled up to his prickly wife and blown a stream of air to tickle the back of her neck, which he knew she hated. She'd have yanked the top sheet up to shield her skin from his breath and despite herself laughed. "Men the world over," she might have said, "Please only themselves."

Do I please you now? he would have whispered.

Hermina sighed. She knew Sam was gone, but did she have to acknowledge it right now?

****

Millicent's cold front continued but Alice came visiting the following afternoon. "I'm glad you like the locket," Hermina had commented.

"When I was at Bompa and MiMi's, I couldn't wear it though."

"Why not?"

"MiMi would get mad and maybe she'd hit me again."

"She *hit* you? Your grandmother?" Hermina remembered now that she had been surprised to see her photo facing Millicent's in the locket rather than one of Alice's grandmother.

The whole story came out: the lilac dress from her father, the sweater from MiMi, the slap. Alice's voice made it all sound like it was no big deal, but her eyes searched Hermina's.

Hermina stopped herself from towing the adult party line: *Well, grown-ups don't always behave well.* Or, *I'm sure your grandmother felt sorry afterwards*.

"What did your mother do?" Hermina asked Alice.

"She got mad and told MiMi *never ever* to hit me again."

"Did your mother make you wear the sweater?"

"No. I wore my Dad's dress."

"Then what did *he* wear?" They both laughed.

"Anyway, we stayed home."

This was the tyranny Millicent and Geena had grown up with and, apparently, their father had never intervened. It should stop here. "Your mother showed you by standing up for you that no one has the right to hurt you. No matter what you've done, no matter who that person is – your teacher, another child, even your own grandmother. Nobody should be allowed to hurt you, just as you shouldn't hurt anyone else."

"I have an idea," Hermina said. "Let's throw a belated surprise birthday party for your mother." Millicent's cold front had persisted. "I have a recipe for an exceedingly gooey, chocolate upside-down cake. If you can find a reason to visit me after dinner, we can bring your mother the cake together."

"I'll leave *Cicciobello* here. Then I'll say I have to get him and I won't even be lying."

Right on cue, while Millicent was washing the dishes, Alice wailed, "Oh, no! *Cicciobello*!" and slammed her palm against her forehead like someone from a silent film. "I left him at Hermina's!"

"It's almost bedtime, Drama Queen. Don't let her waylay you," Millicent said, drying the spaghetti pot.

Walking carefully, Alice came in first with the cake; the good luck candle was taller than the rest and had been relit three times since leaving Hermina's kitchen.

"What's all this?" Millicent tried not to smile but failed. "I already had my birthday."

"As with the *cantos* of Dante, thirty-three is a significant number," Hermina announced and handed Millicent an embossed card. Using her special ink, she'd written the first line of the Dante's *Inferno*. "'*Nel mezzo del cammin di nostra vita.*' As you are – '*Midway upon the journey*' of your life."

"Christ died at my age," Millicent countered. "I could be at the end."

"Or a new beginning."

"Your lips to God's ears," Millicent said, using her best Yiddish accent; she realized that Hermina was regaining ground.

Since the cake proved even gooier than expected, they dished it into bowls and ate it with spoons. Alice sucked the chocolate off all the candle stubs then, under supervision, brushed her teeth. Millicent and Hermina tucked her into bed.

Before leaving for the evening, and as if there'd been no breach between them, Hermina took Millicent's arm.

"You know I didn't mean to cause offense. I *think* for a living, or, I did, anyway. I try to *make sense* of things. Sam was always telling me to feel as well as think. But, may I bore you with something?"

"Sure, why not."

Standing on the landing, Hermina asked, "Are you familiar with Heidegger?"

"Are you serious? Heide-Who? Come on, Hermina. I'm a dummy."

"It may seem a little far-fetched, but this has to do with you."

"OK…"

"He made a distinction between primary and secondary perception. Do you know about that?"

Millicent shrugged her shoulders and pulled a face.

"It's this: we're only able to grasp that a door has slammed because our sensory equipment, our primary perception, has registered the thud. Then we use secondary perception to explain to ourselves what the sensation was, to interpret it. But the visceral immediacy of our primary perceptions can be so frightening that we run away from them, racing after the illusion of control that comes with secondary perception, with 'making sense.' So, instead of experiencing our life we end up telling our life what we think it should mean, what we wish it meant."

"Ok, I get that."

"So, am I right to think that, over the years you've been trying to *make sense* of the cruelty you experienced as a child? Find a way to 'think' it into having been okay when really it wasn't?"

Millicent shifted uncomfortably, but indicated for Hermina to continue.

"And that you often interpreted that as love, so that in some way the two – cruelty and love – became intertwined?" Hermina paused to gauge Millicent's reaction before going on. "I think it started with your mother, but now it's happening with your Fabrizio. You feel at home when love is combined with cruelty. You've 'made sense' of it. It's even become central to you. Do you see?"

Millicent's face flushed with alarm, but then a stillness fell over her as if the contents of her mind were physically realigning. She looked as if that sensation might have been surprisingly pleasurable.

"I don't know, Hermina. I just don't know…" She had no words. She just took Hermina's hand.

****

Heidegger? You're not going to reach the girl that way, Numina, she heard Sam say that night. Hearing her nickname, usually reserved for their intimate moments, she snuggled deeper under the covers. *Your students sought you out because they loved what you love. Millicent only stumbled upon you. And she's a very wounded soul.*

"Many of my students were, too."

You'll need a different voice for her. You might need to learn a whole new song to sing her. Love was not her mother tongue, Hermina.

"Why don't *you* talk to her?"

I'm dead.

"So shut up and let me think." Hermina sat up and put the pillow she'd been hugging behind her head.

"Both of these girls have been damaged, Sam – by maternal cruelty and paternal neglect. They just show it in different ways. Apparently, Geena gouges it into wood while Millicent strokes it over men's parts as if she had no value other than sex. They're both starving."

Nu? So run across the landing with your brilliant analyses and see if you can fix anybody.

"How I wish I could," Hermina sighed. She lay down and once again hugged the pillow. "I wish I could awaken the dead, too."

You're doing a fine job of disturbing at least one man's eternal rest.

"I suppose that's something."

3

Millicent thought that "feel more, think less" might be a normal person's summary of Hermina's Heidegger lecture. Now, she found herself *thinking* more, but not feeling less; feeling, in fact, might even be her forte. At first, Millicent had discounted her students' positive reactions and the waiting lists for her classes as beginner's luck, but maybe she had grasped something instinctively about language teaching.

Maybe she wasn't so dumb after all. All cunt and no brains. Think about that. Think. On her way home for lunch, *"Think!"* Aretha Franklin's classic, blared out of Millicent's internal radio. It kept playing, as if on a loop – which gave her an idea for her next lesson plan.

This time before leaving for Milan her excitement was focused on the teaching while her packing-for-Fabrizio ritual seemed routine. Vibrator? *Check.* Massage oil, French-slit panties, birth control pills? Three times *Check*. As she packed her tape player and her "*Aretha Now*" casette tape, however, a spurt of fear filled her. What if Fabrizio sensed a change in her priorities and dumped her? She'd better follow the advice she'd read in a woman's magazine interview with Brothel Madame X: "Rule One: Mind your fucking."

She arranged the desks in a large circle, exposing her uprooted students to each other's gaze. "I'm going to play for you a song by Aretha Franklin, the Queen of Soul and Rock and Roll, with her hot, syncopated back-up girls. It's an anthem in praise of the freedom you get when you demand that someone see how badly they've been trying to treat you." Handing each a blank sheet of paper, she said, "Listen and write down exactly what you hear." She punched the play button and turned them over to "*Think!*"

After a few verses, Millicent stopped the tape. "Now. Write down what you heard." Then she pushed play again. Then stop. "Write!"

Millicent suppressed a smile at their earnest concentration, as if this were calculus or nuclear physics. When they'd written their way through the entire song, phrase by phrase, she asked them to push the desks and chairs back, all the way to the wall, and stand in the center of the room.

Drifting about awkwardly, fifteen adults regressed into shy teenagers.

"Now," she said. "I want you to dance it. I want you to feel the words through the music. Come on, here we go! *'Think!'*" Gradually, irresistibly, Aretha worked her rousing magic, particularly on the younger women, a secretary and a housewife wearing straight skirts and high heels, who clapped their hands and wagged their rumps. By the time the song had played through twice, all were, to some extent, moving. At the refrain, Millicent shouted, "Sing it with her! Loud!" and they did. With gusto. When the song ended they were laughing and out of breath but fully prepared to go another round.

No. Millicent had them drag their desks and chairs, albeit reluctantly, into a semblance of a circle as she rewound the tape and gave each of them a clean sheet of paper. "Now write what you hear." *"Think!"* When the song ended this time, she handed out copies of the lyrics and talked them through all the slang, and the poetics. "Compare your pre-dance and post-dance attempts," she said. "You all did better the second time, right?"

"*Chiaro*. We heard it more, *tante volte.*"

"Of course, these 'ain't no' scientific research results. But I'm convinced you heard better because you let the music pull you in, body and soul – the same way you learned your mother tongue."

The chatter during their cigarette break was louder than usual. Afterwards, Millicent stopped two of the men from pulling the desks back into rows. "It's not fair that the teacher can see everybody but the students can't," Millicent said. There'd be no more desks in rows for her, no more "pedagogical missionary position" in her classrooms.

In Fabrizio's car afterwards, she broke off their kissing to tell him about the class. "*Bene, bene. Che brava che sei,*" was all he said, then nibbled and sucked her lips. He asked her nothing more during the drive to the apartment. Each time he shifted gears, he returned his hand to her crotch. She was careful to giggle.

****

While she was in Milan, a slow drizzle had been falling in Rome. On Monday, when Colin reappeared, Millicent told him about the "Flight of the Fur." She supposed she'd better retrieve it and asked for his help.

Intrepid Colin had once ventured into the bowels of their palazzo to rescue a fallen brassiere, deluxe, lacy and beige, for his previous tenant, Enchantée. "Dare you journey with me to that Underworld?" he intoned.

Millicent changed into old pants and a sweatshirt wondering if Enchantée had found some excuse to avoid the trip.

On their way down in the elevator, Colin became the second person to quote Dante's opening lines to her: "*Midway upon the journey of our life / I found myself within a forest dark / for the straightforward pathway had been lost.*"

The "Keeper of the Gates" proved to be the owner of the corner bar, who knew more about his neighbors than they liked as evidenced by the fortuitous timing of certain local robberies. Since Man-of-the-world Colin was one of his favorites, he ushered them behind the counter, through his windowless storeroom and to the cellar door. He handed Colin his keys and left.

The dank, low-ceilinged passageways stank from sewer gas, from the black mould that thrives on aged masonry and from the rotting of who-knew-what-else.

"*O mad Arachne…sad upon the shreds of fabric wrought in evil hour for thee!*" Colin quoted when his turning of a lever-shaped light switch disturbed a large spider. "*Purgatorio*, Canto XII" he said, then, "Look at that pre-war wiring," pointing to the fabric-covered cable from which a bare bulb dangled. (*Great or Second?* Millicent wondered.) When nothing lit up after Colin turned the next switch, he brought out what he termed an "electric torch." *Suppose the batteries died,* she thought. *Suppose Colin died of a heart attack or something. How would she find her way out?*

Like the "Boy in the Bin" who'd never found his way out, even though he never existed. Millicent was seven. She and her sister shared a bedroom and Geena told her the secret: a neighbor family kept their deformed son locked in their cellar storage-bin and all the grown-ups knew it. "He's too weak to scream," Geena explained, "because they almost never bring him food." Geena embellished this tale night after night and each night Millicent cried. She still caught herself holding her breath sometimes, as she did now, straining to hear the Boy in the Bin's calls for help.

At last, she and Colin reached a short, padlocked door which Colin pushed up and out like a flap. In the weak light that reached the bottom of the open air shaft, Millicent saw the soggy fur. It lay splayed at their feet in the damp dust like a TV crime victim around whom a chalk line would soon be drawn. *Did she fall?* the detective would wonder aloud, *Did she jump? Or:* (da-dahh) *Was she pushed?*

Colin aimed his flashlight at the coat-corpse, leaned down and lifted the edge of the hem nearest his foot, slowly, as if he knew what was coming.

Rats!

A family of big and little rats skittered out from under their muskrat home and disappeared into holes at the base of the ancient masonry shaft walls. Millicent screamed – silently, on the inhale, as she did on roller coasters which she hated because she never could scream out, could only suck it all farther and farther down.

"Dear girl," Colin dropped the coat hem back down onto the dirt, "to these rodents your moist fur is both a *filet mignon* and a Roman *Versailles*."

"Get me out of here!" she whispered, and valiant Colin did.

It won't bother anybody lying down there, Millicent intended to say that night on the phone when she narrated the "Fur's Fate" escapade for Geena. Instead, she heard her herself say, "Down there, it can't hurt anybody."

4

A week later, she checked the calendar but, no, she wasn't about to get her period. Why, then, did she want to hit somebody? Alice, for example, who was refusing to get ready for school unless she could wear a certain flouncy dress.

"It needs washing."

"Who cares?" Alice sassed.

"Don't mess with me right now, Alice."

"*You can't wear that, it's too dirty*," she mocked in nasal sing-song and Millicent pictured slapping those fresh little lips. Alice remained on her bed holding two of her Barbies who were engaged in vigorous dialogue.

"We leave in ten minutes!" Millicent hurled on her way past Alice's room. In slow motion, Alice stood up and, feigning absent-mindedness, donned the dirty dress she'd sneaked out of the laundry basket the night before.

"*No*!" Millicent shrieked.

"Why don't you ever do the laundry?"

"Why are you such a God. Damned. Messy. Kid?" Oh, it felt great to be fighting, even with someone smaller than she was.

Millicent won: Alice, in a tearful fury, pulled on clean clothes. But Millicent also lost: having missed the bus, they waited in front of *Castel Sant'Angelo* in the rain, huddled together under their one umbrella while attempting to ignore each other. Millicent got Alice to school on time but missed her bus to work. The driver of the cab she, eventually, flagged was in a rage at the downpour and the traffic jams. Hearing him honk and swear as he inched along the Tiber felt almost as good as hitting somebody.

If she wasn't pre-menstrual, why was she feeling this way? Not just angry but, what? Worried. Scared?

Pre-dawn on Thursday, a dream woke her, a song, some cliché, lonesome-teenager plaint which she couldn't catch hold of. Why wasn't her unconscious profound like everybody else's? And, why, oh why, was she crying?

She considered actually exploring her dream but she needed to blow her nose and she had to pee. Back in bed, as she sank once more into drowsiness, her sly, internal disk jockey turned up the volume on an even dumber ditty: *Nobody likes me, everybody hates me / Think I'll go eat worms.*

"Shut the fuck up!" she ordered before turning over and falling back to sleep.

Unaccountably, when she woke up she felt better.

****

Of course, the fact that Fabrizio hadn't phoned might have something to do with it. She never knew when he'd call but rarely had so much time passed without hearing from him. At first, she had invented benign justifications – maybe a kid's birthday party or school play. As the days dragged on, her scenarios had grown more dire: his son had meningitis, he'd been arrested for tax evasion, his car had careened off a cliff. If something ever did happen to him, how would she know? Would his Roman friend, Massimo, think to call her?

Maybe his silence was a protest. Had she been too busy strutting her brilliance as a teacher last time they'd met? Too egotistical? Too boring? The acid of fear burned in her bloodstream. Was he about to leave her?

She mocked up a semi-normal persona to inhabit, but her worry lest she miss a phone call dominated every distraction – the jolly after-dinner jaunts with Alice to the swings behind the *Colosseo*, to the pastry bar at *Piazza Navona*, to *Fontana di Trevi*, again, tossing in coins and making futile wishes.

By the weekend, the tether binding her to the telephone could bear no more stretching. Millicent used the rainy weather to justify their not going anywhere. To keep Alice from climbing the walls, they invited a classmate of hers to visit. When Alice complained that her guest was being mean to her, Millicent served the girls too much *gelato* and too many of the precious Oreos and Reece's Peanut Butter Cups they had transported from the States, and then returned to her bedroom with the phone.

The fear chemicals coursing through Millicent's system polluted her every thought. She *knew* she was nothing but a pathetic whore nobody would ever want. What an idiot she was to imagine that a man of Fabrizio's caliber would choose her.

Ha! Ha! Ha! Stupid whore: a weirdly familiar voice mocked her all day Monday and Tuesday, sounding distant one moment, like an argument heard through the walls of a neighbor's apartment, and shrieking the next, right there inside her head. Through force of will, she managed to enact her role as teacher and then rested from her struggle to keep *The Real Truth* at bay by yielding to the attacks during her breaks.

Wednesday came. It was now two days before her next trip to Milan, and still no word.

Nauseated and shaky, she stood on the landing, phone in hand; she would have to confirm her plans for Alice with Hermina before she left. The moment she knocked at Hermina's door, the phone she was holding rang. Her adrenalin surge nearly knocked her down.

Hermina must have been just inside the door because she opened it in time to witness Millicent's breathy, "*Pronto?*" and see her collapse against the wall then slide, slowly, to the floor, her eyes filling with tears, jaw slackening, chest caving in. "*Ciao, Fabrizio. Ciao. Come stai*?" Hermina backed into her own apartment and closed the door quietly.

He was calling from a phone booth on a highway just this side of the Swiss border and Millicent could hardly hear him above the traffic noise. He warned her that he was almost out of *gettoni* – the phone tokens Millicent collected for him and rolled carefully in paper so he'd always be able to call – but wanted her to know that he wouldn't be able to meet her in Milan this weekend either. He didn't say why. "*Mi manchi,*" he shouted.

"I love you, too," she said, though he'd only told her he missed her.

"I'll call next week," Fabrizio promised.

"When?" she yelled. "It would be easier for me if I knew *when* you'd be calling!" but the *gettone* had dropped and the connection had been broken.

She sat on the floor with the receiver clutched to her chest until it occurred to her he might call back. She hung up but didn't move. When Hermina opened her door a crack, Millicent looked up at her. She saw those eyes, so much like her mother's in shape and color, but not mean, not ridiculing her at all, and nothing like the murderous eyes she'd been seeing in the mirror these past horrible days and nights.

Right there on the cold landing between the two apartments, Millicent let herself fall over onto her side and cry. Hermina sat down and placed all of herself around the sobbing, tender knot that was Millicent. "Yes, *mamaleh,*" she whispered in Yiddish, "*shaina maidel, sweetheart*."

"Real love is kind, my dear child," Hermina whispered as she shepherded the bedraggled Millicent home. She asked permission to make them some proper British Cadbury cocoa and advised Millicent to splash cold water on her face, in the meantime.

Hermina pulled up a chair beside Millicent's bed. For a long while, they sipped their hot drinks. When they finally spoke, Millicent's voice sounded hollow and depleted while Hermina heard her own as gentle, as if she were, indeed, practicing some new song. They agreed, easily, on the details for Alice's weekend stay.

Before leaving, Hermina sat for a moment on the edge of the bed. "Someone will love you well, my dear girl," she said softly. "Look what a fine young woman you are. How good you are at loving." She kissed her left and then her right cheek. "Sleep well. I'll lock your door when I leave. I have the key."

****

Once Hermina had locked her own door, she dropped down onto the hall couch, the empty cocoa cups in her hands. "Thank you, Sam, for having loved me so well," she said aloud.

And then, she knew. "I think I need to go home. I miss our boy."

She entered Sam's room which was full of the recordings he'd chosen and placed so carefully over the years, some of which she'd found for him. She walked up the stairs and through the living room lightly touching one object they'd chosen together and then another; she passed the bathroom where she could picture Sam in front of the sink, shaving his final beard. She carried the cups to the kitchen sink then stood listening to the pulsing silence that sets in once the guests have left and the voices, laughter and scraping of chairs have all, suddenly, stopped. In their bedroom, she pulled back the spread. There was Sam's pillow. "My dearest, my sweetheart," she said, crying gently, her hands cupping her own cheeks, "You're gone."

5

Millicent had an awful weekend in Milan without Fabrizio. She had left her apartment in chaos, left Alice's maddening, *No, I won't and you can't make me!* Refusals to clean up her Barbie-mess. She was pre-menstrual, with an explosive temper, pimples, rat-oily hair and cramps that were even worse since her IUD. Freezing slush pummeled her while she elbowed her way to a cab at the Milan train station. And, to top it off, she had to teach phrasal verbs.

The only way to learn them – if you hadn't choked them down with your mother's milk (or formula) was the hard way: rote and repetition. And since she felt like shit, that was what they were going to do. She covered the white board and flip-over chart pages in a pedagogical frenzy with lists – *Get: Get on, get off…Look: Look at, look out…Give: Give in. Give up.* She hated her students, they hated her, and they all detested the English language.

****

Back in Rome, it struck her that enjoying herself might be a juicier way to avenge Fabrizio's neglect. She knew she took too much crap from him. That "strong women" he'd let slip at the *Porto Venere* hotel. *Donne forti.* Plural. Cheating on his wife, okay, but cheating on *her*? What had Hermina said about real love? "Real love doesn't hurt," or something like that? Bullshit. She felt hurt most of the time. Even when she was with Fabrizio, she felt anxious. What if she didn't please him enough? How could she hold his attention except by wafting her privates at him?

Maybe, she strategized, a threat of having to share her might scare him into shape. Jocasta had seated a man beside her at that party she'd thrown after Millicent and Enrico split up. She'd described him as "A journalist at the margins of the Roman political *cognoscenti.*" He had invited Millicent out to dinner once and up to his apartment which occupied the top floor of a 14th century tower in *Trastevere*, the Roman corollary to a Greenwich Village artist's loft. Nothing had happened. His name was something like Toboggan, or was that one of the politicians who'd been assassinated? Where was his business card?

She found the card: Sergio Lo Chiano, in his forties, grieving over a wife who'd left him "for another woman." Fabrizio read *La Repubblica* just like everyone else in advertising and the arts – just hearing the name Lo Chiano would turn the jealousy knife. He'd know what the guy wrote but not what he looked like: the paunch, the chain-smoker teeth, the tobacco stains yellowing his gray beard.

She felt a sneaky smile creep across her face as she dialed Sergio's number. She knew just how she'd take Fabrizio's crap from now on. She'd take it lying down.

That Wednesday, Sergio treated Millicent to *spaghetti alle vongole*, then, up in his tower, she screwed him. She couldn't stay the night, she apologized, because Alice was home with the opera-singer sitter. Not with Hermina – Millicent wasn't about to mention her Sergio-project, not to Hermina or to Geena.

Home again, afterwards, as Millicent took a long shower, the word *squallida* tinted the atmosphere a yellowish beige.

When she made her dramatic confession to Fabrizio at their next meeting, his eyes lit up. He wanted all the prurient details; precisely what had Millicent done to the famous Sergio Lo Chiano? And what had Sergio Lo Chiano done to her? "Did he do this?" Fabrizio asked as he licked her inner thigh, "or this?" She played the game, glorying in the impact she'd had on him, in her power, in the ground she knew she had gained as she felt the ferocity with which he reclaimed her, planting his flag as only he could.

****

Two days later, Millicent almost jammed the door key in her unabated fervor to answer the telephone. Might he be calling again already?

"*Pronto*?"

Silence. Her racing heart sank. Then, "*Ciao, bella! T'ho trovato!*" It was him. He needed to know right away if she could meet him this coming weekend. "I'll be photographing *Carnevale. A Venezia!*"

"*Assolutamente!*" she cried. She gloated that the thought of Sergio Lo Chiano might be tormenting him.

Would Hermina and Alice hate her for leaving two weekends in a row? She'd have to risk it. At the first opportunity, she went to ask Hermina in her most adult voice, as if she hadn't already promised Fabrizio she'd go. She really was a selfish bitch.

"Leave again? When you don't even have to?" Alice cried out.

"I know you'll miss her, Alice," Hermina said, "but this is a wonderful opportunity for your mother. The Venice Carnival is famous all over the world. Besides, we'll have lots of *gelato* while she's away."

Having slightly mollified a still sulking Alice, Hermina culled books from her living room shelves and, leafing through glossy photos, set about informing her girls about Venetian architecture, its unique military history, the *Commedia dell'Arte*, the origin of the Harlequin, about *Carnevale* as part of the Grand Tours young aristocratic men took during the 1800s. "It's only just been reinitiated; Mussolini banned it and before him, Napoleon. Sam and I had planned to go this year." In her element once again, Hermina seemed to soar.

Millicent promised herself she'd be nicer.

6

"You see only what you choose to," Sam had told her when David, at fifteen, papered his bedroom walls with Fidel Castro and Che Guevara posters.

"Who would *choose* to see a fanatic ideologue in her own son?" Hermina had retorted. "I acknowledge objective reality and expect others to do the same. You, on the other hand, look for excuses for everyone. Except me, of course."

"It's a few posters. Some heroes to irritate his parents with."

"But that revolutionary ideology they glorify," Hermina had bristled, "the *machismo*, the misogyny, the idealization of violence, the duplicitous peddling of liberation fictions while plotting a tyrannical *putsch*."

"He wants to prove he's his own man. Not a carbon copy of his mother – whom he so closely resembles."

"He's flirting with extremism."

"He's experimenting with life."

"Would you have said that had he turned Nazi in the '30s?"

"Enough hyperbole, Hermina. Let David be. Trust him."

Now, two decades later, David spouted things like "One for the Gipper" and "trickle-down economics" and other romanticized, ingenuous, cruel, greedy, *Newspeak* shibboleths. His transfer of loyalty from Castro to Reagan, which she labeled as "Revolutionary Left to Revolting Right," had required a mere shift of polarity; he'd apparently remained the same adolescent champion of demagoguery she and Sam had left unchallenged.

She'd believed for years that she had made a colossal error by caving in to Sam's *laissez faire* parenting. Until she'd comforted Millicent that night on the landing, and she'd seen – no, worse: she'd *felt* – how wounded and vulnerable even grown-up children can be. David had been fifteen, less than half the age Millicent was now, when Hermina had silently erected a wall against her own child. How lonely he must have been.

She'd felt driven to balance Sam's unconditional approval with ever colder and more intrusive judgment which in turn may have left David little choice but to rebel. Was there no Golden Mean?

"Why did we fight over him instead of talking to him? Like we do with Millicent? We can even talk a little now about her wounds, and how we might help her to heal."

Of course! she could hear Sam laugh. *It's easy to talk about wounds we're not responsible for having inflicted!*

Not that they had ever behaved toward David with anything resembling Phyllis Milner's brutality. They'd never terrorized, beaten or humiliated him. But there was no denying that they had made mistakes. Despite – or even because of – their passionate yearning to be good parents they had, indeed, made mistakes.

The yearning to lay such remorse to rest added to her willingness to have Alice with her two weekends in a row. She called it "research." Perhaps she could both help the child and spare the mother future regrets. "This is for me and for David," she told Sam. "And, for you, as well. You mustn't expect any retroactive absolution just because you're dead."

****

The previous weekend, Hermina had detected a tinge of sadness in Alice, but when she had asked, "What's the matter? You seem upset," Alice hadn't answered. She'd only wanted to lie on the bed and read *Tintin* and *Topolino*.

Now, on the first night of Millicent's Venetian fling, as Hermina sat beside Alice's bed she saw that same look and vowed that this would be a conversation rather than a lecture.

"You appear to be sad about something, Alice. Are you?"

Alice was quiet for a long time; Hermina somehow found the patience to wait. *See, Sam? I am educable.*

When tears ran down Alice's cheeks, Hermina said, "You *are* sad. Do you have any idea what you're sad about?"

"I miss my dad," Alice answered, but so quickly it reminded Hermina of a suspicion she'd had about herself: she'd been wondering how often she deluded herself these days by hanging all her worries on the one strong hook of her widowhood.

"Of course you do," Hermina agreed. "But I wonder if something else is bothering you, too, something happening these days."

"You mean at school?"

"Or at home?"

Before Alice could say, "No. I'm not so sad at home," Sam's admonishment echoed: *Don't tell her where she should be sad! She asked if* you *meant at school because* she *meant at school.*

"Is something at school making you sad?" Hermina corrected, thanking Sam for his immortal wisdom. Alice broke into sobs and the whole story poured out.

****

"*Deficiente,*" Alice heard her teacher say, under her breath. She didn't know exactly what it meant but Pietra rolled her eyes and whispered to the girl who shared her desk, and they both snickered.

Sra. Cau had sent her to the board during their arithmetic lesson. Alice had added 19 to 49 just right, remembering to carry the "1" and everything. The piece of chalk had broken in the middle of the 6 of "68" so she didn't press as hard with the stub and the 8 went fine. Everything would have stayed fine if she just hadn't opened her big mouth to proudly announce the answer: "*Settantotto!*" which meant "78"; "s*essanta"* and "*settanta*" were so alike she couldn't keep them straight. That's when Sra. Cau had muttered, "*Deficiente*" and Pietra and her friend had giggled.

"Tell the American what number this is, class," the teacher said.

"*Sessantotto!*" they called out in sing-song chorus. Now, everybody laughed, including Bruna, the retarded girl who shared a desk with Alice, the kid who never grasped when she was being made fun of but just laughed along with everybody in loud snorts, her horsey mouth wide open. Sra. Cau called Roberto to the board and Alice didn't know if she was supposed to stay up front or go sit down until Sra. Cau said, "Is your name Roberto?" and again everybody laughed. "*Stúpida,*" Sra. Cau said out of the corner of her mouth. That, Alice understood perfectly.

"Boy, are you in a pissy mood," her mother had commented the next morning, but she hadn't asked Alice why.

After school that day Alice had renamed one of her Barbies "*Stupidessa*" and then cut the doll's black hair down to her plug-holed scalp. She drew all over the doll's face with black and red marker pens and made her put her clothes on backwards and upside down. When Alice was alone with them, all the other Barbies, especially Alice's red-haired favorite, laughed and laughed and stomped on *Stupidessa*.

"What have you done to that Barbie?" Millicent asked when Alice brought *Stupidessa* to the dinner table one night, but it wasn't a real question. She only shook her head and asked if Alice wanted more cheese on her *pasta*.

****

"I'm not stupid at home," Alice cried. "Only at school."

"You, my dear, are not stupid anywhere at all," Hermina declared. "The stupid person is that awful teacher of yours. Oh, these educators who fluff their own feathers while clipping students' wings! You're a *child*. Your mother needs to be told. We must stop this."

"Don't tell anybody!" Alice sat up and said with panic in her voice. "It will make everything worse. Promise you won't tell!"

"How can your mother protect you if she doesn't know?"

She might of course have asked Alice, the way you just did, Sam said. "I wish you had told us right when it happened."

"It always happened. All the time."

"How awful for you, sweet child," Hermina whispered and gathered Alice up onto her lap, blankets and all, to rock her rather vigorously and kiss her forehead again and again.

****

The day was nine hours younger in California, an ocean and a continent away, so Hermina dialed David at his office as soon as Alice was asleep.

"My dear David."

"What's wrong?" Apparently, he could sense her nascent tears.

Hermina paused, swallowed, and said: "I'm sorry."

But she couldn't continue. This was silly, the wrong way to do it, the wrong moment. She didn't need to talk to the balding executive she had interrupted. She wanted the Mr. Tough-Guy Revolutionary still somewhere inside him, that gangly fifteen-year-old who had struggled for hours in front of the mirror to pomade his curly hair into a D.A. – a 'Duck's Ass.' Or the thirteen-year-old with black fuzz above his bow-shaped upper lip whose voice-change had begun with a sudden and embarrassing falsetto, like metal chair legs scraping on concrete. "I'm sorry to bother you at work. I just wanted to hear your voice," she said.

"That's sweet," he said after a moment, but it could have been a question. "It sounds like something is up, though. Will you still be awake in two hours? I'll call you back."

"You don't need to."

"Oh, yes I do."

He didn't sound angry, after all she'd done, or rather, all she should have done and did not do. He loved her; no question about that. Hot tears slid down her cheeks in a path made crooked by her wrinkles. "How is Ethan?" she asked, gently.

"Fine. He's at field hockey. I'm leaving early to go to his match." For Chanukah, Hermina had bought Ethan the knee protectors he wanted and the special baggy shorts. "I'll call you back after that. Two hours. You sit tight. Okay?"

"Yes. But, wait. David?"

"Yes?"

She paused. "I love you. You know I love you, don't you?"

He paused. "Yes," he said, then added, "And you know I love you, too," in a satiny whisper as if a colleague were in the room. "Two hours," he repeated, in his usual robust tone.

Things were rarely if ever all one way. Not doing something right wasn't the same as doing everything wrong. How could she have forgotten that? She couldn't have closed her heart to him entirely or he wouldn't have been able to treat her so sweetly now. That's what he'd been, there at his desk. Sweet.

"Sam!" Hermina called out, softly since Alice was asleep. No answer. Was she to be left alone to sort through the consequences of all her actions throughout the years? The bad acts – and also the good ones? Was it harder to bear her guilt, regrets, anguish on behalf of those she'd injured or let down? Or this terrible new tenderness? Would she die of this? Feeling so much love that her heart burst its banks?

She couldn't return to these emotions two hours later when David phoned. "What are you going on about?" he asked. "You've been a fine mother." The real problem, he said, was that she was all alone over there. With too much time for worrying. Why didn't she come home already?

"Yes. I've been thinking I would." She regretted saying that immediately.

"That's great, Mom! Wait till Jill and Ethan hear. When? When will you come?"

"Certainly not before the *yahrzeit*. One of us will have to put the stone on your father's grave."

"That's months away. What are you waiting for?"

"I have loose ends to tie up here. Some people. No one you know."

"Okay," David said, grudgingly. "We'll get rolling now, anyway. I want to re-do the basement bathroom for you, rip that tile off and put up a new membrane. That should solve the mould problem. We've talked about opening a window on the south wall of the big room to bring in more light for you."

Suddenly, she wanted to run away from this man, David. She didn't want his basement rooms. She wanted to stay here. With Sam. Why couldn't anything stay simple? Be only love or only distance?

7

At the Venice airport, Millicent boarded the empty boat taxi that was to deliver her to *Piazza San Marco* where Fabrizio would meet her and pay her fare. She'd expected a *gondola* not an ordinary motorboat, but the black-bearded young boatman wore the gondolier's distinctive blue and white sweater and the stripes curved nicely over his pectorals. At his invitation, she sat outside, beside him, enveloped by the scent of the sea and early spring. His muscular forearm brushed Millicent's chest each time he reached across her to point at the landmarks. She was a jewel in the crown of *Carnevale*, he proclaimed; whoever she was to meet in Venice was the most enviable of men. He told her he was making an especially broad turn in the Grand Canal so they would approach *Piazza San Marco* head on. He wanted to see her face when she saw his breathtaking city.

The scene exploded any preconceptions Millicent had about the limits to man-made beauty. She saw the ornate cupolas of the Doge's Palace where, Hermina had told her, aristocrats throughout the centuries had faced scandal but never military defeat. A massive winged lion stood atop a corniced pillar, guarding the harbor. Not far away, dwarfed by the piazza's ninety-nine meter tall brick bell tower, the *Campanile*, stood Fabrizio. The boatman surrendered Millicent to his rival with a flourish of his non-existent cap.

The piazza teemed. Men wearing black capes and beaked-nosed masks promenaded slowly, holding the hands of women in billowing gowns and feathered headdresses of bright red and iridescent blue. Juggling or playing the fife or drum, revelers in Harlequin costumes danced through the piazza in snaking lines.

Fabrizio deposited her suitcase at a hotel reception desk, took out his camera and plunged them into the crowd. He clicked off shot after shot, running backwards without bumping into anyone, leaning this way then the other, never, she noticed, aiming at her. She realized that she was holding Fabrizio's camera bag with the same sincerity with which she'd held nails for Daddy when, at four years old, she'd "helped" him build a picket fence.

He chose their restaurant with care and ordered *Fegato alla Veneziana* for them both – sautéed liver, the gods' own repast, accompanied by a wine Millicent was sure had been born to fulfill that one dish. "I missed you, Millicent," he confided, eyes averted. "Too much. I wouldn't be the man you know without the life I live."

"Who's asking you to change?" Would she be glad to find him on her doorstep, divorced and broken? She wiped the question away fast. If he registered doubt in her eyes, he might dump her.

The next morning, she lay naked watching him organize, sort and mark his films and brush and polish his lenses – private rituals he performed with a shyness she hadn't seen in him before. *This was his profession,* she thought, *his mestiere*. A word she'd misheard initially as *mystery*.

As they left the hotel, she guided his fingers deep into her dress pocket through the hole she'd left unmended. As she wasn't wearing underwear, he could diddle her all through Venice, him feigning innocence and her with a Mona Lisa smile.

They spent the day dipping into the fizzy *Carnevale* crowd currents and then withdrawing; one or two arched foot bridges away from *Piazza San Marco*, all was quiet. These neighborhoods had been inhabited throughout centuries by regular people, loyal not to *Italia*, that recent historical construct, but to *Venezia*. The only sounds came from kids playing, a woman calling down from a window to her friend standing on the walkway below, a man whistling while his quiet motor boat ferried him on his errands along the canal that was his street. As if it were ordinary Life.

At the *Palazzo Veniere dei Leoni*, formerly Peggy Guggenheim's home and now a museum, Millicent discovered a sculpture she wished Geena could see. A gaping crack along the equator of a polished bronze sphere three feet in diameter revealed a hidden complexity, an interior tumult of molten metal frozen in free fall.

Later, back in crowded *Piazza San Marco* in the fading daylight, they heard a deep, slow drumbeat coming from behind the *Torre dell'Orologio*. Grabbing his camera, Fabrizio waved for Millicent to keep up as he followed a procession entering the *piazza* to the mournful beat of drum and fife. Men holding flaming torches lit the way for those who shouldered a wooden pallet which bore the papier-mâché effigy of a great, horned bull. Harlequin jesters pranced around them setting off firecrackers.

As the full moon rose, the procession zigzagged between the bell tower and the lion's pedestal toward the banks of the Grand Canal where a wooden barge waited loaded with straw. Men in *gondolas* held thick braided ropes to keep the barge fast against the current while the bearers of the bull boarded and placed the sacrificial beast at the very center of the straw mound.

A long drum roll, silence, and then one bass voice began to chant words Millicent could not grasp. To the pounding of a single drum, one chosen torch bearer on a *gondola* beside the barge lifted his light high for all the crowd to see. He bent forward, reached out and ignited the straw beneath the bull. Flames engulfed the animal who stood apparently unscathed as the gondoliers towed his pyre farther away from shore. At someone's signal, they all cast their ropes onto the burning barge. The hushed crowd watched from the banks as the bull caught fire sending sparks high up into a blood red sky.

When the waters of the Grand Canal had extinguished the last embers of the bull, darkness took over and revelry broke out. Millicent made Fabrizio pause in his picture-taking to give her a long, deep kiss.

****

Millicent entertained Hermina and Alice with a PG-rated report of *Carnevale*: the murky canals, the Bridge of Sighs so named because prisoners passed under it on their way to the gallows, the Baroque music, the winged lion, the *Torre dell'Orologio* clock tower with two bronze Moors who chimed the hours by hitting a huge clock with sledge hammers, the burning bull.

She made no mention of Fabrizio. Alice knew of his existence, but she'd never met him. Except for Enrico, Millicent hadn't dragged any men into Alice's life only to rip them out again. Such brutality, Hermina had pointed out, Millicent reserved for herself.

In her bed, Alice held the souvenir statue of the winged lion that her mother had brought her and made him dance in the air in time to their counterproductively rousing lullabies. As Millicent prepared for bed, she heard a soft knock on her apartment door.

Hermina wondered if she might have a word. *Just when I'm really happy, I find out I fucked something else up*, Millicent thought, but only said, "Come in."

8

While Millicent was in Venice, Hermina happened upon a fortuitous image to convince Alice to let her tell her mother about her school day torments. “To remain silent, Alice, my dear, about what is happening to you at school would be like peeing in your snowsuit in order to keep warm. You might feel cozy at first, but soon, I promise you, you’ll freeze.”

Alice burst into belly-cramping laughter. When it subsided, she acknowledged that Hermina was right.

“OK. You tell her, though,” Alice commanded. “No. Wait!” she grabbed her doll. “You can make *Stupidessa* tell her.”

Now, alone in the loft with Millicent, Hermina steeled herself for her task and handed *Stupidessa* to Millicent. “She would like to tell you something.”

Hermina’s outrage had been moderated, slightly, by the portion of crow she’d had to eat regarding her own less-than-perfect mothering. Alice’s teacher should also be entitled to her human frailties – though, as a trained educator, she ought to know better. Was a mother’s lack of training any excuse? Of course, Hermina had never ridiculed David. No. Only rejected him. Well, not completely. Wearisome though it was, this incessant moral parrying ignited within Hermina an unfamiliar – if rudimentary – humility. Her characterization of Alice’s teacher, Sra. Cau (as in “coward”), shifted: not necessarily the Devil Incarnate, she was merely an ignorant, frustrated, incompetent hag, unworthy of the sacred trust of shaping young minds. To wish her dead might be, indeed, to over-react.

If Alice’s suffering could break Hermina’s empathic heart and elicit such intense rage, what would it do to the child’s own mother?

Hermina was unprepared for Millicent’s response. Millicent listened without interrupting, and fell back into her chair like someone stuck in quicksand up to the neck, too exhausted to go on struggling.

"Well?" Hermina said when she could wait no longer. "What shall we do?"

"*Do*?" Millicent repeated as if unable to grasp the meaning of the word and fell deeper into silence.

"Millicent!" Hermina resisted the urge to shake the young woman out of her surfeit of powerlessness. "Speak to me."

"I guess I was the age Alice is now," Millicent's voice emerged, as if from a distance. "We were still living in the town house where Geena told me about the boy locked up in the cellar bin…"

"Locked up?"

"Not really. Never mind. I was standing on the landing outside my bedroom door. I'd just told my mother about the girls at school making fun of me. I had that 'I want my mommy' feeling in my chest, so I just told her. Maybe I didn't make it clear enough how hurt I was." Millicent struggled to go on. "She put her face close to mine. I was expecting a kiss. But you know what she did? She pinched my cheek really hard and said 'Ha! Ha! Ha! I'll toughen you up. Ha! Ha! Ha! Get used to Ridicule. Life is hard!' That's what she actually said, like it was for my own good. She hated me. I saw it in her eyes."

"My poor girl. What did you do?"

"I went to my room, sat on the bed and fell into a hole. Falling, forever. You don't die just because you wish you would."

"So now, what about Alice?"

"I never do that to her, Hermina! Make fun of her? How could you think I would do that?"

"Not you. Other people are doing it. Your child is being humiliated."

She stared at Hermina with a horrifying, slack-jawed blankness. "I can't help her toughen up. Look at me. I'm useless."

Hermina had to struggle not to be sucked down into the morass. And if Phyllis Milner's quicksand logic could muddle the mind of Hermina Neumann, from a distance of twenty-five years and eight thousand miles, imagine being her daughter! No wonder Millicent pranced and toadied and never dared to rage.

"It's not about toughening Alice up, Millicent. It's about teaching her to take action by our taking action on her behalf."

****

“Call me ‘Cuba,’” Millicent said to Geena on the phone two days later. “I told Hermina I’m a subsidized economy and she’s my Soviet Union. If she pulls out, I collapse.”

She described how Hermina had been in full swing, railing at Phyllis’s treatment of her young daughter and about how it would be foolhardy for any child to dare to defy such a mother. “Hand that woman a hatchet!” Geena said.

Hermina had insisted that Millicent was no longer powerless. “May that bully of a teacher tremble before the forces protecting Alice,” she’d said. It was fine in theory, but Millicent knew she’d end up tip-toeing into the principal’s office and squeaking, *Oh, please, Signora, do not hurt us anymore,* like some Olivia Twist. The principal would dismiss her as a problem parent and stand loyally by her staff. That was when Hermina had offered to go with her.

“When I told her how pathetic I felt that I couldn’t do it alone, she said that I had to stop looking at myself through Mother’s eyes.”

“Deep, huh?”

Her hands and voice shaking, Millicent had phoned the school in the morning and launched into her list of arguments as to why the Principal should see her. “The secretary cut me off and asked if nine this morning would be okay.”

She had promised Alice that if this didn’t help she’d take her out of that school altogether. She felt like an eleven-year-old playing the role of Mom in a school play, but noticed that Alice looked at her as if she thought she was the real thing.

She had hurriedly freed up her morning schedule so they could all take a taxi to Alice’s school. “Alice looked like someone anticipating the cessation of her known world.”

“Is that a Hermina quote?” Geena quipped.

“A Milli-mina, actually. I think I’m starting to sound like her.”

Once they’d arrived at school, Alice had gone grudgingly to her classroom to be Cau’ed while Hermina and Millicent waited by the secretary’s desk outside the polished door to the Principal’s office. Hermina left for a quick trip to the bathroom, and the secretary chose that moment to send Millicent into the Principal’s office, alone. Millicent recalled thinking then that she’d never in all her years of school been sent to the Principal. Or to the Dean.

Hermina had reminded Millicent over and over, while they’d rehearsed the night before, that she was coming as back-up, that Millicent should do the talking. “So, what did I say, sweetly, standing in front of that permed, dyed ash-blonde matronly lady with her rheumy eyes? 'Mrs. Neumann is in the ladies' room.' What a coward."

Without even looking up from the papers she was perusing, the Principal had gestured for Millicent to sit down on the very low chair in front of her desk. Just as Millicent was fantasizing about Hermina having a heart attack in the bathroom, in she came. She marched all the way around the acre-wide mahogany desk, with her hand outstretched, leaving the well-mannered Principal no choice but to stand up and shake her hand. Hermina may have out-aged her by decades but there was no mistaking her for a harmless old lady. Her 'In-No-Uncertain-Terms' glare packed a knock-down wallop. Millicent had heard the panic in her own voice as she explained Alice's struggles like a salesman trying to peddle something nobody would ever buy. The Principal looked at her impassively and said nothing, while Millicent continued nonetheless to hurl shrill counter-arguments at her. *Yes, Alice understood the language enough to know when she was being called stupid. No, this wasn't simply a matter of their coming from a foreign culture.*

All the while, Hermina sat beside Millicent in a chair just as low as hers, except she placed herself on its front edge with her pocketbook bolt upright on her lap and her stockinged knees smacked together. Once Millicent's voice reached high C, Hermina had placed a hand gently on hers, and Millicent finally shut up. Hermina began. In her most intimidatingly formal Italian, she asserted that, if the cruel conduct being sanctioned there were to become public knowledge within the echelons *she* frequented, it would leave an indelible stain both upon the principal's own reputation and on that of this school. No doubt, she then went on, in the subjunctive, emphasizing the very doubt she denied, a professional of the principal's standing must share their outrage and would surely intervene such that this mistreatment would cease as of today.

"Then she said, as if all that hadn't been enough, 'You, of course, will maintain adequate oversight to guarantee that no reprisals are visited upon Alice as a consequence of our bringing this unacceptable behavior to your attention.' She's good, huh?"

"All this from a low chair?" Geena said admiringly.

"Imagine! I started listing in my mind all the people I wish Hermina would zap for me." When Millicent had tried to sense how her head would feel if such words had come out of her own mouth, she'd had to go down to the bottom of her guts to find them, to the basement of herself. She only managed to feel that sense of non-negotiable authority for a few fleeting moments, but did she ever like it! "As a parting salvo on our way out of the principal's office, she added, 'And, of course I'm sure you'll see to it that *la Sra. Cau* apologizes to Alice directly.'"

"She actually expected the Cau to do that?"

"She would accept nothing less."

"Did she do it?"

"After a fashion. Apparently, in a fake, butter-wouldn't-go-rancid-in-her-mouth voice, she said 'You know I was only joking when I called you *stupida*, don't you?' Know what our girl answered? 'You hurt my feelings. I'm not stupid. And I speak English really well and you don't.' She's a lot braver than I am!" Millicent said.

"Her mother doesn't hate her."

"Know what, Geena?"

"What?"

"I opened the kitchen window a while ago and looked down the air shaft. The rats have eaten almost the whole fur coat!"

****

Sour Sra. Cau's major concession was to have Alice and the class troublemaker exchange places. His exile to the back of the room benefited everyone except Alice's old desk mate at whom he directed all his agitation. She brayed and laughed more now, but Alice didn't think that was because she was any happier.

Even though the teacher's new strategy was to ignore Alice's existence altogether, the *Stupida* branding festered. Verb conjugations, arithmetic – especially multiplication tables – became too scary for Alice to study or even to think about.

Her new desk mate was Tizia, a funny name since in Italian it wasn't really a name. It meant *somebody*, *anybody*, like *Jane Doe*. She was really named *Natasha* but her Russian immigrant parents wanted her to sound Italian. Small and dark-haired like Alice but with bushier eyebrows, Tizia was so good at dodging harassment by blending into the background that Alice had never noticed her. Now, Cau's neglect left the two of them free to design and color Barbie ball gowns and horse-drawn carriages.

Tizia emerged during the following weeks as a friend, someone to invite into Alice's secret Barbie World cupboard, to play and fight with, to never want to see again and then to make up with and love. Life began to feel almost okay.

Hermina began to offer Millicent various lamps, chairs, vases, as gifts which she accepted without an inkling that they might be divestments. With no awareness of Hermina's impending abandonment, weeks went by during which Millicent noticed herself beginning to exhale. A luxurious sense of routine had emerged: Enrico had taken his child-bride to live near his parents in far-away Bologna; her burgeoning following of satisfied and committed students not only made her proud but also assured her a reliable income; and, within clearly demarcated limits, she felt she could count on Fabrizio, or, at a minimum, trust his desire to continue to see her. Her Roman spring budded and bloomed in an unprecedented absence of pain.

III.

1

Geena's phone call came at 5 a.m. one Saturday toward the end April while Alice was sleeping over at Tizia's. "Mill, it's Daddy. He has pancreatic cancer. Inoperable. He's dying. You'd better come home." Millicent sucked in air, and then held it. Could she bear this?

She could neither be alone with the news nor imagine waking Hermina so early. Trembling, she dressed and left the building with no destination in mind. How could dawn air be so soft when her father was dying? She wandered down *Corso Vittorio*, disoriented by the early morning silence, the absence of traffic. She passed Mussolini's balcony at *Piazza di Venezia* and the "Wedding Cake" monument to Vittorio Emanuele II then followed the road as it curved towards the Capitoline Hill. She walked up the ramp to the Santa Maria in Aracœli Church rather than climb the hundred steps, even though she remembered a tour guide saying that the staircase had been financed six hundred years ago by some plague victim in gratitude for having survived the disease. As if pulled toward the austerity of the church's façade, she only glanced toward the view of the Forum from Michelangelo's perfectly symmetrical *Piazza del Campidoglio*, or at the stone lions, the caged she-wolf, Marcus Aurelius on his horse. When she saw the open church doors, she knew she wanted to go inside and cry.

Alone in the chill of the dimly lit *chiesa*, she approached the altar. No chairs had been set up yet. Hoping no one would mind, she seated herself on the bottom step of a spiral staircase that led to a high pulpit. She first heard a distant drone then saw the procession of friars in their coarse brown robes and rope belts enter in pairs through a side door. An elderly monk led the way using his tall, ritual staff as a cane while his partner held his other arm to steady him.

Could her father actually be mortal?

Without even glancing at their congregation of one, the monks gathered in a semi-circle before the altar. The aged cleric performed some morning ritual, and then the youngest monk, more boy than man, stepped forward. In what she thought must be an act of initiation, he spoke with shy sincerity of God's love, his thick, southern dialect echoing through the massive, empty church. The old priest smiled at him, nodded once, and again, and the friars filed out, chanting, through the side door, eldest first, youngest last.

A few moments later, two monks re-entered the church, their hands holding their elbows inside the sleeves of their robes, and approached Millicent. The more heavyset of the two spoke to her.

"*Piangi, figlia mia?* You cry, my daughter?" Both his bulk and his tonsured head reminded her of her father. "Are you in trouble?"

"My father is dying," she said.

"Ahh, my child. Man is not born to live forever. Man is born that he shall die."

"I love him."

"We will include him in our prayers today. And you, also."

"Thank you."

"Do you have a place to stay?" he asked, his brow furrowed.

"Yes. I do. Thank you. "

"Are you hungry?"

"No. No, I'm not." Millicent smiled.

"If you *are* hungry, go around the side of the church. Knock on the small door there and we will feed you."

"Thank you. So much."

"May God bless you."

The two monks left by the side door. Millicent stood, blew her nose, and then walked toward the main entrance, counting the pairs of towering, mismatched columns that flanked the long center aisle. She was halfway down the nave when the rising sun flooded in through the open front doors and enveloped her in a thick shaft of light. *"Nel mezzo del cammin,"* she laughed, listening for the moment's ideal soundtrack. She exited into the sunlit morning to what she could recall of the triumphant chords of Mahler's 2nd Symphony finale, *'Light that Shineth in the Darkness'*. Ancient, Medieval, Renaissance and Modern Rome spread out before her. Flocks of birds sang so ardently that not even the din of buses, Vespas, cars and blaring car radios could drown them out.

That monk had it backwards. Millicent proclaimed, with Mahler and Hermina, *"We are born that we shall live!"*

****

The approach of Death into her girls' lives hurled Hermina back into Sam's illness and death. One well-meaning doctor had ushered her into a quiet room determined to convince her that he'd seen it all before and that time would heal her pain. Nearly a year of practicing loss hadn't helped. She was still being ripped from sleep's merciful amnesia, awakening to the agony of grief's hatchet deep in her breastbone and the shock that she was *not* lying in a pool of her own blood. Disoriented then, she knew something was terribly wrong. But what? Oh, yes. The deafening absence of Sam's glottal half-snore, the freezing absence of his body's heat. Her life with Sam was over. His precious life had been lost with all he'd left unlived, all the music he'd never hear. He would never come home again, never be in her arms. Never again.

"Sam!" she cried out now to their Roman bedroom ceiling. *Sweet Numina*, Sam whispered.

Sympathy was not an emotion that the thought of Phyllis tended to evoke, but surely the woman had some good qualities. Hermina's heart went out to her now in her impending widowhood.

"Take care of yourself, Millicent, not just of them," Hermina warned. "Suffering does not ennoble us, nor does loss turn us into better people." She wasn't as worried about Alice, who was going to be with Neal until Millicent was sure it was right for her to join her in San Ensayo. But Millicent seemed gripped by the delusion that the force of her compassion would suffice to lift her family up and away from its cruel history. More likely, when the capsizing swells of widowhood hit her, Phyllis would drag them all under.

Millicent didn't seem to hear her warning but responded with a request. "May I please leave my phone in your apartment? Both our doors can close and lock even with the cord under them. That way, you can tell Fabrizio what's going on. His friend, Massimo, doesn't answer and Colin is away. I know Fabrizio would worry if there was no answer day after day."

How in the world, Hermina wondered in silence, could she exchange words with that philanderer without giving him a piece of her mind? *'Now, Hermina...,'* she heard Sam chide.

"On one condition," she said and slipped a hundred dollar bill into Millicent's hand. "If you promise to use this to phone me whenever you want, as often as necessary. Or call collect and use the money for something else. Don't worry about the time zones; I'm up several times each night and have lots of practice falling back to sleep. Call rather too often than too seldom."

She accompanied Millicent and Alice to the airport though their flight left inhumanely early. After lingering embraces at Passport Control, her girls walked through the sliding doors and were gone.

When Hermina turned to face the bustling departure hall crowd, she became dizzy and sank gratefully onto a nearby metal chair. She felt as if her skin had lost its capacity to encase her *being* and that the component parts of *her*, of her *Hermina-ness*, were drifting apart, farther and farther, beyond her, out, and up, beyond the airport terminal building, the city of Rome, beyond country and continent, up into the borderless atmosphere – as if she were dispersing and the very illusion of existence were losing sway.

If this was death, how light, how lovely! *Let go!*

The sensation – most likely a precipitous drop in blood pressure, she hypothesized – faded eventually, and she returned to the state of being she experienced as so *normal* that she usually didn't notice it at all. She looked down at the liver spots on the backs of her hands, at the crooked, thickened joints of her fingers, her wrinkled flesh. *Don't you dare die on Millicent now, you selfish old thing,* she told herself. *She has enough to contend with.*

To defy gravity and stand up required a forceful push. *You're getting old, my dear.* She said these things to herself. Sam, it seemed, was not with her. No, the wound of Sam's death wasn't healing with time; if anything it seemed more inflamed. Here she was, alive, in Rome, Italy, alone.

2

Flying westward toward her dying father, Millicent again remembered painting the bungalow's picket fence with him when she was four. He must have been as old then as she was now, just starting out. His excitement had filled the house, when, that is, he took the time to be there. Watching her father, she'd learned that working could be a consuming passion. Unlike him, she couldn't indulge that joy without restraint. He'd never had to say, *Sorry, I can't work that day – Geena and Millicent need me*. Raising them had been their mother's job. The Milner's deal was for Herb to make the family rich while Phyllis took care of everything else. If Millicent had grown up to be the daughter they'd wanted, she would have been doing that now for some ambitious man.

All the way to Chicago to deliver Alice to Neal, Millicent strained to seem upbeat, chatting and joking even as she blew her nose and dabbed her eyes. She flew on to San Ensayo alone. She needed to gauge what she'd be putting Alice through before she let her join her there.

She took a cab straight to the hospital. Saying the magic words, "I just got in from Rome," the nurse ushered her into her father's room, although, visiting hours were long over. She slipped into the chair beside his bed without disturbing him or his roommate by the window.

In the four months since Chanukah, cancer had reduced her father to his ideal weight. When had she last seen his face that handsome? It must have been when they lived in that stone house with the stucco walls and steel beams where they'd been happy for a while. He'd taken a normal job after one of his bankruptcies, took the commuter train home each day by six and was free on weekends. Thirteen-year-old Geena had Daddy to debate politics with at the dinner table, and ten-year-old Millicent had him in the garden.

They planted rose bushes together outside the kitchen door. She ripped handfuls of peat moss for him from the bales he kept in the wild, shaded area behind the garage, or showed off by lifting the whole bale. His muscular arms were coarsely veined, his wrists thick, his fingers huge, yet he could pluck a lady-bug from a rose petal or a thorn from Millicent's outstretched palm with graceful precision. He taught only by example, explaining nothing. He didn't turn any corner of the garden over to her care. But he never criticized her, never ambushed her with trick questions to prove what a fool she was. They worked and sweated together without speaking. He whistled tuneless music that allowed her thoughts to range free. Together, they breathed garden-in-sunlight, garden-at-dusk.

Now, he was dying. She could see that on his face. She put her lips to his forehead and inhaled him, as if she could *incorporarlo*, as if her lungs could fill her bloodstream with him, distributing *Daddy* to all her cells.

The taxi from the hospital brought her to her parents' apartment late. Deniza must have been asleep because Phyllis herself opened the door. *Their hug,* Millicent thought, *was like two worried women.*

****

When Millicent returned to the hospital the next morning, her father's bed was empty. She ran to the nurses' station where they reassured her he'd only been taken down for tests. She retraced her steps but wasn't sure it was the right room. Three men and a woman surrounded the room's other patient, in the bed by the window, all talking at once. They spoke American English but laughed and carried on like her Italian students.

A tall man approached her. He introduced himself as Leo Lombardi and said he was visiting his father. She'd heard that name before. The Lombardi's construction company had done most of the building work on the San Ensayo Urban Development projects, an agency her father had cozied up to when seeking to have his building permits approved.

"This is Bettina," the man named Leo said, "my big sister. She's the other 'son' in Lombardi & Sons. And these two cut-ups are the guys at work most likely to make the old man laugh, when they don't drive him crazy. This is my father. Franco." He was a man of Hermina's generation with a similarly direct gaze.

In courtly, Italian fashion, Leo apologized for having commandeered all the chairs. He offered her his chair and asked

Bettina to pour her a cup of *caffelatte* from their thermos. Millicent was soon deep into tales of her life in Rome, interrupted by rowdy reminiscences from Lombardi pilgrimages to their namesake, *Lombardia*, the lush, rocky countryside around Milan.

Bettina looked at her watch and, with a demonstratively loud intake of air, reminded her crew that work awaited them. They kissed the patient on both cheeks, *all'italiana*. "I'll be back this afternoon," Leo said, his voice soft with affection, as he equitably redistributed the chairs. Before he left, he drew the curtain separating the two beds, "So they can both have a little privacy," and reached out to take Millicent's hand. "My father tells me that your father is quite ill. We wish you and your family all the best."

From behind the curtain, Millicent heard Franco Lombardi's wracking cough.

She had hoped that arriving early at the hospital would assure her some time alone with her father. But just as they rolled him into the room asleep in a wheelchair, Phyllis arrived. With her coat still over her arm, she opened the curtain between the two beds.

"I've told you, Mr. Lombardo. It's much too dark on our side of the room with this curtain closed. We don't have the luxury of a window." She looked at Millicent, shook her head, and hissed "Laborers!" under her breath.

"Lombardi, not Lombardo," the elderly man said, as if he'd told this woman that before. He turned his drawn face to the window and closed his eyes.

****

"At it again, is she?" Geena asked that night at their parents' apartment as they lay on the two single beds in Millicent's room. "You missed last week's heavyweight bout. Undefeated Phyllis vs. Challenger Leo."

"She has something against the Lombardis?" Millicent asked.

"She considers it an insult for a man of Daddy's stature to be stuck not just in a double room but on the lower-status side of it. She'd have been outraged by *any* gang of Italian construction workers reigning over the best real estate. But Franco Lombardi! According to a friend who knows the family, Lombardi once walked out of negotiations when he caught Daddy trying to sneak some small-print clauses past him. The sleazy outfit that got the contract did a shitty job on the wiring, which may have caused Daddy's fire, though nobody could prove it. In her screwed-up logic, Mother blames the Lombardis for the fire. You should marry into the Lombardi family – that would kill our mother."

"Geena!"

"Anyway. Last week, she called Dorfman – you know, he's the big cheese at Urban Development, she claims he's a close personal friend."

"He and his wife came to our house once, didn't they?"

"Yeah. Once. Mother wanted him to intimidate the hospital administrator into giving Daddy a private room at no added cost. Apparently, he refused. Her only option then was to go after Lombardi himself. If he had the window open, she wanted it closed; if he had the curtain between the beds closed, she wanted it open. The guy's family made excuses for her the way people have always done: the lady's husband is sick, she's probably distraught, etc., etc."

"That's all true, though."

"Come on, Mill. What she wants is total control. Anyway, there was a showdown a few days ago."

Geena described the scene: Herb had been given a sedative before some grueling test and he was sleeping it off. Geena was sitting with her back to the Lombardis while Phyllis, on the opposite side of Herb's bed, faced them. The Lombardis were looking at blueprints with the bed lamp on and Phyllis had called out, "That light is shining in my eyes. Turn it off." Apologizing, they tilted the shade. "Turn it *off*!" she'd snapped again, and again they apologized, politely, and pulled the curtain closed. At which point Phyllis had stood up, walked around Herb's bed, pulled the curtain open, marched over to the old guy's bed and turned his lamp off.

"She didn't!" Millicent cringed.

"It was awful. She said, 'I will *not* have my husband disturbed,' in that shrill voice, and then she sat down again.

"Leo Lombardi, the son you met today, came over, really quietly, stood in front of Mother and asked to have a word with her in the hall. He said it softly but you could tell he meant business.

"She refused. He didn't move. The atmosphere was so thick I stopped breathing." After a short, silent stand-off, Phyllis let out a puff of air and yielded. "She went as far as the door frame and stood there with her arms crossed, but he gestured toward the hall like a *maitre d'* at some classy joint pointing the way to a table."

Geena had followed them out. He'd sounded like a benevolent school master forced by circumstances to be strict as he explained that both their families were going through a very difficult time and that, surely, none of them wanted to make the situation any harder than it already was.

But Phyllis had cut him off. "Mr. Lombardo."

"Lombardi," he corrected her. "Leo."

"Nothing and no one will stop me from protecting my husband from the likes of you." Phyllis's lip had actually curled.

"I *beg* your pardon?" Leo was clearly shocked, and Phyllis spat back, "No you don't. You don't care who you hurt or inconvenience, you boorish people."

Horrified, Leo had flashed Geena a look as if to ask if this lady was for real. When Geena raised her eyebrows and nodded, all softness went out of him. "I sure as shit wouldn't want anybody to glare at me the way he did at her, Mill. Then he let her have it:

"'If you continue to disturb the tranquility of this sick room, a space which is to be shared in a civilized manner, we will have the authorities remove you. *You*, Mrs. Milner. Do you understand me? Your harassment will stop.' She was about to say something back, but then he cut her off and said 'Stop. Now!' And he just left her there."

He then returned to his father and drew the curtain between the beds closed.

"She stomped back in a huff and I could tell she was toying with pulling the curtain open again. But you know what? She didn't dare. How my heart sang!"

"Oh, Geena!" Millicent's hands were covering her face at the thought of the scene.

"Ask yourself, Millicent: Why, in all these decades, has no one ever stopped that woman before?"

"What good did it do?" Millicent said. "She's still at it. I saw her pull the curtain open again today."

"Maybe. But I bet Leo, wasn't there," Geena said.

"He'd just left."

"I'm not talking about *changing* her, Millicent – she's too fucked up for that. Just *stopping* her. Every single time. If a stranger could stop her, why didn't Daddy? And why the hell haven't *we*?"

3

The curtain wars were soon moot. As Millicent told Hermina, treatments that might have bought her father a few extra months had caused such complications and side-effects that Dr. Erskine agreed to send him home to die in peace. They installed a rented hospital bed in the area Phyllis called the "sun porch," an elegantly curved space just off the dining room with sky blue walls and cloud white drapes. From there on the twelfth floor, he had a panoramic view of the city in which he'd been a player. The Milner women and Deniza would take care of him until he couldn't make it to the bathroom anymore, then they'd hire nurses. This death, Dr. Erskine told them, would not come slowly.

Millicent phoned Neal to speak to Alice. "Would you like to come and say goodbye to Bompa?" Alice's voice was muffled. "I can't hear you, Alice."

"I said okay."

"Does 'okay' mean you'd rather stay at your dad's?"

"No." Alice sounded the way she did when she had her bottom lip sticking way out.

"How come only 'okay'?"

There was a pause. "MiMi."

"I told you and I meant it: I won't let her hit you ever again. Geena's here, too, you know. How is it at your dad's?"

"We went clothes shopping and ate at Snappy's Pizza. They have pinball machines and I got a really high score."

"Sounds like fun. So, what are you thinking about Bompa."

"Mom? Why does he have to die?"

"I wish I knew the answer."

"Are you gonna die?"

"Someday. Not until you and I are both very, very old."

"Older than Hermina?"

"Much, *much* older."

"Bompa isn't older than Hermina."

"No. But he's very sick. And thin, not like the usual big-bear Bompa."

"How do you know you won't get sick and thin and die, too? Or my dad?"

"Well, I'm going to work very hard not to. And I bet your dad will, too."

"Didn't Bompa work hard? Maybe God is mad at him. He should be madder at MiMi."

"I don't believe it works like that, Alice, that God goes around punishing people. He's not mean."

"Then how come He won't let Bompa live anymore?"

"I don't know, Alice. God could have a reason we don't understand. We can ask Him for help, though."

"To make Bompa live?"

"Yes. But mostly to help us love each other a whole lot."

"Even MiMi?"

"We have to be good to her."

"Why doesn't she have to be good to us?"

"Oh, Alice. You ask such hard questions."

"Mom? Will I die?"

"Yes, but you better not! Not before me, and by then I'll be so old I'll creak and rattle and have no teeth and be all bent over and shout 'Heh? Heh? I can't hear without my teeth!'" Alice laughed. "Call your dad to the phone. Alice? Are you still there?"

"My dad says I should stay here."

"I'll talk to him. And, Alice?"

"What?"

"I love you."

"I love you, too, Mom."

When Millicent brought her daughter straight to the sun porch to see Bompa, Alice leaned against her and wouldn't kiss him. "Show Bompa your Barbie pictures," Millicent said softly.

"Come sit by me, here," Bompa said. He still sounded like himself, so Alice explained the pictures she'd drawn and answered his questions about Italy and about how to say different things in Italian, as if everything were regular. She said nothing about him dying, and neither did he. She couldn't say, "Goodbye, Bompa," as she'd imagined because he wasn't gone; he was right there listening to her and looking at her drawings. When Deniza came to say she'd cooked eggs-and-birdies, Alice hugged Bompa. And kissed him.

"Bompa smells funny," Alice told her mother, later. "Like metal."

Some afternoons during the four long weeks it took her father to die, Millicent went to the sun porch with a book. While he could still manage it, he sat on the side of the bed leaning toward the right, supporting himself with his right hand, his naked legs and bare feet dangling down toward his house slippers. Was there a tumor in there that needed extra room, Millicent wondered? Every so often, a comment would seem to fall from him as if by accident. "Well," he said once, "I don't have to worry about my weight anymore. Or the bad circulation in my feet." And, "I wonder what they'll do with all my shoes?" Most of the time, though, he said nothing, as if directing all his focus inward, as if dying were a complicated puzzle requiring immense concentration.

One morning, he asked Millicent to please wash his feet. "How Biblical," she said, laughing, as she gathered the bowl and sponge and towel. She was careful to keep her touch nonchalant, as if she were washing the dishes. Those legs, she'd always thought of as tree trunks now were thin, and that bear-hair he used to have all over him, had time worn it away?

Coming back from the kitchen where she'd deposited the bowl and sponge, she saw Geena sitting beside their father's bed. At one time, she would have felt jealous, but now she felt happy seeing the sweetness in Geena that she tried so hard to hide. She was speaking to their father softly, but he didn't seem to respond.

4

Millicent wanted time away from the apartment to think. Deniza said she'd watch out for Alice, that is, keep Alice safe from Phyllis, who yelled at Millicent for leaving. "Just like you to parachute in, leave all the work to us, and you go off and indulge yourself."

"I'll be back soon. Deniza says Alice is okay with her."

"This is not a hotel, you know. And what about all the time you're on the phone to that Willamina?"

"*Hermina*."

"Who's going to pay for those overseas calls?"

"I told you. I'm leaving money for the phone bill."

"That'll be the day. Go on. Get out."

Millicent picked up her purse, nodded goodbye to a pained-looking Deniza and kissed Alice. "I won't be long. Keep away from MiMi. She's on the warpath."

With Daddy dying, the time had come to try to talk to her mother, really talk to her. Millicent rehearsed what she wanted to say, over and over, adjusting, editing, restating as she walked purposefully through the park. She pictured herself seated before her mother, holding her hands. She would say: *Of course you're feeling desperate because Daddy's dying*. And: *Of course, you feel helpless and that makes you angry, so you take that anger out on me.* Her mother would melt, tears would fill her eyes and she would answer, *I'm so sorry. You're so right. It's not your fault Daddy is dying. Poor child, you're about to lose your father, and your mother is too upset to comfort you.* They would embrace and cry together, grieve together.

As soon as she returned home, she asked her mother if she had a minute.

"I'm busy."

"Please? Just sit down for a moment." But Phyllis refused to.

“Mother.” Standing, Millicent began to recite her speech as gently as she could.

When Phyllis started to speak, Millicent stopped her. “Please let me finish. You take your anger out on me. That’s okay. I know you don’t really mean what you say. You know I’m a good person.”

A pause followed Millicent’s carefully reasoned plea. As she readied her arms to reach out, to hold and be held, a look of panic spread across Phyllis’s face. She looked the way Alice had when she was four years old, waking from a nightmare, before Millicent had taken her on her lap to rock her and drive the bogeyman far, far away. Slowly, Phyllis’s lips thinned, and a knifelike glare glistened in her eyes. “Don’t you dare patronize me! Shifting the blame onto me. You brat. Who the hell do you think you are?”

Millicent retreated to her bed.

Had she deluded herself into believing she’d had a good mother? What about her father, then? He’d never shut her out the way Geena said he had done to her when she’d hit puberty. Millicent remembered herself twirling for him in her tutu, how his face lit up, how he beamed during those living room fashion shows when she was a child and then a teenager.

What about as an adult? She remembered how she’d stood by his side when his business was burning – as if she weren’t his daughter but a dear *friend*. What was her obligation to him? Should she help him to reconcile himself to his approaching death? No. Help him to struggle against it. She washed her face; if she was to be his one source of courage then he shouldn’t see that she’d been crying. She hurried to his bedside on the sun porch and exhorted, “Daddy. We can fight this. We can. Please?”

A faint smile came to his lips. “I need to sleep now, honey.”

The next afternoon, Herb said he wanted to speak to Millicent alone. She pulled a chair close to his bed.

She was expecting him to talk about his happy memories, his regrets, his losses, his hopes for all of them, and, now, his experience of dying. Or, for him to forgive her for her post-adolescent rebellions and the mess she’d made of her early adult life. For some praise, perhaps, for the child she was raising, for the clean-up she was engaged in, some consolation for her history of always choosing the wrong men.

Instead, he looked at her for a long moment, and then asked her about her long-term finances. She reported that she was making a good living. He said that was good to hear because there would be no inheritance for her or Geena, yet. In his will, he'd left everything to their mother; all their property and investments were in her name; she was the sole beneficiary of his life insurance policies; and, years ago, he'd inserted a clause into their contract with his partners that, if he died, his widow wouldn't be liable for the business's debts. He wanted to know that Phyllis would be all right after his death and also not become a financial burden on Millicent and Geena.

"That's no problem, Daddy," Millicent said. Money – all that stuff about mortgage payments and insurance premiums – none of that mattered to her. She waited, presuming he'd now broach the real topics.

Her father looked at her for a moment and smiled. Did he expect her to start the conversation? Now that they were alone together, should she apologize for all the times she'd ever disappointed him, and tell him that she thought he was the most wonderful man ever?

She said nothing; she'd let him lead.

Was he formulating in his mind what to say? Was he embarrassed by what was in his heart? Was it too hard to express?

Millicent focused all her wit and receptivity on reading this climactic silence, which was bursting with expectation and hope.

Slowly, slowly, the moment passed its peak and Millicent felt herself deflate.

She pictured somebody at a podium, gathering up papers, closing a notebook; she could hear the muffled silence as of an audience putting on coats, preparing to leave the hall.

It was over. Daddy had not spoken and now he was asleep.

She returned to her father once he was awake again and sat on the edge of his bed and lay her head on his chest. "I love you so much, Daddy," she whispered. "Please don't go." He lifted his hand and stroked her hair, slowly.

"Go to the table, Millicent," Phyllis came in to say. "Dinner is ready."

"Start without her, please," Herb answered. "She'll be there soon."

For a long while, her father stroked her hair.

5

The death of Herb Milner began, as Millicent later described it to Hermina, with a quiet slide from an increasingly distant presence into unconsciousness. At four o'clock one morning, the night nurse woke them. Millicent didn't have the heart to awaken Alice, and no one thought to include Deniza, which Millicent later regretted. She held her father's right hand and Geena caressed his forehead; they told him how sorry they were that he had to die this early in his life, that he'd been a good man, that they'd always loved him and always would. Phyllis leaned over to kiss his cheeks and his lips. As she thanked him for the adventure that had been their marriage, Millicent peered, as if through a crack, into her parents' private bond.

For some minutes, Herb still breathed. Millicent had read the phrase 'death rattle' but never dreamed such breathing might have beauty, a rhythm, like music. One deep and labored inhalation followed another. Then, no more.

She felt her own chest fill, empty, fill again. *There does exist a last breath,* she thought, *but this one was not hers, nor this one, nor, most likely, would the next one be.* She neither saw nor sensed any miraculous or dramatic transformation at the moment of his death, no spirit leaving or presence of some god showing up. Her father died. *There was nothing wrong with that moment,* she thought, *although, it changed everything.*

When the first emotional wave ebbed, Herb Milner's three women left his bedside and filed into the living room. This was their '*Hour of Lead*', Millicent recognized, when, "*After great pain, a formal feeling comes.*" It came, and seemed to supersede, if only for the moment, the struggles among them.

Millicent and Geena sat together on the gold velvet sofa holding each other's hands, their heads touching. Phyllis, solemn and upright, a calm, tearful, wife-turning-widow, sat on a chair, as if her daughters were not there.

The doorbell rang. The nurse had phoned the funeral home. Though it was only dawn, they'd come for the body. Millicent stayed where she was, but later, Geena told her how the men had bagged their father then strapped him onto a special gurney, hinged in such a way that Daddy "stood" during his final descent in the elevator. Geena looked on as Phyllis, still crying, skittered in front of the men all the way from the sun porch and out the front door making sure the gurney didn't scratch any of her furniture.

The *formal feeling* returned later that morning as Millicent and Alice cried together over Bompa's passing. As Alice went from room to room in an attempt to grasp that he was gone, Millicent's remorse grew. Why hadn't she woken Alice up to witness Bompa's passing? Whether that would have helped or hurt, she would never know.

At Herb's well-attended funeral a few days afterwards, his 'secret profligacy', as Phyllis referred to it – "Charity" was Geena's more customary attribution – was laid bare for all to see. Total strangers he'd apparently rescued over the years approached Phyllis to express their profound gratitude for Herb's largess. Phyllis learned that, more than once, he had fronted bail money for the brother of their toothless, Polish janitor. He'd let years pass without raising the rent on an old, Jewish, immigrant tenant on a fixed income. He'd paid the doctor bills when Deniza's teenage niece was in trouble with euphemistic 'women's problems'. And on and on. All without a word to his wife.

Standing in the receiving line at the funeral parlor, Phyllis hurled herself into a Lady-Bountiful-Widow-of-a-Jewish-Saint persona without missing a beat. On their way home, alone with the girls in the car, Phyllis raged over Herb's audacity in unilaterally depleting their estate.

At breakfast the morning before Millicent and Alice were leaving for Rome, in an ostensibly offhand comment, between bites of the hot, buttered *challah* – from the specialty bakery which Phyllis still insisted Deniza walk the extra four blocks to reach – Phyllis revealed to her daughters how determined Herb had been to take care of her and protect her. In fact, she said, he had begged her, his beloved wife, with almost his last breath: "Promise me you won't let the girls rip you off."

"Bull! Shit!" Geena shouted throwing her napkin onto the table and storming out. Phyllis shot a long-suffering look at Millicent, that day's Good Daughter. Millicent excused herself from the table.

"Lying bitch!" Geena grabbed her purse. "There's no one to keep her even moderately civil now that Daddy's dead. Not that he ever stopped her when he was alive. Let's get the fuck out of here."

Deniza agreed to take Alice shopping with her.

"It can't be true," Millicent protested leaning both her arms on the wobbly café table. The way her father had stroked her hair must have meant that he'd forgiven her.

"Okay. They were in it together, those two," Geena said. "But that 'Us-Against-Them' crap, that wasn't how *he* worked. Only *her*. He probably was genuinely worried she'd be left with only us to rely on, two husband-less flakes with the combined financial acumen of a cotton ball. You watch, though. She'll find a way to use it all up, to make sure we don't get a penny. If she ever deigns to die, we'll find ourselves in some lawyer's office hearing that her Last Will and Testament leaves whatever is left of her money to the Association for Syphilitic Unwed Schnauzers."

Geena and Millicent looked each other in the eye. An uncanny silence enveloped them despite the hum of coffee house conversations and the hiss of the *espresso* machine. Each one saw her own thought come alive in the eyes of the other. They held each other's gaze. Geena gave their shared thought a voice:

"We could kill her."

A delicious and evil solution. An exhilarating frisson. They spluttered and then exploded with laughter. "Okay, okay," Geena said with sad reluctance. "We won't murder our mother."

This outburst had been more complex than mere relief at pulling back from a moral precipice. They realized they had made a choice, consciously, *not* to exercise the power they'd had all their lives, with no awareness of having it. When Leo Lombardi had said, "Stop it," Phyllis had stopped. Now, they, too, could stop her, with just the lift of an eyebrow.

"Remember: This is not a pardon. Only a reprieve," Geena said. "One she's done fuck-all to merit. We had no mother to teach us goodness. We invented it ourselves, as kids, by loving each other. She lives on because we've renounced our Birthright of Cruelty. We are good people, and no bloody thanks to her."

The last morning, Millicent went directly to her parents' bedroom. She opened the top drawer of her father's dresser and removed the watch he'd worn for many years, the gold one with a disc that rotated on the dial, creating the illusion of an eternally expanding mandala. She found her mother in the kitchen and, with Geena-like boldness, informed her, "By the way, I took Daddy's watch." Phyllis blinked and blinked and blinked again.

6

As she and Alice left San Ensayo, Millicent felt guilty that she couldn't crank up the pathos a fatherless daughter owes her newly widowed mother. She'd said the proper, "I'll miss you so much," but failed to squeeze any moisture from her disobliging tear ducts. Once the cab left for the airport, she allowed herself to acknowledge her relief at getting the hell out of there.

Arriving in Rome, before the familiarity of routine blinded her, Millicent also admitted that her shuttered apartment wasn't a home and that she wanted one. For one brief moment she even let in the awareness that she wanted a husband, one of her own, rather than a man married to some other woman, one he cheated on.

Among the letters Hermina had stacked on the hall table were four missives from Fabrizio. The one with the earliest April postmark was a plain postcard wishing Millicent's father good luck. Two others, Easter postcards sent from photo-shoot locations at Verona and Messina, dripped with innuendos for every mail-handler to see. The most recent, dated early May, instructed her to inform him of her return by ringing his old friend Massimo.

He didn't answer. Nor did an answering machine.

Meanwhile, Alice had gone to knock on Hermina's door. Hearing their excited voices, she joined them. Millicent took one look at Hermina and knew something was terribly wrong. She'd aged and seemed sadder. Was she ill? As Millicent looked past Hermina, she grasped the disaster: Hermina was dismantling her home.

"What are you doing?" Millicent asked, alarmed.

"You were gone so long. I couldn't wait anymore."

"You're moving? Nearby, right?"

"To California, to my son in Orinda. But not until the end of August. We'll have the summer together."

In her bed that night, Millicent knew that it was as true for her as for Dante that midway through her journey the straightforward pathway had, indeed, been lost, if she'd ever followed it to begin with. It was becoming increasingly difficult for her to stay lost. Her favorite artifices had begun to fail her. Hermina was leaving her but Millicent couldn't zip herself into her *I-Don't-Give-A-Crap-About-the-Old-Bag* camouflage suit. The *Daddy's-Little- Princess* costume seemed ludicrous, and not only because Daddy was dead. Both her *Independent-Single-Mother-Career-Woman* outfit and her *Every-Woman's-Sexual-Rival* ensemble were passé. And the very notion of donning a *Femme-Fatale-Mistress* get-up mortified her.

How to describe these feelings? *Loss of innocence*? What's left when that's gone? Guilt.

No. *Reality*.

She didn't have time now to invent a New Reality – she had to be a mother, a breadwinner, win bread. Over the next few days, she kept away from the Old Reality. If she chanced to meet Hermina, she assumed a jaunty air. How else could she bear the coming loss?

****

After their long separation, Tizia and Alice greeted each other with one hug after another and began immediately to plan frequent sleepovers.

Charlotte didn't hail Millicent's return to Rome with such enthusiasm. She had stepped in to teach Millicent's private students and now expected to keep them. "They learn better from someone who has English as their second language, just the way they do," Charlotte argued. The students themselves, with the exception of the young buck whom Charlotte had begun to entertain in her off-hours, expressed relief at having Millicent back. Secretly, Millicent glowed at this affirmation of her superior teaching skills and smiled when one of her pupils complained, politely, that it made no sense at all for Charlotte to teach him English by speaking Italian.

By the end of the first week, Millicent's life had returned to what she'd considered normal, including her frustration over hearing nothing from Fabrizio. Over the weekend, Millicent reached Massimo's answering machine with a message for him to relay that she had returned to Rome and was planning her regular trip to Milan at the end of the coming week. Fabrizio was uncharacteristically prompt in calling to confirm their meeting.

As she packed for the trip, she realized that she was furious. For the privilege of being in some man's arms for a very short time, she had to travel for hours (the calluses would form again on her palm from carrying her suitcase), then crank up a big courtesan extravaganza number.

There is another alternative, you asshole, she imagined Geena whispering in her ear. *It's called 'a good marriage'.*

She was wondering whether the arms she longed for might actually be Hermina's when it struck her that she hadn't planned a special treat for Fabrizio, as she customarily did. The familiar fear of being dumped caused her apparatus for adrenalin production to sputter into gear. A dangerous acid – she'd once seen how somebody's flesh had charred after his surgeons leaked adrenalin onto him.

She stuffed her silky travel robe, unironed, into the suitcase, zipped the whole affair and slammed it down by the door in her unseasonably cold front hall. Returning to her room to collect her purse and keys, she stopped abruptly and closed her eyes for a moment.

"Sam," Millicent said aloud, shyly, never having addressed him directly before, "please send me someone of my own."

****

Millicent had let each of her Milan students know that she, not a substitute, would be coming to the final classes of the semester. They'd all paid in advance, so she wouldn't have suffered financially if some dropped out. But most had been with her since the beginning; she wanted to see them again. She was touched when they all showed up. They even handed her a bouquet of lilies and a condolence card written in very good English. Though she worried about being unprofessional, she couldn't stop tears of gratitude from trickling down her cheeks.

That evening, after Fabrizio screwed Millicent with an intensity that almost made her believe that he, too, had been faithful, she talked to him about her father's death, in economical, telegraphic phrases. He made no comment, refraining as always from engaging in the details of her life.

Later, they reclined together fully dressed on the newly made bed, waiting until it was time for him to drive her to the night train. She heard herself announce as if into an empty atmosphere, "I'm about to lose Hermina, too." Her voice echoed deeper than usual, her cheek muscles lacked even the memory of a charming smile, and his presence held an irrelevance which she only found remarkable in that she'd never acknowledged it before.

His quiet, even breathing told her that his thoughts, too, were elsewhere. Whatever reality these trysts distracted him from – or reassured him about, or compensated or avenged – had little or nothing to do with her, personally. That she might be an interchangeable tool in service of something or other constituted no betrayal. There was nothing to be angry about. He was, after all, more a thing than a person to her as well.

Who was she anyway? An unexceptional thirty-three year old divorcée, with an adequate if impractical job, with a dear if lonely daughter, in a country where she did not belong, clinging to a man who was bound to someone else. She had a sister whom she loved but who lived far away, a mother whom she feared, a flawed father, now dead. And a beloved, elderly neighbor who was leaving her.

This is what I've managed to make of my life so far, she said to herself silently. She ought, perhaps, to have stood up, kissed Fabrizio on both cheeks, said a sincere, "Thank you," and walked out.

She didn't. Instead, as Fabrizio leaned down to cover her mouth with the last deep kiss of this encounter, with one hand on her breast and the other on her rump, habit cranked Millicent into action. She nibbled his lower lip while grinding her pelvis slowly against his accommodatingly clenched thigh. This time, however, even if only for a moment, she noticed herself doing it.

As she reclaimed Alice in Rome the next morning, Millicent stood in Hermina's doorway and looked directly yet softly into her eyes. "I'm going to miss you," she said, her voice unstrained. Her own.

7

Millicent had been going regularly to Martino's chic, white hair salon to trim the split ends from her nearly waist-length hair. She paid a fortune and endured the scorn that Italians direct at those they deem deficient in their sense of fashion.

Today, she asked him, "What would you do if I let you decide?"

"*Finalmente*!" He threw his hands in the air. Then, standing behind her, he looked into the mirror and played with her hair, holding it up, folding it all under. As she watched, she wondered when the college-aged Millicent, the girl who had decided she should wear her long, straight hair parted in the middle, had ceased to exist.

"I'd chop most of this witchy mess off and turn the rest into curls!" Martino declared at last. "What do you need all this hair for?"

She did not say to slide its heft, slowly, slowly, across Fabrizio's groin. To comb through with her fingers, soothing herself as if she were her own pet cat. To hide behind, styleless, in the wings while other women took center stage in the daily fashion cavalcade – envious women, poised to pounce if she dared to make an entrance. No one could ridicule her for losing a competition in which she so obviously wasn't a participant.

"Not too short," she whispered as the radical notion struck her that her hairstyle might not be the only thing about to change.

Her heart kept pace with the salon's blasting rock-and-roll and her clammy palms clutched the chair arms as Martino held the collected mass of her hair aloft between the gaping edges of his shears. "*Guarda!*" he called out and everyone stopped and turned to look. "*Sono Dalila*!" his voice boomed. Then, snip! Martino flourished Millicent's amputated hair high in the air.

Two hours later, he paraded her and her curly, shoulder-length lion's mane around his salon. *"La mia Sansone,"* he bragged. When she left, he kissed her on both cheeks.

****

"Mother's asking me to help her move," Millicent told Geena on the phone later that Monday. "I can't afford to go back there. Really, I can't. But guess what she said." Millicent turned on her prickliest Phyllis whine. "'You're selfish. You have an income. What I have now is all I'll ever get.' She's totally predictable, so how come I'm shocked every time?"

"Resist, Millicent. She has Deniza to help and the bucks to hire movers."

"But she is on a fixed income."

"Right. Of *thousands* a month. Their investment manager told her the stocks Daddy left her are up several percentage points already."

"He said that with you in the room?"

"She hissed at him to shut up. The doorman said she's selling their old apartment for much more per square foot than she'll have to fork out for the new one a few floors down. She's already collected mounds of curtain and carpet samples in luscious colors. Don't get pulled into her 'widowhood-is-a-financial-catastrophe' moaning."

"She said we shouldn't expect her to be as open-handed now as when Daddy was alive."

"The only thing she's ever done with an open hand is slap us. Anyway, she's raising cash by selling off loads of stuff that won't fit in her new place. Every now and then, she remembers to snivel."

"Imagine breaking up that big apartment all alone though."

"Okay, okay. She is terrified. And humiliated. Strangers are walking through, fingering her personal belongings so they can haggle down the prices. And Daddy's presence is everywhere. Going there hurts. An empathy overload."

"I feel bad that you have to carry the whole burden."

"Don't worry. I don't go often."

"Hermina's packing, too," Millicent said. "Alice and I spent the weekend helping. She kept trying to send us out into the sunshine, but she can't drag those heavy boxes around by herself. It's a slow process. Every time she's emptying a dusty cupboard, she calls out, 'Come look at this! I'd forgotten we had it.' She keeps saying I mustn't feel obliged to take the stuff she offers me because I'll only have to pack it up next time I move. Which got me to thinking she's right. *Via Scarlata* probably isn't the last place we'll ever live."

"Is there a whiff of change in the air?" Geena asked before hanging up.

****

"We're usually unaware when we experience the last of something," Hermina mused as they sat on Millicent's roof terrace. "You were privileged to witness your father's last breath knowing that's what it was. I was able to do the same with Sam. But, the last time I could still lift my sleeping son to carry him upstairs to his bedroom, I had no idea I'd never do it again. It didn't occur to me to take special delight in the way his legs dangled against my shins and his hair tickled my face. But I know these are my last months in Italy."

"You might come back to visit us."

"Or might we meet in California?" Hermina asked with a glint in her eye. "But, until then, I have a request. Would you and Alice accompany me on a trip? *Siena*, for example. Have you been there?"

"No."

"I long to spend one more night at our favorite hotel there. And to see the *Duomo*; Sam always hummed the rhythms he heard in the patterns of its black and white marble stripes. That stunning, white Piccolomini Altar is there, too, with four Michelangelo statues. I'd rent a car and we could share the driving. You grew up behind the wheel, didn't you?"

"I can't afford a trip, Hermina. Italy closes during August. There'll be no money coming in."

"Silly girl! I'm inviting you and Alice as my guests. If you're available and have no other plans."

"Plans? Fabrizio will be off with his wife, fixing up their fairytale *Lago Maggiore* cottage. I have no plans. And Alice will be thrilled."

"We can go other places, too, if you'd like to," Hermina remembered to add, lest Sam reproach her for being domineering.

****

Not having forged lasting Italian friendships, Hermina's *addio* would be to *Italia,* its culture, art, history. She'd feast again on fresh ricotta, fill empty bottles for Millicent with newly pressed olive oil more virgin than Maria, and walk with Alice through the fields of seven-foot-high sunflowers, called *girasole* because they turn all day to face the sun, staining the atmosphere yellow. She'd let Michaelangelo jolt Millicent's amorous proclivities from the untried ripeness of his *David* toward the musky virility of his grown-up man *Nettuno*.

As a highlight, and to honor Sam, Hermina ordered tickets to a production of '*Le Nozze di Figaro'*. Could Mozart's sleazy Count Almaviva awaken Millicent by personifying the high-handed failings of philandering Fabrizio? Might clever Susanna inspire Millicent to protest?

8

Millicent wove the silver Alfa Romeo through the luxuriant countryside toward *Siena* while Alice, in the back seat behind Hermina, wriggled her bare toes out the window. Millicent belted out songs from musicals like "*Oklahoma*" and "*Guys and Dolls*" that she and teenage Geena used to sing washing dishes on Deniza's nights off. Alice treated them to endless rounds of "*PIcolomini / PiCOlomini/ PIccolomini picCO…*" and Hermina chimed in with what Sam used to sing in her honor, *"Boom ain't it great to be crazy / Boom ain't it great to be nuts."*

That night, they sat together at Hermina and Sam's favorite hotel watching the light change over the Tuscan plain below. After Alice went to bed, Hermina described for Millicent the beautiful funeral they'd held for Sam. Jill, Hermina's *goyishe* daughter-in-law, had unobtrusively and generously opened their home the whole week after to all the loving *shiva* calls.

"Can we defect and become Neumanns?" Millicent asked. "Or is the plural *Neumenn*?"

"*Numina.*" Tears welled in Hermina's eyes. "Sam used to call me that, his combination of 'Neumann' with 'Hermina'. *Numen*, you know, means the divine spirit of a place, or a god conceived as a person."

Hermina hesitated. "When I move, I'll be going to David's, initially. I hope to buy a place of my own, eventually. I love my son," she said, "but I've never understood how to be close to him. He's not an intellectual or an artist; he's a good, solid, concrete thinker. You know the saying, 'The cobbler's child always goes barefoot'?" Hermina said, laughing. "Well, the anthropologist's child is always an alien culture. Then, here you come, you and Alice, right into my aging life. I could just as easily ask your permission to become a Milner – though you'll forgive me if I say a polite 'no thank you' to your mother."

She paused and then looked at Millicent directly. "Would you and Alice ever consider moving back, too?" *To our newly constellated loving family*, she thought but didn't say. "I have no right to ask that of you, but I want you to know that I wish for it."

"She's right," Geena said when they next spoke. "You should come home. And I don't mean to *Cruella di Milner*."

Millicent tried to sound glib. "I can't afford to. I'm not an heiress anymore. Mother got it all."

"You could teach."

"You may not have noticed, but Americans already speak English."

"Lots of foreigners in the U.S. don't. There must be language schools for them where you could work. Maybe you should start one, near some university."

"But…Fabrizio…"

Geena was silent, then said, "No comment."

****

After the opera, Millicent phoned Geena again in a thrill of excitement. "I actually understood the words!" she exclaimed. "And you should have seen Alice." In her latest swirly dress, she'd looked like one of those delicate aristocratic children depicted in Renaissance portraits. Millicent had watched Alice and Hermina hold hands and glide across the blood-red carpets up into their red velvet box.

"Naturally, I thought of Anna Karenina."

"And the opera?"

"Made me want a wedding. No. A *marriage*."

"Fabrizio'll never leave his wife, Mill."

"Shut up and let me finish." What had really thawed her into slush was Hermina. "During Act Three, when Marcellina discovers that Figaro is her long lost son, she sings, '*Io sono tua mamma*' (I'm your mother). And he sings back, '*Mia mamma?*' (My mother?) In the opera, it's hilarious. But Hermina gave me such a tender look. Like no-one else ever has in my entire life – well, except you, and Alice." Hermina had held Millicent's right hand in both of hers and stroked it for a long time, whole minutes, even after she'd turned back to watch the stage. "Not absent-mindedly, Geena. *Present*-mindedly. With *love*."

****

At the end of the last week in August, the movers maneuvered Hermina's things down the stairs, cursing the stuck elevator. The *donna di servizio* who'd kept house for Hermina and Sam for years arrived with a plastic vase filled with chrysanthemums: she departed, tearfully, with an extra three month's wages wrapped in an *Orvieto* lace doily.

Hermina spent her last night in Italy with her girls. Millicent made up her own bed with freshly ironed sheets for Hermina and prepared the top bunk in Alice's room for herself.

A familiar *formal feeling* resonated throughout their dinner. Ceremoniously, Millicent and Alice presented Hermina with their going away gift – a tooled, leather photo album they'd filled with pictures. The first, the most recent, was of Hermina seated contentedly in front of Millicent's fireplace. Next came photos of their apartments – Hermina's dismantled, both unpeopled. Millicent had taken a picture of the elevator stuck between floors and another looking straight down the air shaft outside her kitchen window, documenting how few traces of the fur coat remained. There were pictures of Alice playing an Egyptian slave in the school play, climbing on the statues at the Garden of the Monsters, and one taken earlier of Alice lying in "her" bed at Hermina's. In a photo of Millicent, newly arrived in Rome, she had long hair; in another, which Alice had just taken of her, she had her short curly mane. She'd also had a copy made of her favorite picture of her and Geena: five-year old Geena sat behind two-year-old Millicent on their rocking horse, Presto, with her arms tightly around her sister.

From her wallet, Hermina extracted a recent picture of David, Jill and Ethan, a fraying close-up of Sam looking tender and in his prime, and another of David, at about Alice's age, with a wide, shy smile. Now, she said, with the exception of Inanna, she had everyone in her album.

In Millicent's imagination, the sliding door at passport control the next morning transformed into a giant razor blade as Hermina walked through it to leave them. When it swished shut, Millicent pictured it slicing through the tether that bound them to one another, and all that had flowed from Hermina's being into hers spurted red from the severed cord onto the airport floor. *I may be melodramatic*, she told herself, *but that's exactly how I feel.*

Alice cried all the way home from the airport and slept in her mother's bed that night, trying to catch a whiff of "Hermina-smell" on Millicent's pillows.

Once Alice was asleep, Millicent, using the key she was to hand over to the real estate agent the following day, entered Hermina's apartment. The empty rooms reminded her of her father's body just after he'd died – an echoing shell around a waning presence.

One of Hermina's heavy, personalized note cards was propped up against a plastic vase of flowers on the kitchen counter. Addressed in her cobalt blue fountain pen ink to the new owners, the embossed envelope was unsealed. Millicent took the note out and read it. It began with home-owner details about uncooperative radiator taps, how to regulate the gas for the hot water heater, the names of a plumber and an electrician who could be trusted, and Hermina's phone number and address in the U.S. in case there were any questions. Hermina had ended the letter with:

Please know that the pain of my recent widowhood has been profoundly ameliorated by Millicent Milner and her young daughter, Alice Kadison, who live across the landing – my dear friends, my heart's adopted family. Though they will most likely be naught to you but neighbors, I would be extremely grateful if you would keep an eye out for their safety. Knowing that you do so will ease my leaving as they have eased my life.

Kindest regards,
Dr. Hermina Szivesen Neumann

Millicent's tears now were unfamiliar. They weren't about pain, or humiliation or despair. They weren't even tears of loss; she had been wrong at the airport – the tether connecting her and Hermina hadn't even been crimped much less severed. *This must be what it feels like to be loved*, she thought. Hermina was right. Real love is kind.

IV.

1

Hermina felt snow-blind – her entire field of vision was filled with the spackled, low, white ceiling of the renovated basement bedroom at David and Jill's. It was already September. An entire month had passed. She hadn't adjusted.

She took in the bile-yellow walls, yellow birch furnishings, vomit-chartreuse wall-to-wall carpet and matching drapes – which blonde Jill had chosen and described as '*Danish Modern with clean lines*'. Her aesthetic body revolted. If she had unpacked her Etruscan figurines, they would have run screaming off the boxy shelves in desperate flight from the tyranny of geometry, which, according to Hundertwasser was, "alien to humanity, life and the whole of creation".

"I don't mean to be an aging, ungrateful brat," she told Sam, sighing deeply and propping her pillow against the rough-hewn low plank which Jill considered a headboard. She was loved here. But to be yanked from Renaissance Rome and then stuffed, Sam-less, into an ugly, upscale Orinda, California, suburban tract house? Good décor does not guarantee happiness – after all, Phyllis Milner's daughters had been miserable in exquisitely decorated homes. But *bad* décor? Over time?

One didn't have to be an anthropologist to grasp how privileged Hermina was, how America's brutal racism afforded her advantages simply for being white. And, between her Social Security and University pensions, Sam's life insurance, their investment income and the proceeds from the sale of the apartment in Rome, she'd have more than enough money for the rest of her life. With good health insurance and the means to pay for a reputable nursing home if she needed one, she'd never be a burden.

"Plus," she whispered to Sam guiltily, "even at these sky-high mortgage rates, I could afford a small place in Marin County. *Not far from Millicent's sculptor sister, Geena*. Maybe she'd be willing to help me fill these empty hands of mine." Abandoning David's basement very soon was a scheme she hadn't dared mention to anyone but Sam.

Hermina phoned Millicent in Rome. "You remember my empty hands? I need to fill them, to create something with them. Maybe out of clay. I've been thinking that your sister, Geena, might help. She lives near my son. Would you give me her phone number, Millicent?"

"Sure, why not." Millicent had said, but she hated the idea. Hated it. "You do know that Geena's pretty crazy?" Still a fucking traitor. But, why? Why shouldn't Geena have Hermina?

"Maybe a bit of crazy is exactly what I need right now!"

"You're 76, Mom," David objected when she found a place at Stinson Beach. "Think of the humidity!"

She smiled. "The inhabitants of the world's coastal cultures don't all move inland when they are old, you know," she said, laughing.

"But the doorways are narrow. What if you need a wheelchair someday?"

"I'll find someone with a chain saw."

He shook his head. "You'll be lonely out there."

"I'll miss you, too, sweetheart," she said tenderly. "But I won't be in Rome. It's only an hour away." Actually, an hour and a half.

By early December, she was installed in her elegantly rustic, four-room, redwood cabin, carefully sited to suit the contours of the land, the shifting light, the winds. Seated on her deck with a proper *espresso*, Hermina found herself wrapped 360° in Nature: to her left a eucalyptus forest, to her right, a grove of California's cypresses twisted, scoliotic, in the direction of the prevailing winds and, before her, the never truly pacific ocean. Proverbially, seas pound, but, as she discovered listening there with Sam, they also hiss, whisper, growl, clatter. Howl. The redwood groves nearby had sprouted before Julius Caesar was able to tie his own toga. Who could feel old here? "Perhaps I have a decade left," she said to Sam out loud. "If I'm careful, wise and lucky, maybe a decade and a half. This would be a fine place for me to step off and join you."

2

Geena started up the industrial sized, 1948 *espresso* machine she'd salvaged from a coffee bar. She grabbed the mallets and chisels and record albums she'd strewn across her daybed leaving the negative image of them behind in the sawdust. Although fairly clean now, her overalls, eyebrows and knotted hair would be dusty by the end of the day. With her forearm she swept wood chips off her workbench and climbed onto it to wrap electrical tape around the wiring of one of the hanging loud speakers whose overloaded bass had blown out in a display of sparks.

With John Lee Hooker's "*It Serves Me Right to Suffer*" tinting the atmosphere of her white, sheetrocked cabin walls to a down-and-dirty Blues blue, Geena flopped into her rotating rattan chair to contemplate the previous day's hewing.

Unless her sister signaled – one ring, hang up, call again – Geena always let the answering machine take a message so their mother couldn't ambush her. Geena caught a certain tone in the voice leaving a message now that made her think it might, in fact, *be* her mother. She turned down the volume on Mr. Hooker in time to hear a polite, "Thank you and goodbye."

She rewound the message: Dr. Somebody had lived across the landing from Millicent in Rome. Millicent might have mentioned her calling? She'd recently moved to California to be near her son, and was wondering if Geena ever took on beginning pupils.

Geena jabbed the stop button then started up her chain saw.

So this was Millicent's Roman neighbor lady. Scourge of school principals. Wasn't one Milner sister enough? Geena didn't take students and the macho, hacking art of sculpture was no place for an aged dilettante anyway.

Two days later, she called again suggesting that if Geena would ring she promised to call her right back so that she didn't incur any costs. A few days after that, as her buzz saw wound down, there was that voice again with its straightforward, patient formality, neither irritated nor demanding, perhaps – watch out – even kind. Geena was tempted to answer. Instead, she listened. The voice expressed the hope that Geena would make allowances for such early and frequent phoning driven as she was by her awareness of death, of the fleeting nature of life. Geena must not feel pressured by this fervency, however, as she would seek another's assistance were Geena unavailable. "Thank you and goodbye."

Geena rewound the tape. Had this Hermina spoken of *death* to an answering machine? Geena's mother had been warbling the death ditty for decades and Geena had fallen for it for years. Ten thousand cubic feet of empathy, squandered. No way she'd be suckered into taking responsibility for fulfilling this stranger's needs, no matter how nice Millicent thought she was.

She'd call and tell her that. Geena ripped off a piece of sketch pad paper, scribbled the number and "twx 7-8AM" and wadded it into the breast pocket of her overalls. Then, she picked up her chain saw and accidentally gouged the cheek of her seven-foot tall female version of Laocoön struggling against the snakes. "Mother fucker!" she hollered and kicked Laocoöna's base; the metal reinforcement in the toe of her work boot left a dent. She grabbed her goose-down parka and the keys to her truck, slammed the studio door behind her and abandoned Laocoöna and her freshly scarred wooden face which now looked more tender than fearful, more vulnerable than enraged.

Without having to think, she drove north, signaled a turn and tore up the steep incline leaving behind a dust trail that could choke a forest.

She was going to get laid. Since she first moved to Point Acuerdo, L.D. was the man for the job. A mortifying number of years younger than Geena, he had two large Chinese dragon pectoral tattoos. He was almost always game.

"Pull it out, Larry Dean. I'm gettin' on!" she called out of the truck window before she'd even arrived at his cabin.

It was only 10 a.m. She'd be waking him up. Or maybe, *them*. Fine, as long as the other woman would leave and he wasn't all fucked out.

"Hey, man! Anything left in that thing for me?" she shouted, slamming on the brakes in front of his collapsed woodpile and honking her horn.

He opened the door wearing only a T-shirt, rubbing his eyes and then his arms against the chill that lasted until noon in the ravine.

"Couldn't come at a decent hour, Geena?"

She pulled off her parka, unlatched her overall top and, before she reached his door, had thrown off her T-shirt, liberating weighty breasts which bounced to each of her long strides. She reached L.D. about the time her overalls hit her ankles. She grabbed him, bit his lips, sucked for his tongue, even though it tasted of 3 a.m. bourbon and unbrushed teeth, grabbed his left bicep with one hand and his as-yet-unstirring cock with the other. "Sport-fucking," they called it.

A short time later, she dismounted and strode outside to find her clothes. When she lifted her overalls, the note about Dr. N. fell out. She crumpled it up and shoved it back into the pocket.

"This round's on me," L.D. whispered, coming up behind Geena and reaching for her breast.

"I gotta go to work, L.D. I have faces to hack." But she stayed for one more for the road.

The following morning, Geena dialed the number at 7 a.m. but hung up after the first ring. Immediately afterwards, her own phone rang and Geena answered it.

"This is Hermina Neumann. You tried to call me just now but the line must have fallen."

"How did you know it was me?"

"You, your sister and my son are the only people who have this number. He's still asleep and Millicent is at work at this hour in Rome. I'm grateful for your call, Miss Milner."

Silence.

"Hello? I apologize, this phone does seem somewhat unreliable. Hello?"

"I'm here." Geena hadn't planned what she'd say. Tell her she didn't take on apprentices, not of any age? But when Dr. Neumann asked if it were possible for them to meet the following week, Geena said, "I need to check my calendar," knowing full well she had bracketed these next three months for intense work toward a group show and that every day was her own.

"Shall we meet at your studio? I want to inconvenience you as little as possible." Geena would remember that sentence having included the word *'dear'* though she knew it hadn't.

"OK, Monday," she blurted out. "No. Wednesday. That would be better."

When she hung up, Geena flung herself down on the cluttered daybed wondering what it was that had changed her mind.

3

Geena called Millicent who reminded her that Hermina had turned out to be okay. Still she wished she hadn't agreed to let the old lady come. She mustn't let her fuck up her work.

She'd set Laocoöna aside for a while to focus on an up-ended tree trunk she'd found after a storm. With a borrowed fork-lift, she maneuvered it into the studio where it now stood, balanced on its jagged top, its wide spreading root mass piercing the atmosphere. She brushed off only some of the soil and applied a matte finish glue mixture to preserve the rest as Fact, as Hard Truth. Today, New-Noo-Neu-woman or not, Geena would begin to maim it, meticulously. The prospect pleased her. A scream made of wood shrieks forever.

Mutilation tools in hand, Geena didn't hear the doorbell over Little Richard's '*Rip It Up*'. Hermina simply appeared. Geena watched her stamp rainwater off old-lady galoshes and remove her coat. Her pleated wool skirt and pale pink twin set accentuated the curvature of her spine, which made Geena think of a breeze frozen in time. "Want an *espresso*?" Geena shouted and crossed the room to turn her music down.

"Yes, please."

"I think you've come to the wrong place," Geena said once they'd settled on the high bar stools in front of her work bench.

"Because?"

"I don't teach." With a thin black marker pen Geena embellished a sketch of her snake-strangled Laocoöna. On the same sheet, Hermina saw horrors worthy of Bosch or Dante: eyes pierced by spears, limbs ripped from torsos, giant spiders sucking lap dogs dry. "Never taught anybody anything, not even myself," Geena said, still drawing.

"All I want is someone with space and equipment and who's willing to explain the nature of the materials to me. I'd prefer to experiment without interference."

“Maybe. But clay’s not easy. I don’t mean to be rude, Mrs. Neumann.”

“Hermina.”

“If you keep at it long enough, the object you’re shaping is going to talk back to you and you might not like what you hear.”

The two women looked each other in the eye for the first time. Neither smiled.

“OK. I’ll set you up. Then I’m going back to work. I have a group exhibit in two and a half months and if I can’t work with you here, you’ll have to go. Millicent’s friend or no. Also, I play music loud.”

“I heard.” From a paper bag, Hermina pulled out house slippers, an ironed apron and a man’s paint-spotted shirt.

Geena slammed the hunk of clay she’d clawed out of a garbage bag onto a board.

“You knead it. Like bread?” Hermina commented as Geena leaned her weight into the clay.

“No. You knead dough to get air bubbles *into* it. You wedge clay to get them *out* and to force all the silicone crystals to lie in the same direction.” Once the mass yielded, Geena filled a bowl with water.

“There,” she said and flung a mix of cutters, spatulas, wires and sponges onto the counter. She wiped her hands on her overalls, turned on Jimi Hendrix’s off-key “Star Spangled Banner” screech, and picked up her own tools.

Seated on her stool at the work bench, Hermina began, with thumb and forefinger, to pluck small gobs of red clay from the mound. She planned to create sarcophagus figures in honor of Sam, complete with those haunting faces the Etruscan artists had mastered.

During the next hours, in an escalating fury over their refusal to come alive, she had punched flat every single one of her abominations. Recalcitrant substance! Geena was right. She was a deluded old lady.

Enough. She amalgamated the clay back into the mound and sighed. She’d better remain in the domain of intellect where she knew her way around.

At precisely that moment, Geena whooped “Yes!” and, “Of course!” and continued her internal dialogue out loud as if Hermina had been privy to it all along.

“These are two parts of the same piece! Can you help me out here?”

Hermina followed Geena to the tall wooden figure of a naked woman who stood, apparently under siege and only half-emerged from a tree trunk, like one of Michelangelo's slaves. Snakes – three of them – were at her, terrifyingly close to a gash in her cheek, right beside her mouth.

Hermina managed to stabilize the statue while Geena dragged the tattered rag rug it stood on into the center of the studio, next to the spreading root.

"Poor schmuck, Laocoön," Geena went on. "Athena blinded him and Poseidon sent snakes to strangle him and his kids for trying to warn the Trojans about the Greeks' loaded horse."

"I know my classics," Hermina grumbled as Geena crossed to the other side of the room and viewed the two pieces of wood from a distance.

"It'll take more than the two of us to hoist her down into the roots." She turned to Hermina and, for the first time, spoke as if in normal conversation. "It's a miracle, this process, don't you think? I mean, you have no idea what you're doing and then, suddenly, you get it. I can't understand why anybody does anything else." She paused. "Now, keep Our Lady balanced while I drag her back into her corner."

Geena went back to her work. So did Hermina.

"The two sisters are so different," Hermina said to Sam that night. "Graceful little Millicent tries to please but tall Geena is a natural phenomenon. She looms and bellows. She's gritty, with her mass of black hair tied in a knot, her overalls torn, her fingernails ragged, her work boots impervious. When she walks, she seems to thrust her whole being forward, belligerently, displacing the air, as if taking up space required a powerful Act of Will. She seems to emanate light, which certainly makes her hard to ignore, but painful to look at. Impossible to really see."

****

As Geena had offered no objections, Hermina returned and again filled her hands with clay. Gradually, the hum of Geena's concentration soothed her cramping brain, allowing her Etruscan aspirations to recede. Then, for a few charmed moments, Hermina's inexperienced hands moved in a sort of harmony and a shape emerged, a face which Hermina liked and might even have been able to love. When she tried to make it happen more, her hands stiffened.

She tried harder, grew even clumsier, and soon there was no face left at all.

What had facilitated those moments of creative grace, however brief? If she leaned back and relaxed, her hands would work on collaboratively – *as long as she didn't think about it.*

Did Geena's talent and courage for tolerating chaos, for navigating abstraction, explain the intensity of her physical presence? She seemed oblivious of the fact that she was teaching Hermina anything at all. Or rather, Geena herself *was* a teaching. Her concentration exerted a force that created an opening, allowing Hermina to enter. During those seconds of freedom into which Geena, however unwittingly, shepherded Hermina, something genuine filled her hands, came into being right before her eyes. Hermina felt happy. She hadn't been happy since they realized Sam was sick.

****

"Tuna sandwich?" Geena called out at lunchtime.

"No thank you. I brought my own food."

Geena retreated to the alcove next to the wood stove, where she had a desk of sorts, a hotplate and a heap of unsorted mail. She turned her rotating chair toward the desk while Hermina, having spread her apron carefully over the sawdust, sat on the daybed.

"I've been thinking a lot about what being here is teaching me. May I tell you?"

"Long as you don't expect a response."

Hermina described, as best she could, her brief moments of harmony and inevitable falls from grace last week. "How do you remain so long in the realm of creativity? It must be some special skill."

"My problem," Geena began, her mouth full of sandwich, "is that I can't stand being anywhere else."

"How did you start? Did you study?"

"Yup. With Dolores."

"An art teacher?"

"No. A croquet ball."

"I'm serious."

"So am I. But it's too long a story. And I have work to do." Geena strode off across the studio. "You can stay or go; it's up to you."

"I'll stop now. I'm rather tired. May I come tomorrow?"

"Don't see why not. You being here doesn't seem to screw anything up."

Did you hear that, Sam? Hermina thought, smiling.

4

During the following weeks, Hermina's forays into that elusive creative space yielded several small figures. She enjoyed the increasing sense of peace she felt working alongside Geena. She found the gentle way Geena placed Hermina's pieces into the kiln quite touching.

They began taking breaks at the same time. To Hermina's surprise, when she asked permission to sit with her feet up on the daybed one afternoon, Geena jumped up, removed all the tools, record jackets and dirty laundry, beat the sawdust off the spread and even plumped up the pillow. "You act so normal I forget you're old," Geena said.

Hermina sighed as she put her feet up. "I don't mean to pry," she said, "but who is 'Dolores'"

"She was my first sculpture."

"Not your teacher? When did you create her?"

"We were living in the bungalow then, which means I was around ten. It's easy to remember dates and ages because they moved us a lot, as Millicent probably told you."

"She's said very little about your family actually, though you have my condolences for your father's death," Hermina spoke gently.

"Yeah. Thanks. The Great Bamboozler."

"Bamboozler?"

"Daddy could charm money out of the trees for his business start-ups, but he was lousy at running them and always over-stretched himself. Hence his three bankruptcies. Borrowed money off my aunt and uncle and never paid back a dime. And that's the least of it."

"Does Millicent know that?"

"She's still in flagrant denial, desperately clinging to her technicolored fiction about the Milner family. I'm working on her.

But if anyone could fool people it's those two. Mother's got no conscience and Daddy was really clever."

"Go on with Dolores."

"She was born in the basement, Daddy's domain, birthplace and tomb for the carpentry projects he never finished." Geena described the concrete stairs outside the house, covered with two slanting, wooden bulkhead doors that led to the cellar. "Mother rarely went there, except to inventory the household items she bought in bulk. She used to brag, 'I give very little and I get a whole lot.'"

"What a motto."

"Since the cellar entrance was at the back of the house, I came and went, unnoticed. Not that anybody gave a shit where I was." Geena described an afternoon when she was roaming through an abandoned building site near the house and found a big rusty rivet, two long steel construction staples and some bent wire, one-inch thick, which had fallen out of a retaining wall. She saw a chunk of wood there, too, a burl, and suddenly, pictured it as a torso, with staple arms and a rivet for a neck.

"I sneaked everything into the cellar, cleared the workbench, hung the rusting hammers and screwdrivers back on the pegboard where Daddy had painted their outlines, swept the floor and set to work." She needed something to be its head and ended up stealing a croquet ball from their set, even though it was too small. She struggled to mount it onto the metal rivet and finally succeeded, thanks to Daddy's hand drill, a penknife and a stolen box of Band-Aids . She described how she'd lie in bed at night imagining tools and run to the cellar in the morning to see if Daddy had anything similar. If not, she cased Ace Hardware. "I adore hardware stores."

The head had needed a face but the ball was too hard to whittle and too varnished for water paints to stick to it. All she had to show for her attempts at burning a face on it was her scorched and blistered thumb. She grew so pissed at that uncooperative bastard ball that she threw it against the wall. That only chipped the cement without leaving a mark on the ball.

Finally, she remembered the existence of glue. She glued on empty almond shells to create eyes, rimmed them in black and painted black pupils; she broke lath strips from Daddy's unfinished bookcase into little squares and rectangles, painted them all different colors and glued them on, decorating the entire head. She cut curly wood shavings with Daddy's planer and stuck them on for hair; she let some hang down in ringlets and draped others across the scalp like a bald guy's comb-over.

"I even cut a vest for her out of a burlap bag. She wasn't only my first piece: I *invented* sculpture making her. And I named her 'Dolores'. I had no idea that meant 'pains'. Just lucky, I guess. And add this to the image – I can't believe I'm telling you all this…"

"I'm so grateful that you are. Please go on."

"I jammed the metal staples into a crack on her back so they stuck out to either side with the 'hand' end of the staples facing forward. There she was with open arms, looking at me. Lovingly. Dolores loved me. And I loved her. Only, I didn't realize that until after I murdered her."

"*Murdered*?"

"Forget it. I've bored you enough," Geena said and stood up brushing imaginary sawdust from her overalls.

"You can't leave me there, Geena."

"Sure I can." She picked up a chisel. "Anyway, you look whacked."

The women worked silently for the rest of the afternoon. As Hermina was preparing to leave, Geena said, with a sly smile, "You could bribe me to continue the story."

"Bribe?" Suddenly flustered, Hermina exclaimed, "Oh, how rude of me! I haven't reminded you to tell me about your fees."

"Fees?"

"For materials, your time. Your teaching."

"Yeah. Right." Geena hesitated. "Listen," she continued, "if you want more stories from me, let me draw you. Naked."

Hermina could hear Sam laugh. *Pricey school she runs!* "I was thinking more in terms of money."

"I don't need money."

"This old body?"

"Yup."

"And you'll promise to return to Dolores?"

"Yup."

"Then I'll think about it."

"Take your time. But life is short."

"You don't say."

****

Neither brought up Dolores or nude posing the following morning, but later that afternoon, Geena left her work and pulled one of her bar stools up next to Hermina. She pinched off a clump of clay and moulded it as she spoke. Each time a form took shape, she squashed it.

"I still miss Dolores," Geena said, looking into Hermina's unflinching eyes. "So does Millicent. She cried back then when I told her what I'd done. Which is probably why I had the guts to keep on making things."

"What *did* you do?"

Geena took a deep breath. "It was the day Mother's canasta club was coming to the house. I was at work in the cellar. Since Dolores had no legs, I wanted to build her a stand. I hammered and hammered, still unaware of the advantages of screws, bending one nail after the other, forgetting the noise factor. Forgetting that Mother was just up the cement stairs on the patio with all her friends.

"Suddenly, she flung the cellar doors open and stood there, backlit by the glaring sun. Her fancy skirt billowing. Even in silhouette I could see she was in a rage. I've made a whole bunch of pieces using that furious puffed-up form of her on the stairs.

"She came down shrieking in a hissing whisper, 'I have *company*, stop making all that *noise*!'" Startled, Geena had gasped in air that felt like barbed wire, and she'd dropped the hammer. "It clanked, loud, and Mother raged across the room toward me with her hand raised. That's when she saw Dolores.

"'What the hell is that?' she said it in an almost normal voice, and her slap-hand wafted down and pointed at her. 'What. Is. That. Ugly. Thing?'

"She smirked at first then she laughed full out. 'I can't believe it! You've made the ugliest thing I ever saw.' Then she ran up the stairs and called out to her girlfriends, 'You've just *got* to come down and see this!'

"I was paralyzed, searching frantically for a way to hide Dolores that wouldn't damage her, while the entire Gaggle of Girls filed down in their high-heels, taking the steep stairs sideways, with my mother in the lead like a tour guide in hell.

"'Have you ever seen anything funnier?' She was laughing, pretending to be good-natured. Her friends, now that I think of it, looked confused. Polite. Natalie, one of them I actually liked, caught my eye. She looked at me the way Dolores did – tender, sort of sad.

"Then Mother said, 'Oh, Geena, the things you waste your time on!' and tousled my hair, faking niceness. 'Excuse the mess,' she said, all smarmy. 'This is Herb's territory and I let him do whatever he wants. Men!' She shook her head. 'Come on, Geena,' she said, sugar melting in her mouth, 'it's too nice a day to spend in a dark cellar making messes.' She chuckled as she held the slant door up and ushered all of us out."

"Oh, my dear, dear girl." Hermina put her hands, briefly, on top of Geena's. "And Dolores?"

"I got my great idea a few days later when Dickey Valdevia showed me his new air-gun." Geena had brought the neighbor kid to the cellar and together they'd wrapped a blanket around Dolores and carried her to the demolition site she'd come from, with pieces of her falling off along the way – her crown of hair, mosaic chips from her face.

"I leaned her against a tree and we took turns shooting BB's at her. I told Dickey that whoever hit her right between the eyes was the winner. Poor Dolores. I won."

****

Hermina could never have predicted the explosion that she triggered in Geena the next day. While rotating the turntable to examine the spine of her latest clay figure, Hermina said, almost as an aside, "Your mother does, indeed, sound mean, but don't you think you paint her as a somewhat two-dimensional caricature? Like a *commedia dell' arte* villain? Surely she has *some* good qualities as well, no?"

She didn't register Geena's glare until she heard a loud clang. Geena had thrown her hammer and chisel onto the floor. She strode across the studio, grabbed Hermina's coat and purse and shoved them at her. "That's it," she snarled. "You're done. Leave."

"What?"

"Out. Go! Get your ass out of here!"

"I don't understand." Hermina sat stunned. Slowly, she untied her apron as she watched Geena march to the alcove, throw herself into her rotating rattan chair and turn her face to the wall. Hermina hesitated but then sat at the foot of the daybed, close to Geena.

"What did I say that upset you so much?"

Geena clenched her jaw. "All that stuff I've told you, that Millicent must have told you, and you still don't get it?"

"What?"

"I can't believe you even have to ask!" Geena spat back. "You're as bad as my sister, and everybody else. You'd much rather believe my mother is just a little nasty but basically sane. *Normal.*"

"Geena, I know you've both suffered. But…"

"Shut up and listen: Some. People. Are. Dangerous. Broken, at the core. Sick. Yes: even some *Mothers*. Too thoroughly fucked up to love or to be loved. No one wants that to be possible," Geena glared. "People say, '*Surely*, every mother, deep down, wishes her child the best.' They say, 'But your mother is so intelligent, so talented, so *charming*.' They say, 'Have you no compassion, no forgiveness? She's your *mother*!' They say," Geena's voice turned caustic, "and I quote, 'Aren't you painting a two-dimensional caricature of her?'" Hermina looked away. "No one wants to know, *not even you*. Hell, it took me years to let myself get it that The Happy-Milner-Family fable was pure bullshit, a forced lie. I was an idiot. But I didn't think you were one. Until now."

"But, Geena, surely…"

"*Surely* what?" Geena stood up and shouted. "You're not listening to me!" She backed away. "Because I never knew what I did that made Mother turn on me I could never avoid doing it again. Since I never knew when it was going to happen I was *terrified all the time*. Do you get it?"

Hermina sat blinking as if to clear away a fog.

"It's precisely when my mother seems to be showing some 'good quality' that she's really dangerous. Take some supposed tenderness, like a hug." Geena was pacing. "The moment – I mean the very moment – I relaxed and melted into her, the moment something 'good' seemed to have switched on inside her, her wiring sizzled and she attacked. *Slash!*

"'You're fat, Geena,' pinching the flesh on my hips in the middle of a hug. 'Everybody is laughing at you behind your back, Geena.' Can you imagine what that's like?" Geena's body shook. "Not only am I disgusting but suddenly I find out I've been shamed in front of the whole world and I've been too dumb to even realize it."

"So that's what that was!" Hermina suddenly understood the terror she'd seen on Millicent's face the first time she and Alice had hugged, on the landing in Rome.

"Awful, right? When sick mothers seem 'good' is *precisely* when the danger is greatest.

"When you're a little kid and your mother picks you up and holds you on her lap and rocks you and hugs you, you don't say to yourself, 'Watch out – pain's coming!' You say, 'What a Magical Mommy I have' and you love her and she seems to love you and you think you're safe.

"Then, right then, out of the blue, she hates you! Can you imagine? A grown woman spewing hatred all over her little child? *What a bad girl I am!* You think since it must be all your fault that a Witch has come in and taken over your Mommy." Geena shook her head. "I never let that woman anywhere near me physically anymore. Just the thought of it, makes me want to puke. Hermina, I was sure you understood all this already. It makes me crazy that people don't want to know that some *mothers* are actually that fucked-up. Permanently."

Hermina sat in silence and then said, "I've let you and your sister down, haven't I?" Geena nodded. "I think I've been afraid I wouldn't be generous enough, not a moral person, unless I gave everybody the benefit of the doubt. I do prefer presuming that everyone has redeeming qualities. Even someone like your mother."

"Who the fuck wouldn't prefer that? But some of us don't have the luxury of keeping up that self-delusion. It's too dangerous. If we let down our guard, we're totally exposed." Geena slumped down into her chair, exhausted.

"Do you ever wonder why she's the way she is? What happened to her?"

"Are you kidding? All the time. *Ad nauseum*. Daddy told us that Mother's father beat her brother, then her brother beat her, while their pathetic mother cowered in the corner doing fuck-all. She is to be pitied. Of course.

"But everybody talks about having compassion for the mentally ill. Who looks at their kids? Who ever steps in to protect their children from them? Because, Hermina, whether my mother was born broken or that it was her hard life that turned her vicious doesn't make the damage she inflicted on us one bruise less horrendous."

After a long pause, Geena said, "You don't have to go, Hermina. In fact," she said, "please, don't go."

Curbing an impulse to place a kiss on Geena's forehead, Hermina walked heavily to her clay figurine, took her time wrapping the protective sheeting around it and then made them some cocoa.

"What I am about to say cannot make up for my clumsiness…," Hermina said as she leaned back into her pillow on the daybed.

"You mean, your Refusal to Face Reality?"

"…As I was saying: I find your sanity and clarity breathtaking," Hermina went on. "If you and Millicent hadn't had each other, goodness knows what might have been your fate."

Geena offered her a conciliatory smile. “Poor Millicent still can’t bear to Face Reality. Or, if she has a lucid moment, she starts flagellating herself immediately for having had such evil thoughts. Drives me crazy. Makes me want to do a brain transplant on her – without anesthesia. She learns and forgets, learns and forgets.”

“Don’t we all?”

“Millicent is worse.”

5

"Apprentice I may be," Hermina called out to Geena late one afternoon, "but I am getting some control here." The clay girl who stood before her was lumpy but nonetheless vibrant and harmonious.

"Beware the Sirens of Competence." Geena's oracular tones echoed across the studio.

Hermina would have liked to receive a bit of praise or encouragement now and then, but she bit her tongue. Chaos might work for Geena, but for herself, Hermina felt some modicum of artistic control was needed to allow her to succeed, to do with clay what she'd failed to do for her students, or her son: *impose* the balance and harmony she wished for them. She carefully wrapped her figure in a damp cloth and plastic for her drive to Stinson Beach.

Once at home, sitting outside at her low table, the Baroque music she played seemed to organize the molecules of the environment into inspiringly orderly shapes. She unwrapped the clay figure and was shocked: the proud, peaceful head of earlier had drooped. "My sweet child!" she exclaimed. "Whom have *you* lost?" She gazed at the girl's sorrow-filled face and said, softly, "I know precisely how you feel."

She made no attempt to "control" the new tilt of the girl's head. Instead, she allowed her hands to stroke the figure, to slowly smooth her arms and help her plant her feet more securely. To the best of her limited technical ability, she attempted to assist the very essence of that young clay woman's intrinsic nature to become visible.

When Geena stopped by later, she stood with her arm around Hermina's waist as they regarded the figure together. "Looks like you showed up," Geena said and kissed Hermina's cheek.

****

Geena showed Hermina her archives and took her around Point Acuerdo and Marin to see pieces she'd sold. They talked about sculpture and usually agreed – the Etruscans, George Segal, even Louise Bourgeois. They talked about music and tended to polarize – Hermina marveled that anyone would '*seek to exacerbate their anxiety*' by listening to Coltrane's '*A Love Supreme*'. Geena dismissed Richard Strauss' "*Four Last Songs*" as '*grief masturbation*' until she saw Hermina flinch, and then added, "Of course, what do I know about a real death?"

"I'm excited about this, Hermina." Geena handed Hermina drawings for a new project. "It feels like it could be something." Inspired by Hermina's talk of Italian architecture and sculpture, Geena had been leafing through her books on Florentine art. "Do you want to know what stuck in my head?"

"Tell me."

"Michelangelo's tomb for Giuliano de'Medici in Santa Croce. It's something about being architectural and sculptural at the same time. I even had a dream about it. Want to hear?"

Hermina nodded and Geena began.

"I'm climbing this broad flight of stairs up to a stone building with fluted columns – like some Hollywood Parthenon mock-up. And there's this frieze above that names the building '*THE GREAT SECURITY INSTITUTION*'. I enter through a heavy, vault-like door. Inside, it's cold and dark, there's an echo of footsteps. Straight ahead is a marble wall, like the one Michelangelo put behind his figure of Giuliano, only with three arched Bank Teller Windows instead of niches. In front of them, open graves have been dug into the marble floor. Inside each one is the same stylized figure: a gilded man. Think Oscar statuette, but without that sword.

"A 1940's Bank Teller Lady with a bobbed hair-do and eyeglasses dangling from a chain is standing frozen in mid-stride on her way to her Teller Box. Nearer the entrance, a balding man in a tailored suit and silk tie is mumbling something nasty. His starched shirtfront is partly open, and you can see his hairless chest is smooth – and gilded. Then the huge entrance door creaks and slams shut. I'm trapped inside. End of dream."

"Strange…"

"So here it begins: '*THE GREAT SECURITY INSTITUTION*' installation. I'm applying for money from the National Endowment for the Arts and I sent for Guggenheim grant application forms. Hell – why not be rejected by the best?"

6

Hermina was gone. Millicent was all alone in Rome.

She couldn't ask Tizia's parents to keep Alice for an entire weekend work trip, nor the icy Canadians who'd bought Hermina's apartment. An evangelical missionary couple she tried out declared after one weekend that they didn't want a child to keep coming to their home whose mother hadn't accepted Christ as her Personal Savior. Their piety had apparently not saved their own daughter who, according to Alice, delighted in tormenting her. Eventually, Millicent reached an agreement with Italian friends of Charlotte who had a new baby, a low income and an extra cot.

Alice kept in regular touch with Hermina, although, Millicent knew that phone calls and letters were a poor substitute for sharing confidences while baking or on their daily walks. Whenever Hermina asked, Millicent felt that she could accurately report that Alice was okay – even if sometimes she had to push away the thought that Alice might be crying herself to sleep in Rome while she was off in Milan. Whenever Millicent checked in with herself, she felt that she was fine, too: a well-established, successful and happy working woman. Her passion for Fabrizio sometimes felt compulsory, tiring, hard to rev up; sometimes the word *lonely* surfaced in her mind during lulls in her conversations with him. That didn't mean she was dissatisfied with their relationship. Anyway, she'd left Neal, she'd called it quits with Enrico; this time, she wouldn't run away. Eventually, something had to give – maybe that something would be Fabrizio's marriage.

"Everything's all right. We're fine. Just fine," she repeated to her sister, and accepted Geena's gravelly, "Terrific," as a straightforward confirmation.

****

Millicent had established a routine with Jocasta which involved staying to talk a while after each lesson. Today, Jocasta ushered her to the roof terrace where the withered foliage clung to the plants in their massive terracotta pots. The teak recliners and Jocasta's fluttering scarf reminded Millicent of a luxury liner movie. Jocasta smiled as she sipped the *caffelatte* her maid had served her on a red enameled tray. "And so?" she said. "The next installment of your *Odissea, signora Ulisse*?" Jocasta leaned back, closed her eyes to the low, late autumn sun and waited to be entertained.

As Millicent dutifully revealed superficial yet amusingly piquant details of her most recent Fabrizio assignation, she pictured herself as a medieval lady-in-waiting, the Queen's *confidante*. Whenever Jocasta opened her eyes, Millicent saw the gleam that fresh gossip elicits. *What a good story my life makes,* she thought. Dismissing her, Jocasta handed Millicent her pay envelope, brushed her cheeks lightly against Millicent's while her lips kissed the air, and then locked the door. When Millicent reached the pavement she remembered she'd left her workbooks and papers on the kitchen table.

The maid let her back in. Standing in the kitchen, Millicent heard foreign words thundering from the living room. She didn't understand the language but recognized the tone of sarcastic ridicule – she knew far too well the sound of a mother's hatred. She stood and listened. At first, Atlas whimpered, then he whined, then began to protest, and when his falsetto crescendoed into a shriek, his mother hit him. A backhanded blow – Millicent could tell from that familiar thud and from the grunt it knocked out of the boy's chest. Atlas sobbed. Jocasta hurled some final, contemptuous epithet at her son and slammed a door, probably to the private quarters, into which Millicent had never been invited to enter.

While Millicent gathered her papers, the elderly maid stood silent at the kitchen counter with downcast eyes, her face a portrait of helpless pity. Millicent muttered a barely audible, "*Grazie*," and let herself out.

When she arrived home, Daniela was somewhere upstairs and Millicent found Alice sitting alone on her bedroom floor with her Barbie world spread around her. Alice looked up at her. She saw her daughter as one might see a separate person and she winced: No. Alice was not 'all right'. Not 'just fine'.

That night, she invited Alice to sleep in her bed. She lay awake picturing them huddled together in a blizzard, their shared body heat insufficient to keep either of them alive. Another of her famous exaggerations? What was a realistic image, then, for the oppressive dinginess she had allowed herself to glimpse around Alice? They were a *family fragment,* not a family. The aspects of her own life that didn't hurt – *Roma*, *Milano*, cat-calls, a photographer lover, *palazzi, la lingua italiana* – weren't enough. And none of that was for Alice. Were their lives too narrow, too isolated? All work and no play? Hermina had taught her to look for what she could *do*, to define conditions she could *fix*, for both of them. But when she pulled Alice's sleeping body closer to her, the sad aura she'd seen around her child evoked such regret and fear that Millicent plummeted into unconsciousness, into merciful sleep.

The following day, she took action. She made enquiries about enrolling Alice in an after-school Arts and Crafts program three afternoons a week, vowing to watch carefully and make sure it wasn't some custodial warehouse for kids of working parents. She found a ballet class for herself, though it wouldn't begin until after the holidays.

Despite her best efforts, their Christmas was gray-beige – despite the colored lights Millicent had draped over the fichus, most of whose leaves had been lost in the dull winter light, despite the stockings hung by the fireplace filled with *carbone* candy and despite the roast "*Pollo*-urkey" as Millicent called the big chicken she'd stuffed with their favorite apple, celery, walnut, and raisin turkey dressing. Neal usually sent great gifts for Alice; none had arrived yet. And those that Millicent chose failed to strike a chord. Neither the presents from Geena and Hermina, nor the forced gaiety of posing for pictures to send back to them, lifted their gloom. *Natale senza i tuoi.* Christmas without your family.

The new year found Millicent climbing the stairs to the fifth-floor of a run-down *palazzo* not far from her office. Millicent had loved ballet as a child but her mother had made her quit when puberty hit because, "You're not cute in a tutu anymore." While giggly kids from the previous class raced around the dressing room in their underwear playing keep-away with some girl's socks, Millicent and a few other shy ladies pulled on their own tights, leotards and ballet slippers.

The aging, stringy teacher knew how to make students work. "*Glissade, arabesque, glissade, tour jeté*," she called out. "Your legs scissor in midair. You can't avoid gravity, you will come down, but gravity has less to grab hold of if you keep your torso straight.

Land first on the ball of your foot with your toes bent, *then* bend the ankle and only *then* the knee. Gliiiide down in *un atterraggio morbido*, a soft landing. Then the leap! *Sì*! *Sì*! *Così.* Across the room in pairs this time."

She felt as if she were eight again, in the mother-free domain of a demanding but respectful ballet teacher. In pink toe shoes, white tights, a pink leotard and a stiff, flower-petal, white net crinoline, little Millicent's spine lifted as if she were suspended from puppeteer strings braided into her dark hair. Her head tilted slightly to the right, jaw loose, lips touching but not tight, forehead soft, arms curved in front of her as if embracing a fragile globe. She held her hands straight but not stiff, with Pinky, Ring Finger and Tall Man curved together but not touching. Most important, she raised her ribcage, not like a show-off, not so high that her spine was forced to arch, but rather, lifting subtly upward, an upward floating of the neck, an upward rising of the head, up, up into the music – and toward heaven. Today, twenty-five years later, that upward lift reawakened her ballet body's wisdom: Everything depends on how you place yourself. How could she have forgotten that? Boredom, depression, loneliness, these were *results* of a problem rather than the problem itself. Might the problem simply be incorrect placement? Should she and Alice be near Geena and Hermina?

When she phoned Geena that same night, they both cried as they imagined being together again.

Millicent didn't mention how unsure she was about leaving.

****

"Which language schools did you apply to?" Geena asked a few weeks later.

"It's not that simple."

"You're not going to '*yes-but*' me again, Millicent, are you? You're lonely. You told me so. And Alice is miserable."

"Yesterday she asked me in Italian how to say *Tuesday* in English. Maybe it wouldn't be fair to uproot her."

"You can't uproot something that doesn't have any roots."

"You don't understand."

"Try me." Geena heard her sister sniffling. "What, sweetie? What's wrong?"

"You'll get pissed. Or think I'm dumb."

"What is it?"

"Fabrizio."

Geena said nothing.

"I love him, Geena. You don't know him." Silence. "Are you there?"

"I can't keep going through this with you, babe," Geena said softly. "You get it, then, suddenly you're thick again. Why won't your brain let you keep what you learn?"

"You have to let me live on my own premises. You have to respect my choices."

"Call me when you make some."

Geena hung up.

If anyone had ever attacked Millicent, Geena would have rushed to the rescue, a one-woman Marine Corps. But when it was Millicent doing the damage, to herself and to Alice, did she have to sit by and just watch? *Respect her sister's choices*?

Geena attacked her wood pile since she knew she risked damaging whatever sculpture she approached. Raising the axe made her think of her ultra-cool, bastard, high school boyfriend, Dan Fell. (Changed from Feldenstein.) A budding psychiatrist, he'd informed her after fucking her purple that she was his research experiment to determine how much shit a girl would take in exchange for exceptional sex. He didn't say "a fat girl"; he grabbed her midriff roll and laughed as if it were all a joke and Geena, like the idiot she was, laughed with him.

Who was she to say what Millicent should or should not accept in a relationship?

7

Dare-devils, Millicent thought, *aren't brave; they're numb to risk.* Courage means realizing that you're doing something hard, like deciding to move home, then doing it anyway. Even though she wasn't brave enough yet, she knew she had to apply for U.S. jobs now so Alice could start at the beginning of the California school year. If they moved home.

She began with a résumé. She neither lied nor dissembled. On the page stood irrefutable proof that, during these last two years, Millicent had established a respectable, credentialed *career*. She filled out the job applications Geena had gathered for her and hid them in her underwear drawer; some conversations still needed to take place before she could mail them.

The first and most important conversation would be with Alice. If Alice wanted to stay in Rome, the job applications would go right into the fire.

The second and easiest would be to let Colin know he should look for new tenants.

The third conversation would be with Enrico, whom she still loved and to whom she felt a debt of gratitude for opening the door to her professional life. Ethics required her to warn him, and soon, that *Lingua Nuova* might need to find a replacement for her. Besides, she wanted him to write her a letter of recommendation.

The last and worst would be with Fabrizio. Cut herself off, intentionally and with forethought, from her life's first sustained supply of passion? She might as easily drive a car full speed into a brick wall, climb up a mountain and then jump, rip her heart out while it still beat, as the Aztecs did to virgins. She remembered what she'd thought as they'd rolled her into the operating room for an appendectomy at sixteen: *Shouldn't I run away when someone plans to slice me open with knives?*

Hermina, in one of her more strident moments, had described Fabrizio's treatment of her as, "debasing exploitation and neglect in flattering surroundings." Yes, okay, there was some truth to that. But no one knew her body as he did; no one before him had cared to explore her. There it was. No one, before, had cared. That's not nothing.

Was it brave or stupid to give him up on the slim hope that a good marriage lay in store for her? A bad bet – check out the divorce statistics. Why should she be an exception? Unstable, over-emotional, single-parent her. True, men like Sam did exist (*had existed*), a man who'd chosen demanding, bossy Hermina. (Nurturing, generous, unstintingly kind Hermina.)

She imagined Hermina behind her whispering in her ear, *you may consider Fabrizio a nice man, but as long as you are bound to him, your full life cannot unfold.*

Hermina wouldn't say, *be grateful for whatever crumbs you get from that cheating s.o.b.* Fabrizio wasn't really a selfish bastard. Neither one of them had succeeded in creating a whole life, but, together, each had made the other's unwhole life more bearable.

And here she was, about to leave him on purpose. To wound them both, on purpose.

Maybe Alice would let them stay.

Millicent mailed out her applications, without having asked Enrico for a reference. She put off the conversation with Alice; rather than throwing her into uncertainty it seemed kinder to wait until some concrete job offer had come through. And, since the entire proposition might be hypothetical, there was no pressing need to mention to Colin anything about leaving.

Or to Fabrizio.

They met. She had ironed her silk robe. When she'd brought out the special aromatic massage oil she'd purchased because the label promised it would open a man's heart, he'd called her "*strega mia,*" his little witch. Millicent was determined to bask in the full force of his enchantment. He compared her to a little pink cloud that seemed harmless but could block out the sun and turn the whole world dark. The glint of fear in his eyes made her feel powerful, though a bit silly – like a kid who believes in her own Halloween costume. In the morning, she gave him head while he slept and he awoke to his own orgasm. *Dà tutto, non chiedere nulla.* ('Give all. Ask for nothing.') Show me the wife who can top that.

****

She sat up in her loft in front of the fire late one Wednesday evening correcting student essays while luxuriating in her vacation from waiting for the phone: their *Via Scarlata* neighborhood had been informed that, due to repairs, telephone lines would be out until Thursday.

The doorbell rang. She ran downstairs to pick up the *citofono* receiver.

"*È Massimo,*" a voice came through, scratchy.

"*Massimo chi?*"

"L'amico di Fabrizio." Fabrizio's friend. Their messenger. Was Fabrizio okay?

While Massimo was on his way up, Millicent quietly closed Alice's bedroom door, threw her best robe on over her nightgown – and put on lipstick. She and Massimo had never met, though he knew all about her and Fabrizio, undoubtedly in prurient detail. She was unprepared for such a broad-shouldered man, over six-feet tall, with a square jaw and cleft chin, decked out in full Italian regalia: pressed black jeans, an ironed black t-shirt (did he have a wife?) and a black leather jacket like the one in ads for men's expensive cologne. He smelled of expensive cologne.

In one hand, he carried a small envelope and in the other a bouquet of mimosas.

"Fabrizio has to cancel your appointment this weekend and he's been unable to reach you by phone," Massimo explained standing in the doorway. "He asked me to deliver a note to your mailbox. But I thought, why not to your door? May I come in?"

Millicent was never able to reconstruct *how* their quick and quiet fuck had come to pass. She had ushered him up to the loft. She was almost certain, nearly dead sure, Massimo had made the first imperceptible advance as they spoke together in front of the fire, their voices subdued. And the next advance, too, which couldn't have been difficult since a nightgown offers easy access. Apparently she hadn't resisted. She had not helped him unzip. She could have sworn that he'd managed that himself, smoothly, had smoothly slipped inside her, and, when it was over, smoothly slid out. She remembered him zipping his pants, remembered him finishing off the brandy she'd poured for him before, remembered going down the stairs with him, still with no awareness of what she'd done, closing the front door quietly behind him and then going up to the kitchen to put the mimosa into a vase – all in a trance-like state.

The trickle down her inner thigh woke her up.

Terror struck.

She was afraid all of Thursday, afraid all of Friday on the trip up to Milan, all of Saturday during her teaching and at every pause. She was afraid when she woke up on the train early Sunday morning. She hoped that Massimo had not 'confessed,' but scoring with Millicent was sure to win him more points than Fabrizio had earned for plucking that bride on that cruise ship. Besides, she knew men, especially Italian men: Massimo's victory required that Fabrizio learn in explicit detail not only that he had been vanquished, but also how easily.

Tuesday's mail brought a business envelope addressed to her in Fabrizio's hand, with, as usual, no return address. On a sheet of lined paper ripped from a spiral notebook, he'd written one word: "*Puttana.*" Whore.

Whore shoved a stick into her oozing sore and spread its poison. *Shame* shrieked. She longed to phone Geena and tell her everything. When *panic* took over several days later, she phoned Massimo. Would he please ask Fabrizio to call?

"I'd be delighted to help you, *cara Millicent*," he said, his voice silky, "but Fabrizio and I are not currently on speaking terms."

Is this how it feels to be crazy? She thought as she called Information for the forbidden number then dialed it, digit by digit. She hung up when the woman who answered said Fabrizio wasn't there. Had that been *her* voice pouring into Millicent's ear? Would *she* ask Fabrizio who this telephoning woman had been? Millicent would probably never know; she had no leverage anymore, no currency for coercion.

For days, the telephonic silence boomed throughout the apartment. For days, she tormented herself about how men shoot their wives or girlfriends so they won't leave them. Here she'd taken aim with her own weapon – the smoking cunt – so that her lover *would* leave her.

She was dangerous. Neal should be the one to raise Alice. Millicent hurt people through simple neglect or wanton acts. She'd fucked her way through college, fucked her father's tenants, her parents' friends' sons. She should be pilloried. Not the usual way, with her neck and wrists locked into the holes in the wooden post in the public square. A special pillory chair for her, with holes for her ankles, locked there naked, her legs spread wide apart.

During the days that followed, Millicent managed to carry on, to teach, to cook, wash dishes, fake her way through mother-putting-daughter-to-bed rituals. But each night, the demon voice went wild and the thought, she kept coming back to, was *Death.*

The Tiber, with *sampietrini* filling her pockets like Virginia Woolf, the train with her body under it like Anna Karenina, the stove with her head in it like Sylvia Plath.

Poison.

The drain cleaner under the sink.

When? She asked herself and answered: *Now.* She opened her bedroom door.

"Mommy?" Alice woke up.

"What?"

"I'm thirsty."

"I'm on my way to the bathroom, Alice."

"I love you, Mommy," she said, drowsily. Millicent said nothing. She stood shivering in the hall until she was sure Alice had fallen back to sleep. Then she locked herself into the bathroom.

What she saw in the mirror shocked her. She recognized that swollen face, the crimped look of disgust on her mouth, her greasy, ratty curls. But those eyes – they weren't hers. Were they Geena's? Or Hermina's? Behind the panic, she saw…*tenderness!* A soft voice said, *Sweetheart,* almost drowning out the hatred. Was that Geena's voice? Hermina's? Had they merged? *Sweetheart,* the voice repeated with quiet force. Millicent began to cry. Those kind mirror eyes held hers as the voice rose in volume. *Yes, you've made some hurtful choices, but you're not a bad person. You're losing someone you've cared about, and of course that's painful. But you don't need to die. You need comforting.* She looked and looked, drinking in the antidote instead of the poison.

After a while, she splashed cold water on her face, turned off the bathroom light and went back to her bed. She slept as if in a coma.

8

Many days passed before Millicent told Geena, everything, including the Massimo fuck.

"An Orgy of Shame and Regret," Geena said, softly. "Didn't use a rubber, did he?"

"I'm on the pill."

"That won't keep you clean, babe. But how are you now?"

"Shaky." She thanked her sister for saving her life. "Imagine that I came so close to putting Alice through something like that!"

"Bullshit. You're a wimp. One whiff of Drano and you'd have run gagging out the door. Besides, you know I'd kill you if you ever tried to hurt yourself. Have you told Hermina?"

"Only in my imagination."

"In your imagination, how did she take it?"

"She raised her eyebrows, sighed deeply, looked down at her folded hands, one thumb stroking the lifeline of her other palm the way she does. And she said, 'Think more and feel less; secondary perception *can* be liberating.'"

"That's our Hermina!"

"You know it hadn't dawned on me until now, but, actually, I silenced some of my demons all by myself. You and Hermina weren't really here! I'm the one who ended the relationship with Fabrizio – of course in a mean and sneaky way. But maybe it's not too late for me to grow up."

"Are you going to hang on to this new dawn? I can't bear many more rounds of your 'get-it / forget-it' dance."

"You'll see. When you and I hang up, I'm going to take drastic action."

"What?

"I'm unplugging the phone."

Washing the dishes that night, Millicent thought about being unkind to Fabrizio. As the hot water ran over her hands, Hermina's phrase, "*ethically appropriate guilt*," sneaked through. Awful how rarely she let herself feel that. She'd *hurt* her father by fucking everyone around him. She'd *hurt* Fabrizio, now, not just wounded his macho pride. And – this one was hard: she'd certainly *hurt* his wife. The woman had a name: Teresa Donizetti. Millicent didn't know what problems in that marriage were caused by, or provoked by, Fabrizio's philandering, but one thing was irrefutable: Teresa bore none of the blame for Millicent's participation in (if she should now call things by their proper name) their *adultery*.

****

Alice awoke that Saturday morning, sat on the floor with her back against her bunk bed and picked up her latest failed sewing project. She was making a cap for Cicciobello from a piece of purple velvet that Millicent called '*velour*'. She'd just discovered *scampoli* – remnants. Geena had cartons of them in a zillion colors with names like "brocade" and "corduroy" and 'burlap', but Alice hadn't realized before that fabric stores sold them.

Yesterday, using thick thread and a fat sewing needle she'd brought home from the after-school Arts and Crafts Center, she had attached woolen strings on either side of the velvet circle she'd cut out. But the pancake hat kept falling off Cicciobello's round head. Her plan for this morning was to do what Hermina had taught her: needle in, out, in, out, pull and, *ecco fatto*, a drawstring.

Alice had told Millicent that Arts and Crafts was okay, except for the big boys who broke stuff and shouted and scared everybody without any of the grown-ups stopping them. Once, they'd stripped one of her Barbies naked then run around sticking her crotch under all the girls' noses. After that, Alice had kept her Barbies home.

"Morning, sweetie." Millicent sat down on the edge of the bottom bunk.

"Morning," Alice mumbled and licked the tip of the wool, again. No matter what she did, it kept bunching up instead of staying pointed so she couldn't get it through the needle's eye.

"Can I talk to you?"

"Yeah," Alice said, and now she got it! She pulled the wool through and had to keep on pulling. The thread often ran out before she was done sewing so this time she'd cut a really long piece.

"Alice. I've been looking for a new job. I've applied for jobs in California. For us to move there. This summer. As soon as the school year ends. Near Geena. And Hermina."

Alice wanted to make a knot at the end of the piece of wool but each time she tightened it, it was in the middle. So she had to take the knot out. *Again.*

"What do you think about that?" Millicent said, quietly from behind Alice's shoulder.

"What?"

"Please put that down and listen to me for a minute. This is important."

"Wait!" She was picking at the knot with the point of the needle, but it just frayed. She stabbed into the strands, plucking at them with more and more force, making a 'tsk' sound with her tongue each time but the dumb knot still wouldn't loosen.

"Alice?" Millicent put her hand on top of Alice's so she had to stop those jerky, picking movements. Alice dropped what she held and shouted at her mother, "Leave me alone! You're ruining everything! *Lasciami stare porca miseria*!"

"Sorry," Millicent retreated, and then said "Ouch!" very loud because she'd stood up so abruptly she'd banged her head on the metal frame of the top bunk.

Alice hunkered down over her knot again and didn't look up.

When she heard her mother climb the stairs to the kitchen, she dropped the needle and the thread and threw herself onto her bed with her back to the door. She grabbed a *Topolino* comic book and leafed through page after page, but without really looking.

A wonderful smell wafted down the stairs. French toast. Her favorite. She was hungry. She shuffled up to the dining room and flopped down at the table.

"It's almost ready," Millicent called from the kitchen. "Come get the syrup." Without a word, Alice pulled a chair over to reach into the cabinet.

Millicent served them both. Alice poured an excessive amount of syrup onto her French toast then cut it all up, bite-sized. With her elbow on the table and her head propped up on her hand, she stabbed a piece with her fork, hard, and put it in her mouth. She chewed and swallowed. She put another bite in her mouth and, as she chewed, tears started to roll down her cheeks. One more bite, one more swallow, and Alice put her head down onto her arms and sobbed.

Millicent moved her chair next to Alice's, wrapped one arm across her shoulder, and, with her other hand, stroked Alice's head as she cried and cried.

9

Alice cried often during the weeks leading up to their departure and raged at her mother for changing everything, again. Besides being parted from Tizia, the worst was packing her Barbies. When her stack of empty shoe box houses filled two whole cartons, her mother wanted her to throw them away. "We pay for shipping by volume not by weight," she'd said. Alice protested they didn't make any noise at all. "Volume," Millicent explained, smiling, "can also mean how much space something takes up."

She suggested folding the boxes, but Alice yelled, "Smash their homes? When you bend something, you never ever get rid of the line!" At last, they agreed she could fill the shoe boxes with Barbie stuff and pack her own clothes around them.

Millicent heaped praise on Alice for the gargantuan effort she'd made in Italy. She helped Alice pick out matching stationery sets for her and Tizia and address Tizia's envelopes to her, in care of Geena. Alice set to work making Tizia a red brocade Barbie cape and glued cotton balls around the hem like fur. When Tizia and her mother came to say goodbye, they all kissed and hugged and cried. They gave Alice a small, gilded icon she'd always admired. The lady at their breakfast coffee bar gave her the store's biggest "Kinder Egg" and said, "*Che fortuna che hai*!" How Alice was lucky to go to California. She promised to look Alice up if she ever came there. Colin, meanwhile, expressed his sincere regret at the departure of his 'little family' by presenting Alice with a book of Italian fairytales in English as a parting gift and an iridescent blue butterfly, framed, her favorite from his collection. Slowly, Alice began to talk about how good it would be to go home, to Hermina, to Geena, to her Dad.

****

Determined to leave Rome responsibly, Millicent put aside money to pay Daniela an extra month's wages. Hardest to leave – besides Fabrizio – was Atlas. She'd told him several weeks earlier that she'd be moving away; she spent time talking about it at each lesson hoping to soften the blow. She had a goodbye present with her on the day of the final lesson, an Excalibur-shaped pen complete with leather scabbard, and a used, leather-bound copy of the Arthurian classic, *The Once and Future King*. But he had locked himself in his bedroom before she arrived and wouldn't come out.

Sitting on the floor during the entire hour, she spoke to him through his closed door. He was crying but wouldn't speak. She told him how lucky she felt to have had him as her student, how much she'd miss him and then slipped a note under his door with her name and Geena's address on it. She promised to send pictures from her new home. "I would love to hug you goodbye," Millicent said when it was time for her to go.

Perhaps he heard the tears in her voice because, at the last moment, he unlocked the door and flung himself into her arms. He said something but his face was pressed into her chest and she had to ask him to repeat it. "Take me with you!" he pleaded.

"I can't, Atlas," she whispered, holding him tight. "I'm sorry." No way would she utter any *Think-how-your-mother-would-miss-you* crap. She handed him the gifts which he carefully unwrapped. "Promise me something," she said. He looked up at her. "Promise me you'll never believe anybody, not even your mother, who tells you that you're a bad person. You are *good* and *caring* and *smart*."

Using her best Hermina voice, she told Atlas, "This pen is magic. Whenever you touch it, it will remind you, in a loud voice inside your head, what a fine person you are. If you lose it, don't worry. Absolutely every pen you touch from then on will do the reminding. And every pencil and every paint brush and crayon and piece of chalk. Okay?" He cried. "Okay, Atlas?" He nodded. She kissed him goodbye.

As she reached the front door, she thought of the terrifying stories Geena had needed to make up about that boy locked in the cellar storage bin. How many real children, behind how many elegantly draped windows, ought to have been rescued? A memory came to her now from when she was seven. A woman had marched up to her mother as they walked along the street and hissed, "You vicious, neurotic bitch!" at Phyllis and then stomped off. Millicent hadn't had a clue as to the meaning of the woman's words; she just knew that someone had finally dared to tell her mother something

True. After that, Millicent felt a little bit less alone. She regretted not having done something similar for Atlas – told Jocasta in his presence to either be kind to him or get the hell out of his life.

Millicent had no goodbye gift for Jocasta, nor was there anything extra from her in the final pay envelope. It was some comfort, however small, that, passing Jocasta on her way out, Millicent had been too angry to be anybody's sycophant.

****

The entire *Lingua Nuova* staff showed up at the dinner held in honor of Millicent's departure – except Enrico and Mariangela. They sent "regrets" and a gift, an ornately wrapped leather passport case, embossed with Millicent's initials. It was undoubtedly Mariangela's way of underlining which of Enrico's women had to hit the road. As a parting present, Charlotte handed Millicent an oversized bouquet and vowed she'd miss her immensely, which might even have had some element of truth to it.

At Millicent's last Milan class, a student named Rosanna told everyone how she'd moved north to *Milano* from *Puglia*, the heel of the *Italia* boot, two decades ago, yet still felt like a foreigner, and was treated like one too. Making matters worse, she now felt alien in the rural village of her childhood and was no longer suited to living there either. "Homeless" was the English word she'd learned. She worried for Millicent, going back to where she'd come from. "In *Puglia*, they do not know what to make with me."

"*Of* me," Millicent corrected, gently.

"Do not go," a young man warned her. He confessed now that he came from the slums of *Napoli* – which everyone knew already from the traces of dialect he'd never be able to erase. Back home, he said, they'd sneered at him for working toward a university degree in sociology. "'Who the shit do you think you are? Your father sells lottery tickets!'"

"I'll miss you Italians," Millicent said. How would it be different to teach English to people whose first language was German, or Urdu, or Chinese, all of them living somewhere that was foreign to them? Wouldn't they all be worrying when or if they'd ever see their people, like in Carole King's song, '*Home Again',* that she now played for her class? Would she feel foreign in California? Could she be an adult anywhere other than Italy, where she'd learned how to be one? Dear *Italia.*

"Invite us there!" Rosanna cried out. Everyone laughed, but she was serious. "Really. Invite us. We could be some sort of language tourists. I would come."

"Me, too," the man from *Napoli* claimed. "*Anch'io,*" cried another; then they all talked at once about the Golden Gate Bridge and Disneyland and baseball. Millicent interrupted the excitement. It was an intriguing suggestion which she promised to consider seriously. But they shouldn't neglect their own impending losses. Yes, she was leaving them, but they were also about to leave each other.

She distributed copies of Mary Oliver's poem, *In Blackwater Woods*, as much as a going away gift to them as it was an educational exercise. When Hermina had sent it to her, she had guessed, correctly, that she wouldn't be able to read the last two stanzas aloud to her students without crying. If you hope to keep on living, the poem said, you'll have to learn how to love what you know will someday die, to hold it close to you because your very survival depends on it,

"*...and when the time comes to let it go*
to let it go."

V.

1

Their direct flight "home" was filled with European tourists. The first American they saw was the San Francisco Customs Agent they queued for, a white guy with a crew cut and a chunky torso that strained the buttons of his uniform. "Mr. Tush Face," Alice whispered pointing at his pudgy cheeks and Millicent hushed her.

A short, Italian couple stood in front of them. He radiated *capo famiglia* authority despite his homespun clothes and missing teeth while the woman seemed to Millicent to be the very embodiment of matronly deference. He hoisted their old-fashioned suitcase onto the Customs officer's bench while she continued to cradle their carry-on, which looked very heavy.

"Please unwrap that, Ma'am," the Customs man commanded with the unflinching politeness of one whose jurisdiction is absolute. It was an entire *prosciutto*, a cured pig's leg weighing maybe ten kilos. It became his thankless task to explain that, according to F.D.A. regulations, the only pork they could bring into the country was canned pork. Once she recognized the Italian words *contrabbando* and *confiscare* buried in their English cognates, her protest began. In panicky, rapid-fire, Neapolitan dialect, she explained how they'd raised and slaughtered and cured the ham themselves for their son who was all alone in this strange land. Her boy's *prosciutto* was coming to America! The official didn't have a clue what she was saying but he tried to calm her, as did her husband. She grabbed the hunk of meat, clutched it tightly to her chest and, waving one hand dismissively over her head – Millicent could see her now as the terror of the village marketplace – marched off toward the exit. "*Vaffanculo*!" she growled, ferociously, which Millicent knew meant, "Up your ass!"

Two, burly, uniformed officials entered from the sidelines to head her off. Her husband, apparently appalled at his own impotence, was left to grab their suitcase and follow his wife and the guards to some cubicle where she could lose her battle – and their *prosciutto* – in private.

Millicent and Alice's turn came and Mr. Tush Face waved them forward. After a 'you're-one-of-us-and-aren't-these-foreigners-a-hoot' wink, he glanced perfunctorily at their American passports which Millicent pulled from the travel wallet Geena had given her at the start of the odyssey. Ignoring their suitcases and carry-ons, he warbled, "Welcome home, pretty ladies. You have a real nice day!" Millicent resisted the urge to shout "*Vaffanculo*!" at him, yielding instead to the forward thrust of the major life choice she was now enacting. She rolled their luggage cart out through the massive exit doors which slid closed automatically, blocking all retreat.

Officially inside America, she donned her Italian exoskeleton of irritability so that all this polyester cheer – the *Everybody-is-your-real-good-friend* bullshit her countrymen smeared all over their surfaces while their nastiness lurked just below – couldn't implant itself within her like an artificial heart. *Look at them,* she thought, *slouching around the airport in their pajamas, shuffling their feet, chewing gum, their arms dangling and their bellies flabbing out.*

She didn't even recognize Hermina at first, with her gray hair hanging loose, uncoiffed, dressed in a fluttering, hand-painted, wearable-art tunic and a pair of pants that probably had an elastic waistband. Millicent felt an impulse to turn and bolt back to the *prosciutto* people and beg them to adopt her. '*Andiamo*!' she'd say. '*Qui non capiscono un cavolo. Un tubo. Un cazzo*!' Literally, colloquially, eloquently: "Let's go. Here, they don't understand a cabbage. A tube. A prick!"

Geena, very recognizable in her usual overalls and boots, ran toward her and Alice. Alice hesitated for a second, as if resisting being picked up like a child. Then she jumped into Geena's arms, almost knocking her over, latched her legs around her and they reverted to their puppy game of nuzzling each other's necks. Hermina held Millicent's face and gazed into her eyes with her usual, unwavering sweetness. "Here you are at last," she said and kissed one of Millicent's cheeks firmly and then the other like a proper Italian.

Lying awake that night in Hermina's beach house, with Alice sleeping beside her, something felt wrong. On each of her previous transatlantic trips, after her "Arrival Eyes" had caught a brief glimpse of the essential nature of the place, as if seeing it for the first time, familiarity had sucked her back in. Everything was too well known for her to see it and she'd quickly lost perspective. This time, the unfamiliarity persisted. Of course. She'd never before entered a United States of America in which there was no Daddy. She'd never before crossed this border with such full awareness of her fear, of how dangerous it felt to be in the same country, on the same continent, as her mother.

She surrendered to yet another of her dumb, self-evident revelations: Perhaps this wasn't a 'homecoming' at all since that involved a return, the way Dorothy returned to Kansas at a click of her ruby slippers' heels. Millicent had now arrived someplace entirely new, like E. E. Cummings wrote, '*somewhere I have never traveled, gladly beyond any experience*'. He meant, *love*. She meant, *home*.

****

She had accepted the Berkeley job. The one in San Jose offered more money, but was too close to Phyllis and too far from Geena and Hermina. Finding American abominations such as Levi's and Birkenstocks repugnant, she apartment hunted in her pastel pink, shirred tulle frock and high-heeled Italian sandals. She climbed into the very used, rust-red Volkswagen with a sunroof that she had purchased, but didn't head for Berkeley. The area where she'd be working crawled with scroungy, un-retooled hippies still hawking the same old peace-symbol roach clips and tie-dyed t-shirts. Surely she could find a more suitable home for them in cosmopolitan San Francisco.

Her fancy shoes gave her blisters after she'd trudged around the upscale Union Street area for hours. She stopped for a rest and a treat. While dipping an authentic *biscotto* into a proper *caffelatte*, she eyed a man in an Armani-like suit who nodded and flashed her a smile in that great Enrico/ Fabrizio/ Massimo tradition. Despite months of down-time, the juiciness-producing mechanism within her immediately cranked into action; she parted her moistened lips and smiled back with a soft-focused gaze. Fortuitously, a passing fire truck's siren snapped her out of it. "Thick, indeed," she snarled at herself. She swigged her coffee dregs and left. She had promised herself, Geena, God, Hermina: *No more.* No more impossible relationships, no more directing all her energy toward the most seductive, withholding male in proximity. Was it her fault the message was slow in reaching her nether-lands?

By the end of the day, she had established that every apartment she liked in San Francisco was beyond her means and would also have left her an hour's commute away from Alice, even longer during rush hour. Childcare arrangements would have become a nightmare. So she'd reconsider Berkeley, which, she discovered, was not inhabited exclusively by aging hippies. Plus, it was even further from San Ensayo, cutting down even more on the risk of Phyllis turning up unannounced. Millicent planned to have an unlisted phone number and lie to her mother that she had no phone. The thought flashed through her mind that Fabrizio wouldn't be able to locate her either…unless she called and left him her number…*Stop that!* she scolded herself. She'd vowed, *No more!* But could she trust herself?

She managed to find something affordable in the Berkeley Hills near a grade school renowned for its "racially and internationally diverse student body." She hoped Alice might not feel alien in a school where everybody was different. The furnished "carriage house" – a one-bedroom apartment built over the owner's two-car garage – also had a walk-in dressing room with a window and a wall of shelves that could work as Alice's room. The small living room had a sofa bed for Geena or Hermina and a bay window that offered a sliver of a view of the San Francisco skyline across the Bay.

She'd move to a nicer place once her earnings increased, but in the same neighborhood – no way she'd yank her kid out of yet another school. This prioritizing of Alice was new. There'd be no more following her parents' model: 'We do what's right for us, and the kids had just better adjust.' *No more*!

2

Unpacking, Alice saw to her horror that all Barbie's shoe box houses were bent and crushed and dead. If she'd been folded into a carton and shipped to America she'd have had trouble straightening up again, too. Nothing – not even propping them up with popsicle sticks – could save them.

The landlord had said they could paint and her mother let her choose the colors: "Princess Pink" and "Glacial Turquoise" for the shelves, "Lady Lilac" for the walls. With a frilly, pink bedspread and a matching curtain, her room looked like a Barbie world. But Alice missed the darkness of her Roman cupboard. And she missed Tizia. They'd already exchanged letters on their farewell stationery, but that wasn't the same as being with her.

Nothing was the same here. Her light switch was teeny and glowed in the dark; the toilet flushed so quietly she had to watch to make sure all the *cacca* was really going down. She missed her breakfast talks with the lady at the coffee bar – Alice knew she wasn't ever coming to visit. Hermina lived here, but not right across the hall. She'd miss waiting in front of *Castel Sant'Angelo* for the bus but wouldn't miss Sra. Cau, not one little bit. Here, she'd walk to school with a neighbor, Caroline. She seemed okay, but she wasn't Tizia. "It's supposed to be great to move to California," she said to her mother, in Italian, one night at bedtime, "but everything is different here and nobody knows that but me. They think this is how everything always is, always, everywhere."

****

Alice was leaving for her visit to Neal before the school year began. Millicent felt guilty that they hadn't seen MiMi since they'd returned – not even once – and decided to have Alice fly out from the San Ensayo airport. Though Alice objected, Millicent refused to budge. "She's my mother and your only grandmother. We'll only be there for one night. Besides, we'll have fun on the trip down."

The four hour drive took them six hours. They rolled down their windows and sang as loud as they could. They stopped in Gilmore, "Artichoke Capital of America," and ate fried artichoke hearts at a restaurant which featured a ten-foot tall, faded green cement artichoke outside. They stopped along Highway 101 to watch the glider planes soar silently overhead. At a fast food drive-in, teenage girls roller-skated up to their car to hook a tray with hamburgers, onion rings and Cokes onto the lip of their rolled-down windows. This certainly wasn't *Italia*!

To clear them for entry, the security guard phoned upstairs. In the elevator, Millicent looked at Alice. The fear on her face matched the sensation Millicent had been ignoring in her own belly and chest. "It's only this one night, sweetie. Then you're off." Alice nodded.

When Phyllis opened the door, Alice walked past her as if looking for Bompa and Deniza somewhere in there, and the stuffed lion, too. The small apartment, on a lower floor of the same building where Herb had died, lacked a panoramic view and was crammed with the decorating treasures Phyllis couldn't bear to part with.

Millicent reached out for a hug but her mother pushed passed her. "I'm so excited," she said, with a gleeful smirk. She'd finagled a position for herself on the Board of the building's Owners' Association and she'd be addressing them in only half an hour. "There's a trouble-making widow here! Only owners are allowed to live in these apartments. But she moved out and 'loaned' her place to her son and daughter-in-law and their spoiled-rotten three-year-old, who screams constantly and smears ice cream on the elevator buttons and the lobby carpet. I have spearheaded a campaign to enforce the building's regulations. Your father understood all this. Let people start subletting and the property's value plummets. This asset is all I have left in the world. I'm not about to let that bitch ruin me. I want you at that meeting!"

"What about Alice?"

"You want her to see me in action, don't you?"

Phyllis's performance was impressive: a well-researched, logical, stern, almost eloquent citing from the by-laws. The errant widow's representative then pointed to conflicting clauses regarding "transitional accommodations to familial exigencies" and the Board postponed its decision until lawyers had been consulted.

"I thought this was a democracy!" Phyllis objected loudly.

"That's exactly why we must abide by our own regulations," the harried but patient chairman responded.

"Shit!" Phyllis hissed to Millicent in the lobby afterwards. When the offending widow walked past them, pale and shaken, Phyllis grabbed her arm. "You make me sick, thinking you can do whatever you want. I'll stop you!" Alice backed off and shot a horrified look at her mother as the widow broke free and retreated in silence.

"Mother, please," Millicent said placing her hand softly on Phyllis's shoulder. "Let it go. The elevator's here."

Phyllis turned on Millicent. "How dare you! Wait till I get you upstairs."

"Disloyal brat!" She began slapping her daughter with words even before the apartment door shut. "Whose side are you on? You were nowhere to be found after your father died and I needed help. Now, you come waltzing in and gang up against me, humiliating me in public. If you aren't adult enough to be responsible, just stay away!"

Millicent opened her mouth, but, to do what? To argue? Explain? Beg for forgiveness? Her *de facto* abandonment, her absence during the terrible time of her mother's move, was indefensible, and Phyllis was her *mother*. But how mean! The Fifth Commandment, "*Honor thy mother and thy father*" stacked the deck against the child.

In the car on the way to the airport the next morning, Alice said, "I hate MiMi."

Somewhere along Highway 101 on her lonely drive back to Berkeley, it hit Millicent that her mother had used the same poisonous voice with the widow that she used so often with her and Geena and Alice. Might that nastiness be part of who Phyllis was, not only as a mother or grandmother, but also as a human being?

All her life, whenever her mother had yelled at her, "You selfish bitch!" or "You worthless brat!" Millicent had believed that to be the irrefutable *Real Truth*: she was bad, always had been, always would be. But Millicent as seen through Hermina's eyes was good. Who was she really, as a human being?

Did she even deserve to live? She heard Ferlinghetti trumpeting, or was it E. E. Cummings, *"listen: there's a hell of a good universe next door; let's go."* It would be so simple: a single, abrupt, leftward jerk on the steering wheel would send her car swerving into the path of one of the huge trailer trucks careening down the steep grade she was climbing just outside San Jose.

No! *No more!*

No, she admitted at last to herself: She didn't love her mother. But that crime was not punishable by death, neither her mother's death nor her own death nor the death of some innocent truck driver. She focused her mind on the image of Alice's sweet face and drove on toward safety.

3

To Geena's astonishment, local funding came through for "*THE GREAT SECURITY INSTITUTION*" project. With the Arts Council grant in hand, she'd convinced the Hector Hernandez Gallery in San Francisco to exhibit her installation when it was ready.

"Patient ferocity" was Hermina's term for the way Geena entered into the long preparation period. At a friend's recording studio, she made the sound tracks for the creaking door, the echoing, stony footsteps, the Effigy Man and Teller Lady's mutterings. Another friend posed for drawings and she made one clay prototype after another of her rhomboid-chested grave figures. Four graves would suffice, lined with sheets of paneling made to look like cobblestones, and with the gilded figure in a different posture in each one, from standing up to lying down. A funeral director agreed to keep the installation supplied with rotting floral arrangements, delivered in their fetid water. Ah, the aroma of decay.

No – she would need a fifth grave. But this one she'd keep empty and available to the public, make it deeper than the others with stone steps leading down into it. Upholstered in burgundy velvet or Naugahyde, and maybe with a soft pillow. She'd hide loudspeakers at ear-level when inside the grave, repeating the words of Dante's inscription over his gates of hell: '*Abandon hope, all ye who enter here'*. She could post a sign, '*This Way, Please*' with an arrow pointing down. Or maybe not.

****

As Millicent had expected, not one of her new students was Italian. The Norwegian guy seemed straight off some farm, blithe and without a clue. The Israeli, GI-Joe-doll / Soldier-of-Fortune type had a look in his eye as if he might suddenly pull an Uzi submachine gun from his book bag. He directed his aggression at the Moroccan girl who resembled a beaten dog offering her throat.

Meanwhile, the Polish woman with her pasty face and drab headscarf shot nasty looks at the Rwandan woman. A tall Tutsi, she was living proof of how differently blackness can be carried by someone upon whom America's racism hadn't been heaped since birth; she radiated a presumption of supremacy, an air of *noblesse oblige* that forced even Millicent to struggle to remember her own authority.

Sometimes it seemed as if a geo-political war might break out right there in her classroom, but Hermina warned her against stereotyping. When Millicent waxed nostalgic about Italian inter-regional prejudices seeming less virulent, more innocent, even sweet, Hermina had chided, "Don't idealize them, dear. They adored their Mussolini."

The worst, however, was that the school she worked for adhered to the "Audio-Lingual Method" with its pre-packaged modules and language lab drills designed to prepare students for standardized exams. "McLanguage," as she called it, might teach students vocabulary and grammar, but her preferred "Communicative Language Teaching" also taught them to live in the language, to grasp and appreciate its soul and beauty.

Her case for teaching CLT fell on deaf ears, so McLanguage it would have to be. She'd park her heart outside her classroom – goodbye literary lesson plans, songs, laughter, dance – and take the ALM curriculum materials home and study them.

Gradually, routines emerged for her and Alice. Millicent left for work each morning after Alice left for school and returned before Alice's after-school program ended. She took her turn as Room Parent. Evenings, after she supervised Alice's homework, they'd walk to the Rose Garden playground, or drive to Tilden Park to watch the sunset or wade in the brooks, enveloped in the scent of eucalyptus. Sometimes they went down to Shattuck for cheese pizza or Thai food with peanut sauce.

Alice stayed home alone while Millicent taught her Monday and Thursday evening classes. She watched TV and she sewed, practicing what Hermina had taught her about chain stitches and feather stitches and how to make the back side of cross stitching look almost as nice as the front. And, she'd just discovered patchwork; her class was making a quilt.

Her new school classroom was much, much nicer. It smelled of modeling clay and milk. The walls weren't bare but covered all over in things the kids had made. In America, they didn't wear *grembiuli* over their dresses, in fact, nobody but Alice wore dresses. Her mother bought her tops and pants, but she still felt pretty weird anyway.

At first, she acted like she was better than everyone else because she could talk a language that wasn't English until she discovered that other kids knew different languages, too, like Spanish which Alice thought she could understand then realized she couldn't. Sometimes when she talked, kids looked at her like she'd suddenly turned into a giant, pink flamingo or something and she'd realize she'd been talking in Italian, which she still liked. The teacher, Mrs. Milligan, caught a girl teasing Alice. "See? What do you see? I don't see anything!" The girl had mocked her because she kept saying "*sì*" instead of "yes." The teacher leaned down and insisted she apologize for hurting Alice's feelings. Nobody in Italy would ever have done that, except her mom or Hermina.

****

One Saturday, Millicent drove Alice to Geena's for an overnight then returned home for some quiet time alone. Looking through the treetops at the moon hanging over the Bay, she scanned her inner world. Her job, though boring, brought in enough money to cover her bills. Alice was okay now, this time, for real. Millicent's mother was far away while both Hermina and Geena were nearby. Although Ferlinghetti's line, "*Something's missing where the hole is*" kept repeating in her mind, she'd hardly slept with anyone since she'd moved home. Geena assured her that cunts don't ever seal up no matter how long they go unused. The thought of all those strangers she'd allowed inside her body over the years made her nauseous. Despite the occasional temptation, she hadn't phoned Fabrizio.

Tonight, she had an unfamiliar pulsation in her gut along with some sort of flickering in her chest. Was it caffeine? She searched the words she knew best: *Loneliness*? No. *Horniness? Panic? Fear*? No. Maybe *empty* was the word? What about, *silent*? The noisiness of her Italian life was gone. Switched off. Was the exciting part of her life over? Junkies probably miss their addiction once the withdrawals are over. Maybe misery, too, was a habit that was painful to kick.

But this gut dither wasn't only the *absence* of pain; there was also the *presence* of something new. What? As she felt her way into it, it expanded, filling her chest, taking possession of her face where it became…*A smile.*

"Shit," she said aloud, smiling more. "What I am is…" here she tongued a drum roll, "…*Happy!*" Well, my, oh my, just look at that: She didn't need a man to make her happy. She just was. All on her own.

She phoned Geena.

"I'm having a happiness attack!"

"Keep breathing, babe," Geena said, laughing. "It'll pass."

"Know what else, Geena? I think I'm finally learning."

"I'm stunned. What's got into you?"

"You know how Mother asks on the phone, 'How are you? What's happening?' as if she's really interested? Well, I used to actually *tell* her. Now – you'll be proud of me Geena – I remind myself in advance that the whole conversation is going to be about her, so I shouldn't be disappointed or hurt. I give her some smarmy stuff she can brag about to impress people and the rest of the time I just let her whine. It's like a game: how many ways can I say, in my most sincere-sounding voice: 'Gosh, poor you!', or, 'How frustrating for you!'"

"No wonder she compares you to Gandhi."

"She still tries to play us off against each other of course, but I've warned her I'll hang up on her if she starts badmouthing you. I'm not such a traitor anymore."

"You realize that after she talks to you she immediately phones me to say how wonderful my sister is. She's such a bitch."

"You like my new strategy, right?"

"No."

"Why not? I thought you'd be proud of me."

"It's manipulative. Dishonest." Geena's voice slowly filled with anger. "We should confront her, hold her fucking feet to the fire. Hermina says that since Mother is a grown-up, she deserves to be shown the respect of being held accountable."

"That never works. She still doesn't get it."

"It's not only for her sake that we shouldn't let her off the hook. It's for ours. To hear ourselves tell the goddam truth so maybe we'll remember it. Shout it to the world, whether she can learn or not, whether justice will ever be done – or not."

"Whenever I try to tell someone our mother hates us," Millicent said, "they look at me like I'm a messed-up teenager with a case of arrested development."

"They don't want to know that some mothers are cruel."

"She is charming, though. I learned the entertainer part of my teaching from her." Millicent thought for a moment. "Plus, she sure can decorate."

"Now there's a eulogy showstopper if I ever heard one."

"I wonder how we'll feel once she's dead."

"Cheated. What will we have lost? What could we possibly grieve over?"

4

Alice and Millicent argued more and more often, especially about chores now that there was no Daniela-the-Maid. Alice hated vacuuming since the threads from her sewing projects jammed the rotating rug attachment, but she flew into a fury when asked to stick her hands into the toilet, even after Millicent bought the smallest sized pink rubber gloves.

Millicent asked Alice why she seemed even angrier after she came home from Christmas vacation with Neal. She said it was like a scraping feeling inside her that made her say mean things at school, to Millicent, and even sometimes to Hermina. At her dad's, they ate at Taco Bell or Burger King. He bought her candy bars and tons of clothes – if she said she liked something he'd go and buy it for her. They'd go to *Marx Brothers* movies and she said once he laughed so hard he fell right off his seat. At his house, she decided when to go to bed and often fell asleep on the couch while he watched television.

By contrast, Millicent set limits on how loud and long Alice could play marching songs on her kazoo and insisted she clean her room. When Alice yelled, "I hate you!" Millicent sent her for time-outs in the bathroom until she was "fit to be around people again." It wasn't too early for her hormones to be kicking in – she was eleven and Millicent, Geena and their mother had all started to menstruate at ten. Geena told Alice that she used to be angry a lot, too, when she was a kid and that hammering nails into planks had helped her. Alice tried hammering at Geena's studio, but she missed the nail so often she threw the hammer onto the floor with all her might and its head broke off.

From school, reports came of disruptive behavior. What they called "Think-It-Over Time" was given to her frequently now as a corrective. The night after an emergency parent-teacher conference, Millicent sat by Alice's bed and asked her what she thought was going on. She started to cry. She missed her dad and would have to wait weeks, until Easter, to see him, and then, be there for only ten days.

After that, Alice and Millicent went to a guidance counselor to see if they couldn't navigate their way through this, and for a time things started to feel less scratchy. Alice earned gold stars on a chart on the refrigerator for not blowing up, for finishing her homework without her mother having to nag her and for setting the table after only being asked once. She also earned stars at school for being the class monitor without bossing people around. When she had enough stars, she and her mother went to the Exploratorium as a special treat.

****

After Easter at her father's, Alice was standing by the kitchen sink in her pajamas while Millicent washed the scrambled eggs pan. "I have to tell you something, Mom. Okay?"

"Sounds serious. I'd better pour myself a cup of coffee," Millicent said. She sat down and put her feet up.

"My dad. He buys me whatever I want. He never yells at me. He never makes me do anything. He's nice. Not fakey nice like MiMi, like I'm a guest he invited over so he has to be nice to me. I know you're gonna be mad, but, do you know what I think?"

Alice waited until Millicent asked, "What?"

"I should go live with my dad. Go to school there and everything."

Millicent's brain exploded. Her mind dripped down the wallpaper, her heart shrank to walnut size and rattled in its shell, her breath blew out of her and tore the curtains off their hooks. *He'll take you from me, he'll say he has custody now, you'll be gone, I won't survive. He doesn't phone you, write you, visit you. I'm the one who pays the bills and even your goddam airfare to visit him and you want to reward him? Him, the absent one, the one who's never been there? Don't leave me!* Millicent silently shrieked.

Though Millicent succeeded in keeping all those words from escaping, she apparently failed to wipe the horror from her face. Waiting for an answer, Alice grew pale, then paler and her tears trickled toward her chin. She waited. She didn't move. She hardly breathed.

At last, Millicent spoke. "Oh," she said.

Alice seemed to take this as a signal to continue. "Do you think he wants me, Mom? Could we call him? I don't know if he really wants me!"

You'll suffer if you stay with him. I left him for a reason, Millicent managed not to say but only mumbled, "I don't know, Alice." By this, she meant she didn't know what the hell to do, but she suddenly realized Alice might have thought she was saying she didn't know if Alice's father wanted her. Millicent had ripped Alice from Neal's loving albeit incompetent arms and moved her to Italy, five thousand miles away. How could he have been expected to handle that loss well, emotionally stunted as he was?

"Your dad loves you, Alice. No doubt about that."

"I love him so much, Mom."

Millicent knew there'd be no reprieve. She couldn't rewind this movie, continue the breakfast clean-up without Alice's bombshell, launch into their Sunday activities without this mutilation of her future and her heart. Perhaps she could beg for a deferment?

"What you want to do is huge, Alice," Millicent said, softly. "I need some time to think about it."

"I have a room there. I could bring my posters, my Barbies, my..."

"Alice. Stop! Please. I can't talk about this anymore. Right now. Okay?"

"I know he's home on Sundays, I think. We could call and ask him now."

Slowly, Millicent stood up. She yearned to hold Alice in her arms, to rock her back and forth and whisper, *I love you, baby, don't leave me,* over and over. Instead, she placed a single, controlled kiss on Alice's wet cheek. "I'll think about it. I promise," was all she said. She went to her room and closed the door.

Alice turned the volume up on *Rocky and Bullwinkle*. The noise allowed Millicent to bury her face in her pillow and let the bottom fall out without worrying, too much, that Alice might hear her sobs.

The loud television sounds took Millicent back to another morning, long ago, when she'd wished she *could* send Alice away to stay with Neal. When was that?

After the divorce but before Enrico. Four and a half year old Alice had taken refuge from a monster dream, curling up in a tiny ball in Millicent's bed then, later, stretching out her arms and legs, leaving Millicent only the edge of the bed to lie on like a soldier at attention.

Millicent had reveled in her Saturdays off. No pulling on smelly-footed nylons, no clear nail polish applied to stop a run sticking to the hairs of her badly shaved calf, no packed lunch for Alice forgotten on the counter, no lateness because the car wouldn't start, no secretarial kowtowing to the English Department staff.

When they woke up, she'd grabbed hold of Alice's feet, held one to her ear and shouted into the sole of the other, "Hello? Who's calling? Who do you want to talk to?"

"Poo-Poo Head!" Alice had hollered, giggling.

"Hello? I'm having trouble hearing." She'd shaken Alice's foot. "Something's wrong with this phone. Louder, please!"

"I said, HELLO, POO-POO HEAD!"

Millicent dropped both little feet, lifted Alice's pajama top and gave her tummy a juicy honking 'pwoof' with her lips. Alice wriggled and laughed, threw one leg over her mother's shoulders, knocked her flat on the bed and then rolled over so they both lay on their backs, feet up in the air, forming, Millicent said, "two phone booths waiting for a call."

They'd planned the day: first the park with the swings and slides, then home because Millicent had stuff to do. Laundry, for one thing. She spat her first slurp of coffee into the sink because the milk had gone sour. She set a bowl of dry corn flakes and a spoon in front of Alice on the living room rug, turned the TV to Saturday morning cartoons and went to take a shower because she stank.

She'd gathered up the stinky towels and dirty clothes lying draped across the radiators, under chairs and beds and stuffed everything into a big garbage bag which she dragged to the back door, planning to haul it to the machine in the building's mouldy, spidery cellar. If she had enough quarters.

When she poured a second cup of coffee, black which she hated, she realized that, oh shit: she also had to shop. That fact bowled her over. She flopped onto the sofa and stared at the animated bears dancing in unison. Why didn't she ever get a day off?

Alice must have seen her mother crash because she started the morning's first whine. "Let's go, Mommy."

"Later. We'll go later."

"I wanna go *now*."

"Don't push me, Alice. It's Saturday." Millicent lay, fully extended, on the sofa.

"Poo-Poo Head," Alice had muttered under her breath heaping the remaining dry corn flakes from her bowl onto the rug. She lined some of them up on the carpet and played vacuum cleaner with her mouth, sucking them in along with rug lint so she had to spit the dirt out in small popping "t-puh" sounds. When she looked up, expecting to get yelled at for spitting, she saw that her mother had her forearm across her eyes.

"I'm going back to bed, Alice. For a little while."

"You said we'd go to the swings!"

"Later, Alice. I promise." Millicent went to her room and closed the door.

She had a right to feel sorry for herself. Couldn't Neal take Alice for a while? Her period was coming, her skin was oily and pimply, she was alone with a kid, had a badly paid job which she hated, and nobody to fuck her. Her wet hair dampened the pillow first, then her tears did.

"You really are a poo-poo head," Millicent said to herself while Porky Pig's, "That's All Folks!" blared in the living room.

****

Now, Alice waited for Millicent's decision. One day, two days, careful not to bug her mom. Several times, she overheard her mother on the phone to Geena or Hermina, sounding serious and close to tears. Finally, on Wednesday evening, Millicent asked Alice to sit beside her on the couch.

"I know you miss your dad," her mother said looking serious, and tired, "but I've moved you around a lot. You've been in four different schools already and you're only in sixth grade. Rome wasn't that great for you. You've worked hard to get used to Berkeley, to the new kids, to speaking English again. It's okay here for you."

Alice shook her head no, but her mother said, "Wait, let me finish. I have a suggestion: Let's ask your dad if you can stay with him all of this summer, all eleven weeks from when school lets out until Labor Day. Try it and then come home. If you still want to live with him, we can start planning for the following school year. What do you think?"

This whole summer would be nice. After that, she'd only have one more year here. Here wasn't so bad.

"Let's call him now!" Alice said, brimming with controlled excitement.

5

"It's time for me to meet your mother," Hermina announced.

"Don't!" Millicent and Geena cried out, hoping to spare her.

"I need to experience her myself." Hermina didn't admit her concern about the rigidity in her own nature which her struggles with clay had exposed. She'd prided herself in basing conclusions on evidence as opposed to preconceptions, fantasies or fads, but then, all too often, she turned *certain*.

"What a dogmatist I can be," she'd admitted to Sam. Rather than rail against her certainties as David and many of her students had, Sam refused to take her arrogance seriously. He'd flash her an indulgent affectionate smile which of course drove her wild with fury. On the other hand, Geena had accused Hermina of giving Phyllis the benefit of the doubt because imagining their Reality had caused Hermina too much vicarious pain.

But either way, to have assessed Phyllis Milner without having met her seemed not just arrogant but unethical.

****

Phyllis appeared to be neither evil nor monstrous. She was *radiant* when she entered the cliff top San Francisco restaurant wearing a robin's egg blue jacket and yellow scarf over a floral dress whose print played upon those same tones. Her incandescent smile seemed to illuminate the room and reminded Hermina of Tuscan fields of sunflowers. Despite how many obviously expensive bracelets, rings, necklaces, earrings and pins she had on, she managed to appear bejeweled rather than gaudy.

Hermina allowed herself, uncharacteristically, to be drawn into a (heavily perfumed) embrace, as if this were a reunion with a dear friend. "Thank you," Phyllis spoke into Hermina's ear in a loud stage whisper. "For all you've given to my two, dear daughters." The sarcastic smirk Hermina saw Geena and Millicent exchange reminded her not to let her guard down. She wanted to look into Phyllis's eyes and communicate the warmth she had for the girls. Phyllis's glance was already elsewhere, sweeping the room.

She took the chair with the best ocean view. "My husband and I were soul mates," she began in a resonant voice. "Remarkable, isn't it, that neither of my wonderful daughters has found a man to love her? But, maybe someday," she'd deepened her pitch and turned her voice raspy. "As my mother used to say: 'Every crooked pot has its lid.'" Phyllis's hearty laugh might have proved contagious if Hermina had not seen Geena wince. "They do have their work, of course," Phyllis warbled, re-shaping her face into a portrait of archetypal maternal pride.

"Your daughters are artists," Hermina said, "one with language, the other with space." She recounted briefly for Phyllis their positive impact on her life. "What a privilege to have Millicent share her creative development with me and to work alongside Geena."

"Art was always at the center of our home," Phyllis responded. She and Herb had combed rural junk stores for antiques whose real value the bumpkin shop owners didn't grasp. "'*Junque*', we called it," she said in a French accent and laughed.

"Geena and Millicent have told me about the beautiful homes you created," Hermina said and Phyllis beamed.

Charming echoed in Hermina's mind while Phyllis entertained them with one story after another. Alice squeezed in an anecdote of her own, describing how they'd made bread at school with too much yeast and then set it to rise overnight in the refrigerator. Up and up it rose until it tipped the racks above it, spilling ketchup and mustard all over the dough like blood and ooze. Hermina was thinking to herself what talented raconteurs these Milners were when Phyllis's voice, caustic now, stopped her cold: she interrupted Alice's story to compare her refrigerator mess to Millicent's teenage acne. "I used to call her 'Pizza Face'. Just look at her," Phyllis went on, laughing and pointing at Millicent. "Imagine someone with such a Jewish nose choosing that short a haircut!"

"Both your daughters are beautiful," Hermina said severely. Phyllis shrugged.

The waiter arrived with their meals and Phyllis focused on the food.

As they'd planned in advance, Millicent, Geena and Alice took a walk on the beach between lunch and dessert.

"I have wanted to meet you," Hermina said once she and Phyllis were alone, "As I said, your daughters and your granddaughter have become important to me."

Phyllis looked suspicious for a moment, then almost shy. She exhaled deeply. "I am the mother of one child who might have become a famous artist and of another who could have danced professionally." *Was her tone confessional,* Hermina thought, *or conspiratorial?* "Their father and I tried to encourage them. But Herb had important ambitions, too. I'm sorry you didn't get to meet him; he was a very special man."

"So I've heard."

"He started from nothing and made an acclaimed contribution to the development of San Ensayo. I worked by his side." Tears came to Phyllis's eyes. "Excuse me. It's not easy to be a widow, as you well know."

Hermina's look was intended to acknowledge the losses they had both so recently endured.

"No one ever phones a widow," Phyllis continued. "No one invites a widow anywhere. No dinner parties, no cocktails before concerts, no sailing parties. We widows are invisible!"

Phyllis had placed her hand on the table and Hermina sensed she wanted her to reach out and pat it, but she didn't. "You'll see. Slowly, a new life emerges," she said, gently. "It's happening for me, thanks in part to your remarkable daughters."

"My *daughters*!" Phyllis said. "My two *defective* daughters. They're a whole lot more helpful to strangers than they are to me, someone they're actually related to. Herb warned me they would turn out badly."

"*Defective*? What are you talking about?"

"Herb blamed me for how they turned out," Phyllis continued. "He took care of the business and they were my job. Was it my fault that Millicent disgraced us, jumping into bed with anything in pants including our best friends' sons? Or that Geena dresses like a laborer, lives in shacks and smokes who knows what? You have no idea how badly they hurt their father." Tears ran down her cheeks. "Oh, Hermina, I'm so lonely, so totally alone now." She drew an ironed and perfumed monogrammed handkerchief from her purse and blew her nose.

She looked deep into Hermina's eyes, her glance now apparently brimming with love and admiration. "Listen to me going on and on! You're so easy to talk to, Hermina! I can see why my girls speak highly of you." Her face brightened. "I know! Why don't you come visit me in San Ensayo? Forget them," Phyllis added. "Just the two of us – two widows on a fling!"

Hermina said nothing as a grotesque image arose of Phyllis attempting to climb into her lap to be cuddled. She pushed her chair out of range.

"Actually," Phyllis said, shifting her tone with breathtaking agility, "you might be a bit too old." She raised one eyebrow. "Or maybe you've already realized you're not in my league."

Hermina was relieved to see the girls returning.

Before they'd settled into their chairs, Phyllis sent Alice off for chocolate ice cream from the dessert table. When she returned with strawberry since there was no chocolate left, Phyllis attacked her. "Spoiled brat!" she feigned a smile, but the set of her jaw revealed her boiling rage. "You get exactly what you want. But do you bring *me* what *I* want?"

Tears welled up in Alice's eyes.

"Stop it, Mother," Geena said as Millicent pulled her daughter close.

"Phyllis," Hermina said. "This is about *ice cream*. Surely, that's not worth making Alice feel bad."

Millicent and Geena held their breath. Their mother pushed her dish of ice cream away. Her pasted-on smile transmuted into a sneer. "Mind your own business!" she snarled at Hermina.

Hermina paused. "When someone hurts a child," she said, "the protection of that child becomes the business of whomever is present. Their moral *obligation*, in fact."

"Didn't you hear what I said?" Phyllis glared intensely into Hermina's eyes. "I said: Don't! You! Butt! In!" as if each word were a blow.

Hatred! Annihilating hatred poured into her from Phyllis's eyes and Hermina felt fear. What was Phyllis capable of? Was she insane? *Sam!* She called out inside herself.

Hermina stood. "I need to use the rest room," she said stiffly, "but I'll be back in just a moment." She hoped the girls would be safe in her absence.

She stood shaking behind the locked stall door, wishing Sam were there to protect them.

Slowly, she regained her composure and then her courage. She concluded there'd be no point attempting a discussion with someone so unbalanced. However, even if she couldn't have an impact on

Phyllis, she owed it to the girls to confirm their reality – in their presence.

She found the waiter, paid the bill and checked that Phyllis would be returning immediately to San Ensayo – no one would have to be alone with her after Hermina had spoken.

She placed herself in front of Phyllis and said to her, in an authoritative yet kind voice: "I don't believe that you are evil. But, clearly, you are often cruel. You have done real and lasting damage. Actually, I think that you are suffering from a psychological imbalance. You have an obligation to your family to seek professional help."

No one breathed. Phyllis's face seemed to fill with horror. She grabbed her jacket and purse and stormed from the restaurant without saying a word. Geena stood at full height; Millicent pulled Alice to her; Hermina nodded slowly to her girls.

****

"I had no idea, Sam," Hermina exclaimed as she drove home. "I thought I did. I thought my empathy was well-tuned. But being the target, having that poison aimed at *me*. No: *into* me! And I'm not a child, not *her* child.

"Even in utero, before they were even born, Geena and Millicent were drenched in that vitriol I choked on today. What perspective could they have? Suckled on venom, how could they possibly recognize milk? Only brutal cruelty would feel like *Home.* They'd presume that's just how *Life* is. And, worst of all, that's what *Love* is."

She couldn't have been clearer about how wrong she had been back in Geena's studio, how devastating it must have been for Geena to hear her glib comments about Phyllis's "good sides" – as if Phyllis Milner were a normal woman whose "little murders" were part of some "takes-two-to-tango" mother/daughter conflict. Theirs hadn't been a conflict. It was a one-sided tyranny: a toxic adult with all the power abusing children who had none.

"Did you see what she's been doing, Sam? *Come close. Love me!* Then, slam! *Get the hell away!* Again and again, throughout their lives."

Hermina needed air. She walked from her cabin through the cypress forest to the ocean, the blessedly indifferent sea. *Mother Nature.* "None of your *Jewish Mother* jokes, please," she said as if angry at Sam. "My mother was Jewish and *good.*" Her loving

Jewish mother had died so early that Hermina had always ached for anyone suffering maternal *absence*. She saw now that she hadn't had nearly as much insight into the long-term consequences of a damaging maternal *presence*.

"I know she'll never seek help – with no capacity for empathy or insight, she hasn't a clue that she's disturbed. That means she's doomed to remain the same caricature of herself for the rest of her life!" Phyllis was certainly to be pitied. The girls must feel compassion for her – even abusive people deserve that, though from afar. But they shouldn't expect themselves to love her.

"She's *dangerous*, Sam. I have to help them see her as she is – and give up their hope that she'll change. Give up on her, unkind though that might sound. Alice, especially, must be kept away from her."

Yes, Numina, she heard him say, and then, *But, it's enough now*.

"Taken one cruelty at a time," she added, defensively, although, Sam had never accused her of exaggerating about Phyllis, "her crimes might seem banal. But the unremitting acid drip of them decade after decade has etched deep wounds into those girls' lives. She didn't murder them, though she well might have, but she did maim their psyches. They're still struggling to recover. They may always be."

Please, Hermina. Go home and rest. He loved her.

****

The following week, Geena and Millicent came for lunch at Hermina's, but the door was locked and she wasn't answering the doorbell. "Think something's wrong?" Geena said while digging in her purse for her set of keys.

"Hello?" they called out. Silence. They crossed the living room and opened Hermina's bedroom door. The drapes were closed. They saw the mound under the covers. Was she breathing?

"Hermina?" Millicent said softly.

"Yes," they heard through the blankets.

"You're *not* dead. That's a relief," Geena said.

"Are you sick?" When Millicent folded back the edge of the covers to check for fever she found that Hermina's cheeks were wet with tears. "Has something happened?"

"Yes."

"What?"

"Sam died."

Hermina blew her nose but then withdrew again beneath the covers. "Talk to us, Hermina," Geena said, almost crying. "Please sit up." While Millicent went to get Hermina a glass of water, Geena pulled open the drapes.

Reluctantly, Hermina dragged herself up to a sitting position. She was still in her night clothes. "Don't believe anyone who says grief gets easier with time," she began, "it only changes."

Millicent and Geena exchanged a look. Neither had devoted much thought to Hermina's grief, as if, of course, it was behind her. "We're both so thick," Geena said.

In the beginning, Hermina said, she'd felt like one of those houses after the London Blitz where the whole front has been blown away and everyone can see into the rooms – the sofa, the dining table, the wallpaper. Exposed. Shell shocked. "I was still in shock when we first met."

"I didn't realize," Millicent shook her head. "I'm sorry I was so mean to you back then."

"I didn't want to know either. Nothing has happened to *me*, I told myself. It was *Sam* who'd lost his life. But I felt flayed. The initial rawness passed, and then came the noise and uproar of living on, even if I didn't want to. Packing, moving. Starting over." Hermina raked her fingers through her disheveled hair. "Now, suddenly, when at last I'm not pummeled by that King Lear tempest, here comes a different pain. Worse. Deeper – the wound of Sam's death cuts deeper now. I've been a widow for over three years now and I feel like the hardest part has just started. His death is final. Real. My Sam is *dead*."

Seated on either side of her, they stroked her arms, her forehead. She looked at their hands. "He will never touch me again. I won't touch him. Ever. It's as if I just found that out. I want him back!" She shook her head. "And I can't have him."

When Hermina's crying subsided she said with a soft smile, "See? I throw futile tantrums."

Geena handed her the glass of water and she drank.

"He is around, though. And I have dreams about him. Every night before I fall asleep I tell him that I love him." She added, with a wan but genuine smile. "You know that I still talk to him. And he hasn't stopped answering. Like now, he's saying, *Hermina, you'll feel much better if you get up*. So I will." She turned and slid her feet into her slippers. Holding onto her as if she were elderly, Millicent and Geena helped her to stand.

They went to the kitchen and prepared lunch together, slowly.

"Sometimes, though, like right now," Hermina said, her voice still quavering, "I feel 'storm washed'." She looked out the window at the forest and the ocean beyond it. "As if, the squall has passed, and the sun is glinting, and the air smells fresh of sea and salt." She looked at them. "Then I think, it's okay. I can go on."

6

"*The Great Security Institution*" installation opening was imminent; Geena's work had progressed from drawings through maquettes and now, in early April, it existed and filled the actual space.

Her exhibition at Hector Hernandez's high-ceilinged, converted San Francisco warehouse gallery was a far cry from her Beau Jangles bar-*cum*-discotheque venue a decade ago. Hector, a Costa Rican-born, gregarious, rotund, faux blond charmer, worked a circle of the best-heeled avant-garde curators and Northern California celebrity collectors.

The gallery's main door faced the street and opened into a labyrinth of brightly lit rooms where a selection of Geena's more saleable sculptures, drawings and small carvings were displayed. Here, among others, were three of her major pieces – her 'Laocoöna on a Half-Stump', a hollow, prickly sculpture she called 'Body Braille', and her father-shrine, a stuffed tuxedo she'd named 'Studs and Links'. Unsure she could bear to let these go, she'd priced them high.

Rows of plastic champagne glasses, bottles of California's best sparkling wine, soft drinks and trays of *hors d'oeuvres* would be set up on a long table in front of the receptionist's counter. Geena promised Alice that most of the canapés wouldn't have stinky cheese.

Geena figured she might actually make some money, even after the gallery took their 40%. Not that Geena or Hector expected "*The Great Security Institution*" installation to sell in its entirety; installations almost never did. But Hector was convinced that, between Geena's talent and his cachet, many people would be wanting a piece of this event. He had hired a top-notch photographer to document the installation and create numbered, boxed sets for the gallery to market. He'd convinced Geena to part with her maquettes as well as her gilded grave figures and their clay prototypes. He'd selected dozens of her preparatory drawings to frame. He'd bought his favorite for his own collection and hung it in the gallery with a red "sold" dot on the wall beside it – a Business Man effigy sketch around which she'd calligraphed a funereal border in black Gothic letters that read: "*I draw that I may not butcher*."

Before the opening, she spent her last sleepless nights on her sister's sofa bed. She hadn't let Millicent inside to see the installation yet.

But she took Alice with her for a final check and shared every secret with her.

The entrance to the installation was around the side of the building. Geena had draped that entire exterior wall (*à la* Christo) with a thirty-foot tall canvas tarp painted with hyper-realistic, *trompe-l'œil* Parthenon columns – just as it had appeared in her dream almost two years ago, including the words, "*THE GREAT SECURITY INSTITUTION*" painted across the frieze in two-foot tall letters that looked as if they'd been hewn into stone.

In between the faux columns was a real door, ten feet tall and six feet wide, originally designed for warehouse deliveries. Geena had added thickness to it and slanting sides, like the inside of a vault door. Covering the entire outside of the door was a giant, metallic-gray, winged scorpion with a female face and torso – *Geryona,* Geena's version of Dante's *Geryon*, the Monster of Fraud.

Alice screeched when saw that door, and then covered her mouth as giggles spurted out. "MiMi is gonna to be so mad at you!" *Geryona* had Phyllis's face.

To Geena, *Geryona's* two-foot long stinger was undoubtedly her best feature. Curving up and out, it served as the door handle, though Alice couldn't bring herself to touch it. Geena demonstrated hydraulic-hinges which she'd designed so the door would swing shut slowly, creaking until it slammed. Once inside the dim light, Alice moved closer to her aunt.

"Feel how chilly it is?" Geena asked. "That's air-conditioning. I want it stone cold. Do you hear those footsteps? They're from speakers up by the ceiling. And, that smell? That's dead flowers, leftover from real funerals."

"Yuck!"

Twenty feet ahead of them was the mock-marble wall. Geena explained how the three Teller Windows she'd cut into it were placed high so even grown-ups would feel small. She held Alice up so she could see. Behind the bars covering the first, Alice saw a life-sized rag doll collapsed on the floor, through the second, a wooden rocking horse with a broken rocker, and through the third, in strobing light, Alice saw the shards of a smashed glass lamp gleaming blood-red. "Please put me down," she whimpered.

To their right and spot lit was the white plaster Teller Woman effigy from Geena's dream (*à la* George Segal). Geena had dressed her in real clothing (*à la* Duane Hanson) – a green pleated wool skirt and matching twin set, costume jewelry, and eyeglasses dangling from a fake gold chain around her neck. Through speakers hidden in her stiff hair, a voice murmured a list of items: "Blue shirred lampshade, purple doily, trimmed in gold braid…"

Next, Geena walked Alice to the far left where, under another spotlight, the plaster Business Man stood, clad in tailored, gray tweed. "Put your hand in his pocket," Geena said, but Alice was afraid, so Geena reached in and removed a small speaker that muttered snippets scrounged from the *Inferno*, "*The fraudulent stand lowest…Fraud is the malice that most displeases God…*"

"Weird," Alice said, shaking her head.

"Look up there, over the door – but don't tell your mother about it, I want to surprise her."

"Bompa!" Alice cried out.

"And, look over there," Geena said, pointing to the graves sunk into the floor in front of the Teller Windows. In three of them were stylized, life-sized 'corpses', gilded and naked, at various stages of lying down. Instead of burying them in earth, Geena had heaped mounds of costume jewelry around them – fake diamonds, pearls, emeralds, rubies.

A fourth grave was covered by an iron grate, but instead of a corpse, two pairs of gilded feet stuck up from between the bars, as if a couple had been shoved, head first, deep into the jewels filling their shared grave. Geena had painted the feet a charred red, like in Dante, she told Alice, where the soles of sinners' feet were burned.

"Ouch!" Alice said, but very softly,

The fifth and final grave was empty. Available. No corpse, no jewels, no bars. Three stairs at one end led down into it. An upholstered pad of crimson leather lined the bottom. From a speaker tucked behind a matching leather head pillow, Geena's version of Dante's warning kept repeating: "*No one who fails to repent should ever be absolved.*"

"Want to climb in?" Geena said as if she'd expected Alice to treat all this as only fun. But Alice seemed on the verge of tears.

"What's wrong?" Geena asked.

"I want to go. I'm cold."

****

The night before the opening Geena was terrified. She pictured herself entering the scene with Millicent to her left, Alice to her right, Hermina covering her back, each of them packing a Smith & Wesson in a fringed leather holster. But she knew that nothing could protect her from the major Bay Area newspaper art critics who routinely covered Hector Hernandez exhibitions.

Nor from her mother. She'd made the mistake of mailing her a photo of the final maquettes as if to say, *Look, Mommy. Look what I made.* (And she accused Millicent of being a slow learner?) Phyllis had responded, "Your father and I went broke putting you through art school so you could build dollhouses?" She didn't bother to challenge her mother's distortion of history by mentioning the massive student loans Geena was still paying off.

Where is it written, *Thou shalt invite thy mother to all major life events*? Geena remembered how her mother had "worked the room" other times when her art had been on display. A pin-pulled grenade of envy and self-aggrandizement, Phyllis had sought out and cornered the "Valuable People" to inform them that her husband's influence had shaped the city of San Ensayo and that it was her own decorating artistry that had shaped Geena's talent.

There was no way to win. If Geena didn't invite Phyllis and she found out about the exhibition from someone else, she'd be mortified and attack. If Phyllis came and the exhibit was a success, she'd be envious and attack. If she came and recognized herself and Herb, she'd be wounded and then retaliate. Geena mailed her an invitation.

7

"You clean up nice, babe," L.D. said when Geena was dressed and ready to go. Hermina had helped her choose an elegant suit of armor for the opening – a raw silk, mauve kimono to wear over black gaucho pants. When the time came, however, she dressed the outfit down by pulling on her tooled cowboy boots. "To prevent irony deficiency," she said to L.D. With an *aw-shucks* blush spreading above his beard, he handed her an unwrapped gift: the genuine "Leatherman PST" (Pocket Survival Tool) she'd coveted. She kissed him and they set out for the ordeal.

Geena didn't know what to do with herself. She tried to help the gallery staff replenish the canapé trays, but they shooed her away. L.D. asked her to show him the tomb but she refused to go near it saying she'd be damned if she'd listen to any asshole's comments, good or bad. Hermina approached her, frequently, with smiles, hugs and reports on the daunting, hushed atmosphere prevailing within the installation. She'd encouraged her to "mingle," which Geena knew didn't mean "work the room" as her mother would have done, but the prospect made her ill nonetheless.

"Have you seen my mother?"

"No," Hermina said.

"I don't think she's here yet."

Hector came over to convince Geena to chat up the mucky-mucks. She knew enough not to risk it: too often, she'd failed to stop herself from telling schmucks with clout where to shove their opinions. After all, the bleeding bush she'd carved to frame the winged scorpion *Geryona* on the door was known in the *Inferno* as the "tree of suicide."

****

From her experiences at the smart restaurants Colin had taken them to in Rome, Alice had learned how to behave. Consequently,

Millicent was shocked when she entered through the creaking vault door and saw her daughter clumping around doing a monster imitation, to the hearty laughter of some man.

In full Frankenstein mode, gamine Alice eased herself stiffly into the grave Geena had left empty for the public. Holding a champagne glass (filled with ginger ale), she semi-reclined in the open pit, at the same angle as the half-seated, gilded corpse three graves over. The newspaper photographer snapping shots of Alice bragged to Millicent that one of these images would fill the front page of the "Arts & Entertainment" section.

The next time she looked, Alice was talking intensely to the man. He squatted down beside the grave and whatever Alice was saying made him laugh again. Millicent had seen him before. Odd that she couldn't place him. She had a good memory for attractive men.

She sauntered over.

"Hi," she said, hoping she sounded nonchalant.

"Mom!" Alice climbed up the steps, out of the grave and ran to her. "Didn't we go to *Lombardia*? That's his name, 'Mr. Lombardi'! Geena says he speaks Italian!"

Apparently recognizing Millicent, he reached out to shake her hand. "Hello! You're Geena's sister, right, and Alice's mother? I'm Leo Lombardi. We've met. Our fathers shared a hospital room - briefly."

The memory flooded back. The world's first Phyllis-stopper.

"No, Alice," he went on, "I only know the Italian phrases I grew up with, like *babbo* and *mamma*," he said, then smiled to Millicent, "plus the raunchy swear words guys use at building sites." He looked around. "Strong stuff, huh?"

That was when Millicent looked up. High above where Leo stood she saw the piece that Geena had kept hidden from her: the huge and brightly lit head of Herbert Milner hung suspended over the entrance door, the size it would have seemed to his girls when they were little. She'd carved, sanded and painted it – Geena hadn't burned or brushed or wounded him this time – then mounted their father's head on a glossy, oak platter like a taxidermied trophy she'd bagged, with Herb's white beard, his somewhat pointed, bald forehead, his Tevye-lips, and his eyes, those warm, inaccessible, enigmatic, distant, cold, unyielding, love-promising eyes.

"What's wrong?" Leo asked, staring at Millicent as if her hair were on fire. He turned and saw what she was seeing. "Oh. Your dad," he said softly. "Some tomb, huh?"

"'The Tomb of the Unknown Family,'" she blurted out, then flinched. That was too true.

She located Geena hiding on a low stool behind the receptionist's counter in the main gallery. Millicent knelt beside her with tears in her eyes. "It's incredible," she said, then noticed that Geena was trembling. "What's wrong? This is a huge success."

"Oh, fuck," Geena said.

****

When Geena didn't answer her phone, Hermina drove up the coast intending to leave the Sunday newspapers, with two very good reviews, outside the door. But she heard music blaring and knocked, then banged. At last, Geena opened the door, pale, shaking and in tears.

"You must not have seen these reviews. They're wonderful." Hermina turned off the music and spread the newspapers out on the workbench. "'Michelangelo's *Inferno*…a howl given substance…a box of anguish…a paradoxical freezing of outrage, pity and grief into hyper-modern, neo-Classical form…like Rodin's 'Cubic Truth'…'"

"I read 'em. L.D. dropped them off," Geena said, weakly.

"And the one from that lady critic who's usually so cutting? 'Milner holds our feet to the fire…' Nothing wrong with that one either, Geena."

"What the hell am I supposed to do with this shit?" Geena demanded.

"Enjoy it."

"I didn't work for this."

"Nonsense. You've been at it all your life."

"I didn't do it for the reviews."

"If you had, they probably wouldn't have been this good."

"I feel exposed."

"You've accomplished an authentic piece of work. There must be some joy in that, no?"

"And for an encore? Geena Milner, Tomb Queen?"

"Stop picking at it like it's a sore. Take a few days off. Rest. Listen to Beethoven – he knew something about rejoicing in accomplishment. Then, go back to work. You know how to do that."

Geena stood close to Hermina, looking down at the newspapers. "I miss my dad," she said at last. "He might have been proud of me."

"Or angry. Or wounded. Or confused. Be proud on your own behalf."

Geena nodded. Then she whispered, "She didn't come."

"Oh, so *that's* what this is about. Your mother. She's another kettle of worms. How silly of me not to realize. You seem to have caught on to her so insightfully that I keep forgetting how vulnerable you are. And that you're still yearning."

Geena walked unstably to her rattan chair. Hermina followed her, sitting down at the foot of the daybed to be near her. "I'd pictured it," Geena continued, "how she'd walk in with her tight, fake smile and say, 'Mmm,' the way you do when you taste something you hate but the hostess is right there. She's my mother, for chrissake." Geena bent forward clutching her knees while shoving a fist into her gut to stop the pain. "She'd see herself and Daddy in the work," Geena continued, still curled up, "and say, *we never liked you either*. And, *You're not an artist. You're an assassin.* And she'd be right…instead, she just didn't come."

"I never expected her to," Hermina said.

"You would have come, if I was your daughter."

"I'm not mentally unbalanced. She probably couldn't bear to see your glory since it isn't hers."

"She doesn't love me, does she?"

"No, I don't believe your mother will ever be capable of that." A brutal reality to have to take in. Was she being too honest? "But, Geena, I haven't known you long but do you know what I realize?" Hermina waited. She needed a sign that Geena was within her reach.

"What?"

"I've already grown to love you."

"Don't you dare!" Geena winced.

Sam, give me courage, Hermina said inside, feeling close to tears. "You're not alone."

Geena let a tear trickle down her cheek. "Millicent and Alice love you too. And Sam. Maybe we four, together…important pieces come from you, Geena, work other people need to see."

"What do you mean?" Geena asked, with hardly a pause now.

"'The art of living is to make use of suffering'. That's what you succeed at doing." Hermina thought of her own excruciating loss and, for a moment, could hardly breathe. "Many of us live much farther from the bone than you do and are grateful that someone does our feeling for us."

"I don't do it for you."

"No. But you do it. And that gives the rest of us something. Your work gives me something."

"What?" Hermina struggled to resist the comfort of pontificating on the functions and functioning of art. At last, she found the personal words: "Your sculptures make me more alive. That's it. In fact: You yourself do that. You *enliven* me." *Yes!* Sam would have cheered. "Your courage. How exposed you dare to be. How you're angry when you're angry and, now, how you are sad when you are sad. Most of us don't have such direct emotional access."

"I wish I didn't."

"Do you really?"

Geena laughed a little as she said, "No. I don't envy thick people."

"You didn't have to invite your mother, you know."

"But I hoped, maybe this time…"

"Sweetheart," Hermina leaned forward. "Look at me and I'll say it again: Hope is your enemy here. You long for *a* mother. Have done so all of your life. You don't long for *your* mother. Not Phyllis Milner. You must give *that* woman up. Please, Geena. Bury that hope in the empty grave you dug."

VI.

1

Several of Millicent's Italian students had kept in touch. In fact, repeated requests had arrived from Rosanna, from Puglia, to please invite some of them to America as 'language tourists.' Half a dozen of her fellow students had said they'd come. Millicent had given it little thought since Rosanna made the suggestion back in Milan. At first, Millicent had loved the idea, but now doubts crept in. She drove over to Geena's studio where she knew she'd find Hermina who went there most days.

"Too much trouble, too much work, too unprofitable," Millicent volunteered, seated in Geena's rattan chair sipping a *caffelatte.*

"It might mean release from indentured servitude to McLanguage," Hermina said. "And besides, you could try it out without giving up your job. Take some unpaid leave and see if it's a viable enterprise."

"Why do I feel like Wile E. Coyote when the Road Runner drops a seven-ton weight on him?"

"Fear, perhaps."

"Or, *Realism*." Millicent had little reason to trust herself to start any venture, however small, she said. The only overt business teaching her father had ever offered was two sentences when she was seventeen when he wanted to put in a bid to buy HMS Queen Mary and develop it as a shopping center. "Choose the scale you want to operate on. Pick a banker and dial the number." How sound would his advice have been?

"Not all ambition is self-delusion," Hermina said. "Do research. Investigate if the project is realistically feasible. And, if it is, whether you would want the life it would bring if it succeeded. Sam used to say how often people fail to explore that second aspect."

"I finally have a routine with Alice, a predictable schedule, a steady income, you and Geena nearby, my mother far away, and no *putzy* men around to suck up to and dazzle. Why ruin all that?"

"I promise to warn you if I see you over-inflate. But I do consider you capable of this."

Geena, chewing the end of a pencil, wandered in. "I know. Call Leo Lombardi. He could to help you see if it's do-able, if you'd need to borrow money – that sort of thing. He helped me a lot when I was planning my installation."

"He's a builder."

"And a business man. From a family that didn't fuck him up. Or go bankrupt."

"Is he expensive?"

"Offer him a home-cooked meal."

Assuring herself she wasn't an idiot for seeking help since no one can know everything, Millicent left a message for Leo at the San Ensayo office of Lombardi & Sons. When he called back, he warned her that he knew nothing about either the travel industry or language schools but he did know about planning projects. He would be happy to help her think through what information to collect and who she ought to contact.

As she assembled their tacos and poured a beer for Leo, Alice took him on a guided tour of her Barbie housing complex. She told him her Grand Plan for what she'd take to her father's next month where she'd be spending, "the completely whole summer!" Leo made appropriate noises. The somewhat stiff dinner conversation ranged from Alice's school to the culture of Italo-Americans to the future of Geena's installation.

"So. Tell me about this course you're planning," Leo began once Alice had gone to bed.

Millicent had been imagining maybe two events a year which would involve a tour that was part culture tourism and part language lab. The extra money could make a big difference to her and Alice. As a free-lancer, she'd be able to teach the way she wanted to again, with music and movement, literature and reading aloud to her classes.

"Imagine being paid to do what I love," she said, not mentioning that she used to presume prostitutes had that luxury.

By the end of the evening, they had talked through who she'd need to approach and what she'd need to ask. She couldn't sleep after he'd left; one idea after another caused her to turn the light back on and make notes – what if Enrico would agree to advertise a course in the *Lingua Nuova* brochure? Her brain tingled.

"Feel free to call," Leo had said, and during the next couple of weeks, she did over various things.

Enrico had agreed without hesitation to advertise an October course for intermediate and advanced students. Might he be regretting how shamelessly he'd treated her and Alice and considering this an opportunity to improve his image? Might the blush be off his teen-bride's rose? Or was his enthusiasm an expression of entrepreneurial glee? *Lingua Nuova*'s co-hosting of the first "*Italia Parla America*" ("Italy Speaks America") U.S. tour would add an extra touch of class to his autumn line-up. Enticing well-heeled students to sign up for expensive courses was what Enrico did best.

Despite or because of Millicent's bubbling enthusiasm, Leo was adamant that before Millicent took it any further Enrico should sign a detailed contract, which he was happy to help her draw up. It took some doing, but Leo, eventually, convinced Millicent that if Enrico expected to make a percentage out of this, then he had to bear a share of the risk. That meant making an upfront contribution. When she presented Enrico with contract terms it must become apparent to him that this Millicent was not going to be a pushover.

Fortuitously, Geena had a friend whose wife was a San Francisco travel agent. Sigrid knew her way around the globe and thought Language Tourism might prove "quite the Golden Goose." The dollar exchange rate was unfavorable at the moment, so the travel industry was offering attractive transatlantic deals, and Sigrid could secure a terrific group rate at Hyatt hotels – reducing the price from outrageous to merely expensive. There would be guided tours, a Broadway show and the afternoons reserved for teaching.

Starting in New York, and taking in LA their last stop would be San Francisco's Hyatt Regency, a fabulous, new, Embarcadero building where glass-encased elevators slid silently up and down the seventeen story atrium's fern-festooned walls. And, serendipity! They'd be there just in time for Bruce Springsteen's "Born in the U.S.A." concert at the Oakland Coliseum.

The final teaching weekend would consolidate, confirm and celebrate their expanded American-English mastery.

She didn't feel burdened or stressed making these plans – and despite the upfront payments she would have to make (subsidized equitably by *Lingua Nuova*) for concert tickets and hotel rooms, she reasoned that the hotel deposits could be refunded and she'd know her numbers before the cut-off date. Sigrid liked the thought of scalping the theater and concert tickets. Hell, they might even make a profit if the tour fell through!

Was Millicent behaving just like her father and betting her life's savings on a fantasy? Leo reassured her: she'd be taking a risk, but a calculated one. He thought she should go ahead, get herself a tax accountant and an attorney.

At the end of May, Millicent signed papers establishing "Mother Tongue, Inc." The night Hermina suggested that name for her company, Millicent dreamed she had a huge hole in her belly, like the one the cartoon detective, Dick Tracy, always ended up with after getting shot. Everybody could see right through her stomach to the wallpaper and the sofa and the end table and the lamp. Then, slowly, under Hermina's watchful eye, the hole began to close up. Once Millicent was all fleshed out again, Hermina explained, in her most pedagogical, dream voice, "This, my dear, has been a demonstration of the verb, 'to incorporate'."

2

"It isn't a date," she told Geena, when Leo invited Millicent out to dinner. "He just wants us to celebrate my new business."

After they'd delivered Alice to Hermina, he parked in Sausalito so they could walk all the way to the middle of the windswept Golden Gate Bridge. This was the first time they'd been alone together out in the world. Although she struggled against it, Millicent couldn't help conflating the Pacific and the Arno, expecting Leo to merge with her, Fabrizio-like, into the awe-inspiring, sunset-stained panorama.

But he launched into an animated discourse on the forces carried by each of the pylons, the dimension and weave of the cables bearing the road bed and their unique "catenary" droop, the rust-provoking impact of salt spray and the rust-inhibiting properties of the specially designed paint. Once the work crew had finished painting the entire bridge, he told her, they began immediately to paint it all again.

Leo must have noticed that Millicent was shivering. He wrapped his jacket around her and said something she couldn't hear above the thundering of the late rush-hour traffic whizzing by at their backs. He brought his lips closer to her ear and she listened for her internal string section to crescendo, preparing herself to melt again at long last. She held her breath. "You know, Millicent," she heard him say, "one reason why this bridge is elegant is that nothing is over-dimensioned. It's as strong as it needs to be to carry the load it has to carry and that's it!"

He took her to a homey Chinese restaurant, where he detailed the geological quirks of the San Ensayo soil he'd worked with all these years, as well as its impact on building foundations.

He obviously delighted in expounding these monologues and that kept her listening, despite their deadening duration. Double entendres – about pipes-and-fittings, plugs-and-sockets – came to her mind from force of habit but she deemed them too adolescent to interject. Instead, she wedged in an anecdote about her lisping high school algebra teacher they all called 'Mithter Tholomon'. He spoke only to the blackboard and the boys. She knew she wasn't fawning when she claimed that, had any of her teachers explained things as well as Leo did, she might have enrolled in more than the required minimum of science classes.

A drowsiness crept up on Millicent during dessert as numbing boredom threatened to take hold. Then, Leo said, "Geena's told me a lot about your parents, but not much about you." Now, he listened. And did she ever talk.

What the hell, she wondered later, had made her say so much? She talked about her father, about the fashion shows that her mother had insisted she perform for him. She told Leo how it had struck her, too late, that her father had been trapped in having to appear larger-than-life and that they'd all had a stake in pretending he was powerful. She told him about her mother – the beatings, the ridicule, the crazy-making way she flipped between glorifying and demeaning first Millicent and then Geena; how her behavior in the hospital had been nothing but consistent. She even told him about the men. "I believed until very recently – until I found out I can teach, until I met Hermina and realized I'm smart – I believed…," she spoke more softly now, "that the only power I had was sexual." She then gave him a brutally short summary of the Fabrizio affair. All of this without standing outside of herself to monitor her shame.

When the waiter brought the check and she finally stopped talking, Millicent felt as naked as Eve after the bite. Did she seem like a pathetic nut case? A whore? "You must think I'm crazy!" she said. But while holding her breath waiting for his response, a burst of rage replaced her panic. Shoving spikes out through all her pores, she looked him in the eye and promised herself that if she glimpsed even the slightest twinge of pity or contempt, she'd be gone, outta there. *Forget it, Bud!*

"Crazy? The exact opposite," Leo said. "I think it's remarkable that someone who's been through all that has landed so firmly on her feet. *Complimenti*, Millicent."

3

Geena was grinning as she told Hermina and Millicent about the money that was still rolling in. Not only had the *Geryona* door relief sold, but also the effigies and the gilded corpses. The buyers had all agreed to make them available if the installation were ever reassembled, a possibility which Hector was exploring aggressively.

Geena enjoyed peeling dollars from her wad of 'well-gotten gains'. She'd built a "family room" addition to her cabin and furnished it with folding bed-chairs for Millicent and Alice and a proper bed for Hermina. One afternoon while Alice was off with a friend, they inaugurated the new space, feasting on the homemade chili L.D. had left for them. Hermina showed off her "drunken vessels" as she called her early attempts at using the potter's wheel Geena had bought for her.

"What's next for you, Geena?" Millicent asked.

"When I told the College of Fine Arts that I don't teach, they offered me a semester as Visiting Artist."

"I meant, what are you going to sculpt next?"

"Beats me. During this roosting part of the process, this sitting on the eggs – it's best not to bounce too much. In the meantime…," she looked at Hermina. "May I?" Hermina nodded. "When we first met, I told Hermina the price for using my studio was permission to draw her. She has finally paid up; she's not a welsher, after all. Just a laggard."

"She said 'nude' back then, but, fortunately, she eased her terms," Hermina added.

"We've been playing, haven't we?" Geena said as she spread out her drawings. Hermina as Abraham's old Sarah, with a wrinkled face and a pregnant body, laughing; Hermina curled up as an aged fetus; Hermina as a cypress tree, her scoliotic spine twisted as if after decades exposed to the prevailing winds.

Millicent examined them closely, especially one full-face charcoal portrait. What courage Geena had to gaze long and deep enough into Hermina's tender eyes to capture such a poignant likeness. "Your work has changed, Geena," Millicent said. "These drawings are soft. Loving, even."

"It's our new art movement: 'Post-Exorcism.'" Geena winked at Hermina who smiled back. "And how's your 'Mother's Tongue'?"

"Shit-can that apostrophe," Millicent said laughing. "Leo's been great help. He never says anything *personal* but he gives wonderful lectures. They're long, though, and he doesn't notice when his listener's eyes have begun to glaze over."

"Sam would say that means he's a bit like me," Hermina said. "So, perhaps, he's clumsy. Or might he be shy?"

"Hermina presumes that men are people, don't forget," Geena said.

"Something about him let you confide in him. Consider trusting yourself."

"Ha!" Millicent snorted at that concept.

"Have you asked him questions about himself? He's likely to appreciate your interest if he's a fairly normal man. Especially if you ask because you want to know him better rather than to ridicule male reticence in general."

"I've never fallen for a 'fairly normal' man."

"Don't blame men for that, my dear."

"Hardly anybody out there is like Sam, and you know it."

"My firm conviction, based on long experience, is that men as a class are better than their reputation. If, that is, you understand how to appreciate them, and if you don't conspire either with their baser indoctrinations or their inflated sense of entitlement. Ask Leo questions. Get to know him."

"I don't think he's gay, but he might be celibate."

Now it was Geena who snorted. "Are you nuts? Don't you realize the guy's market value? Definitively hetero. He's even *nice*, for chrissake, with a successful business, no small kids and no preening awareness of what a hunk he is. A good man in his forties has three or four decades of horny younger and older women to fend off. He'd have to be a *castrato* to withstand the continual pressure. He may not be involved with anyone right now, but that doesn't mean he always keeps it zipped."

Why doesn't he want me, then? came to Millicent's mind, but it sounded false, habitual. Had she outgrown such refrains?

"You don't need to go to bed with a man to make friends with him," Hermina said gently, as if Millicent could find that an alien concept.

"He's invited us, me and Alice, on a picnic, but she said she'd rather be with you, Hermina, if that's okay. She's leaving soon and for such a long time."

****

He drove Millicent to his favorite spot among the redwoods. During his long, though admittedly interesting, tutorial on the ecology of redwood forests, Millicent clung to Hermina's word 'shy'. He took a bite of a sandwich and she seized the moment. "Tell me about you," she said.

"You met my family at the hospital. My mother passed away when I was in my twenties. You know about my work. What else? I married young. I have two grown kids away at college. And I'm divorced." He stopped and took another bite.

"Why?"

"Why what?"

"Why did you get divorced?"

Leo paused. "It wasn't in the plans," and then shook his head. "Funny I should use that expression. That's exactly what my father said when he heard his cancer was terminal."

****

When Millicent returned to Hermina's, Alice was asleep after her long day of embroidery lessons and beach combing.

"I did it," Millicent announced to Geena and Hermina as they sat on the moonlit deck sipping their wine. "I pried a personal narrative out of Leonardo Lombardi. I think you'd like him."

"I already do," Geena said. "What did he say?"

Millicent almost launched into the tale, but she checked herself as an unfamiliar ethical qualm stopped her from betraying his confidences, even to them.

She re-ran his story for herself that night in bed. He had begun by explaining what had been "in his plans": a narrow, two-story house for his family that he'd designed and that Lombardi & Sons had built. It was modeled on a hotel overlooking Sienna that he and Patsy had discovered while exploring their Old World roots, his

Catholic-Italian, hers, Protestant-Northern Irish. Situated on a narrow ridge overlooking the San Ensayo canyon, the house had one wing for their kids, Meg and Brandon, another for him and Patsy, and, in the middle, a central section for the whole family. Each room had one windowless wall, which faced the road. The huge windows on the other side of each room offered an expansive view of the forests across the valley and of the city below.

After Leo moved out, the absence of street-side windows meant that he couldn't check how family life was continuing without him – whose light was on, who was in which room. Nevertheless, he had stood outside often, staring at the blank area of wall he knew belonged to Meg's room or to Brandon's and, of course, the wall he still struggled to call '*Patsy's*' instead of '*ours*'.

He hadn't seen it coming, he told Millicent. "With no warning, Patsy announced she wanted a divorce, and you know what I answered? 'A horse? But you don't ride.' Then she had to repeat it. '*Divorce*', and I said: 'But we're happily married!' She said, 'Maybe you are, but I'm not.'"

Why hadn't she spoken up earlier? What had he done or not done or been that was so intolerable? How could she do this, pull his whole life out from under him, send him out of his own home, away from his bed, his closets, his tools, his workshop? "…My kids." His voice cracked.

He'd wanted them to see a marriage counselor but Patsy had refused. "I'll do anything!" He'd begged and he still felt no shame about having pleaded. It was wrong. It shouldn't have been happening.

Patsy offered to let him stay that night, in his workshop, but he went to Bettina and Hank's, his sister and brother-in-law. They moved their TV into the living room for their kids, opened the sofa bed in the den and left Leo alone to sob in loud, rusty spurts, like the faucet at the cabin they used to rent in the spring.

They must have heard him crying through the thin walls that some second-rate company had built, since he could hear every word they said, even with their bedroom door closed. "Leo should get everything, not that fucking Protestant Ice Queen Bitch," Bettina had proclaimed. "Including custody of the kids. He's the one who pays attention around there, and the bills!" His first impulse had been to storm in and defend Patsy, yet again, from Bettina's belligerent faultfinding. But he hadn't. He wasn't angry, not yet, but there was comfort, however cold, in someone raging on his behalf.

He recognized the numbness he felt as shock; he'd gashed his thigh once with a chainsaw and remembered shock's anesthetizing mercy. And how short-lived it was. Real pain, he knew, was on its way.

Millicent asked him what the worst part had been. He answered that it was probably a tie – between realizing his own guilt for the break-up versus telling the kids. But, really there was no contest. Eleven-year-old Brandon had taken a huge stride backwards when they'd told him, as if he'd caught a body blow that slammed a breathy "No!" out of him, then a second backward stride as he begged, "No! Daddy, no!" And a third, which left him standing, silent, as if pinned against the windowless living room wall by the force of life-as-he-knew-it ending. And eight-year-old Meg had curled up into a tiny ball, the thumb she'd quit sucking three years before shoved back into her mouth, to the hilt.

"That was the worst," Leo said softly. He looked into Millicent's eyes. Then he changed the subject.

Thinking back on it, Millicent understood that what she'd seen in that moment had been more than the anguish he was reliving. She'd recognized in him that same sense of astonished wonder she had experienced after she had revealed so much of her history to him. Leo, she now realized, didn't speak about these things easily. Or to just anyone.

4

"My Dad just told me he signed me up for YMCA day camp and he bought me a ghetto-blaster for my room!" *Here we go,* Millicent thought as they climbed into the car to go shopping for summer clothes, "trainer bras" for her rapidly bursting breast buds, and the rosy-toned lip pomade Alice was desperate for, but which Millicent worried was almost like lipstick. They'd never before been separated for eleven whole weeks.

Alice would turn twelve while she was away. Millicent had stocked up on the smallest sanitary belts and pads available and insisted that Alice practice how to use the equipment before she left. She stashed some at Geena's and Hermina's and had a supply ready to pack for Alice's trip in case her period started at Neal's. Millicent hoped, though, that she and Alice would be together when it happened.

Indeed, one morning, four days before she was due to leave, Alice nonchalantly asked her mother for a clean sheet and then started closing herself up in the bathroom every ten minutes. Millicent didn't understand until Alice whispered, "You have to go buy more of those stupid things."

Millicent gave her a big hug and said with a tender smile, "You don't have to change pads so often, you know."

"Yuck!" Alice said with tears in her eyes and then went to wash her hands, again, while her mother made her a cup of cocoa.

She lay on the sofa all afternoon with her forearm covering her eyes, sniffing the air to check if she smelled funny, wondering if she'd faint from loss of blood. Wondering if the pad would make a huge bump at the back of her pants that everybody would point at and then laugh. How come her friend Merilee's mother didn't die of embarrassment when her period gushed out in a movie theater all over the seat like Merilee said had happened and then an ambulance came? Could she make it stop somehow?

Millicent tried to comfort her talking about her *little girl growing up*. But when Millicent admitted that she'd told Geena and Hermina and that she'd need to warn Alice's dad, too, Alice stormed into her bedroom and slammed the door screaming that her tush was her own; her mother had told her that in no uncertain terms, and now she'd gone and phoned everybody in the world to talk about Alice's tush. She didn't understand anything anymore.

It must have itched in the night because the next morning, she woke up with blood under her fingernails. People were wrong about blood. Blood wasn't red. It was an awful, rusty-brown. She washed her hands using the nail brush, hard, then washed the nail brush, then took two wash cloths with her into the shower, one for down there only.

There wasn't much blood that day and, mercifully, none the day after. This wasn't the last time, though; it had only just started. That's what they said: "Alice started." What if she started bleeding at school? Nobody else did.

She was positively sure now. She was going to her dad's and never coming back. And she'd never use rusty-brown cloth or thread in her patchwork and embroideries ever again.

5

One afternoon after Alice left for Chicago, Millicent stood in a queue at the bank. As she searched through her purse for the Mother Tongue, Inc. statements she had questions about, she became aware, subliminally, of a male figure to her right. A dark, masculine force. Not a threatening darkness, but heavy, impinging, too close for the etiquette of queuing. With her mind occupied elsewhere, her body had registered the darkness of the brown lapels within her peripheral line of sight and the dark, curly chest hairs protruding below the open-collar button of a coarsely woven, beige shirt. She inhaled the layered odors of the clean but not perfumed male of the species, awash in pheromones. She felt a strong, animal pull and an equally strong instinct to flee this presence that hovered so close to her right side that her elbow had brushed against him as she hunted through her purse.

She raised her eyes. Leo stood there, his face alight with an easy smile.

"I saw your car," he said. He hugged her and placed the familiar, Italian kisses of greeting on her cheeks.

She needed a moment to quiet herself, to transit up, from animal, to female, to woman, to herself, a person in a very public line in a bank. When the man in front of her turned around and looked at them, Millicent, flustered, heard herself explain, "We know each other."

****

Each time Leo's business brought him north, he phoned and then dropped by after work. Though she worried about exploiting him, making a project out of him in order to avoid missing Alice, she found herself surprisingly adept at getting to know him.

"If telling your children was the worst, what was the second worst?" Millicent asked him.

He paused, but knew the answer. "That would be Patsy hollering at me: 'Just because I put it into words that our marriage is over doesn't mean it's all my fault it ended!' She said it in the Irish-brat style she used when she felt guilty but would sooner die than admit it." Millicent had seen a photograph and could picture Patsy, her tight, reddish curls trembling, her wiry form primed like a runner on the starting block.

It had dawned on him later that Patsy had been sending out oblique warning signals for years. Her sarcastic asides had flown past him like goblins which he presumed weren't real and thus could be ignored. Standard stuff, like he worked too much, cleaned house too little, entertained their kids while she did the hard part, the disciplining and the rules.

Couldn't she have warned him in some way that he could hear, before the axe fell? She had to carry her share of the blame for years of simple faking or was it outright lying? "Did you ever come?" he admitted shouting, to their mediating lawyer's immense discomfort, "or were you protecting our domestic harmony there, too?" Since when is leaving dirty socks under the bed a capital crime? he'd protested in the office of the lawyer who reminded them, again, that he wasn't a therapist.

"Problem was," Leo said, "I knew she was right." He confessed to Millicent that knowing that the fault was also Patsy's hadn't helped him one damned bit. He had loved as best he knew how. It hadn't been good enough. The unbearable truth that skewered Leo was that his way of loving had left his wife feeling – her word; he couldn't believe it – *lonely*.

Lonely? He said that he had loved her intensely. He'd loved her bouncy form, so small he could grab all of her in his arms as her protector, or hold her the way he'd hugged his little bear when he was a kid falling asleep. "I'm there feeling battened to her, wing-nutted and soldered, and she's feeling *alone*?" If that were so, and Patsy assured him that it had been, then everything he believed he knew about himself as a man, even as a person, was built on a steep slope of landfill.

How the hell, and based on what premises, was he supposed to go on?

He let her keep the house. His kids were about to lose him – try as he might to view it otherwise, that was how he saw it – they shouldn't have to lose their home as well. He couldn't afford a place where they both had rooms of their own. He settled for a two-bedroom apartment in a building his company had built so he trusted the solidity of the walls.

His apartment overlooked, through its one living room window, the ever more densely populated San Ensayo valley. The view included not only McDonald's arches, which, he discovered, glowed even when seen from above, but also acres and acres of strip mall parking lots plus housing developments laid out in regular, repeating sequences. Okay, not rigid grids, but suffocatingly predictable patterns. In the past, he had countered any cocktail party complaints about developers by blasting, "Go ahead. Be the first to give your house back to nature. I'll tear it down for you for free." Now, he was face to face, daily, with the extent of the damage Lombardi & Sons had been actively and profitably complicit in, with how they had helped to destroy a huge amount of San Ensayo's natural beauty as one complex after another stole luxuriant hillsides to create the now sprawling village-*cum*-city.

He felt fortunate that, in his efforts not to notice his grief, he'd only needed to wake up in a few wrong beds to figure out that sexual conquests proved nothing, neither to Patsy nor to himself, about the quality of his love. He discovered also, though somewhat more slowly, that alcohol didn't erase his sense of failure, though strong *grappa* and melancholy jazz temporarily eased the ache. Gradually – he couldn't reconstruct the stages traversed – he realized he would survive. "I sort of poured cement into the wounds, I guess," he said.

He had been with one woman for a while. That relationship had been chosen precisely for what it wasn't, what it couldn't touch or stir up, and it had, eventually, withered and died. Since then, he'd kept pretty much to himself. He worked a lot. He believed he'd grown used to being alone and, perhaps, he even preferred it.

Millicent felt some sort of pang hearing of his preference for being alone but decided not to take it personally. In fact, she was proud she hadn't tried to push him toward sex.

6

"Leo and I are *friends*, Geena," she answered when her sister asked if she and Leo had done it yet. He'd invited Millicent south to see *his* San Ensayo. "It was fun. Bettina cooked homemade *ravioli* for us. Lots of laughing and reminiscing about her brother's bizarre experiments growing up, breaking things to see how they worked, blowing stuff up. He would have made a great engineer, but he knocked Patsy up when they were still young."

They had stopped at his apartment on the way back. It was small and smelt like *Eau de* Man, with tools covering the counters, piles of books all over the floor, and rolled up blueprints stored in empty industrial drums. It seemed as if no woman had been there for a hundred years, but multiple photos of his kids at all the stages of their growing up covered the walls.

"According to him our father wasn't nearly the major player Mother makes him out to be." Millicent had pressed Leo for the truth and had learned that Daddy screwed some families out of their patrimony to get the land he built on. And he tried to hoodwink the Lombardis into signing a construction contract with unfavorable terms slipped into the small print. "Leo's father just walked away."

"I already told you that. Why don't you believe shit when it comes from me?"

"It sounded worse coming from Leo. Anyway, we joked that our families could be the Montagues and Capulets of San Ensayo."

"Or the Guelphs and Ghibellines."

"Who are they?"

"Read your Dante."

"And…we went to visit Mother. He knew I dreaded seeing her and offered to come with me."

"You don't have to go there. Why the hell did you even tell her you were down there?" Geena asked.

"Same reason you invited her to your exhibit – I was afraid I'd bump into her and she'd be pissed."

"*Touché*. But I learn from my mistakes."

"You make lots of noises about having learned. But you're still scared of her too."

"Okay, okay. So – how was the visit?"

"Shall we say…brief? Geena, I think she's losing it."

"I'm sure you're right. But what actually happened?"

"A wave of too much *L'Air du Temps* hit us hard when she opened her door. She was dolled up in a baby-blue skirt and a sky-blue blouse with a plunging neckline, accessorized by an obscene amount of costume jewelry – rings, necklaces, bracelets, earrings, pins. You think she sold her real jewels?"

"Nah. She's hiding them from us in some safe."

"Anyway, when Leo reached out his hand and expressed his belated condolences on Daddy's death, she embraced him and then snuggled into his chest. It would have been comical if she hadn't seemed so sad."

"And creepy."

After Leo pulled away gently, Phyllis said, in a suave and urbane voice, "So you're the latest man to have my daughter."

Millicent gasped.

Phyllis took no notice. She pointed to the tool box she'd apparently readied for Leo. Eyebrows high, head tilted, eyelashes batting, she'd warbled, "You Lombardos are construction workers, right? You'll do a chore or two for me, won't you?"

"Mother, he's a guest," Millicent protested.

"And I'm a widow in need of help," Phyllis snapped back. "Compassion is not Millicent's strong suit," she said and left the room. Leo put his arm across Millicent's shoulder and pulled her to him, hard.

Phyllis returned lugging a step stool. "We can save the clogged drain for later. But, first: You hear that? My smoke detector batteries are beeping day and night." She'd reached into her skirt pocket. "I bought new ones."

"I should be able to manage that," Leo said, politely.

As he stood on the stool reaching up toward the ceiling, Phyllis wrapped her arms around his hips – and nuzzled her face into his crotch. Millicent saw him flinch. "I'll stabilize you," she said winking at Millicent. "Wouldn't want you to fall and sue me for damages." Her grin was salacious.

The batteries in place, Phyllis took Leo's hand. "Plumbing next. Sit down, Millicent," she commanded, "and wait for us here." As she began maneuvering Leo off toward the kitchen, something rose up within Millicent, some sense of propriety, some long-overdue determination to stop subjecting herself, and now this decent man, to her mother's seductive, mean, pathetic ploys. *Enough! No more!*

"No, Mother," she said. "That's it. We're leaving now."

Amid a hail of protests and accusations of neglect and ingratitude, Millicent had taken Leo's hand and hurried him out of the apartment.

In the car afterwards, they sat in stunned silence looking straight ahead. "Oh, please don't believe what they say about daughters becoming just like their mothers," Millicent murmurred. Then they looked at each other and both erupted into laughter.

Leo shook his head from side to side. "Millicent," he said, "I've never ever met anyone quite like your mother. Not in all my life."

7

Leo took Millicent on a tour of the routes he and his father had followed back in the early days of the San Ensayo post-war construction boom. His lean, laborer father's workday began at seven and ended by three. He'd often be waiting for Leo when his elementary school let out and together they'd comb San Ensayo looking for building sites.

"What did you and your dad talk about then?" Millicent asked, taking hold of his arm.

"Nothing personal," he answered. "Stuff about site mishaps or problems he had solved that day. And he taught me about tools and materials. He taught me how to balance on beams by having me walk the sidewalk curbs, the park bench backs, the length of any fallen tree branch we came across no matter whose yard it lay in."

Later, as they sat together on his sofa, he corrected himself. "Actually, maybe all of that *was* personal." He reflected aloud on how those walks with his father had shaped Leo's life, his work, his sensibilities, his love of tools, his curiosity about absolutely everything. They had walked through their town enveloped in an intimate world of feeling; there'd been no need to name it. "Dad had this phrase, 'Love in Action'," Leo said. "It's what he'd say when my mom handed me back a shirt I'd torn on the way down a tree, all mended. He'd say, 'There you go, son. That's love in action.'"

Millicent smiled ruefully at having no such acts of maternal care to recall.

"Patsy criticized me for not talking about my feelings, but maybe it was *her*," he said, as if realizing it for the first time. "Maybe it was her who was insensitive and distant. Maybe she didn't understand how my heart used to swell when I ran out of school, across the playground and saw, yes! There he is. Dad.

"I was proud; nobody else's father was out there waiting to take them around, show them the world, teach them the town. But back then, it simply was. Love just is."

He looked down at the floor; both were quiet. "Which is all fine, except," he paused, "when Dad was lying in that hospital bed, apologizing and saying, 'This wasn't in the plans,' all I said was 'No. It sure as shit wasn't!'" He described how his father had shaken his head slowly, his eyes darting as if he were searching blueprints for some missing detail. "I changed the subject. I said, 'You know that circular saw you bought me last Christmas?' I had to clench my throat to keep from crying. 'I found a stand for it for only twenty bucks. I can lift the blade easy or drop it with one single lever. You'll love it.' '*Bravo, Leonardo,*' he said and patted my hand and sort of rubbed my forearm." Millicent could see it, a big-knuckled, calloused hand caressing Leo's muscular arm.

He looked at her now with sad eyes. "Millicent, I didn't say to him, *babbo, I love you*. I hardly ever said that. Not then, not before, or later. And then he was gone." Leo looked at her as he confessed, "I haven't said that enough to anyone in my life. Not to my mother even while she was dying, not to Patsy, not hardly to my kids."

She moved closer to him. She took his face in her hands and kissed his cheeks where the tears would have run if he hadn't choked them back. She kissed the furrow on his forehead.

He kissed her lips. Once. Softly.

Without thinking, she kissed him, again, differently, this time.

He pulled back to look at her, smiling seriously.

When they were naked, he stood by the bed pulling back the covers. His erection was beautiful to her. They lay down together. He gathered her body to his and held her.

Aroused though she undoubtedly was, she knew that attempting to wow him was out of the question, nor could she imagine the two of them taking turns performing or applauding. Again, he pulled away to look into her eyes. She used to challenge Fabrizio by keeping her eyes open as she maneuvered him to the right place, but this wasn't like that: Leo looked at her *tenderly*. What was she feeling? *Shy!* She felt shy. *Idiot,* she thought to herself when her mind served up the word, *virginal*. She listened for some romantic soundtrack, but there was none. Just the sound of his breathing and hers.

When she came, her orgasm was intense. She didn't disappear into it, the earth didn't move, but something major had shifted.

Alone in her apartment, Millicent struggled to find the right word. *Having sex* was too anonymous, *sexual intercourse* too clinical, *fucking* left no room for the (apparently mutual?) caring from which their arousal had slowly and undramatically emerged. She couldn't think the phrase *making love* much less dare to apply it to them. She would gladly *see* Leo again. Do again whatever she wanted to call whatever they had shared. *Shared.* This word caused tears to slide down her cheeks. What if she was out of touch? She certainly had been before – deceived by her own yearnings again and again, imagining that men had feelings for her and intentions toward her which they had never signaled. What she and Leo had done together, they had, indeed, *shared*.

But the word she heard growling in her heart next was *hungry*. Had the word been *hot* – as in the flaunting of one's enjoyment of sex as an art form reserved for some equally gifted and sensual partner – that would have been a source of pride. *Hungry* was an accusation. Beggars are hungry. Rejects. *Hungry* equaled *shame.*

Who was she kidding? Leo choose *her*? A man whose life had taught him that "love just is" would pick somebody who also took such luxury for granted. Not the likes of her. She had better keep her *hunger* well hidden.

"We did it." Millicent told her sister.

"When?"

"In San Ensayo."

"You waited a week to tell me?"

"I have the right to a private life, you know."

"Well? How was it?"

"I don't know. Nice. No big deal."

"You mean he isn't big?"

"Actually, he is. Maybe too predictable, though, too domesticated."

"Try: 'normal'? Or: 'not likely to manipulate or betray you, cause you anguish or grief.'"

"It wasn't very passionate. It was okay. But there wasn't a lot of foreplay."

"Your cunt isn't the only organ in your orchestra."

"It's the one I play best."

"Practice the others."

8

Five weeks into the planned *whole entire summer with my dad*, Alice phoned, collect.

"Mommy, the kids at the 'Y' are mean. I wanna come home. Please?"

Millicent said nothing.

"Mom?"

"Have you talked to your father about it?"

"No."

"Talk to him."

"It won't help."

"Give him a chance," she said. "Learning to be more than just a vacation father can't be easy." They practiced then how Alice might speak out on her own behalf at camp and Millicent promised she'd talk to Neal about how to support her.

"Check out what's going on at the 'Y'," Millicent suggested to Neal, in as non-confronting a voice as she could muster.

"There are no problems here," he shot back with his customary flat-voiced, tight-lipped dismissiveness; no wonder she'd divorced him. But she had taken Alice from him before he'd had time to figure the fathering thing out. She had been a full-time parent all these years yet had needed Hermina's help to confront the Italian school principal. Poor Alice, stuck with two incompetent parents.

She had a sneaking suspicion that her hoping that Alice wouldn't need to come home early was selfish – that she didn't want to cut short this quarter-year vacation from single mothering. When they married and had Alice, she and Neal were emotional adolescents. This would be her first chance to get to know herself as a grown-up on her own. By mid-July, she'd received ten hefty Language Tour deposits, from six former students and four new ones. She was free to focus on herself, her life, her work. On Leo.

****

At summer's end, Millicent met Alice's evening flight home. She almost failed to recognize the twelve-going-on-twenty-year-old who teetered out of the gate in platform sandals, red lipstick and mascara, heavy black eye-liner, glittery blusher, dangly clip-on earrings and fake nails. Alice cut off their hello-hug by shoving a huge, battery-driven tape player into Millicent's hands while she rummaged through the contents of her orange vinyl, rhinestone-covered purse. It wasn't Neal's fault that Alice's breasts had grown so much in only eleven weeks, but the tank top that showed off her brand new cleavage was. And those very short shorts.

She drove them home to the banging of rock-and-roll and then endured an uncomfortable evening, as if Alice were some unsavory stranger in the house.

The next day, when Alice was about to leave to meet her friends, Millicent stopped her.

"Alice. I wish you'd wash that stuff off your face," she said, "and cover up a bit. Okay?" She was hoping she sounded good-humored.

But challenge filled the air as the haughty tilt of Alice's delicate chin and her silent sneer seemed to proclaim, *you can't make me! You have no power over me,* and, *I'm out of your control!*

"Come on, babe. Wipe off the lipstick, and while you're at it, please wipe that look off your face, too." Millicent turned, intending to walk away.

"Why should I?"

She swung around. "Because I am asking you to."

"That's no reason. Dad lets me," Alice threw back, as if she knew that would be a hard one to counter.

"Alice. Look at yourself!"

"Why? What's wrong with how I look?"

"You're twelve years old, for god's sake!"

"What's that got to do with anything?" Alice snapped back.

"Because a twelve-year-old shouldn't go around looking like…like a…a…*Slut*!"

Millicent had been biting her tongue since Alice had stepped off the plane to keep that slur from escaping. Now she'd said it, and the force behind the hurtling epithet seemed to hit Alice's gut like a cannon ball.

But Alice stood up straight and in a renewed wave of belligerence declared, "I'm not changing!" with her arms folded, one hip flung, saucy, out of kilter. "And you can't make me!"

Millicent raised her hand as if she wished she could slap her fresh daughter's face when the doorbell rang and Leo walked in, carrying a bouquet of wooden tulips for Alice.

With Millicent's back to him, he must not have seen her jaw-jutting, squinty-eyed maternal fury. *Otherwise,* she thought later, *he would have been furious at her, and rightly so; she was the grown-up here, the one who ought to have known better.* From his vantage point in the doorway, he saw only Alice and exclaimed, "You look so unhappy! What's wrong?"

Whereupon Alice's rigid chest armor loosened and she melted into tears. She uncrossed her arms and, to Millicent's grateful relief, reached out to wrap them around her startled mother. Alice wanted comfort from her? Maybe she hadn't disappointed her too much or too often, been too much like her own mother. Maybe that awful insult hadn't ripped through the child's too taut body and collapsed her into agreeing that, *yes*, she was bad, wrong, and she knew it and her mother was right, so right. Her wounded daughter whom she didn't want to wound even more!

When they all sat down together, Millicent teased out the full tale of the Chicago YMCA day-camp disaster. From the very beginning, Alice had broken local codes which she had no idea existed, by approaching whoever she thought she might like. How was she to know she should have classified people by skin color? It wasn't like that in Berkeley or in Italy, not for her anyway.

As her skin tanned, the black kids at the "Y" pegged her as Hispanic – the enemy. Some bigger girls taunted her, shoved her, hit her and one even threatened her with a knife. The Hispanic girls, who called her "White Toast Wonder Bread," wanted none of her hot-shit pretending that she was one of them. Alice explained to them, the way she'd practiced with her mother and also with Hermina on the phone, that their teasing made her feel bad. She told them how she tried to treat people and how she thought people should treat her. This approach actually worked with a couple of *Latinas*, who began to soften toward her until they, too, succumbed to pressure and backed off. That left only the white girls. They were *really* tough.

Except for Vicky, a scrawny, bleached-blonde fourteen-year-old white girl who stood up for Alice, though not against the girl with the knife; everybody, regardless of color, steered clear of her since it was obvious that she was crazy. Vicky taught Alice about make-up and about cleavage and how to make her breasts look even bigger, Alice told her mother, but not until Leo was out of the room. She trained her in flirty looks and "booty-shaking" until, at last, Alice aroused calls of "Check out those knockers!" from whatever group of boys she wobbled past on her platform sandals. Vicky claimed to have "*done it*" and Millicent asked her if she knew what that meant. "F. u. c. k." Alice spelled it out and said she didn't "*do it*" at all, no way, although, she confessed, she had kissed a couple of the boys. But when their hands found her breasts, she'd run off as fast as her shoes permitted. She also admitted that Vicky had introduced her to Tampax.

Millicent waited until Alice was asleep before venting her rage at Neal to Leo. That stupid man never considered that dropping a naïve girl into an inner-city environment would cause a culture shock she couldn't handle, no matter how world-traveled she was. Another "Y" might have offered more supervision. If Neal had claimed that money was the issue, she would have contributed to the cost of some place better for her. He'd done nothing to protect her. She'd hardened because she was suffering. Did Neal not see? Or did he not care?

9

"Why, one may well ask, would some Wacky Creator cause full breasts to pop out on the chest of a straight-hipped, four-foot-ten-inch twelve-year-old?" Millicent said, entering circuitously into her revelations about Leo and Alice. Hermina and Geena were visiting Millicent in Berkeley and Alice was out with her friends.

"I remember that shock," Geena shook her head.

"Boys have it easier – it's their feet that grow first," Millicent lamented. "All of us mothers were happy to coo at how cute and clumsy the pubescent son of a friend of mine was when he walked through the kitchen with his big feet flopping like a puppy in swim fins. But when my Alice walked through and the screen door slammed behind her – silence – more silence. Followed by envious, bitchy tit jokes.

"Then, oh my god, we go to the beach! Alice runs, hopping and waving, straight to her friends. In full sunlight, in her bikini, with those porn-star boobs bouncing."

"She is still a kid," Geena protested.

"You and I know that. But grown men leer. Have you forgotten how it was, Geena? Oh, for a bell jar to put over my Alice."

Millicent described how vigilant she'd been, watching as the teenage boys' eyes followed Alice, joking, whooping, making gawky geeks of themselves. And how one Lothario, who surely knew he was too old for Alice, walked right up to her. "He put his arm across her shoulder and guided her toward a grove of trees and cupped his palm right there, looking as if he thought he was one clever guy. And Alice, she leans into this wannabe Don Juan and looks up into his eyes while licking her ice cream cone. I *mean*…"

Millicent raced up to them and Mr. Young Buck unhanded the girl. He was defensive at first and then indignant. "Take it easy, Mama," he said, with all the arrogance he could muster.

Murdering her mother with a glare, Alice zigzagged among the beach towels and plunged into the very cold water – which she'd previously proclaimed she wouldn't do because it would mess up her hair. She paddled frantically to the far side of the lifeguard's rowboat that was drifting around a buoy and held on to it as if this was a game of tag and her mother couldn't get at her because she was safe on base.

When Millicent beckoned for Alice to come out of the water she shook her wet curls, no. Millicent beckoned again, adjusting her face so she looked serious rather than what she was – lost, frightened and, to her shame, angry. Alice shook her head, less emphatically, then swam to shore. When Millicent reached out to wrap a towel around her narrow shoulders, ostensibly to provide warmth, Alice flinched.

"Sweetie," Millicent recalled saying, hoping she didn't sound panicky, "I've never had a kid your age before so I don't know how to do this. Let's take a break. Grab your things and let's go home."

Alice shook off her mother's hands with a huff and marched back to her girlfriends. From the look on her face, she seemed to be snarling something like, *my mother's such a bitch!* She sulked all the way home in the car, went straight to her room and slammed the door.

Millicent phoned Leo, determined not to fall prey to the fear that he might reject her as a fallen woman with a rapidly falling daughter. She admitted to him how incompetent she felt to help young Alice bear the confusing burden of such over-dimensioned beauty. She couldn't yet confess her terrors of facing Alice's puberty alone – being the horny single mother of a ragingly hormonal child. Her fear of Frankensteining into a rival who attempted to seduce all the luscious young guys Alice would attract. Or, an alternative nightmare: that she'd want to be so insanely strict that, to protect Alice from her over-protection, she'd let her run wild.

Leo said he'd be there right after work and reassured Millicent that everything would be okay.

When he arrived he hugged Millicent and suggested she invite Alice to come out of her room so that they could talk to her together. Millicent sat on the sofa and he on one of the swivel chairs. Her mascara smudged, Alice glowered in a sweatshirt and jeans as Leo gestured for her to sit in the other swivel chair. Instead, she crossed her arms and perched on the far end of the sofa, ready to bolt.

"Have you heard the phrase, *body language*?" Leo began, in a friendly manner, as if Alice weren't bristling. He didn't seem the least bit afraid of her, Millicent noted.

"No," she stated bluntly, but her tone said, *I don't know and I don't care.*

"It's the message our body sends out even if our words are saying something else," Leo explained. "Know what I mean?" No answer. "So, are you aware that sometimes your body language may seem to be saying something that you don't mean to?"

"Like what?" Alice said, unimpressed.

"Like, *I want to do it. Let's do it?"*

Her jaw had dropped and her face cramped. She craned her neck forward and shot her mother a look – a rich blend of contempt and fear. Blinking hard she engaged her entire mouth in saying, "*What?*"

Leo smiled. "There's nothing wrong with that as such. Sometime, when you're older that will be just the message you'll want your body to give. But if you're sending out *let's do it!* messages without meaning to, boys might think you are telling them to *go ahead*. If they start to fool around with you a little and suddenly you won't let them do that, they might feel tricked. Maybe even angry. Boys your age and even older aren't always good at controlling themselves – some don't even try to be good at it."

Alice and Millicent remained silent, but Alice uncrossed her arms. She looked confused.

"Here's what I suggest," Leo said. "Now that you're aware that your body might be sending out a *let's do it* invitation, check to see if you like how the boys react. I'm not your parent but I think you're too young to *do it*, and I'd bet that your mother agrees with me." Millicent nodded, emphatically. "When you're older and really ready, it will be important to let her or some other grown-up know – because there's things you'll need to understand then."

He paused, but he wasn't finished. "Know what else, Alice?" he went on. "You could experiment with sending out *different* kinds of messages, maybe friendly, hello messages – and check to see how you like the way the boys react then. And the girls, too. Does that make any sense?" Alice sat mute.

"I expect your mom would be glad to talk more with you about all of this. Right, Millicent?" Millicent had bobbed her head again as if it were on a spring. Alice looked from Leo to her mother, to Leo again and back to her mother, as if she were adrift in foreign seas. Millicent didn't know how to navigate now either. Somehow, she had to figure out how on earth to behave like a grown-up, like the female counterpart to this informative, respectful, grown-up man.

Millicent explained to Geena and Hermina her sudden revelation: *So this is what fathers are for!* Lucky Alice. "Can you imagine, Geena, the grief we could have been spared if Daddy had explained all of that to us when we were twelve?"

Alice's 'body language' had softened; she looked close to tears and as if she would gladly hug someone if the distance hadn't been too great to cross. But then Leo stood up and did the crossing for her. "You're a fine girl," he said, giving her a quick, *paternal* hug and kissing the top of her head. Alice's arms jerked up and, as she was returning his hug she looked at her mother as if to ask permission. A smile had spread over Millicent's face and tears came to her eyes. "It's okay, baby," she said.

Alice went to her room and closed her door, quietly. Before Leo left, he and Millicent shared a long embrace. They'd agreed that, for now, he'd sleep over only when Alice wasn't home; the girl had enough of her own hormones to balance without theirs leaking through the thin walls.

Millicent and Alice spent that evening together as if nothing major had transpired. Alice washed her face and tamed her hair into a pony tail and they agreed to play 'CLUE'. Alice won – the Butler in the Dining Room with the Rope – speaking with a British accent while Millicent made choking noises. They laughed a lot.

"There's more," Millicent said, eying Geena and Hermina over her glass of sparkling water, enjoying the intensity of their listening. "Want to hear the rest?"

"You bet," they said.

"Yesterday, Leo suggested that we go to the beach together," Millicent continued. "He asked if I'd mind if he had a word with Alice's would-be seducer."

"This should be good!" Geena grinned.

Leo walked up to the boy and made it clear to him – "young man," he called him – that someone his age had no business messing with a twelve-year-old. "He seemed genuinely shocked that she was *that* young. And worried when Leo promised him there would be consequences which he would not like if Leo ever had cause to seek him out again. What a metamorphosis: tough stud to guilty twerp."

When Millicent finished the story, the three women sat silent.

"Sounds like you may have found yourselves a very nice man," Hermina said.

Millicent looked down and said, as if to herself. "I know. He's great. Especially for Alice. But is he right for me?"

****

"We are well and truly screwed, my dear Millicent," Geena said when she phoned one morning, her voice trembling.

"What's wrong?"

"Somebody I know from San Ensayo just called to congratulate me on the marriage of my mother."

"What?!"

"Unbelievable, huh? Apparently, there was a little announcement in the San Ensayo paper, but the lady who called had the inside dope. I couldn't tell if she'd phoned to torment me or to probe for more juicy details."

"Geena! Are you serious? What is this?"

"According the woman, our brand new 'step-father' – I may puke! – is a notorious gold-digger, a con-artist high-roller somewhere in his 70s who decks himself out in glitzy, Las Vegas-type sports clothes, most likely over a girdle to hide his paunch. He's a member of the Owners' Association of Mother's building. That's where they met." Millicent tried to remember if she'd seen somebody who looked like that at the attack-on-the-subletting-widow meeting she'd witnessed when she first came home.

"The third of this guy's contentious divorces apparently just made headlines down there because he sued to have his ex-wife pay *him* spousal support and he lost. Millicent – I do hope you're sitting down – he and Mother went to some shyster lawyer together to draw up new wills, naming each the *sole* beneficiary of the other. So much for our patrimony. Mother's bragging all over town that he divorced a witch to marry an angel. *She* will make sure he's cared for in his twilight years. And she's totally convinced he'll do the same for her. Stupid dupe."

Disinherited? Millicent felt dizzy. Even after all she'd learned, this would take some time to shake down within her.

"I wonder if she plans to tell us," Millicent said, amazed that not being invited to her mother's wedding could actually hurt her feelings. "You think we'll ever see her again?"

"Oh, yes. She'll expect a gift. Mother did claim to have promised our dying father not to let us rip her off."

"Daddy would be horrified," Millicent said, "I'm sure! And worried for her."

“I really don’t know about that, Millicent. We’ll just have to believe whatever we need to about the past. And in the meantime, as Billie Holiday warned, Mommy and Daddy might be rich, but God blesses the girl that’s got her own.

10

Waiting in New York for her October Language Tour students to land was almost as bad as waiting at the airport for Alice. Millicent's shoulders relaxed, her chest expanded and her belly unclenched when Rosanna, her student from Puglia who had proposed the tour in the first place, waved at her wildly as she exited Customs, then ran to embrace her. "*Lo sapevo fin dall'inizio! Avevo ragione! E qui ci siamo!"* ("I knew it right away! I was right! And here we are!") she said as the other returning students gathered around, the three men and three women looking at Millicent as if she were a beloved relative.

Rosanna introduced the new students, a young, corporate-looking, Milanese couple with wide, formal smiles and two middle-aged Roman women.

A van took the jet-lagging group to the Hyatt Hotel near Grand Central Station. Their full-on itinerary would begin the following morning when Millicent turned them over to Maya, the Argentinean tour guide whom Sigrid had recommended, who would herd them to the Empire State Building, the Museum of Modern Art, then back to Millicent for their afternoon lessons and the evening's entertainment.

"Whoopi Goldberg on Broadway", the centerpiece of their first weekend, left Millicent's Italians wide-eyed, thrilled. And overwhelmed; they didn't understand a word. Millicent took copious notes during the performance and then decoded Whoopi's sly cultural send-ups for them the next afternoon.

Ciccia, one of the Roman ladies, assumed the role of the Class Clown, sprayed streams of juicy language in a *romanaccio* dialect to mimic Whoopi's "Fontaine" character – a black, male, globe-trotting, junkie thief with a PhD in literature. "English please!" Millicent shouted back good-humoredly above the laughter.

On Wednesday in Los Angeles, however, Maya warned Millicent of a fomenting revolt. Ciccia and the other new Roman student, Flavia, had joined forces to stoke each other's discontent: the New York jazz clubs had been squalid and the view from their Manhattan window seedy; the Italian food in West L.A. was lousy; the La Brea tar pits were only pits of tar; the homework was too demanding and kept them from enjoying the sites. When even Disneyland evoked gripes, the other students complained that "*le due rompicoglioni*" ("those two ball-busters") were souring the trip.

The griping ebbed once they reached San Francisco. The cable car bell clanged precisely as expected and the deliciously steep descent left several of the women shrieking, "*Frena! Frena!*" ("Put the brakes on!") like kids on a roller-coaster. Their meal at Fisherman's Wharf reduced their contempt for American cuisine and the quality of Union Square shopping suggested that "American Fashion" might not be an oxymoron after all. Each student seemed to grasp what a privilege it was to be among the 50,000 ecstatic fans at Oakland Coliseum for Bruce Springsteen's iconic, "*Born in the U.S.A.*" concert.

There were many experiences Millicent wouldn't be able to offer: no Alcatraz, no boat trip under the Golden Gate Bridge, no chilly Pacific beach combing, no Exploratorium, no Palace of Fine Arts, no eighty-five meter tall, two-thousand-year old redwood trees. But filled with enthusiasm – for the experience, the country, their teacher – most of them assured her, "Don't worry. We'll be back."

She'd prepared essay questions for a final exam based on the new film of Orwell's "*1984*" starring Richard Burton and John Hurt, which they'd be seeing together. Ciccia and Flavia, however, stood up in class and announced that they weren't coming. They had made other plans. When Millicent reminded them that failing the exam would cost them their course certification, the lid blew off. "It's your job to please us," Ciccia hollered. "We're the ones bankrolling this stupid course, financing that fancy, red cashmere blazer of yours. *Che te ne frega, figlia di mignotta?*" ("What the fuck do you care, you daughter of a whore!")

As she explained, step-by-step, the pedagogical structure of the course she had designed, Millicent's voice shook. But Ciccia's tirade went on so long and so loud that a Hyatt House security guard came to check what was wrong.

Sneering and whispering, Ciccia and Flavia stood arm in arm beside the van and refused to board. Millicent held her breath waiting to see if the others would join in the mutiny, but everyone except the two "*maladette megere*" ("damned bitches") climbed in.

Throughout the film, and afterwards, in her hotel room, late into the night, Millicent's mind assailed her with the merciless internal diatribes she'd hoped she'd grown beyond and would never hear again. She was a failure, an incompetent, a useless organizer, unfit for any position of authority. She was a bad person, loved by no one, deserving love from no one, hardly deserving to live.

She picked up the telephone, then hung up. Once, twice. Finally, she dialed. Leo was at her apartment in Berkeley, ready to celebrate the end of the course with her the following evening.

Crying, she had hardly choked out three sentences before he said, "I'm on my way," and hung up.

For a few moments, she lay on the bed feeling relieved. Then, a full regressive panic struck. Berkeley to San Francisco at 1:00 a.m. – maybe half an hour to get ready. She showered quickly, nicked her ankle shaving and when the bleeding wouldn't stop she stuck on a wad of toilet paper. Then she ransacked her luggage in vain looking for something sexy to wear. Unlike with Fabrizio, she wasn't worried that Leo might not show up. He'd come. But then what? She was a mess, a mortifying mess.

She wrapped a hotel bath towel around herself like a sari, but it was too heavy and kept falling off. She put on a bra and panties instead – she needed to have something on for him to take off. She applied lipstick and blusher. Her hand shook while she put on mascara; she poked the wand into her eye which burned and watered and made her nose run. When she put on her high heels she ripped the toilet paper off her ankle and re-opened the cut. Why the fuck had she phoned him?

He knocked, she unlocked the door, he came in and looked at her, confused. "You're getting dressed? Are we going out?"

She threw her arms around his neck and shoved her tongue deep into his mouth, but he eased her away. "What's happening, Millicent? You look so…"

She stepped back. "I 'look so…' what?" Why had he pushed her away?

"Well, like Alice when she first came home from her dad's."

"*Slutty*?" She stepped farther back. Pissed off. Belligerent.

"No. Lost," he said, then added, softly, "and scared."

Those eyes. Like Geena and Hermina's in the mirror in Rome when she didn't drink the Drano, telling her, tenderly, *you're okay, sweetheart*. Millicent saw him look at her that way. She let herself be held.

He undressed, she washed her face and put on her warm pajamas, they climbed into bed and she told him everything – not just about tonight, but also the Drano story and the San Jose trailer truck she'd resisted the urge to crash into. Afterwards, he said, "It sounds like hating yourself is sort of like riding a bike. Once they teach you, you can never forget. You'll always know how."

He kissed her, gently. Then harder. Soon he entered her, and when she came, the pulsating waves spread upward to her chest. She pressed her chest to his. She needed to. For a long time.

He was asleep when she got up to pee. She caught a glimpse of herself in the bathroom mirror. Could it be? Those eyes she saw looking at her – they were *her* eyes. Was this an illusion? Could that really be *Millicent* looking at *Millicent*, with love?

She'd learned to be the good mother she'd never had, thanks to Geena and maybe even their father. This moment was different. New. Now she was learning to be the *daughter* of the good mother she'd never had. Letting good mothering in. Why had that taken longer? Maybe it was easier to *give* what she'd yearned for and needed than it was to *receive* what she'd yearned for and needed.

Back in bed, she thought about what Leo had said. Maybe loving and being loved were also like riding a bike – or even better, like speaking a new language. Once they teach you, you never forget how. Not completely, anyway, even if you'll always have a funny accent.

The following morning, Ciccia and Flavia shuffled, pouting, into the class conference room. Millicent, exhausted, but in no way humiliated, directed a redemptive gaze at them that was like the one she'd seen last night, although, more formal. She told them quietly that she had arranged for tickets and transportation for them to see a matinee showing of the film they'd missed. She hoped they would go. She did not want them to fail this course.

Their bravado wilted, they went to the movie, took the exam and even passed it. That evening, as the group hugged and thanked Millicent before boarding the shuttle bus to their flight to Italy, a subdued Ciccia looked almost as if she might apologize.

****

Enrico phoned just before Thanksgiving. *Lingua Nuova* had been receiving glowing responses from the participants. The relief she heard in his voice was predictable; the extravaganza had proved profitable. But she also heard a new quality of respect. She contracted for a Language Tour next Easter, this time to Silicon Valley, to New Orleans – and to Chicago, a city Millicent knew well. She warned him that the applications for this course would have to include screening questions. She was determined to weed out the Phyllis-like Ciccias. But there was something more in Enrico's voice. Was it softness? They could have been quite a couple, if he had dared. Okay, if *they* had dared. They reminisced on the phone about those first summers in Chicago, about how hot they'd been together, and about Alice twirling his long hair around her finger as he read to her. Enrico had acted like a shit, but he wasn't a bad man. They'd both been young and culturally stupid. She missed him. Maybe she always would.

She noticed that Enrico hadn't mentioned Mariangela and she hadn't referred to Leo as anything but her business consultant.

11

Alice was still in her pjs when Leo arrived to pick them up for their first shared vacation trip, Thanksgiving weekend. “You didn’t see me!” she yelled as she ran past him to her room and then reappeared, her hair neatly braided and her clothes on straight. She nodded hello, but Leo pulled her in for a quick and gentle hug; she explained what she had packed and they talked through what else she might need. Millicent watched them speak directly to one another – two individuals, separate from her.

In the cabin, she caught herself having tickling bouts with Alice, playing games of indoor catch with a rolled up sock, as if Leo weren’t there; she was aware momentarily that, for once, she wasn’t performing for a man. Occasionally, she checked his eyes for judgment of her, but in them she found no condemnation of her as a single mother who treated her child like a sibling, or as a mother who needed to keep her child a child.

He didn’t join in their games; instead, he shared his own – guy-stuff, like off-trail hikes which they never would have risked alone. He had bought Alice a pocket knife and helped her build a lean-to in the woods.

When Millicent awoke from an afternoon nap in the cabin bedroom that she and Alice were sharing, she heard voices and wondered who was visiting. Alice and Leo, seated in facing easy chairs, were having a discussion, about capital punishment. He nodded to Millicent as she passed through on her way to the kitchen alcove. She kept her back to them while she buttered toast for herself, unsure if the emotions flooding her were joy for the moment of family feeling or sadness that her own father had never really discussed anything with her. Or, was she afraid? She’d been wrong so often; she and Alice might lean into this apparently nice man only to discover there was something wrong with him. Or, he might not want to stay.

In Berkeley again, Leo helped them with their bags, gave Alice a hug and tousled her hair; then he gave Millicent a solid, PG-rated kiss which Alice watched intently. The moment he left, that old, vestigial Voice of the Grand Accuser blared once again in Millicent's head. The only phone calls he'd made during their five days away together had been to his kids. Didn't the guy have any friends? Was he an isolated creep? Some Humbert on a campaign to gain their trust? Her heart raced, her mouth filled with the metallic taste of fear, her eyes blinked as Terrible Truth, *Real Reality*, made itself clear and she walked into Alice's room.

"Alice?" Millicent's brow was furrowed. "You like Leo, right?"

"Sure," she said and continued composing outfits from the clothes she had strewn across her bed.

"You don't think there's something really *wrong* with him?"

"Are you nuts?" The left side of Alice's top lip pulled up into a sneer and, in a sing-songy voice, she said, "No, Mom. There's nothing wrong with Leo. And I like him a lot."

****

Leo had celebrated Chanukah with them at Hermina's – it was Patsy's year to have the kids visiting for Christmas. By New Year's, Alice seemed to have grown more comfortable with her mother and Leo showing each other affection and he began staying over in Millicent's bed even when Alice was at home. They made sure she was asleep before they made love, which they did far more quietly than Millicent preferred.

As Alice lay awake one rainy, winter night and watched the lights from passing cars rise up the wall, change shape and color, cross the ceiling and disappear, she thought about Leo. He was okay. A lot okay. The air in their house was chubbier when he was there. What color? She was learning about colors from Geena who also loved them. Magenta, maybe. With chocolate-brown.

She liked it when it was just her and her mom – sky-blue and aquamarine. Though sometimes it was ketchup-red and poop-yellow. With just the two of them at home, she could be alone, just her, with her mother around, but not right there. She liked that. Sometimes when Leo stayed over, she felt a different alone. Alone without anybody. That color – a see-through green – scared her. Then she missed her dad.

Other times, though, she and her mom and Leo were like a braid, like in Rome with her mom and Hermina. Each of them had their own colored strings, all the same thickness. What colors were hers? Not Barbie-pink-and-purple – they worked for her bedroom but not for her. Her colors were more like the rain. Not rain on grass. Rain on a sidewalk. Rain on Roman cobblestones – on *sampietrini*.

Earlier that day, her mom and Leo had been sitting together on the sofa and she'd stood in front of them and showed them the patchwork square she'd made for the quilt project at sewing class. When all the kids finished their squares, they'd sew them into a quilt that would hang in the school stairwell. Her square was a house with multicolored calico doors under silvery-gray and silky-white clouds.

She'd been collecting remnants, and also clothes from the health food store's free-box to cut up, taking everything from grown-up's dresses to babies' pants as long as she liked the cloth or the print or the colors. She cut swatches and moved them around and watched how one was happier when she put it next to another. Or madder. Or bored. Sometimes the pieces argued, "No! I want to be next to the checkerboard swatch!" "No! Me! I do!"

A great thing about fabric was that she could cut it and suddenly have *two* checkerboards. Then, the brocade with raised yellow polka dots on a silky pink background and the solid – oh, what was the name she'd just learned for it: *mauve!* – and the solid *mauve* denim could both have their own black and white checkerboard swatch right by them. The checkerboard loved it when they fought over her, how they both wanted her.

She could see that her mother and Leo really liked her school quilt square. While they looked at her holding it up, their heads tilted the exact same way and they had identical smiles. They really liked her, too. Alice saw her own colors then as a beautiful, swirly mix that reminded her of the rainbow spot on the driveway after her mother's car had leaked oil.

Would she be glad if Leo were there all the time? Once, she and her mother were having a fight and he'd put his hand on her arm and his eyes got black and he said, "Didn't you hear your mother tell you to stop shouting, Alice?" She'd thrown his hand off her and yelled at him, "You're not my father! You can't decide over me. You have to marry my mother if you want to be my father!"

If he did, what colors would *that* square be?

And what would that do to her dad's square? She didn't even know what colors her dad's square was. She tried to picture it, but she fell asleep.

****

For a full quarter hour in advance of Leo's arrival, Millicent stood watch at the window: she was determined to learn the *Real Truth* of her feelings for him. He pulled up, parallel parked masterfully (*Laborers park trucks for a living,* came the Phyllis-ism) and climbed down from the truck's cab. No mistaking it: he looked good. For the first time in a long time, her inner radio switched on, blaring insipid doggerel, soppy tunes about never having been in love before, about loving now and forever more. She opened her door and when he wrapped his arms around her, she felt like she'd come home. Maybe not a *happily-ever-after* home, but certainly no *Phyllis-and-Herb* home.

Out of the blue, while driving across the Bay Bridge the other evening, he'd started talking finances. He and Patsy had set up trust funds when their kids were born so their college educations would be covered. His alimony payments had stopped when Meg turned eighteen. His father had left him and his sister in good financial shape. His share of the company yielded him a solid, annual income. And, he said, he was free to move north: Bettina and the San Ensayo staff would cover for him while he focused on expanding Lombardi & Sons' Bay Area operations.

"It was like I was my own father and he was a suitor laying out his honorable intentions before asking for Millicent's hand in marriage," she said on her weekly catch up with Geena.

"How did you feel?"

"As if, somebody had dropped a heavy toolbox on my chest from a great height. I changed the subject."

"Why?"

"You'll think I'm really dumb."

"I know already that you are."

"Maybe we're just not made for each other. Maybe there's something really wrong with him. His wife left him for a reason, though I don't know why I should trust the opinions of someone who calls herself 'Patsy'? He can be as stiff as a board on the phone."

"A stiff man is good to find," Geena said.

"You know me, Geena. If I'm horny enough, I can turn a Pop-Tart into a *Monte Bianco*, so how can I know he's okay for me? Besides, the guy can't play. He isn't a player." She'd never tried the ploys she'd used on Fabrizio on him – it just didn't seem right somehow. He picked up after himself, washed his own laundry, washed the dishes when she cooked – he wasn't like having a second child in the house. But, the more time he spent at her place, the more toiletries and clothes he moved in, and papers, and blueprints. And tools.

His tools had sparked their first full-blown argument. Lombardi & Sons had a San Francisco workshop and a warehouse, but Leo didn't always stop to unload his equipment there after work. She had already filled up the storage space their landlord let them use in his cellar. Leo couldn't leave his expensive electric jigsaw, his drills or his measuring instruments in his truck parked on the street all night or they'd have been stolen. So he brought them into the apartment! Tools, Millicent had proclaimed, are ugly and don't belong in anybody's living room.

"You can't have it your way all the time, Millicent," he'd said.

"Well, Mr. Sense-of-Entitlement, you can't just barge in here and spread out like a fungus!"

She had never factored bad habits into her calculations. He left the radio on constantly, tuned in to hokey stations. He heaped his dusty clothes onto one of the bedroom chairs at night, his socks spreading their blue-cheese stink throughout the whole apartment. He didn't like Bob Dylan. He only liked action movies and fell asleep during sensitive art films that moved her to tears. She had presumed that the opposite of never being sure if a man would ever phone you again was some sort of domestic idyll, to which one ascribed the word *love*. Could it be (was she *still* so thick?) that a real relationship was just regular life with mutual affection and sex added? Like soup-in-a-cup, just add hot water and spice?

It was, she had to admit, a very convenient system simply to turn over in bed and get laid without having to pack and take a train. Neither she nor Alice liked it when Leo spent the entire work week off in San Ensayo. At first, Millicent luxuriated in stretching out across the bed, but when Alice wanted to crawl in with her, she was grateful for the company. Was life in general better with Leo than without him? She switched her inner radio off each time the damned thing started playing, '*Sometimes When We Touch*', especially those confessional lines about wanting to hold on and never let go.

"He handed me a bouquet of flowers he bought the other day like they were some box of nails I'd ordered from Lombardi & Sons." Re-running the moment, Millicent had to acknowledge his wry smile, one of those facial micro-expressions she'd read that policemen watch for to check if somebody is telling the truth. Then he grabbed her up into a big, tweedy hug; foreplay it wasn't, or even romance, but she liked it. Their sex was like heat without flash, a flame that burned blue instead of the red that she was used to. Blue flames, she knew, were hotter.

"So he does have a libido then?"

"Yes. We do it often." But Patsy's word *lonely* continued to haunt her. "Don't be mad at me, Geena, but I'm still not sure Leo's the man for me."

"You really are a jerk," Geena said. "And you break my heart."

12

Hermina waited with Millicent on the couch one afternoon in late February, her lap filled with embroidery thread, hoops, needles. She and Alice had traced a pattern onto a piece of fabric using carbon paper. When she came home from school, Hermina would show her how to make the French knots her own mother had patiently taught her almost seven decades ago.

The phone rang and Millicent answered it. "Will you accept a collect call from Italy, from Mr. Donizetti?" With the air knocked out of her, her eyebrows shot up, her heart galloped and she answered, "Yes!" She mouthed, "It's *Fabrizio*!" to Hermina who looked confused at first, probably thinking she must mean Enrico. But then she shook her head slowly, side to side. Millicent carried the phone into the kitchen.

"*Ciao bella,*" Fabrizio crooned as if no time had passed. He'd called the place in Rome where she used to work and they'd given him her U.S. phone number. He said he'd decided to forgive her. He said he and his wife had split up "*all'italiana*," – they were still living together but slept in separate bedrooms. He'd been offered a gig sailing around the Mediterranean photographing luxury yachts. "*Vieni con me?*" he said, stressing "*vieni,*" meaning "come." He said she could join him at Sorrento.

He referred to the proposed meeting as a *riunione,* the phrase he'd used with her when he'd wanted his colleagues to believe he was phoning a client. He'd know just how she'd picture them 're-uniting.' She fell right back in. All their code words, innuendos, salacious laughter. She felt sophisticated for the first time since moving back to California. She felt aroused. Wet.

She said, "I'll need some time, to plan," then added, "and to think." Her inner radio turned on just then blaring Lucio Dalla's "*Ma Come Fanno i Marinai*" about a sailor who wonders if the heartless women he's left in every port still think about him now and then. She told Fabrizio she'd call him tomorrow. She wrote his phone number on the refrigerator note pad and, after exchanging a few more lip-licking double entendres, they hung up. Her legs shook as she returned to the living room.

Hermina sat there, hands collapsed onto her lap, her face filled with the intense grief that was usually about Sam.

"To what end, Millicent?" Hermina asked softly. "*Per arrivare dove*?"

Per arrivare dove? Millicent's juices dried right up. Good question – to arrive where? In fact, her first reaction as she'd pictured bobbing across the Mediterranean clutching Fabrizio's camera bag in one hand and his dick in the other had been a mix of nausea and exhaustion. Now came shame: Fabrizio calls – *collect* – and what does she do? *Accepts the charges*. He pushes "play" and she bursts into song. Their songs. What's awful is that she loves singing them. Feels flattered to be asked. And even worse: grateful.

Pathetic.

Seating herself on the swivel chair farthest from Hermina, she crossed her arms and said, through tight lips, "I don't know, Hermina. *Per arrivare dove?* Leo can be so stiff. Boring. Unromantic. We go from sitting on the sofa to penetration without a how-do-you-do. I just don't know, Hermina.

"Sometimes, I'm lonely with him. There's so much of me he can't even register, much less meet or play on or with. So much of me is wasted on him."

"And so much of Sam was wasted on me. I had no idea until I met you and Geena how deaf I'd been to some of the music of that man. Now, I miss the whole of him, including the songs I couldn't hear until after he was gone. What *I* wasted. Time doesn't help. I miss him more the longer he's dead." Hermina shook her head.

Millicent continued, as if she hadn't been listening. "Why did I choose Leo? For stability? Because Alice's hormones scare me? He's interesting and smart and a good person. But he's so predictable."

"You mean 'reliable' don't you? Yes. And also he's kind, and so are you. Those are some good grounds for a life together."

"Will they be enough? Will I start resenting him for everything he isn't, start attacking him, demeaning him, turn into a cruel she-wolf like my mother?" She couldn't bear the look on Hermina's face just then. "Don't worry. I'll call Fabrizio and wish him *un buon viaggio* without me.

"My choice isn't between him and Leo. It's between Leo and *not* Leo. I was happy before I met him. If I choose anyone at all, it should be someone who makes my life even better. Otherwise, what's the point?"

After a pause, Hermina addressed Sam softly as if he were in the room with them, something Millicent hadn't heard her do for months. "Forgive me, my love," she said. "First I lose our Inanna and now I fail to fix our Millicent." Tears ran down her cheeks.

Millicent waited until they had subsided to say, quietly, but firmly: "I know you don't mean that, Hermina. I was wounded, yes, even damaged. But I'm so much better now. Now I know I'm not irreparable and it's you who's proven that to me. You and Sam."

Hermina winced, and Millicent sat straighter.

After a pause, Hermina continued. "Yes. But you do still apply the skewed logic you learned in childhood that leaves you ignorant of where your true beauty lies, your value. But then, no one raised in such an abusive family could be expected to have perspective, to even realize *that* they don't know, much less *what* it is that they don't know."

Millicent was listening.

"Of course this next phase you're hesitating to enter with Leo is frightening. Nothing in life is as intimate, as vulnerable, naked and exposed as mature sexual love. But it's worth the risk. You've seen how Sam keeps helping me grow, even from the grave."

"Yes."

"He's still my oxygen – essential. How can I tell you, Millicent? To discover the power that a profound love has to heal and re-shape and bring joy to both people, you have to dare to let it happen."

As several more tears dropped onto the rainbow of embroidery threads spread across Hermina's lap, each one shining like a jewel, Hermina appeared, suddenly, frail. Old.

"Please don't cry," Millicent said.

"Please don't sabotage this precious opportunity to participate in the best that life has to offer."

Hermina blew her nose and then laughed. "*If*, that is, I know what's right for you. Which, maybe, I don't. Sam would undoubtedly remind me to trust you to navigate by your own maturing wisdom. And, sweetheart," she sighed, "he would be right, as usual." Her gaze overflowed with tenderness.

Millicent drank it in. She moved aside the embroidery hoops and fabrics and packets of sewing needles and skeins of thread to make a space for herself. She placed Hermina's arms around her and rested her head on Hermina's breast.

"I know I'm ineffectual as well as arrogant," Hermina said stroking her hair. "But you do feel my love for you, don't you?"

"Yes."

"I've wished my love could teach you about Life to spare you Life's pain. And to help you choose good love," she said, placing a kiss on Millicent's forehead. "Isn't that what a mother is for?"

They sat there for a long time and were still there together when Alice came home from school. They made room for her in between them.

13

Alone in bed that night, Millicent tried hard to forgive herself for allowing Fabrizio's phone call to pull her that far back, to shake her new foundations. She didn't miss Fabrizio, the person; she missed sex as her performance art. She remembered an Erica Jong quote about failed artists, how their creative energy, having no outlet, imploded "…in a great black fart of rage that smokes up all the inner windows of the soul." Leo deserved better from her.

Hermina had told her, "Grown-ups don't use sexuality merely for erotic display, but also to express love." Was Millicent starving for applause to confirm her existence, now that Daddy was dead?

Maybe she and Fabrizio had achieved sexual heights Hermina and Sam knew nothing about.

Or: might Leo, Hermina and Sam know something she didn't, about some art form embedded in Ordinary Life? What the fuck would that be? And: What would *that* fuck be?

Perhaps she could have it both ways: explore the *love* part of *making love* with Leo while also tutoring him in the *art* of sex, the way people offer music appreciation courses. He was good raw material – a lusty, competent, considerate lover – and she was a good teacher, teaching being her second most developed talent.

Terrific start for a life together, like the lady in the cartoon saying, "*You're everything I've always wanted to change in a man.*"

They'd begun as friends which admitted him to the same exclusive club as Geena and Hermina. He and Alice had a friendship, too. She and Alice could talk to him about anything and trust that he'd never shame them. He was never mean, not even when he was angry. He knew they were quirky and they could count on him to object whenever he disagreed, but his endorsement of them as individual human beings was unequivocal.

When she stood on tip-toe to press her chest against his, she didn't feel like a child in the safety of a father's arms, though there was an echo of that. Nor, despite the protective impulses that often washed through her, was she like the mother of a son grown tall. The word '*lover*' pulsed in her, but not as a stopping place. In fact, there was no stopping, only resting, in an eddy in the midst of the dizzying currents of Life. Carrying them toward what? *Love?* That sounded adolescent. Surely, there was a bigger word. Or had she always made that word shrink?

A thought then struck her which made her sit up and turn on the light: *What if it was too late to back out?*

She'd kept Fabrizio away from Alice. But she had let Leo slide deep into their lives, heedless of the consequences. The implications. He had not only told his kids about her and Alice – he had introduced them all to each other at a boisterous family gathering at Bettina's. She'd liked his Meg and Brandon and they'd seemed to like her and Alice.

Here it was, mortifyingly self-evident revelation number umpteen-thousand: If she told Leo he wasn't the man for her, *she wouldn't be seeing him or his family any more*. How could she ever make her heart hard enough to rip Leo out of her life? Out of Alice's? How could she possibly tell him he'd be losing them? *What a body-blow!* She thought of the grunt Jocasta had knocked out of Atlas's chest when she'd hit him, and of her own mother's cruelty, and of the breathy "No!" Leo had described coming from Brandon, when he and Patsy had announced they were divorcing. If she rejected Leo, he would be hurt, and she would see it! She would have to face the wounded Leo. Leo in pain. *Pain that she herself had caused him.*

Her anguish at the thought of Leo in pain, of inflicting pain on Leo, at the thought of him losing them, of them losing him, said it. She loved this person. And he loved her. Them.

There it was: She loved Leo. And she could let him love her. The feel of his hand resting on the nape of her neck as they walked. The way he listened to her elaborately embellished problems, waited, and then offered some startlingly wise, capsule resolution. His respect, his intolerance for disrespect, his subdued, heartfelt laugh, his absence of artifice.

They were an "Us." *Us.* Two separate, fallible people, in it together with everything: the laundry, the dishes, the cuddles, the menstrual blood, the pimples, the contracts and lesson plans, the longings and the disappointments, the conversations, the achievements, the arguments, the outings, Alice, Meg, Brandon, Geena, Hermina, the electric tools, the wounds – the wounds, new and old, the foibles – his and hers, the scent of him, the taste, his erections, their orgasms, the laughter, his loving eyes, their kisses, his tenderness, and her own. The two of them, doing the best they could given what they knew, then doing their best to do better as soon as they knew more.

Two whole Ones. Together.

Epilogue

Leo turned to Millicent in bed one Sunday morning that spring and said, "Yesterday, I looked at a house for sale that might work for us. It's near here so Alice wouldn't have to change schools. There's room for all three of our kids."

He described the layout, the yard, his work room, her office space, at a price that, together, they could afford.

Millicent thought he might be joking since he spoke as if contributing to an on-going discussion rather than trumpeting the arrival of a new era. "Wow," she said, "how cozy my car will be in the garage while your poor truck shivers out there on the street."

"I think, tax and insurance-wise, if we're going to own property together we'd be in better shape if we were married."

Millicent sat up.

"You shit!" she said.

"What? What's wrong?"

"This is it? This is how you do it?" She was, in fact, close to tears.

"It's true. There *are* tax breaks."

"Oh, and by the way, you love me."

"Oh," Leo's smile turned sheepish, "and, by the way: I love you."

"Well, I hate you!" Millicent proclaimed on her way back under the covers and into his embrace. "And I hate having your tools in the living room. You bet your ass, any house we buy had better have a workroom."

"There's space for two cars in the garage, by the way. We could go see the house today if you want."

Millicent grew restless as they cuddled, until, at last, she said, "Well? Do I have to do all the work?"

"Work? Of course not. I'll get the Lombardi guys to help us move."

"Not that work. Do I have to say it all myself?"

"Say what?"

"Figure it out, you dumb, Dago carpenter. Do I have to draw you a blueprint?"

"I don't get it." He pulled away and looked at her, confused.

"Thick as a toe, *porco Dio!* I wait all my goddam girly life for Mr. Right and this is how the story reads? Okay. I'll write the script myself: 'Millicent, my dearest, I love you with all my heart. Will you marry me?' 'Oh, Leo, darling. I thought you'd never ask!' Which, in fact, you never did!"

"Didn't need to. Seems to be a self-service station here, and a fine one, indeed. But don't stop there. What does Millicent answer?"

"How should I know? You tell me."

"Okay: 'I accept your proposal, dear Leo. And after we're married, you can keep your tools anywhere you want – on the dining room table, the couch, next to the bed, in the bed, in the refrigerator.'"

"Let me make it perfectly clear, Leo: I'm not washing your socks and I'm not changing my name."

"You're such a Romantic, Millicent."

She nestled into him. "Leo?"

"Yes?" She paused so long that he said, "What? What is it?"

"I am still afraid, you know," she whispered.

He kissed her. They made love.

THE END

Acknowledgments

What joy it would be to share the stories behind my gratitude for what each of you has given, including to me. Here, however, I only have space for your names:

Kirsten Aasheim, Clare Alexander, Beverly Allen, Synnøve Senstad Andersen, Aleksander Auseth, Jessica Auseth, Simon Auseth, Maggie Barrett, Miriam Barth, Stefan Barth, Merrick Lex Berman, Birgit Bjerck, Christian Borch, Therese Bøckmann, Feliza Gutierrez Cacerez, Sarah-Chanderia, Don Cushman, Berenda Dekkers, Julia Demmin, Franca Errani, Peter Esdaile, Vincent Felitti, Sandra Forman, Lars Martin Fosse, Iole Gandolini, Anna Maria Gandolini, Franco Garletti, Liliana Garletti, Paolo Garletti, Jonny Geller, Christian Gløersen, Linn Getz, Steve Gottlieb, Ane Haaland, Randolph Harrold, Diane Keevil Harrold, Siri Harsem, Irene Hetlevik, Olivia Hetreed, Kari Hildrum, Kevin Hildrum, Lorents Hildrum, Silvia García Hurtado, Gøril Julin Jakobsen, Sven Johansen, Tanny Karunaker, Georgia Kelly, Thomas E. Kennedy, Anna Luise Kirkengen, Ellema Kjær, Chris Knill, Lise Kollsund, Erik Koritzinsky, Carol Levy, Jill Lewis, Sonja Linden, Judie LoGiudice, Liv Lundberg, Jim Loughrill, David MacMillan, Lilian MacMillan, Liv MacMillan, Dagny Mahler, Carole McKenzie, Joel Meyerowitz, Martin Mitchell, Bente Prytz Mjøland, Paul Morrison, Audun Myklebust, Bjørn Naume, Alberto Orsini, Gilbert Reid, Paul Robinson, Grete Roede, John Saddler, Flora Sadun, Ruth Schmidt, Deborah Schneider, Nancy Schroeder, Rudolph Schwartz, Christian Strehlke, Heidi Senstad, Ida Søreide Senstad, Johanne Hadland Senstad, Per Søreide Senstad, Rolf Senstad, Tom Senstad, Alan Shinwell, Carol Deans Shinwell, Anne Simon, Lee Simon, Aarom Smith, Anthony Somkin, Carol Somkin, Ada Spanier, Lee Spanier, Damian Spieckerman, Roberta Spieckerman, Thea Stabell, Hal Stone, Sidra Stone, Britt Søreide, Turi Tarjem,

Jørgen Thorkildsen, Ragnhild Thorp, Tove Træsdal,
Holger Twellmann, JoAnn Ugolini, Barbara Van Noord,
Thor Vardøen, Ann Wakcher, Elisabeth Wakcher,
Carrie McKay Waller, Meira Weiss, Sarah Westcott,
Bente Westergaard, Kirsten Westergaard, Line Westergaard,
Alberto Zucconi.

Thank you!

References

Dante *Inferno.* Canto I, 49-60. *La commedia secondo l'antica vulgata*, ed. Giorgio Petrocchi, 4 vols. Milan: Mondadori, 1966-67.

All translated Dante quotes are from: Henry Wadsworth Longfellow, translation, Dante's "Divine Comedy", First Edition, Leipzig: Bernhard Tauchnitz, 1867.

Mary Oliver, "In Blackwater Woods", from *American Primitive*, Little, Brown and Company, Inc. 1983. First appeared in *Yankee Magazine*, 1979.

E.E. Cummings, "somewhere I have never travelled, gladly beyond", *100 Selected Poems by e.e.cummings,* Grove Press, Inc. New York, 1959.

E.E. Cummings, "pity this busy monster, manunkind" *100 Selected Poems by e.e.cummings,* Grove Press, Inc. New York, 1959.

Lawrence Ferlinghetti, "Overpopulation", *These Are My Rivers: New and Selected Poems 1955-1993.* W. W. Norton & Co., 1994, p. 128.

Erica Jong, *Fear of Flying*, Signet, Penguin Putnam, 1974.

Photo: Joel Summerfield

American born Susan Schwartz Senstad holds Masters' degrees in psychology and fiction writing. She practiced in the U.S., Italy, and Norway as a psychotherapist and communications teacher, and works now as a writer and editorial consultant. Her prize-winning first novel, '*Music for the Third Ear*', was translated and published in five countries, and adapted and broadcast internationally as the 'BBC Radio 4 Friday Play', '*Zero*'. She lives in Oslo with her Norwegian husband with whom she shares three children and five grandchildren.

Printed by BoD™ in Norderstedt, Germany